everything sh...
her fiscal downfa...,
you places'. She loves the ocea... ...,
camping), good food (but not cooking), and shoppi...
no downside.) She lives in Massachusetts with her family.

To find out more visit www.lauraandersenbooks.com
or follow Laura on twitter @LauraSAndersen

'Imaginative . . . an exciting, action-driven plot containing
strong doses of both intrigue and romance... an original and
entertaining read that's reminiscent of the best of
Philippa Gregory'
Library Journal

'Gripping . . . Andersen delves into an alternative Tudor England
geared to rivet period fans and newcomers alike. . . . Perfect for
Philippa Gregory fans'
Booklist

'A surprising gem and a thoroughly enjoyable read'
Historical Novels Review

'[*The Boleyn King*] alive with historical flair and drama,
satisfies both curious and imaginative Tudor aficionados. . . .
Her multidimensional characters are so real that readers will
wish it was history and eagerly await the next in the trilogy'

Also by Laura Andersen:

The Boleyn King

The Boleyn Deceit

The Boleyn Deceit

A NOVEL

Laura Andersen

EBURY
PRESS

1 3 5 7 9 10 8 6 4 2

First published in the United States in 2013 by Ballantine Books,
an imprint of The Random House Publishing Group,
a division of Random House, Inc., New York.

Published in the UK in 2014 by Ebury Press, an imprint of Ebury Publishing
A Random House Group Company

The Random House Group Limited Reg. No. 954009

Addresses for companies within the Random House Group can be found at:
www.randomhouse.co.uk

A CIP catalogue record for this book is
available from the British Library

The Random House Group Limited supports The Forest Stewardship
Council® (FSC®), the leading international forest-certification organisation.
Our books carrying the FSC label are printed on FSC®-certified paper.
FSC is the only forest-certification scheme supported by the leading
environmental organisations, including Greenpeace.
Our paper procurement policy can be found at:
www.randomhouse.co.uk/environment

Printed and bound by CPI Group (UK) Ltd, Croydon, CR0 4YY

ISBN 9780091956493

To buy books by your favourite authors and register for offers visit:
www.randomhouse.co.uk

For

Sandra Lee Lindsay,

1942–2006.

You loved me enough to let me go.

Thank you.

The Boleyn Deceit

PRELUDE

8 February 1547

"You will not tell me what I can and cannot do with my own son!"

If there was one thing to which George Boleyn was accustomed, it was his sister's temper. Anne had never been known for her retiring personality, which was just as well or she would never have caught Henry's eye.

And if she had not become the wife of one king and the mother of the next, George knew he would still be a minor gentleman of enormous ambition and small fortune. That meant he did not rise to Anne's anger. "I am not telling you, the council is. The council that Henry's will put in place."

"My son is king now!"

"In name and spiritual right, yes. But he is ten years old, Anne. In practice, it is the regency council that will rule England until William is of age."

A regency council that had pointedly excluded Anne. There had been child kings before in England, and often their mothers were central to the organization surrounding them. But Henry Tudor, for all his flaws, had always possessed superb political instincts. He had known that even after all this time, passions ran high against his wife. Anne could not be allowed anywhere near her son except in the most limited maternal capacity.

George Boleyn was another matter. Six months before his death, Henry had made him Duke of Rochford, and in his will the late king named him not only a member of the regency council, but bestowed on him the position of Lord Protector of England until William turned eighteen. Not that George had any illusions about the solidity of his position. He was just slightly less hated than his sister and he would hold power only as long as he could keep the other council members from turning on him.

"You are mother of the King of England," he said in a softer voice, gentling Anne into listening. "William loves you and that will never change. I know that you would not jeopardize his position for misplaced pride. You would not risk the Catholics combining against him."

"They would not dare!" But her protest was halfhearted. They would dare all too well, for in their eyes Henry had left only one legitimate child—the Lady Mary, thirty years old and as stubborn and righteous as her mother before her. Henry's son or not, religion made William's position as a boy king precarious.

George took his sister's hands. "Look around you, Anne. Look at where we are standing."

Grudgingly, she ran her eyes around the high-ceilinged privy chamber in the heart of Windsor Castle's Upper Ward, reconstructed by Edward III for himself and his queen, Philippa of Hainault. In the midst of winter, the queen's apartments were a haven of warmth with blazing fires, walls softened by exquisite tapestries, the richness of polished wood, and the sheen of silver and gold décor.

"We have won, Anne," George continued with persuasive conviction. "We have broken the chains of Catholic tyranny and opened the way to a new world. William is the promise of all we hoped and dreamed. I will not let him fail."

As well as a formidable temper, Anne possessed a formidable mind, and she knew he was right. That didn't stop her from saying caustically, "And yet you will allow Norfolk a seat on the council despite his attainder. If Henry had lived just one day longer, the Duke of Norfolk would be *dead*."

"But Henry didn't live one day longer. And to further punish the duke now would only enrage the Catholics. Don't worry about him—I prefer my enemies close enough to control. Besides, Norfolk is William's great-uncle. Pride will stay his hand for now."

Anne shook herself free of George. Fiercely, she retorted, "You had better be right. And you had better be my voice on that council. William is my son, no one else's. Don't you forget it."

"I won't."

But even as George kissed his sister on the forehead, he thought, But if William is to be what we want, the world will need to think of him only as Henry's son. It is a king I am creating now, whatever the cost.

CHAPTER ONE

I have but a few minutes before Carrie must dress me for tonight's festivities. Christmas is nearly here, but tonight's celebration is rather more pagan. There is to be an eclipse of the moon, and coming as it does on the winter solstice when darkness claims its longest reign, even the most devout are unsettled.

So why not dance and drink and throw our merriment into the dark as a challenge?

Also, there is a visitor at court. His name is John Dee and he is reputed one of the finest minds of the age. He has come to court in the Duke of Northumberland's company, and William has commanded him to give a private reading of our stars. Only the four of us—for it would not do to let our secrets, past or future, slip into wider circulation.

Despite the cold, every courtyard at Greenwich was filled and more. No one wanted to miss the rare and possibly apocalyptic sight of the moon vanishing into blackness before their eyes. Minuette had barely room to shiver beneath her fur-lined cloak, so closely were people packed on this terrace overlooking the Thames.

She had managed to keep away from the royal party; below her she saw moonlight glinting off Elizabeth's red-gold hair. William stood near his sister, surrounded as always by men and women. While everyone else's eyes turned to the heavens, Minuette's sought a familiar figure in the flickering torchlight. She rather hoped she did not find Dominic standing near William.

A whisper ran collectively through the crowd, transmitting itself more to Minuette's body than her ear. She looked up: overhead, the edge of the moon's circle was eaten away. Despite herself, she felt her pulse quicken and wondered what terrible things this might portend.

More terrible than a star's violent fall? The voice in her head was Dominic's, an echo of his impatient skepticism.

Minuette fingered the pendant encircling her neck, tracing the shape of the filigreed star, and smiled. This eclipse is no portent of doom, she assured herself, but a sign of great wonder. And that I can believe.

She watched the blackness bite away at the moon until it was half covered and still moving relentlessly onward. There were murmurs around her, some nervous laughter.

A hand came from behind, anchoring her waist with a solidness she could feel even through the layers of fur and velvet and linen. And then, after much too long, a second hand followed until she was encircled. Minuette made herself keep her eyes open, made herself stand straight and not lean back into the comforting weight behind her. Or perhaps comforting was not the right word—for her heart quickened and her breath skipped.

Although she could count on two hands the times Dominic had touched her since the night of her betrothal, her body knew him instantly, as though it had been waiting for this part of her all her life.

Only in the dark did he dare to touch her, for only in the dark could they remain unseen. No one must know, not yet. Not a single whisper must cross the court while William (openly betrothed to the French king's daughter) threw himself in secret at Minuette's feet, offering his hand, his throne, and his country to her. It would take time for the king's infatuation to die. And, until it did, no one must suspect either William's passion or Dominic's love.

So Minuette laughed and played and worked and flirted as though everything were normal—as though William had not lost his mind and thought himself in love with her—as though her own heart was not fluttering madly inside a cage, wanting only to wing itself to Dominic—as though she had no secrets and everything was as it had been before. She saw Dominic every day and behaved toward him the same as always: playful and young and oh-so-slightly resentful of his lectures.

And then, like tonight, he would touch her, and she thought she might weep with wanting to turn into him and cling.

Instead, she kept her eyes open and directed at the sky as the moon's last sliver gave up its fight and slid into nothing.

Gasps went up from the crowd, and in that covering moment, Minuette felt Dominic's mouth alight softly just below her left ear and linger. She did close her eyes then, and swayed back slightly as his arms tightened around her waist and they both forgot where they were and who, and in a moment she would turn and their lips would meet and she might die if she waited any longer—

A great cheer exploded around and below them, and Minuette's eyes flew open to see the moon pulling itself away from the darkness. By the tightness of Dominic's grip on her waist, she knew his frustration. But he was—always had been—the disciplined one.

Within seconds she was standing alone once more, only warm cheeks and quick breathing to betray what no one had seen.

What no one must ever see.

Greenwich Palace had always been a dwelling of pleasure and luxury, of laughter and flirtation, of light and merriment. It was situated on the Thames five miles east of London, close enough to the city for easy access yet far enough to be well out of the crowds and squalor and pestilence. The last two King Henrys had expanded the complex, Elizabeth's grandfather facing it in red brick and her father adding a banqueting hall and enormous tiltyard. Her father had been born here, as had Elizabeth herself. A beautiful palace for a beautiful court.

On this longest night of the year, the palace blazed with candlelight and what heat the fires and braziers failed to provide was made up for by the great press of bodies. Men and women dressed in their finest, drinking and dancing and circling around their king as though he were the center of their world.

But what happens to that world, Elizabeth wondered, when the center fails to hold?

Ignoring the chatter of voices directed at her, she watched her younger brother, worried and angry with herself for worrying. When William had returned from France last month with a treaty and a betrothal, he'd poured out to his sister his ardent love for Minuette along with his plans to wed her, and ever since Elizabeth had carried a thorn of anxiety that made itself felt at the most inconvenient times. It's not as though he's being indiscreet, she told herself firmly. He's behaving precisely as a young king of eighteen should behave. Dressed in crimson and gold, William flirted with every female in sight (and even a man or two), he drank (but not so heavily as to lose control of his tongue), and he carried on several layers of conversation with the French ambassador at once.

And he had not been nearer to Minuette than ten feet all evening.

Elizabeth, being determinedly talked at by a persistent young cleric, swung her gaze to where her chief lady-in-waiting held court of her own, surrounded by a gaggle of men, young and old, all clearly besotted by Minuette's honey-light hair and her graceful height and the appealing knowledge that she was an orphan in the care and keeping of the royal court. With the influence she held in her relationships to Elizabeth and William, Minuette would have drawn an equal crowd even if she had been pockmarked and fat. But the men would not then have been eyeing her with quite the same expression.

A voice, very near and very familiar, broke her distraction. "How long," Robert Dudley said conversationally as he neatly cut out the disappointed and ignored cleric, "is your brother going to continue baiting the French ambassador? William has the treaty he wanted—why make the poor man suffer?"

"Because he can," Elizabeth replied tartly. "And you do the same—only with less care. Everyone knows your father continues to grumble about peace with France. How hard it is for him to swallow, a pact with the devil Catholics."

"My father has moved on to other concerns. He's not one to fight a losing battle."

"As fine a commentary on the Dudleys as I've ever heard."

Robert raised his eyebrows and lowered his voice that half step that made Elizabeth's blood warm. "We choose our battles with care—political, religious . . . personal."

His voice returned to its normal tones and he changed the subject deftly. "Are you looking forward to tonight's audience? I imagine Dr. Dee has found it difficult to read your stars, complex as you are."

She gave him a withering look. "I am exceedingly skeptical, seeing as this Dr. Dee comes from your father's household. No doubt you have whispered to him all the things you most want him to say of me."

"You wound my integrity," Robert said, hand on heart. But his voice was serious when he went on. "John Dee is not the sort of man to be persuaded by anything but his own intellect and the truth of what he sees in the heavens. I promise you, Elizabeth, whatever he tells you tonight will be as near as you will get to hearing God's own words. I only wish I could be there with you."

An hour later, as Elizabeth and Minuette slipped away from the festivities, she wished Robert were with her as well. She understood the need for privacy—anything that approached foretelling a royal's future was dangerous, and though William had commanded the audience, that didn't mean he wanted everyone at court to hear about it—but it was beginning to wear on her being just the four of them all the time. The "Holy Quartet" Robert called them, and not entirely in jest. And now that William took every opportunity of quartet-privacy to fawn over Minuette, Elizabeth's patience grew thinner with each day.

The two young women wound through increasingly depopulated corridors until they came to one only dimly lit by two smoking torches, its brick walls chilly and bare. There was a single guard wearing the royal badge at a discreet distance from the closed door behind which waited their guest, not near enough to overhear but only to keep the curious away.

Elizabeth opened the door to the east-facing room herself, breath quickening with the rare feeling of anticipation. She was not at all certain what was going to happen in the next hour, and she found the sensation unexpectedly delightful.

The room showed signs of a hasty attempt at comfort, from the deep fireplace blazing with light and warmth to the four cushioned chairs ranged along one side of a waxed wood table. Across the table was a single high-backed wooden chair; the man in it rose to his feet and bowed deeply. "Dr. Dee," Elizabeth said. "Welcome to court."

"Thank you, Your Highness." John Dee straightened and Elizabeth took him in. Although she'd known he was only a few years older than she, not even thirty yet, in person she was struck by his youth. Considering all Robert had said and all she had read from correspondents in England and abroad, it was something of a surprise that this young man had achieved such scientific and intellectual stature; then again, Dee had been a fellow at her father's Trinity College at the age of nineteen. More recently the King of France had tried to retain him for his court, but John Dee had declined and returned to England after several years on the Continent, lecturing on Euclid and studying with men like Mercator. He had come to the Northumberland household in the service of Robert's father, and all the court was anxious to meet this man who made things fly and read the stars and charted the heavens with surety.

Elizabeth sat and waved Dr. Dee back to his chair. Minuette sat next to her, uncharacteristically silent. She had been less than enthusiastic about this idea, which surprised Elizabeth. Usually Minuette was the first to embrace the new and entertaining.

Upon examination, John Dee looked like many a scholar or clerk, with his neatly pointed beard and unostentatious clothing. His eyes were deep and thoughtful and steady and he met her gaze without flinching. She liked those who were not cringingly cowed by her—but best not let him take too many liberties.

"Dr. Dee," she said, looking significantly at the leather portfolio that lay between them on the table, "you are aware that it is treason to tell a king's future."

An irrelevant point. It was William who had commanded this private audience, William who had run with the idea of seeing what lay in his stars. Her brother was afraid of nothing, certainly not his future. But casting charts was legally forbidden for royalty, as it might be used as a pretext for rebellion.

Dr. Dee was no fool to fall into such an easy trap. "I do not foretell the future, Your Highness. I interpret the heavens, which is to say, I translate a very little of what God himself has laid in store. And what could God have in store for our good king but glory?"

Would he lie? Elizabeth wondered. She didn't think he was an open fraud—even if Northumberland would fall for that, Robert Dudley certainly wouldn't. But it took subtlety to tell a king what he did not wish to hear without making him angry. How much would Dee avoid saying? Or was William truly charmed, with a lifetime of good fortune inscribed indelibly in the heavens?

The door was shoved wide and William strode in, a little the better for good cheer, followed by Dominic dressed in all black and looking more than ever like a shadow ready to wrest the monarch from danger at any moment.

William went straight to Minuette. Bending low over her chair, he kissed her hand in a lingering and proprietary fashion. Just before it would become uncomfortable for the rest of them, he released her and turned to the visitor.

"Dee!" he said. "Welcome to court. We are always glad to reward those who are useful to us."

No one could have missed the subtext, thought Elizabeth. *Tell me what I want to hear, and you'll be rewarded.*

Minuette had brightened with the men's entrance. "Isn't this thrilling, to discover what our futures hold in store?" She smiled at William (who laughed), then at Dominic (who did not). "Who is to be first?" she asked.

William dropped into the chair next to hers. "You, sweetling, if you wish. What better way to begin, then, with the stars of the brightest woman at court?"

Elizabeth caught the look that John Dee shot at William before dropping his eyes discreetly. Damn, she thought. He may be young, but he is no fool. And that's all we need—someone leaking word of how Will behaves with Minuette in private.

She looked at the one person whom she knew was as concerned with secrecy as she was. Though Dominic had never spoken to her of William's romantic agenda, he radiated disapproval. Now Dominic fixed William with his eyes as though sorely tempted to tell him to behave himself.

As though that had ever succeeded.

Dee cleared his throat and opened the folio. On the top page Elizabeth saw a large circle divided into twelve sections, some of them blank while others contained mathematical and astrological symbols. She knew that each chart would be different, based on the hour and place of their individual births. Despite her wariness, her interest flared as John Dee focused on Minuette. There was something new in his eyes, something that made Elizabeth sharpen her attention and think: This is a man who knows things.

"Mistress Wyatt," he addressed Minuette, and even his voice had a new authority to it. "Our king is right in naming you a bright star. Your birth was a gift—to the king whose hour it shared and to those here who love you. You were born to be loved."

Elizabeth, listening hard for every meaning, felt a twist of annoyance at that. To be loved was far too passive. She herself would prefer to *do* the loving and retain the control. But not everyone was like her—and certainly Minuette could not complain at being loved by a king.

"There has been peril in your life," Dee continued, "and doubt. Do not be too eager to escape either—peril is often the price for doing what is right, and doubt is good, as it makes us search our own motives—"

William interrupted. "Peril, doubt—I mislike this way of speaking to the lady. As the bright star she is, there must also be joy."

For one moment, Dee met William's gaze as an equal, assessing and perhaps understanding more than he should. Then he flickered down a notch and returned to Minuette. "Yes, mistress," he said gravely. "There will be an abundance of joy, for such is your nature. There will be marriage, passionate and deep. Though peril and doubt walk hand in hand with such joy, you will count the price well paid for what you gain."

That pleased William more, for he took Minuette's hand, raised it to his lips, then continued to clasp it as she said, a little shakily, "Thank you, Dr. Dee. You quite take my breath away."

Elizabeth would have bet everything she owned that Dee was not telling all. This was vagueness, but so well finessed that he might not be accused of foretelling an unpropitious future. Peril and doubt? If Minuette were to be William's wife, there would be plenty of both. And even a marriage "passionate and deep" could be a thing of disaster in the end.

"Elizabeth," William ordered Dee. "My sister must be next."

She waited for Dee to search out her page in his folio—though he had not referred to Minuette's at all, as if he had memorized their fates—but surprisingly, he disagreed. "If it please Your Majesty, I had thought to address you next. From the youngest to the oldest—there is symmetry in such a reading."

William had been drinking just enough that Elizabeth wasn't sure if he would snarl in anger or give way graciously. After hesitating, he gave way. "Who am I to gainsay the stars?" Another subtext: *I'll let you take me in turn, but it had better be worth my while.*

Dee gave a flick of a smile as he turned over Minuette's star chart to reveal the one beneath it. "As you say. Despite the fact that you and Mistress Wyatt were born nearly at the same hour and in the same place, the stars reflect the differences between you. You know, naturally, that the comet that marked your birth was a portent of great power. The heavens marked you at birth, Your Majesty, and every moment of your life has been lit with the flame of that comet."

"Flame can be grand or destructive," William replied, not as lightly as it appeared. "Which am I?"

"A grand king in a time of destruction. The powers of Satan oppose you—"

"Wretched Catholics," William muttered.

"—and Europe grows uneasy at England's rise. There is much uncertainty on your path, Your Majesty. But a burning star can blaze the way to a new world—or it can flame out and fall into darkness."

The last words rang ominously into the silent room. Elizabeth's throat tightened. Had Dee just accused her brother of possibly choosing darkness?

William waved it away. "Of course I choose the new world. What of more . . . personal fates?"

Was it Elizabeth's imagination that Dee held the image of William and Minuette's clasped hands in his mind as he answered? "The personal and the public march together for a king. Trouble there will be, and opposition, but you will always keep your own ends in mind. You will never lose sight of what you most desire."

William gave his catlike smile as he leaned back in his chair. "That is a future I can embrace."

But you need hardly look to the stars to know that much of William, Elizabeth thought—or any king, for that matter. Their father had never lost sight of what he desired, and had nearly riven his kingdom for it.

Feeling more nervous than she'd expected, Elizabeth met Dee's attention next. But his gaze was kind, almost . . . sorrowful?

"Your Highness," he began, and this time he did look down at the new chart he'd turned to, as though wondering where and how to begin, "your stars were the most difficult to interpret. They are changeable, one might almost say willful."

"Right stars, then," William said with good humour.

Elizabeth hardly heard him, for her eyes were riveted to Dee's. That cryptic sense she'd had earlier intensified. For a moment she felt that she was seeing the future herself. He is important to me, she realized, or will be. For a long time to come.

As though acknowledging her unspoken thoughts, Dee nodded. "Your future is veiled even to yourself, Your Highness, for the clearest eyes cannot see straight into the sun. You love deeply and your loyalty to your single love will be everlasting."

Did he mean Robert? Everlasting loyalty . . . but that could mean anything from eventual marriage to a lifetime of unfulfilled love.

"You will command men and guide nations," Dee continued, and in that moment he crossed the line of discretion he had been walking so carefully before.

Suddenly alert (though probably he had been all along), Dominic laid a hand on William's shoulder. "Beware, Doctor. Your king guides this nation."

"And as such, he has already given Her Highness her first

command, when he named her regent earlier this year. And before another year passes," Dee returned his gaze to Elizabeth, "you will be your brother's voice in a foreign land."

That did speak of marriage—one out of England. Elizabeth blinked, furious at herself for disappointment. It was hardly news. This wasn't prophecy; this was merely stating the obvious.

But John Dee continued to stare at her and Elizabeth had a queer double feeling that she was seeing him here, now, and also seeing him some years in the future, with white hair and a pointed beard. He was going to tell her how to save England, he was about to tell her what she need do for her people . . .

The moment snapped and Dee cleared his throat as he turned his full attention to Dominic. He took Dominic's measure, the only one standing, protective behind William, with one hand still on his friend's shoulder. "The elder brother," Dee said thoughtfully. "The first, who would be last."

Dominic dropped his hand and said stonily, "I have no need for a star-teller. I choose my own future."

"But you do not choose that of others—and as long as your life entwines with those you love, you are not entirely free. You are the eldest, but you have the most to learn. Lessons of honour and loyalty and, yes, of choice. Not everything in this world is as it seems. You must learn to see gray, where before you have seen only black or white. There will be pain in the learning, and danger if you will not learn to bend."

William snorted. "There will only be pain because Dom thinks too much and makes everything more serious than it needs to be."

"That is your calling," Dee said to Dominic. "You are, above all, loyal, and you speak always to the king's conscience. Who will tell him the truth if you will not?"

A pause, verging on uncomfortable, until William spoke. "Tell Dom something pleasant—how many beautiful women in his future?"

An even longer pause, then: "Only one," Dee said tersely. "There will only ever be the one."

Tension entered the room, on such misty feet that Elizabeth could not say where it centered. William broke it with a laugh as he stood. "Well, that's all right, then. All we need do is identify this one beautiful woman and Dom's future is set."

And just like that they were finished. William went so far as to clap John Dee on the shoulder. "My thanks for an interesting diversion, Doctor. I hope you shall find our court accommodating to your intellect and talents."

Dee bowed. "The most glittering court in Christendom, Your Majesty."

"Ha! I'd love to see Henri's face when he finds that the English have captured what the French could not. You are most welcome at my court, Dr. Dee, if ever you should tire of Northumberland's household."

Then William spoke to the rest of them. "There is still music to be had this night. Dom, if you dance with Minuette first, then no one will find it odd when I come along and steal her from you."

"Not odd at all." Dominic's voice was toneless. "Dr. Dee, if you don't mind, I will stay until you have burned those charts."

"Of course," Dee answered, and emptied the folio. There were only the four pages; Dr. Dee had written down his calculations, not their interpretations. Those would stay locked in his own mind. One by one he fed the pages to the flames.

"Thank you," Dominic said. He and Minuette followed William out the door.

Elizabeth hesitated, then confronted Dr. Dee, who straightened, meeting her on that precarious equal ground that made her both nervous and approving.

"Your Highness?" He made it a question, but she would have wagered he knew what she was going to ask.

"What did you *not* say, Doctor?"

"Many things, Your Highness."

"Why? What is so bad that it could not be told?"

"Why must it be bad? Even glorious futures do not come without cost. And as I believe I said before, this is not exact. God made the stars as he made men. Only He can read them perfectly."

"What did you see?" Robert's wife dead? Elizabeth married for love, as William meant to do? Civil war, as another Tudor king cast aside wisdom for desire? Elizabeth far from England for all the rest of her life as the wife of another royal? As she thought that, Elizabeth's heart pierced with pain and she knew that would be the worst future for her of any—to leave England and never return.

Dr. Dee was silent. The hiss of the flames twisted like cords around her skin, and she had a sudden sense that there were ghosts in the room, pressing into this moment as though they'd been waiting. Her father and grandfather, of course, but even stronger was the sense of her grandmother: Elizabeth of York, whose Plantagenet blood had sealed Henry VII's Tudor victory when they wed. What did that daughter and mother of kings want her namesake to know?

Unexpectedly, Dr. Dee took her right hand, letting her fingertips rest in his palm. "This is the hand of a woman, Your Highness. But it is also the hand of a ruler. The king, your father, spent much effort and pain to secure a worthy heir for England.

If he had been able to see beyond your woman's body, he would have found the heart of the heir he sought."

He pinned her with his eyes, an urgency to his gaze as though there was more he could say but wouldn't. Elizabeth could almost feel words forming along her skin where he touched her hand, and if she stayed here another moment she would know something she had never dreamed of . . .

She snatched her hand away. "Goodnight, Dr. Dee."

CHAPTER TWO

How, ROBERT DUDLEY wondered, does George Boleyn nose out these insalubriously private areas of every royal palace?

He doubted it was the women George took to bed who told him how to find dank cellars and tunneled-out storage spaces—Rochford was liberal in his sexual activities, but also discriminating. His type of woman might not always be a lady, but she would never be a common whore. And Robert could not imagine any woman except a desperate one being caught dead in this particularly foul-smelling section of Greenwich.

Strictly speaking, the walled yard in which he paced wasn't part of the palace itself. It belonged to a dilapidated stone outbuilding that held a jumble of gardening equipment, which on the night before Christmas was in little danger of being used. The stench came from the Thames, running fast and foul only yards away.

What am I doing? Robert asked himself uneasily. It was a question he'd begun to pose with distressing regularity the last six weeks. Working with Rochford had promised so much, but he was beginning to wonder if it was worth it. It wasn't so much the Duke of Norfolk's death in disgrace that bothered him, nor even the continued imprisonment of his grandson, the Earl of Surrey, for an almost wholly imaginary crime. Robert didn't like the Howards and had no regrets about helping the proud Catholic family along their way to destruction.

What troubled him were particular faces and the memories attached to them: Elizabeth's earnest faith when she'd asked him to go after Minuette for her friend's safety; Dominic's stubborn lies about Giles Howard's death—also done in the interest of protecting Minuette. Her face troubled him as well, because he felt guilty for using her and he couldn't pin her down, all of which was eminently frustrating.

But beneath the frustration was the fact that he had been lying to Elizabeth and her friends for months. All right, be honest, it was more like years. It had begun in the late autumn of 1552, when Rochford suggested Alyce de Clare as a likely instrument in their plans. Alyce had been a lady-in-waiting to Queen Anne and was thus ideally placed to report gossip and pass on carefully calculated rumours of Catholic conspiracy. She was also ambitious, which made her susceptible to flattery and promises. Robert had latched on to Alyce enthusiastically when he'd troubled to study her a little closer. Though not really beautiful, Alyce had possessed an excellent figure and a streak of something in her nature—Wildness? Calculation? Animal cunning?—that had readily appealed to him. More than once in the months of flirting and intimacy that followed, he'd guessed that Rochford knew firsthand of Alyce's physical appeal, but he had never asked.

"Contemplating your sins, Lord Robert?"

Not only could the Lord Chancellor move almost silently, it also seemed he could read minds. His voice made Robert twitch in annoyance and surprise.

"Contemplating how many of them I can lay at your feet, my lord," he rejoined smoothly.

"Not a one," Rochford answered with equal smoothness. "A man's sins are his own."

"And you've made sure nothing I've done can be directly traced to you."

"Of course."

Robert sighed. "What untraceable task am I to be given next?"

"One very much to your taste and talents: I want you to attend Elizabeth assiduously this winter. Make yourself indispensable, so that my niece does not have a need that you have not anticipated. I want you in her presence chamber and her privy chamber. I want to know who else is there, and what they discuss when they are."

"I will not spy on Elizabeth." Robert said it flatly. "Not for anything."

"I think that point is debatable, but it is also irrelevant. It is not Elizabeth I want you watching—it is Mistress Wyatt."

"Minuette? Whatever for?" But Robert was afraid he very much knew what for.

"I told you she bears watching. My instincts are never wrong. It is for you to tell me why the girl makes me uneasy."

Because she killed Giles Howard, Robert thought. But even if Rochford knew that, he didn't think the Lord Chancellor would care. Giles Howard had been the last and least of the Duke of Norfolk's sons and he had earned his death with his own violence. Not a matter to sharpen Rochford's interest—so what about Minuette made the Lord Chancellor so uneasy?

"It is in your own interest as well," Rochford said now. "Mistress Wyatt is the one who made all the fuss over Alyce de Clare's unfortunate and untimely death. She suspected Giles Howard was responsible, but does she still? If she believes the pregnant Alyce's tumble down the stairs is not to be laid at Giles's feet, she will not rest until she has found the guilty party. And you wouldn't want her stumbling over your mistakes, would you?"

Robert most certainly didn't want Minuette stumbling over his connection to Alyce. The first person she would tell would be Elizabeth, and their relationship was already complicated by his wife. How could he explain a pregnant mistress as well? Especially one who had died so inconveniently while spying on Elizabeth's mother.

The damned man was so certain of Robert's acquiescence that he didn't even wait for it. The only satisfaction Robert could get was calling out a question as Rochford retreated. "Why on earth has the Earl of Surrey not been brought to trial? I thought your goal was to eliminate the Howard family. And yet Surrey continues to sit in the Tower without any charges being brought."

That stopped Rochford, just long enough for him to look over his shoulder dismissively and say, "Don't attempt to know my mind, Lord Robert. You might not like what you find."

If there was one part of being king that William would have abolished if possible, it was council meetings. Here it was Christmas day, and still his privy council would not let him be. The aftereffects of drought and poor harvests, Rochford said. Torrential rains. People starving. Not to mention Mary imprisoned and the death of a duke of England under taint of treason. A realm does not sleep, Rochford insisted, and her king must be willing to do likewise.

So as the sun rose behind leaden clouds, here was assembled his much reduced privy council, more or less the remains of the regency council that had ruled in his name for years. Six months ago William had turned eighteen and gone immediately to war. Followed by his mother's death, and then more weeks in France negotiating, and then Minuette . . .

William imagined announcing his engagement this very morning, having it preached of in the chapel, setting the bells to ring out his love. Then he imagined the shouting that would follow—mostly from Rochford—and sighed. Not yet.

As Lord Chancellor, his uncle opened the council, which this morning consisted of just over half a dozen men: Rochford and Dominic, naturally, along with the Earls of Pembroke and Oxford and Archbishop Cranmer. Sir Ralph Sadler ran the household and William Cecil, Lord Burghley, the treasury. Most of them were in their forties or fifties—Cranmer was actually in his sixties, though still active in both mind and body—and even Burghley, who was only thirty-four, behaved like a cautious old man.

Age and temperament aside, there were not nearly enough members of the privy council. And that was the true purpose of this meeting. His uncle had been pressing him for a decision for three weeks, and now he meant to force the matter.

"Your Majesty," Rochford began, "before the new year dawns, we must have a complete council. You cannot long afford to overlook some of the realm's most powerful men."

William slouched back in his chair, willing to allow his uncle the chance to drone on and list his no doubt well-thought-out and even better phrased arguments to press his point. Why deny the man his pleasure? William meant to agree—if only to stop the endless tide of pressure—but he could afford to be generous this early in the morning. The Christmas service was still two hours off.

Dominic was not so patient. "Who?" he asked. "With Norfolk dead, and his heir imprisoned, the council already holds the only two remaining dukes in the kingdom."

Rochford himself and Northumberland, easily the two most Protestant lords in England. There had been four dukes appointed to the regency council, but the Duke of Suffolk had died of apoplexy when William was sixteen. Suffolk had had only daughters—Jane Grey his eldest—and there had been no question of naming another duke since then. It was unlike Dominic to make a political point, and William wondered where he was headed with this one.

So was Northumberland. His blunt face (the rough edges of which so perfectly mirrored his soldier image, a man uncomfortable with pomp and elegance) looked skeptical as he asked, "What are you implying, Exeter?"

Even though he had named Dominic Marquis of Exeter just six months ago, William still wasn't used to hearing Dominic called as such.

Northumberland pressed on. "Do you think the realm needs another duke?"

"It is not titles I am thinking of, but opinions. I think the realm needs binding, and this council should represent more than one viewpoint to serve effectively." Dominic, unlike Northumberland, always looked perfectly suited to the finesse of the court. Tall (though William, at six feet two inches, Dominic had finally topped him by an inch), and though soberly dressed, Dominic had a way of carrying himself that reminded everyone that he had Plantagenet blood several generations back. Mostly, though, Dominic belonged because he never bothered to think about whether he did or not. It was instinctive.

"Such as the views of those who meant to march a foreign army upon London and kill our king?" Northumberland countered, brusque and angry. He had not his son Robert's careful guile; he was too sure of his power to play games. "There is no place for traitors in England, let alone welcoming them into the heart of the court."

"Traitors, no," Dominic retorted. "But men of good heart and honest thought, who want the same end but perhaps through different means. No one man holds a lock on all virtue."

William laughed. "Really, Dom, how old are you? You sound like a university philosopher. Not," he added, "that you aren't right. It is a poor king indeed who cannot be trusted to hear more than one voice in council."

"Does that mean you are ready to name new men?" Rochford pressed.

"It does. Wriothesley, Arundel, Paget, and Cheney. We need men as skilled as they are opinionated. And they will be free to speak their minds." William looked around. "That's all."

He was half out of his chair when Rochford said, "Lord Exeter spoke truly, Your Majesty."

Subsiding with a suppressed groan, William said, "He always does. On which particular point do you agree with his truthfulness?"

"We must decide what to do with the Earl of Surrey."

The late Duke of Norfolk's grandson, currently held in the Tower of London for suspicion of treasonable activity, Surrey was heir to his grandfather's title and vast lands that would place him on a footing with Rochford and Northumberland—if he didn't lose his head. Even if William chose to leave him alive, he could seize the lands for the Crown and, say, banish Surrey to the Continent. Or simply keep him imprisoned.

Not that they had evidence Surrey had done anything treasonable.

Not that it necessarily mattered.

Northumberland had already made up his mind; no surprise considering how the Dudleys and Howards hated one another. "Norfolk cheated us of a useful execution—make Surrey take his place. That will teach the Catholics not to play at rebellion."

"Surrey has been raised Protestant," Dominic pointed out. William didn't have to ask his friend's opinion; distaste was written all over his face. The others would agree with the louder voices. That left, as always, Rochford.

"What say you, Uncle?" William asked. "Kill a man for his name?"

Rochford hesitated, and in that unusual moment of uncertainty William saw a momentary likeness to Dominic. Again, a resemblance not wholly surprising considering that Dominic's mother was a second cousin to George Boleyn. They both had long, thoughtful faces and dark good looks that made women pliable. "There is wisdom in the use of a public execution. But there is also wisdom in mercy. You have established a position of strength, Your Majesty: victory in France, betrothal to the French king's daughter, the Lady Mary under house arrest . . . I think, perhaps, it is time to ponder mercy."

"Besides the fact that there is no evidence of Surrey's involvement?" Dominic broke in, barely a step away from open sarcasm.

"That is true," Rochford answered slowly. "In fact, I am disturbed by his consistent denials. Surrey has not wavered, or been caught in a single falsehood. It may well be that he is innocent of any crime."

"Except representing a family that would listen to a foreign pope over our own king," asserted Northumberland. "A pope who insists that the throne belongs to Mary Tudor and our king is naught but a bastard."

The room went very still. Cranmer and Burghley shared a look that united the old cleric and the younger councilor in shared disapproval of such folly. William felt his stomach roil; though he knew it was said of him elsewhere, he should not have to listen to such words in his own council chamber. "That's enough," he said sharply. "I will judge a man by word and action, not by gossip. And certainly I will not rule out of fear. My uncle has doubts. That is sufficient for me to be cautious."

Already a plan was forming, not yet more than a thought and a sense that it would be unexpected and thus fun. As well as useful. He kept the possibility in the back of his mind and dealt with the immediate issue.

"Lord Exeter." He always addressed Dominic in formal terms when he was about to make a political point. "Visit Surrey in the Tower. Not just yet, though—leave it for a month or so. We will let him sit awhile and ponder the error of his family's ways. I will keep the interrogators away from him until then. When you go, speak to his guards, speak to his servants, and speak to the inquisitors."

He dared Rochford to protest, but his uncle seemed, if anything, approving. Hard to tell behind that masklike face. Sometimes William wished Rochford was as openly violent in his feelings as Northumberland.

"What is my brief?" Dominic asked. "Guilt or innocence?"

"Fact," William said. "Did Surrey have any knowledge of his grandfather's plot with the Spanish? If you are satisfied that he did not, then it will be time to speak of recompense."

Dominic was visibly glad, and William basked in that moment of approval. "Yes, Your Majesty."

"That is all." William waved them away, all except Dominic.

When the door was closed on just the two of them, William stretched out his legs and sighed. "Tell me true, Dom, do you think Surrey knew of his grandfather's plans?"

"No."

"That's an awfully quick answer when you haven't even spoken to the man yet."

"I've read the interview transcripts. He's been racked—did you know that?"

Gentlemen were mostly spared torture, but Rochford had insisted. It did make Surrey's denials more plausible. William ignored the underlying disapproval in Dominic's question. "We all know how stubborn the Howards can be, particularly when their lives are at stake."

"Surrey wasn't at Framlingham during the Lady Mary's residence. He had come nowhere near East Anglia for eight months. You appointed him to the northern marches and, except for the time he spent in Paris at your command, there he stayed—where, by the way, he has been remarkably effective on the border. He has ever served well and faithfully, with not a hint of his father's radical Catholicism. I daresay I've never heard the man express a religious opinion before now."

"He'll have to if I let him live. The Catholics will force it of him. He'll have to come down on one side or the other."

"Will he?"

"What does that mean?"

Dominic shrugged, but the tension in his eyes belied his attempt at being casual. "As long as we force men to hold a religious opinion to the exclusion of all else in their life, England will remain unbalanced, liable to be tipped at any providential moment from one side to the other."

"You think I would return this country to Rome?"

"Never. Which is why you will always be a target for those who would."

"Then little has changed. Don't worry about me, Dom. I'm young, I'm handsome, I've beaten the French, and I'm engaged to a Catholic princess. I'd say we're fairly balanced just now."

Dominic shifted restlessly in his chair, but he would not stand until William gave him permission. "If you're thinking about balance, does that mean you would invest Surrey with the Nor-folk title and lands?"

"An almost-Catholic duke against two Protestant ones? I think I shall have to." With a grin, William added, "And perhaps another title as ballast against my uncle and Northumberland. We shall see."

Dominic seemed uninterested in William's hints. "Then I'll speak to Surrey."

Christmas at court was an exercise in furious revelry and ex-hausting entertainment. Dominic had never cared much for the masques, those exuberant displays of costume and dramatic theme and over-the-top allegory, though he had been forced to participate in several in earlier years. But this Christmas he had flatly refused when pressed by several comely court ladies to join the play. Minuette did not press him, though he knew she was part of it. In fact, from the accounts of the Master of Revels, it appeared she was planning the masque single-handedly. Orders had been given for multiple lengths of black fabric, both velvet and muslin; for red velvet headdresses; and for a machine that would produce thunder and lightning. It all seemed silly to Dominic. These days everything seemed silly that wasn't directly connected to the present security of the state or the secret be-trothal of Minuette and William.

But before the Christmas debauchery came Christmas wor-ship. This part Dominic did enjoy, if only because everyone, even William, sat still and he could slip his gaze sideways almost as often as he liked and glimpse Minuette next to Elizabeth. The view of her was one he knew well and never tired of: caught in profile, the line of her brow and throat, the spill of her hair onto her shoulders beneath her sheer black hood . . . Dominic had done little enough praying in church these last weeks, unless God counted it worship to devour Minuette with his eyes.

She didn't seem to mind. Although she glanced his way rarely, there was a wealth of pleasure in those flashes.

William, naturally, assumed those glances were for him.

Today's Christmas service was full of gratitude for the nation's safe delivery from the hands of evil councilors and the whore of Babylon who looked to enslave all the world. Dominic caught William's brief frown as the archbishop hinted at the whore being not only the collective Catholic Church, but the individual person of William's half sister, Mary. Though he might not have cause to trust her, the Tudors were very clannish, and William believed he alone had the right to chastise his sister. But Archbishop Cranmer deftly brought his words around to England's king as the champion of true Christianity, and then the choir was singing and the soaring alleluias brought a shiver to even Dominic's religiously conflicted heart.

If anyone had asked his beliefs, he would have said he believed in honour, his king, and God. In that order. Unlike his mother (who had longed to join a religious order when young), Dominic did not follow Rome and would fight to keep England from returning to the sway of papal power. But he also disliked Martin Luther and the other Continental firebrands who thought a new Earth could only come on the blood and destruction of the old one. What use was any religion, he wondered, that demanded blood? That was the Old Testament. This was the world of the New Testament—did not Christ himself command, "Ye shall love one another"?

These arguments almost never made it out of his closed mouth. He preferred to serve to his strengths, which would never be debate and theology. He was a soldier. He was sworn to his king and country and he would not dishonour that.

Except by loving the woman his king wanted.

Dominic distracted himself from that uncomfortable thought by focusing on the chapel's choirmaster—another man who had once loved Minuette. Jonathan Percy had proposed to her just six months past, and Dominic had never been so glad as when he'd learned she had refused him. Percy had taken the rejection well enough and had even served as Dominic's squire during the French battles, but he had always belonged here—in a royal chapel creating music for kings, both earthly and heavenly.

Dominic wondered if Percy's continuing presence at court meant that he was truly valued as a musician, or if William's past relationship with Percy's twin sister had more to do with it than his talent. Eleanor Percy Howard had been married to the Duke of Norfolk's youngest son in order for William to make her his mistress without complications. She had already borne William one child—a girl—and even now claimed to be carrying another child that she laid at William's bed.

Of course, that claim was being made from the Tower of London, for Eleanor had been caught up in the Duke of Norfolk's plotting, which ended in the violent death of her husband, Giles. The other women of the Howard family were being kept merely under house arrest, but Eleanor had been brought to the Tower almost a month ago. Not because of hard evidence that she'd intended treason, but because she had twice attempted to escape house arrest from the Howard estate at Framlingham. When she was caught the second time—twenty miles away from Framlingham and headed for London—she insisted, as she had all along, that she must be allowed to speak to the king.

But William, wrapped in his consuming passion for Minuette, had sent word for Eleanor to be kept in the Tower since she could not be trusted in a lesser confinement. Dominic thought that had been for Minuette's sake, for she had always disliked Eleanor and no doubt William thought it a sort of gift to his beloved to lock away his former mistress. Dominic did not expect Eleanor to be locked away for long. She was a woman, and the mother of William's child, and had proved herself skilled at pleasing the king. No doubt the king's memories of pleasure would, in time, lead to her release.

When the service was ended, everyone rose for William and waited while he swept out. Dominic was kept from following by Robert Dudley, who left the side of a smiling Elizabeth to speak to him.

"What is it?" Dominic asked roughly. He had a hard time taking Robert's measure, and that made him uneasy. Add in the fact that Robert had been at Framlingham on that last, disastrous night when Norfolk had been arrested and his youngest son killed . . .

Robert did not take offense, though he always seemed to give the impression of understanding and somehow pitying Dominic's unease. "I merely wondered what news from the council this morning."

"Ask your father."

"I'm asking you. Is it true that William means to return Surrey to court?"

How did Robert always manage to know what was going on quicker than anyone outside the privy council? Dominic said as little as possible. "No decision has been made."

"I hear you're going to meet with him," Robert threw in carelessly. "Wonder how he'll feel, dealing with the man who murdered his uncle. Well, not that anyone much liked Giles Howard. Probably you did Surrey a favour removing the least of the Howards."

Before Dominic could frame an appropriate answer without giving way to anger, Robert added in a lower voice, "Have you ever thought that the evidence against Norfolk might have been just a bit too tidy? Penitent's Confessions, Spanish naval involvement, Lady Mary preparing to lead foreign troops against her brother . . . it does sound like a plot made to order by suspicious Protestants. Interesting to think about that when talking to Surrey. The Howards have plenty of enemies themselves, you know. Just a thought."

He dazzled his mercurial smile at Dominic and whisked off—after Elizabeth, no doubt.

Had Robert just hinted that he believed Norfolk innocent of attempted rebellion? The Dudleys and Howards were long antagonists—why would Robert want to see the Earl of Surrey cleared from suspicion? But then Rochford had voiced something of the same opinion in council earlier. What had he said? *I am disturbed by his consistent denials.* Well, so was Dominic, but he would not have expected the naturally wary Rochford to agree with him. Or Robert, for that matter.

He watched as Robert caught up with Elizabeth and bent his dark head to her red-gold one. Even from behind and at a distance, it was clear how he felt about her, and Dominic experienced a surge of jealousy.

How has it come to this, Dominic thought, that I envy a married man in love with another woman? But he knew his envy wasn't about Robert's love—it was because Robert didn't bother to pretend about it.

Minuette's Christmas day was a blur of sound and colour, punctuated by clear flashes: the piercing familiarity of Dominic's dark-green eyes in chapel, the tremor of alleluias in her bones, the headiness and triumph of pageantry. The masque was a fabulous success, everyone said so, even Elizabeth had gasped in delight at the marauding Saracens draped wrist to ankle in black with red velvet headdresses who threatened the court until the gallant Christian knights bearing the enormous papier-mâché dragon of St. George came to rescue the ladies from their clutches. There was smoke and thunder and music and hilarity and dancing and fighting—everything a Christmas masque should be. William kissed her hand before all the court in thanks, and both men and women flattered her with praise. It was very satisfying.

But none so much as when Dominic came to stand beside her and, surveying the crowds, said, "Playing politics, Minuette? That is unlike you."

Even as she replied, "Whatever do you mean?" in pretended innocence, her heart soared that Dominic alone seemed to have caught the small detail at the end.

"The single knight who took his enemy's hand rather than put him to the sword. They walked off together, with a woman between them." He turned his head and lowered it nearer hers so no one would overhear. "Do you mean to be that woman, to bring peace between Catholic and Protestant?"

"Of course not—it wasn't a real woman, she was the symbol of Peace itself. And anyway, the masque was about the Turks."

When Dominic smiled at her, it nearly broke her heart. She so rarely saw him smile. "You could be that symbol, Minuette. You would have that power, if you were . . ."

He didn't say the word, didn't even mouth it, but she heard it nonetheless. *If you were queen.*

Her eyes went to William, laughing at some clumsy wit from his aunt, Lady Suffolk. "I won't be," she said. "Not ever."

His smile had faded when she turned back to him, but he leaned in farther and whispered in her ear. "Happy Christmas, Minuette. I left your gift with Carrie. I hope you like it."

He was gone so suddenly that Minuette wanted to cry out in frustration. Why couldn't he do as William had and hand her the gift himself? The king had seized ten minutes alone with her when he'd come to see Elizabeth after service this morning: one minute to watch with satisfaction as Minuette stumbled thanks for the far too noticeably costly ruby necklace, and nine minutes to thank her for the very simple embroidered missal cover she'd made him. His had been a mostly wordless thanks.

Didn't Dominic want to thank her the same way? She'd given him a missal cover as well, trying to be discreet, as they all must be. Except it seemed that she alone was discreetly in the middle. On one end was William, recklessly sure of himself and not afraid enough of being caught. And on the other end was Domi-nic, so absolutely devoted to control that in public he barely even seemed to tolerate her company these days.

Men.

She was still feeling somewhere between excited and wounded when she escaped to her room far earlier than she normally would have. She had a headache—something she had never been prone to until these last weeks—and yes, despite her frustration, she was curious what Dominic had left her.

She had not expected it to be alive. But when Carrie told her Lord Exeter's gift was in her bedchamber, Minuette flung open the door and was confronted by a pair of silky brown eyes that kept rising and rising as the dog seemed to unfold itself until it stood before her.

The eyes were beautiful, and the cinnamon coat, but good heavens it was enormous! An Irish wolfhound whose nose came level with her rib cage. Minuette could not think of a single thing to say. It was the only animal she'd ever owned, apart from the horse William had given her last year. The hound was nearly as large as Winterfall.

Minuette was even more perplexed when the dog bent his head down and pushed something toward her with his nose.

Hesitantly, Minuette picked up the paper-wrapped rectangle— definitely a book—and sat on her bed to open it.

Il Canzoniere . . . Petrarch writing to his Laura . . . Minuette's Italian was nearly fluent and her cheeks burned as she skimmed the pages. The last time she had seen these poems had been in the aftermath of her friend Alyce de Clare's sudden death and a frantic search to decode a message. Now she took the time to look at the words themselves. If this was a fair measure of Dominic's feelings beneath that damnable self-control, then it was a wonder she did not go up in flames every time he looked at her.

The dog sat and laid his marvelous head in her lap. Minuette stroked him between the ears. "What am I supposed to call you?" she murmured.

Carrie was at the door, ever knowing precisely the moment she was needed. With her glossy brown hair and knowing eyes, she always reminded Minuette of a bird. A wren, perhaps. "Lord Exeter said to tell you Fidelis is his name, and so is his nature."

Fidelis—Latin for loyalty. "Loyal by name and nature," Minuette said wryly. "I could not describe him better myself."

CHAPTER THREE

O N THE FEAST of Epiphany, January 6, Elizabeth attended morning service at Greenwich's Chapel Royal and listened to Bishop Latimer preach from the text of Isaiah chapter sixty.

" 'Whereas thou hast been forsaken and hated . . . I will make thee an eternal excellency, a joy of many generations.' Thus spake the Lord to his chosen Israel, but is not scripture also the Lord's word to us? Has not our own kingdom been hated for the truth's sake, and forsaken by those more concerned with worldly power than heavenly gifts? Hear his promises to us, that we will be an excellency and joy to generations."

Latimer was a good speaker, Elizabeth admitted. Grudgingly, because the more fiery the rhetoric, the more she instinctively wanted to argue the opposite. Not that she didn't agree that God had worked wonders in England, but so often his wonders were hard to distinguish from the more earthly ambitions and plots of men. Did Latimer believe that her mother had been set in her father's path specifically to seduce him into splitting from Rome? That argued a God of sardonic intent and not always impeccable methods.

If William had ever entertained such doubts, she didn't know it. Her brother tended to the practical wherever religion and politics collided, and kept his personal impressions close to his heart. She believed he had them, she just didn't know if God's words to William's heart ever deviated from his personal wishes.

The final prayers were spoken and Elizabeth had just reached the chapel door when Lord Rochford was suddenly, silently, next to her. "May I walk with you, niece?" he asked pleasantly.

"Certainly."

They kept a companionable silence with one another as they passed out of the tiled chapel floor and into the more crowded areas of the palace. Since her mother's death last summer, these informal conversations had been carried out once or twice a week. At first Elizabeth had been surprised that her uncle would seek her out, but she had come to realize how deeply he missed his sister. They had always been exceptionally close and, with Anne gone, Rochford seemed to think Elizabeth the nearest thing to a substitute.

Not that he would ever say so.

When they reached the less public north galleries, frigid enough for breath to be seen if one walked slowly, Elizabeth asked, "What is on your mind, Uncle?"

"I have been brooding on the Penitent's Confession and the aborted Catholic plot in November."

She inclined her head in acknowledgment and waited. There would be more. There was always more than the obvious when George Boleyn spoke. He did not need to elaborate, for Elizabeth had been a full party to the search for the alleged Penitent's Confession, a document the Catholics desperately wanted to lay hands on as evidence that William had not been Henry VIII's son at all, but rather, born of incest between Anne and Rochford himself.

The search for the Penitent's Confession had ended at the

Duke of Norfolk's home at Framlingham in November. Minuette had been sent by Rochford precisely because she could look for the document without raising suspicions. She had found it, all right—and promptly burnt it, for the forged confession had purportedly been signed by Minuette's own mother, once a friend to Anne Boleyn. Elizabeth thought that Rochford had not been exactly displeased at that.

That forged document had led to Norfolk's arrest and subsequent natural death in the Tower. The most pressing question left unresolved two months later was the extent of Mary Tudor's knowledge and support of a plot against her brother's throne. It was no secret that every Catholic in Europe—and England— thought Mary England's only legitimate ruler. Rochford's spies had even reported that Spanish ships were prepared to land on the east coast preparatory to either spiriting Mary away to raise an army or else to land troops in support of her royal claims.

Rochford sighed. "Not a single member of the Howard household has admitted to plotting either to help Mary escape or to help her fight against the Crown."

"We know that Norfolk was searching for the Penitent's Confession—his own brother told us so. And it was your intelligencers who said Spanish ships were sailing to England."

"Anyone who provides information in exchange for money is unreliable. Who is to say my intelligencers were not offered more money to lie to me?"

"Are you saying that you do not trust your own intelligencers?" Elizabeth regarded her uncle, walking gravely beside her. He had her mother's colouring—and William's, for that matter— dark and sharp-featured and watchful. Though William's bright blue eyes softened the resemblance.

"I am saying that anyone who trusts blindly is a fool and deserves to be lied to."

Elizabeth had heard that from him before. She smiled briefly in acknowledgment. "Whom do you suspect of lying to you—and why, Uncle?"

"The Howard family is extremely unpopular amongst the more radical Protestant circles. I can think of any number of men who would not hesitate to work against them."

"By planting lies about the Spanish navy and spreading the vilest rumours about my brother's birth? Do you really think that Protestants would tell such falsehoods in the hopes of implicating Norfolk?" Elizabeth had never been able to erase from her memory the broadsheet Dominic had found at the beginning of all this—the drawing of her mother attempting to seduce Satan himself. Her voice hardened. "That is a perilous game to play, no matter how unpopular the Howards may be."

"That is why I am troubled. If it was all a pretense, if Norfolk was perhaps innocent—"

"Norfolk most certainly wanted his hands on the Penitent's Confession," Elizabeth interrupted sharply. "He was actively looking for evidence of Mary's legitimate claim to the throne, and he would not have hesitated to use it against William. That is not innocence."

It was Rochford's turn to agree. "No, it is not innocence. But if there was another hand at work, one that manipulated the situation to bring Norfolk down, it means there is still another traitor to be found."

She paused, and searched her uncle's face. "You are truly concerned about this."

"I am truly concerned about any threat to William's throne. My sister paid a heavy price for you and your brother to hold the positions you deserve. I will not see that price paid for nothing."

"Why are you telling me this and not William?"

He shrugged and looked down the corridor, as though the

bricks or window glass might provide an answer. "Because I cannot go to William with half-formed fears. He likes hard answers, not speculation. But you . . . it was Anne I always went to in order to work out my own mind. And you are remarkably like her. I find talking to you helps put my thoughts in order."

"I have done precious little."

"You have listened, niece, and that is enough."

"Enough for a beginning. But what will you do next?"

"What I always do—hold multiple possibilities in my head at once and not neglect any of them for the simplest answer. Anne's children need never fear for the throne while I am here. I was born to unearth secrets."

She looped her hand through his arm, her long white fingers so much like her mother's. As they exited the gallery and began to encounter those who bowed and curtsied at their passing, he added softly, "You should watch your expressions while in church. Your dislike of Latimer is plain to be seen."

Born to unearth secrets indeed.

9 January 1555
Greenwich Palace

Since Christmas, William has become a bit more attentive to me in public. He says that, considering how close we have always been as friends, it is actually more suspicious to ignore one another. So he has begun to dance with me more than once in an evening and he has summoned me to play chess with him twice. At least we did actually play chess—I was afraid the game was only an excuse. But apparently Dominic told him sternly that he could not be completely alone with me, so we played in his privy chamber with four or five others in attendance.

Dominic was not among them.

15 January 1555
Whitehall Palace

The court has moved to London for a parliamentary session called by
William. They are being asked to ratify the French treaty and
William's betrothal to the young Elisabeth de France. For the first time
I can remember, I feel confined by the city. Whitehall is sprawling and
enormous and yet I feel as though I cannot take a deep breath here.
There are too many people, too much time spent pretending, and too
little as myself.

There are rumours that the Earl of Surrey will be pardoned. When I
asked William, he said that I should not bother myself with unpleasant
details. I almost laughed aloud, thinking he was teasing, but he meant
it. Love, it appears, does odd things to men. William seems incapable of
remembering that we once told each other everything, that he would
always complain to me about his uncle or his councilors or the intricacies
of politics and that I not only kept up but added my own insights.

As for Dominic . . . it seems love has made him mute.

27 January 1555
Whitehall

Parliament has ratified the French treaty and composed a most gracious
statement to William about his betrothal. Everyone seems in good
humour now that we are at peace and the question of the king's
marriage is settled.

Little do they know. After William beat me tonight at chess, he
whispered, for my ears alone, "I cannot wait to claim my chosen queen.
Then my people's good wishes will truly have meaning."

On the first of February, Dominic took a boat from Whitehall
Palace to the Tower of London to interrogate the Earl of Surrey.

As the boatman brought them alongside the Tower's water gate, Dominic wished he'd chosen to ride instead. He detested this entrance, smacking as it did of political prisoners arriving in the dead of night.

"Just an entrance, milord," Harrington said.

How did Harrington always know what he was thinking? He had inherited the large and quiet man from his time working for Lord Rochford. Dominic never quite knew how to describe what Harrington did—Man-at-arms? Steward? Personal secretary?—but he had quickly grown to depend on him with a trust and reliance he didn't offer most men. It was a pleasure to work with someone who seemed to respect him personally and not simply for his title and position.

And Harrington was right—the river gate was merely a convenient entrance when arriving by water. The Lieutenant of the Tower greeted them at the top of the steps and, at Dominic's request, led them first to the torture chambers. Dominic had been in them only once before—last year, while being trained by Lord Rochford. The Lord Chancellor had required Dominic to see things for himself, but that was one sight he wished he could forget: the man strapped by wrists and ankles to the rack, his joints torn from their sockets from being rolled in opposite directions. Dominic didn't even remember what the man had been accused of.

Today, mercifully, the rack was empty and the only one in the chamber was the man who usually operated it, a heavyset, powerful man named Sutton. He didn't seem to recall Dominic from last year, but his interest sharpened when he heard his title.

"Exeter, is it? You one of the Holland family?"

"No, I'm a Courtenay."

"Titles change with the wind these days. The last Duke of

Exeter was a Holland, he was constable of the Tower in 1447." Sutton said it fondly, as though recalling someone he'd known personally. "He it was who brought this to England." He laid a hand on the rack and added, "The Duke of Exeter's daughter, she's called. Did you know that?"

Dominic had not, and wished he didn't know it now. "I'm not a duke," he said brusquely. "Do you remember the Earl of Surrey's interrogation?"

"'Course I remember him. First time I've had a titled gentleman down here."

"What answers did he give?" Dominic had already spoken to the interrogators themselves, but he wanted the word of a man who had no political interest in the proceedings. Only a physical one.

"I don't pay much mind to what they say," the man replied. "But him . . . they weren't as anxious to get answers as I'd have thought. Usually they press a man to the edge, and well over it, to get him to say what they need. He was a gentleman right enough, held up better than some who collapse the moment they see the rack. He just kept saying no to whatever they asked."

And that tallied with what the interrogators had reported: the Earl of Surrey had steadfastly and continuously asserted his innocence in whatever plots his grandfather might have had in hand.

Sutton continued, not unkindly, "If it eases your conscience, milord, I was gentle with him. Only turned the rollers three times, not enough to damage anything permanently. He'll heal right up."

Dominic could not bring himself to more than nod before gladly, gratefully, escaping. Though it was bitingly cold and wet outdoors, the air was vastly cleaner than whatever guilt and pain and despair had been trapped in that ghastly chamber.

"Right," he told the lieutenant. "I'll see the Earl of Surrey now."

He and Harrington followed the lieutenant to the Bloody Tower and up several flights of ice-cold stairs to where Surrey was being held. The earl had two rooms and three gentlemen to serve him, as befitted his status. But it was still a prison cell, with bare stone walls and deep-set narrow windows that let in precious little light and the plainest of furnishings, and Dominic came close to shuddering at the thought of being locked away. His father had died in such a cell—perhaps this very one—accused and alone, and he wondered for the first time if it was dread as much as illness that had killed him.

Surrey rose to meet him. "Courtenay," he said, understandably wary. "Sorry, it's Exeter now, isn't it? I haven't been at court enough to remember."

Thomas Howard was younger than Dominic; at not quite nineteen, he was of an age with William. His light brown hair had a hint of red to it and he was clean shaven, which argued a greater than usual care for his appearance while imprisoned. He had a straight nose and his eyes were wide and slightly slanted, giving him an inquisitive, intelligent expression. He'd been the Earl of Surrey since the age of ten, when his own father was executed for treason. There was enough of familiarity and pity about his circumstances that Dominic felt sorry for him.

Which, he reminded himself, should no more affect his judgment than his distaste for punishing a man before fault had been found. "May we speak privately?" he asked, and Surrey led him into the smaller interior chamber, which contained only a bed and a single chair, while Harrington leaned against the wall of the outer chamber and prepared to learn what he could from Surrey's men. They had a round table and a deck of cards; men often spoke plainer while their hands were occupied.

Dominic took the chair and waited for Surrey to perch on the edge of the bed before saying, "I'm here on the king's behalf."

"I believe the men who racked me said the same."

"When I say it, you know my commission came face-to-face."

"Right. The King's Shadow, you're called."

Dominic knew it could be worse. Male companions of kings might be called all sorts of things if the king in question were unpopular. Considering how little time he spent flirting with women—exactly none—it was a good thing for his reputation that William was loved.

Surrey eased slightly, though the underlying tension remained. "What is your commission?"

"To determine the truth of what happened at Framlingham."

"You'll know better than I do, seeing as you were there and I was not. I'm not the one who stuck a knife in my uncle Giles's throat."

Clearly this wasn't a man afraid of plain speaking, whatever the circumstances. Dominic met his gaze steadily, though his mind whispered, *It wasn't a knife, it was a shard of glass. And it wasn't me . . .*

"He earned his death," Dominic countered harshly. "What about you?"

"I don't want to die, no more than any man, but how am I to prove a negative? I knew nothing of this Penitent's Confession I've been tortured over, nothing of any Spanish troops or grand Howard design to put Mary on the throne. If I could open my very head to you, you would see that I am innocent of these charges. Since I cannot, all I can give is my word and my past and future actions as bond. If I am to be allowed future action."

Dominic stood up and let his silence settle over Surrey while he circled what he could of the tiny room. Before he'd ever come here, he had believed in Surrey's innocence. But now he was even more certain. At last, he stood still and stared at Surrey, who rose slowly from the bed and tried not to look either hopeful or desperate. It could be hard to distinguish between the two emotions.

It would not do to make promises, but Dominic did say, "The king is inclined to be merciful. He desires to unite his kingdom, not divide it further."

"I would hope . . . to live and to serve is my only aim, Lord Exeter." Surrey stumbled over the words and Dominic realized again just how young he was. How young they all were, and yet trying to do their best for England.

He and Harrington bid goodbye to the earl and his men (with whom Harrington had indeed been playing cards) and exited into the open, outside the Bloody Tower, where Dominic breathed deeply of the frosty air, glad to be out of the confining walls and eager to return to court. But when he gave thanks to the Lieutenant of the Tower, the man said, "Another prisoner has asked to speak with you. She was most insistent, though who can say how she heard of your presence."

She—it could only be Eleanor Howard. He traded glances with Harrington, who shrugged slightly as if to say *Up to you*. Dominic had no desire to speak with William's former mistress, but she was the only female of the Howard family to be confined to the Tower. Guilt decided him. Or perhaps it was merely prudence. Eleanor made an unpredictable enemy.

She was being held in Beauchamp Tower, closer to the Lieutenant's Lodging. Her outer chamber was smaller than Surrey's, but it was warmer and richer, with tapestries on the walls that she would have had to pay extra for. She had two maids with her, both older and plainer women than herself who had the knack of blending into the furniture. From the moment Dominic entered,

Eleanor ignored her maids completely and focused all her attention on him.

She was undoubtedly an attractive woman—with her flaxen blond hair and surprisingly dark eyes—and she had the trick of looking at every man she met with more than a hint of promised pleasure. There were no concessions to prison in her clothing; she wore an extravagant gown of moss green velvet edged with ermine. Though she had claimed to be pregnant at the time of her arrest, there was no sign of it now beneath her tightly cinched stomacher.

Dominic had not seen her since November, and she said almost the same thing she had that last night at Framlingham. "I must see the king."

He opened his mouth to reply and she snapped, "And don't say he doesn't consort with traitors. I am not a traitor. You know that."

He did—reluctantly—know that. She was grasping and ambitious and amoral and had never evinced the slightest grief over her husband's violent death . . . but she was loyal to William. He was probably the only thing she had ever been loyal to.

He promised what he could. "I will speak to him." Surely if William were going to release Surrey and allow him to become Duke of Norfolk, he would set Eleanor free as well, if only for the sake of the child she had borne him. Not to return to court, of course . . . which was best for all concerned.

Eleanor narrowed her eyes, as though she knew what he was thinking, but said only, "You do that."

If Eleanor discovered even a hint of William's passion for Minuette, she would make a relentless enemy.

———

William was shooting with an arquebus when Dominic returned from the Tower. He heard Rochford's queries and, content to let his uncle have the first say, lifted the twenty-pound matchlock gun onto the forked stick and sighted carefully. He squeezed the lever, igniting the flash, and the ball shot out to strike the targeted breastplate. William liked shooting at plate armour; he was close enough to this breastplate to tear through it completely. As the onlookers applauded, he handed the arquebus to his arms master and looked over to Rochford and Dominic, in close conversation.

In the months since turning eighteen, William had found satisfaction in standing his ground and forcing others to come to him. When he beckoned them, he thought Rochford moved a little slowly.

"Walk with me," he commanded. This time his uncle definitely hesitated when William made clear that it was Dominic he wanted at his side.

"You spoke to Surrey," William remarked, leaving Rochford to pace slightly behind them.

"I did."

"And?"

"I am convinced he had nothing to do with his grandfather's treason. The investigation has not turned up any evidence, he went nowhere near Framlingham or the rest of his family for months, and his character—"

"You think there is a specific character type for treason?" Rochford cut in. "That you can know by past action how a man will jump in future?"

"*If* a man will jump, perhaps not. But *how* he will—if the Earl of Surrey committed treason, I do not believe he would lie about it. He would have his reasons, and he would not be ashamed of them."

"Men change when their lives are at stake."

"Then they are not men," Dominic said sharply.

"Enough," William interposed. "I agree with Dominic. Surrey is to be released. He will return to Kenninghall and stay there until further ordered. Which I believe you counseled?" he said pointedly to Rochford.

"So I did."

"See to it."

He watched until his uncle had disappeared inside the ashlar-stone walls of Whitehall. Then he turned back to Dominic on the riverbank path. "What else?" he asked. He knew when his friend was brooding.

"I spoke to Eleanor."

He didn't look at Dominic, appearing to consider the bare landscape of midwinter. He knew he would not have to respond; Dominic was incapable of ignoring anything he felt was his responsibility. It was why William had sent him.

"Is she also to be released?" Dominic eventually asked.

William had made his plans long before today. "Eleanor can go to Kenninghall with Surrey. I believe her daughter is being cared for there." Actually, William knew it for a fact. He had taken care to know. The child, Anne, was undoubtedly his; he had briefly considered acknowledging the baby girl before Eleanor's arrest, but knowing how much Minuette disliked Eleanor had stayed his hand. Still, he would ensure the child did not lack for proper care.

"Eleanor wants to see you."

Of course she does. "No."

"Are you sure that's wise?"

William looked sidelong at Dominic, amused. "Surely you are not counseling me to meet with Eleanor Howard?"

"I am counseling you to take care. She is dangerous, Will. Far more so than the Earl of Surrey, if you ask me."

"Eleanor cannot touch me."

"What of Minuette? Eleanor hated her thoroughly when she was nothing more than your friend. If—when—she finds out that Minuette is much more to you . . ."

"Don't worry about Minuette," William said. "There is no person more important to me. I will keep her safe, Dom. You can trust me for that."

There was a long pause, as though Dominic couldn't decide which condescending and unnecessary warning to issue first. At last he said simply, "Just be careful."

3 February 1555
Whitehall Palace

There are stretches of time in which I (nearly) forget about Framlingham and the lady chapel and the rivers of blood and tears I shed there . . . but today is not one of those times.

William has pardoned the Earl of Surrey. I take no issue with that, for Surrey was not at Framlingham at the end and I do not believe he had any personal involvement in his family's schemes. I do not even mind too terribly that Eleanor has been released and sent to Kenninghall. She is vindictive, but not stupid. She would never have countenanced a scheme to harm William when he is the source of every favour she has ever had. And she did lose her husband at Framlingham. My guilt is enough to soften my dislike. A little.

My troubled mind arises from a message I received this morning from Stephen Howard, youngest brother of the late Duke of Norfolk and my stepfather. He has also been pardoned and asks that I pay him a visit in his London house before he returns to the country.

I shall have to slip away quietly, for both Dominic and William would protest. It is annoying to have both of them watching me so closely.

Minuette knew that she could not, of course, go completely alone to see Stephen Howard. She might be able to deceive the men, but never Carrie. Her maid was a fierce friend and even fiercer guard, and there was no slipping away from her. Minuette took Fidelis with her as well; the enormous hound reminded her of Dominic, padding quietly along next to her and turning a forbidding gaze on all around him. Fortunately, her stepfather's town house was on the same side of the river as Whitehall. She couldn't imagine the boat that could have carried Fidelis across the Thames.

The streets, as always, were awash in humanity and its trappings. Street vendors and darting pickpockets and the shrill cries of argument mingled with the odors of food and, from some of the smaller streets, abundant refuse. At least in winter the odors were not quite so overwhelmingly bad. Minuette had dressed in one of her plainest gowns and a simple wool cloak with no trim—but there was no disguising the quality of the fabrics or the shine of her hair or even the way she moved. Eyes followed her and Carrie as they walked the mere half mile from Whitehall to the edge of the City—that square mile of London that answered to its own Lord Mayor and deigned to pay homage to the king—but Minuette did not feel in any danger, particularly as Fidelis ensured that she and Carrie were given a wide berth.

She knocked on the door of a discreetly wealthy town house and Stephen Howard himself threw it open. He looked much the same as before his imprisonment, perhaps the lines around his mouth and eyes slightly deeper. Though he was in his mid-fifties, he had the lean build of a younger man and his light brown hair had grayed attractively. There were times when Minuette had to admit that her mother might have actually loved her second husband for his person as much as for his position.

Those moments were usually ruined when he opened his

mouth. Today he raised his eyebrows at Fidelis and asked, "What the hell is that?"

"My protection," she said.

"Do you need protection from *me*?"

He always made her ruder than she meant to be. "Are you going to invite me in? I am here at your bidding, not the other way round." He regarded Fidelis dubiously, and she added, "He can wait with Carrie. Surely you have somewhere for my maid to sit comfortably?"

It was pleasant to have disconcerted him, and she thanked Dominic silently for it as Howard led Carrie and the wolfhound—which nearly reached her maid's shoulder—to the kitchen.

When he returned, he took Minuette into an airy solar at the back of the house. The room overlooked a narrow garden that was sunk in the grayness of winter slumber. In addition to the fire in the maroon-tiled fireplace, several coal-filled braziers made the chamber pleasantly warm.

After she seated herself, he studied her and remarked, "My disgrace suits you, stepdaughter. You are glowing."

Uncomfortable with his penetrating stare, as though he might be able to divine the secrets that made her glow, Minuette countered sharply. "What disgrace? You never even saw the inside of the Tower. You ensured leniency when you warned the king of your brother's search for the Penitent's Confession. House arrest can't have been too difficult in these surroundings." She indicated the warm fire, the thick carpet, the silver candlesticks.

"Yes, my familial disloyalty and your intervention spared me the Tower. Nonetheless, the name of Howard is a dangerous one to bear just now."

"As it has been before. You weathered your nephew's treason and brother's disgrace once before—no doubt you will weather it again."

He chuckled. "Can it be that you have grasped the game of politics? Your mother never had it in her—and your father certainly didn't—but then, you've spent most of your life being tutored by the Boleyns and they play as easily as they breathe."

She ignored—just—the slight about her father. Stephen Howard seemed to take it personally that her mother had loved a man before him. But she didn't have time to debate the merits of her father to her stepfather. "What do you want?" Minuette asked.

"To tell you not to play these games," he answered promptly, and all mockery vanished. "I don't like that you were in the middle of everything at Framlingham. And your mother would have been horrified."

"You were the one who warned me that the duke was looking for the Penitent's Confession. That's why I was at Framlingham."

"You were at Framlingham because you are a convenient pawn. Who sent you there? Was it the king himself? Or Rochford?"

He was so annoying that it was easy to overlook how perceptive he could be. "What does it matter? The Penitent's Confession is destroyed and this particular game is over."

"Is it? Why did you burn that confession, Minuette?"

Because I don't trust you entirely. Because my mother's name was signed to that document and you are the one who told me your brother was looking for it . . . Although part of her wanted to pretend that burning the Penitent's Confession had put an end to the ache, the larger part wanted answers.

She countered with a question of her own. "What precisely did you know about the contents of the Penitent's Confession?"

He looked bewildered, and wary. "Only that it claimed William was not Henry's son."

"That is all? No discussion of who might have made such a

claim? No concern that such a convenient document might be a forgery or outright lie?"

"As you said . . . what does it matter now?"

"Who talked about it in your family? Someone besides your brother?"

"Minuette—"

"Who talked about it?!" she yelled, and was darkly amused by the shock on his face. He had not expected her to raise her voice.

Shock quickly turned to anger. "I'm not going to indulge your curiosity while you're in a temper."

She pitched her next words with care. "Who in your family made a mockery of my mother's name?"

"The Penitent's Confession was signed with your mother's name?" Though it was half a question, he did not need her confirmation. "That is why you burnt it, because you did not want your mother's name seen."

She did not trust any of the Howards, but her stepfather . . . She remembered what Carrie had told her, grudgingly, about her mother's death. *He slept in a chair, when he slept at all, and he ordered us around as though he could keep Death away if he just willed it hard enough.*

Stephen Howard had loved her mother, she trusted that. So finally, grudgingly, she told him the truth. "My mother was the supposed penitent, confessing that Henry was not William's father. But that confession was false from beginning to end, including her signature, because it was dated just one day *before* her death."

Her stepfather grasped that detail immediately. "No one in my family would be stupid enough to make such an elementary mistake. We were at Framlingham with the others when she died— everyone knew that your mother was out of her mind those last

THE BOLEYN DECEIT · 59

days. No one who was there would ever believe she was in a condition to make such a confession, false or not."

"What about your nephew, Giles? He would have been a child, only . . . what? Nine, ten? And you said yourself he had a personal issue with me. He might have used her name to hurt me."

He shook his head. "This entire plan was far too clever and subtle for Giles. Far be it from me to disparage family, but Giles was not our brightest mind." He paused, then said, "What about his wife? Eleanor makes no secret of her dislike of you. And she is both clever and cruel."

"And truly attached to the king. Everything she has she owes to William. Eleanor would do nothing to threaten his rule."

"Unless," he argued, "she was playing a double game. Threaten the throne—in order to strengthen it."

It was Minuette's turn to blink. "I don't—"

"Think about it." Stephen Howard leaned forward, hands clasped loosely together, the firelight glinting off the threads of gold in his brown velvet doublet and dancing on the snowy linen of his cuffs. "The primary threat to the king's rule has been neutralized. With my brother dead and his heir under question in the Tower, the Catholic powers are in retreat. Mary is under house arrest, her position has never been weaker, and the king's public approval could not be higher after his victory in France."

"Are you saying all of this was a feint? That Norfolk *never* intended rebellion?" Minuette thought of Alyce, her friend whose untimely death had begun the unraveling of Norfolk's treason, and of how scarcely anyone even remembered her. The thought that her friend had been a casualty of a mere game made her sick.

"I'm saying that these sorts of maneuvers are still well beyond you, Minuette. Go back to court, serve your princess, and keep your head down. I will find out who defamed your mother's name. You can trust me for that."

She did—though she couldn't swear that his intent was to bring the perpetrator to the king's justice. He looked rather as though he would kill the person himself. For the first time, she realized that there were aspects of her stepfather that reminded her of Dominic.

"I will promise," she replied. "On one condition—I want to know who was behind it all. Not just for my mother's sake. There was a woman, my friend . . . Her name was Alyce de Clare and she died at the beginning of all this. Alyce was part of it and in over her head, and she . . ." It seemed wrong to tell him all of it, though most of the court had known. Known, and now forgotten.

"She what?"

"She was with child when she died. The child's father was almost certain to have been part of the whole conspiracy. I thought it was Giles, after you told me he'd lied about being home in March of 1553."

"He was quarantined with the pox that month."

"Well yes, I know that now. If you'd bothered to be specific when I asked about his whereabouts before, I might have saved a good deal of time. But what matters is that whoever fathered Alyce de Clare's child is still unknown. If you really think this was a feint, a double-dealing method of tainting your family, that man could be the key to discovery."

"Yes, he could. Very good, Minuette."

"I have a list of names I was going through, I could send them to you."

"That would be useful. But that is the end of it, do you hear me? No more games for you. Remember that the next time Rochford comes calling. You stay out of this."

Oh yes, she thought wryly. Definitely like Dominic. Although Stephen Howard didn't know her as well, so she was able to lie much more easily.

"I'll stay out of it."

CHAPTER FOUR

"Happy?" Robert murmured.

Elizabeth twitched as his breath caressed her cheek. "You're distracting me," she protested, her fingers moving smoothly across the strings of her lute. Happy, yes; but also suspicious. Robert had been more than attentive this winter. He had been ever on hand, and for once neither her brother nor her uncle had made any comment on it.

William's lack of observance was easy enough to understand—he had eyes only for Minuette. And people were beginning to whisper.

Including Robert. He leaned back and stretched his legs out as he asked, casually enough, "So what do you think of your brother's French betrothal?"

She didn't believe in that casualness. With a quick frown, she stopped playing and laid the lute aside. Before answering, she scanned her presence chamber to ensure no one was paying more than the usual attention to her. Her ladies knew to give her space when Robert was with her.

It would have been easy to parry the question back to him, but she didn't bother. Wasn't that the point of Robert, that he was someone she didn't have to always guard against? "I think that I feel rather sorry for the child. I hear that Elisabeth de France is quite taken with my brother. She spends her time practicing her English and learning our history so that she might do him proud."

"Isn't that admirable in a girl who will one day be England's queen?"

"She's nine years old, Robert! She should be studying for herself, not to impress a man she's met only once."

"Not everyone loves learning for its own sake. Not every princess is you. And most men would be delighted with a wife who thinks only of pleasing them."

"Most men don't deserve such a wife."

He grimaced. "You are harsh, Elizabeth."

And you are married, Robert, she very nearly replied.

But he swung the conversation away with his impeccable instinct for avoiding trouble. "What of your friend, Mistress Wyatt? The king has been most gracious to Dominic—does he mean to bestow any favours on Minuette? If she had wealth, the men of England would be lined up to claim her."

From one dangerous topic to another. "Perhaps then it is wiser not to endow her with wealth. I don't believe those sorts of men are the sort she is interested in."

"Whom is she interested in?"

"Why? Are you thinking of staking your own claim?"

"You know that there is only one woman for me," he retorted in that carelessly seductive voice that made her want to forget herself. "Constancy to true love—that is something King Henry's children know all about." Then his expression turned serious. "William, for one, is a man ripe for constancy. Why do I think it is not directed at his French princess?"

Elizabeth's heart sank. Only three months, and things were

beginning to unravel! William had never been able to control his countenance, and so she'd known it was only a matter of time before people began to realize how he felt about Minuette.

The question was: how did Minuette feel about William? Elizabeth had never asked her, but now she would have to. How could she control the situation if she didn't know everything?

On a sleety mid-February day, Minuette was summoned to see Elizabeth. The fact that it was a formal summons—a written request from the princess, delivered by a page wearing the crowned falcon badge Elizabeth had taken from her mother— meant that she could guess at the subject. It appeared Elizabeth had finally grown tired of her absolute silence on the subject of William's secret proposal. There had never been any chance Elizabeth would simply let the situation unfold of its own accord. She wanted a hand in its unfolding.

Indeed, Elizabeth went straight to the heart of the matter once the two of them were closeted in the princess's private study at Whitehall. The room was lined with shelves of books that most scholars would have sold their teeth to own. Elizabeth approached scholarship the same way she approached everything: with absolute dedication to mastering a subject until all its secrets were known to her. So it was no surprise when she placed Minuette in a chair facing hers and said sternly, "You are going to stay in this room until I know precisely how you feel about my brother and his plans for you. Is that clear?"

After an instinctive moment of stubbornness, Minuette laughed. "Perfectly clear, Your Highness. I am yours to command."

Elizabeth's expression softened. "For now. But that's rather the point, isn't it? My brother is determined that in future you will answer solely to him."

"And that troubles you?" Minuette didn't ask only to deflect the attention, but because she was genuinely curious how Elizabeth felt about William's proposal. They were friends, yes, but Elizabeth was first and foremost a princess royal. One had only to mark the cloth-of-silver dress she wore with such easy elegance, the pearls studded in the coils of her red-gold hair, the ruby ring she wore on her left hand, the indefinable inheritance of privilege that manifested itself in how Elizabeth moved and even thought. What could she think about her brother intending to marry a woman of no name and little wealth? Not to mention the fact that William's intentions narrowed Elizabeth's future course of action considerably.

But Elizabeth proved herself a true and concerned friend when she answered warmly, "The only thing that troubles me is that I haven't the slightest idea how *you* feel. I can be in no doubt of my brother's feelings—he can hardly speak of anything else when we are alone. But you have shut me out, Minuette, and not just since William's proposal. You have kept your own counsel since my mother's death at Hever last summer."

Minuette remembered it well—the burning shame of being found by Elizabeth in William's arms, lost in much more than a kiss in the same room with Queen Anne's corpse. It was with real remorse that she replied, "I am sorry, Elizabeth. It's never been about shutting you out. It is only . . ." *It is only that I don't want to marry Will. It is Dominic I love. And I can't tell you that because William mustn't know, not until I figure out how to get all of us out of this without pain.*

She couldn't say any of that, so she said, "It's a complicated situation. I am doing my best to keep my head and behave well."

Unusually affectionate for her, Elizabeth took Minuette's hands in hers. "I know, and you are. But we are alone here, and I miss you. You know more of Robert than anyone living. Can you not speak to me of William?"

Minuette could feel her barriers cracking, and she let some of her heartfelt trouble come through. "I was, of course, astonished at his proposal," she answered Elizabeth. "I had never dreamt such a thing. I know he is impulsive, but this . . . my immediate thought was that he wanted to make amends for what occurred at Hever. Not," she added hastily, "that he needed to make amends. We were equally complicit. But you know how gener-ous he is in his affections. I do not believe William has thought this through."

"But you do love him." It was not quite a question.

"You know I do. And because I love him, I would never hold him to an offer made in the heat of the moment." She could hear the sleet hitting the window with a hiss that sounded disapprov-ing, as though even the weather could see through her half-told truths.

Elizabeth let go of Minuette's hands. She sat back, once again coolly assessing. "You expect that he will have to retract his offer?"

"He cannot afford to alienate the French now, and with the debts and tax burden from last year's war, that will not change anytime soon. William's affections run hot, but for how long?"

"I don't know," Elizabeth said, frowning, "but my father's af-fections ran blazingly hot for a good six years before he married my mother. Don't underestimate William's devotion to you."

"I would never do that. But I also don't underestimate his de-votion to England. And even you must admit that making me queen would be an exceedingly bad idea for England."

Elizabeth shrugged. "It is true that the nobility is not pre-pared for the elevation of another minor Englishwoman to the throne, even if you come without the burden of an ambitious family, as my mother did. And William is wise enough to know he cannot make his intentions public without causing an outcry greater than any since my father's break with Rome. He will be patient—we must also ensure he is discreet."

"People are talking." Minuette said it flatly.

"Only a little, but that will change if William continues to favour you so openly. As long as he was sleeping with Eleanor, no one thought twice about his friendship with you. But with no other woman to distract him—"

"Are you suggesting we arrange a mistress for William?" Minuette could not decide if she was outraged by Elizabeth's practicality or respected it. And she could not begin to unravel how she felt about the thought of William in the bed of another woman like Eleanor.

"I am suggesting that it might be wise to remove ourselves from court whenever possible. If I am not here, neither can you be here. Perhaps we will visit Mary. My sister has been left in solitude long enough—no doubt she would welcome visitors from court. Or, at least, endure them."

Minuette thought of facing Lady Mary after that last, disastrous stay at Framlingham. It didn't excite her, but Elizabeth was right. It would be better for everyone if she and William were separated.

She tried not to dwell on the fact that leaving court behind meant leaving Dominic as well.

Once thought of, Elizabeth wasted no time in arranging to visit Mary. It worked out rather well for her, since her half sister was currently a reluctant "guest" at Syon House. Just ten miles west of London, Syon House belonged to the strongly Protestant Duke of Northumberland, and his eldest son John, the Earl of Warwick, was Mary's court-appointed guardian. If Robert chose to visit his brother at Syon House while Elizabeth was also there, who would remark on it?

William had not been enthusiastic about the temporary separation from Minuette, but Dominic had backed Elizabeth up, and so her brother agreed to let her and Minuette travel to Syon House at the beginning of March. Richmond Palace was only a little farther west; William planned to catch up to them there after two weeks.

Elizabeth thought she had everything under control, up until the day before her departure. As she was sorting through the books she wished to take with her, Kat Ashley interrupted.

"Lord Northumberland and Lord Robert to see you, Your Highness," Kat said warily. Kat was always wary where Robert was concerned. Alone among Elizabeth's women—except possibly Minuette—Kat Ashley had the privilege of speaking her mind freely to the princess, whose governess she had been since Elizabeth was four years old.

Elizabeth looked up and marked the lines of disapproval on Kat's round-cheeked face. "What does he want?" Robert she would always welcome, but the duke? Perhaps he wished her to convey a message to the Earl of Warwick, or perhaps he himself planned to visit Syon House while she was in residence there.

Kat sniffed, looking very maternal in her blue wool gown and the old-fashioned gabled hood covering her silver-streaked hair. "The duke asked for a private audience. Will you see them?"

"Very well."

Elizabeth's immediate impression was that Robert would have rather been anywhere else than her presence. He stood two paces behind his father, and his normally expressive face was shuttered as though he were trying to distance himself from whatever his father had to say.

Northumberland, shorter and rougher-edged than the elegant Robert, spoke with unusual diffidence. "Your Highness, thank you for seeing us. There's a matter of some delicacy . . . obviously the king will have to know but I thought that you . . . perhaps you will speak to him for my son?"

Involuntarily, she looked to Robert, who met her eyes and gave a slight shake of his head. *Not me.* Well, that was something.

"Which son and why does he require my intervention with the king?" Elizabeth asked the duke.

"Guildford, Your Highness."

She should have guessed—of Northumberland's five living sons, Guildford was his favorite for no discernible reason. He was the youngest—two years younger than Robert—and his only talent appeared to be getting into scrapes.

"And what has Guildford done?" Fighting, drinking, gambling above his means . . . all were distinct possibilities with the Dudley sons.

"He has unexpectedly married."

"Rather young," Elizabeth remarked drily. "He's just twenty, isn't he?" She turned her steady gaze to Robert, who had once again dropped his eyes. "Though that is not the youngest age at which a son of yours has married. And is the young woman— I suppose someone of whom the king will not approve?"

"Lady Margaret Clifford."

If she had been a man, Elizabeth would have whistled at that name, or sworn aloud. No, her brother would most certainly not approve. Margaret Clifford was their cousin, a granddaughter of Henry VIII's favorite sister, and as such she held a place in the royal line of succession. Elizabeth did not mince words. "It is against the law for a member of the royal family to marry without the sovereign's permission. The penalty is death."

If anything could bring Northumberland to humility, it was love for his family. Ashen-faced, he became voluble. "They are young, Your Highness, as you said, and in love. I told Guildford to wait, that I would discuss the matter with the king, but youth is impatient. And the girl—"

"Already with child?"

He nodded.

"That will displease the king even more," she said sharply. "And I do not see why I should be the one to bear his first anger rather than you. Or better yet, Guildford himself. If he is man enough to marry and be a father, then he should be able to stand up and admit what he has done. Where are they?"

"I don't know."

"Don't know—or won't say?"

For a second, she saw the canny flicker in his eyes and was reminded that, anguished or not, Northumberland always played the game to his advantage. But what advantage could he gain from a willful son getting a royal girl with child and then having the gall to wed her in open defiance of the law?

Elizabeth turned her attention to Robert. "Why are you here?" she demanded. "To speak up for your brother?"

He hesitated, then squared his shoulders. "My father thought I might gentle your temper. I told him he was mistaken; that you would not welcome any words having to do with a young and hasty marriage coming from me."

Her laugh was immediate, and bitter. She said to Northumberland, "At least one of your sons is wiser than you. I will speak to the king of this matter and persuade him to kindness—to the girl, at least. As for your son, he has made his marital bed. Now he must lie in it."

As they bowed themselves out, Robert eyed her gravely and she wished—oh, how she wished!—that she had not been speaking as much about him as about Guildford.

9 March 1555
Whitehall Palace

There has been quite the scandal at court. Guildford Dudley and Margaret Clifford are married, and the girl is said to be already with child. She is not even fifteen! William was furious—not the shouting, throwing things kind of anger that I know how to deal with from living with his mother. No, this fury was deep and dark and terrifying even for the onlookers. The Dudleys sent Margaret to court on her own to face William, and I will not soon forget the girl kneeling before the king in supplication while I held my breath along with the rest. For once even I could not predict what he might do.

As Margaret Clifford's mother is dead—and clearly she was not being well supervised—she has been sent to her aunt, Lady Suffolk, along with a contingent of royal guards to ensure that if Guildford attempts to contact his bride he will be found. He has still not had the nerve to show himself. Both Elizabeth and I have warned Robert that each day's delay will only harden William's anger. But in this matter, Robert appears to have little influence with his family.

The tempest has delayed Elizabeth's and my planned departure for Syon House. With the Dudley family teetering on disfavour, William wanted to scrap our visit to Mary altogether, seeing as she is in custody at one of their homes and in the keeping of Northumberland's oldest son. At last he agreed to let us visit, but not to stay at Syon House itself. We will travel directly to Richmond and make the short trip to see Mary as often as we wish.

I do not think it will be very often.

Three days after the women's departure for Richmond, William endured a privy council meeting that was more than usually tense. In addition to the Duke of Northumberland, who sat brooding and watchful as if waiting for someone to badger him about Guildford's folly, the Earl of Surrey was in attendance for the first time. The king had met less resistance than he'd expected from his uncle at naming Surrey to the privy council; Rochford had gone so far as to admit William's wisdom in balancing England's divided religious interests. Still, William kept his eye on the young man, wary for any sign of his grandfather's arrogance or belligerence. Surrey looked unassuming enough; his clothing balanced nicely between the Earl of Oxford's peacock extravagance and Dominic's restrained simplicity.

Both Northumberland and Surrey sat quietly while other council members discussed the early items, which centered on the treasury and the unpleasant fact that William was rapidly running out of money. Though not himself so much as England, a point he was quick to make when William Cecil, Lord Burghley, began listing personal expenses as examples of items that might be scaled back.

Burghley's voice was as inflectionless as his numbers. "In the last year, Your Majesty, you have spent two hundred pounds on books, five hundred pounds on fabrics, and more than eight thousand pounds on property . . ."

"All of which came from my own purse, not England's coffers," William interrupted, allowing a hint of displeasure to creep in. He was not going to permit Burghley to accuse him of plundering England's treasury for his own pleasures.

But Burghley was not easily cowed. "And none of which would matter if your spending confined itself to such trifles. But the treasury is nearly depleted after the French campaign. There have been too many years of drought and bad harvests. Retrenchments will have to be made in public expenditures."

"Then why are you troubling me with figures about books and fabric?"

Rochford intervened, his steady voice still holding more than a trace of authority. "Because your personal life should set the example for the people. You cannot cut back government posts and servants, not to mention increase taxes, while flaunting private wealth in a most public manner."

Piqued by his uncle's intervention, let alone the fact that he was correct, William ignored him and said to Burghley, "What is it you recommend?"

The treasurer's answer was prompt. "A commission to study court expenditures and make recommendations for eliminating unnecessary spending. Now that we are at peace with France, there are certainly cuts that can be made. The sooner the better."

"Fine." William bit the word off to underscore his reluctance, though he knew it was a sensible plan and he was already turning over possible commission members in his mind. His father and Cromwell had proposed the Eltham Ordinances years ago and been lauded for their good sense. This was a chance to show himself as practical and civic-minded as they had been.

After finances, they arrived at the most common, and most rancorous, subject—religious discontent. Although it had been muted for the last four months by his betrothal to Elisabeth de France, Catholic resentment at Norfolk's death and Mary's house arrest ran deep, and they never knew when it might flare into something ugly.

Two weeks earlier, a prosperous family in York had been burned out of their home by a mob claiming they had sheltered a Jesuit priest some months before. If that were all, it would never have come to William's attention, but the mob had been less than careful and, in their haste, neglected to ensure that the house was completely empty before they fired it. A twelve-year-old housemaid had died in the blaze—a girl with no ties to the Catholic

Church, save working for a family who possibly sympathized with Rome.

Tensions had been running high in the North ever since— from the justifiably angry Catholics, who accused the mob of not caring whom they hurt, to the local cleric who had preached a sermon that as good as said the dead girl got what she deserved and anyone even speaking to Catholics was damned by association.

"The Lady Mary's household has remained quiet on the matter?" William asked. The last thing he needed in this overheated climate was any kind of public statement from the half sister who most of Europe still considered England's rightful ruler.

"It has," Rochford said. "Your Majesty, do you mean to continue her house arrest indefinitely? Or is the Princess Elizabeth's visit to her a sign that you will soon restore her some measure of autonomy?"

William looked at the Earl of Surrey, sitting stiffly where once his grandfather had sat and entirely mute until now. "What think you, Surrey?" he asked curtly.

"I think her imprisonment is a mistake, Your Majesty." He had a strong, clear voice that was more remarkable than his other, somewhat forgettable, features.

William indicated that he should continue. Surrey's voice strengthened as he spoke. "Your Catholic subjects are still that— your subjects. Including the Lady Mary. It is my understanding that you have no certain evidence to doubt her loyalty. When you punish where there is no fault, resentment breeds. And you cannot afford resentment."

William raised a single eyebrow. Despite his own recent imprisonment, Surrey was not afraid to be direct, even offensive. But he was honest, and William had ever respected honesty. "What would you do?"

"Continue your course of moderation. Don't confuse matters of state with matters of conscience. There will always be agitators on both sides, Your Majesty, but the bulk of your people understand and admire your tolerance."

Northumberland grunted and finally broke his silence. "Tolerance is earned. And it isn't Protestants threatening the throne."

"It isn't me, either," Surrey retorted. "By all means, punish treason wherever it threatens. But don't confuse the security of the state with personal prejudice."

"Says the man not long out of the Tower," Northumberland muttered, almost but not quite under his breath.

"I would think you would agree with Surrey's call for tolerance, my lord duke," William said with deceptive mildness. "After all, there's more than one way to undermine the throne."

It was the first time William had publicly touched upon the matter of the still-absent Guildford since the day he'd sent Margaret Clifford into Lady Suffolk's care. He felt everyone's attention sharpen—except Dominic, whose attention was always pitched to an extreme. Oxford and Pembroke looked almost greedy as they leaned into the table, eager to watch the arrogant Northumberland be taken down a notch. William wondered if there was a single man at that table who truly cared for anything more than his own position. Other than Dominic, of course.

William also leaned forward, and clasped his hands loosely on the table in front of him while focusing on Northumberland's uneasy face. "I wonder, is your son still in England, or has he been spirited away to the Continent? Not very gallant of Guildford to abandon his girl-bride."

"He knows Your Majesty would not harm her," Rochford interposed in his measured way. Like so much his uncle did, the intervention irritated William.

Harm his young cousin? No, he would not do that. But the

chit of a girl was hardly an innocent—Margaret had admitted to being a wife in all ways to Guildford Dudley and had the belly to prove it. Time to bring pressure to bear before it was said that Northumberland could get away with anything. Let it be seen, William thought, that he could punish Protestant as well as Catholic.

"My Lord Chancellor," he said—for this was a task for Rochford, not for Dominic's more sensitive conscience—"have Margaret Clifford—excuse me, Margaret *Dudley*—arrested. Bring her to the Tower, that we might question her more closely about her husband's whereabouts and . . . intentions." He considered Northumberland for the space of four slow breaths, letting the tension build. "I find it difficult to believe that young Guildford would have been so rash of his own accord. To bed the girl—yes, he would easily do that. But to wed her? A girl in line to my throne? I wonder where your son got the courage to do that?"

He took pleasure in having rattled the normally undaunted Northumberland. "Your Majesty, I assure you—"

"You're excused, my lord Northumberland. I have no further need of you at court just now. You may return when you bring your son to answer for his crime. You are free to retreat to whichever home you choose—save Syon House, naturally."

It was a toss-up whether the duke would go quietly. He did, in the end, shoving his chair back with all the fury he could not give voice to, and William did not envy whatever unlucky soul would bear the brunt of Northumberland's swallowed resentment.

The remainder of the meeting passed quickly, no one anxious to further try William's uncertain temper. He rather enjoyed it, while he pondered Surrey, who'd had the good sense not to react to Northumberland's public rebuke. The late Duke of Norfolk would not have been so circumspect. Although he knew the Howards could be erstwhile friends and implacable enemies, William decided that he liked this young earl.

It seemed Dominic liked him as well, for he took several minutes to speak to him as the privy council was dismissed. When Surrey had left the room, William called Dominic back.

"I need hardly ask if you agree with him," William said.

Dominic shrugged. "I have seen the results of heavy-handed repression. You wouldn't need a lieutenant on the Welsh border if there hadn't been so many generations of brutality on both sides."

"The real trouble with the religious divide is that even when I punish clear-cut wrongdoing, it gets tangled up with religion. There's always someone ready to turn any situation to their advantage."

"I suppose that's why we have a king. To sort the impossible."

William laughed. "All the more reason to buy what books I wish, without meddling from accountants and clerks." He looked at Dominic and made his decision on the spot. "Dom, I want you to head this commission into court spending. Your advice I can live with, for it will not be condescending. Or, at least, no more so than usual. I do have one condition."

"What is that?"

"That you do not protest the expense of any gifts I choose to give Minuette."

Dominic's expression did not so much as flicker. "As long as they're not bought with treasury funds, I promise to refrain from comment." Then, swiftly, he changed the subject. "What made you go after Northumberland today, after so carefully holding your tongue?"

"A man who wishes to openly attack should take care his own

house is in order first. If Northumberland wants to provoke Catholics, he needs cleaner hands. Don't you think he's the one who manipulated Guildford's marriage?"

Dominic shrugged. "Possibly."

"That's a possibility I dislike. Everyone knows his one great regret is that he married off Robert too young, so that he has no chance with my sister. He would have taken care with Guildford to choose ambitiously. Not quite Jane Grey—I'm sure Northumberland still hopes I will change my mind and marry her myself—and Jane's sisters are too young, but Margaret Clifford comes next to them in succession."

"All those women," Dominic said lightly. "Elizabeth, the Grey sisters, the Clifford girls . . ."

William laughed. "Believe me, no one is more anxious than I am to start getting sons. But until then, yes, all those women line up after me, which means I must take great care with the men who come near them."

Always anxious after being confined to sitting for too long, he stood and began to circle the table. Dominic rose as well, used to standing still while his friend prowled. "I've been thinking, Dom."

"Always a sure sign of trouble."

He rolled his eyes at his friend, who for the first time in weeks looked somewhat cheerful. William hadn't realized how tense Dominic had been until now, when his expression was once again open and relaxed. It lightened his heart, and he went on confidently, "I've decided to allow Surrey to inherit his grandfather's title."

"Another Duke of Norfolk? Let's hope this one is less trouble than the previous one."

"It's good for the country," William said. "I won't let him

have all the lands and retainers—I'll clip his wings considerably—but it will soften the Catholics to see that I am not afraid to listen to their advocate."

"Fair enough."

"The thing is," William went on, "as I've said before, it's a balancing act. With Surrey made Duke of Norfolk, that brings us back to three dukes in the kingdom. But when I propose this to my uncle, I actually mean to propose bringing the council to four dukes."

"You mean to create a title?"

"No, I thought I'd resurrect one. There hasn't been a Duke of Exeter in almost a hundred years—what do you think?"

Dominic must have been truly relaxed, because William could see the play of thoughts across his usually impassive face: openly surprised, then shocked, then staggered. He opened his mouth, and shut it without speaking.

"Wouldn't you like to be my lord Duke of Exeter? Come on, Dom. Say something."

"You have lost your mind."

"Say something less insulting."

"Your Majesty—"

"Don't call me that."

"People will say it's favoritism."

"And so it is."

"Damn it, Will!" Dominic ran his hands through his black hair, an unusual sign of aggravation. "Be reasonable!"

"Finished yelling at me?"

They glared at one another.

Then William nodded. "Good. Now give me credit for not being stupid. I know what some will say if I make you a duke. Just as I know what some will say about restoring Norfolk's title to his grandson. People always talk, Dom. I don't care about that. I care about having a council that represents England and a nobility that is balanced."

"Northumberland and Norfolk," Dominic said thoughtfully. "Protestant and more-or-less Catholic."

"Yes. With my plan, I will have one duke loyal to the Catholics and one duke loyal to the Protestants. Then there's my uncle. Protestant as well, but loyal primarily to himself. What I need to round it all out, Dom, is you."

"Why?"

"So that I have one duke in England who is loyal only to me."

Dominic must have been far more shattered than he'd suspected, for he broke royal protocol and sat down in the nearest chair while William still stood. He dropped his head into his hands for a long minute in which William wisely held his tongue. He knew how to bring his friend round. One only had to appeal to his sense of duty.

Dominic groaned. "I don't suppose I actually have a choice, do I?"

William grinned. "That's why I like you—always stating the obvious."

CHAPTER FIVE

Elizabeth, who had not been to Syon House before, had to admit it was impressive. Approached through a park that was in detail, if not size, nearly the equal of royal grounds, the house itself had been built by Northumberland in the Italian style in the years since King Henry's death. Once Sion Abbey, dedicated to the Bridgettine nuns, Northumberland had laid out his house over the foundations of the abbey church.

Despite its grandeur, Elizabeth felt a faint apprehension as she studied the rectangular, flat-fronted house. The nuns of twenty years ago had not taken lightly to their dispossession: indeed, their confessor protested so vigorously that he had been executed and his body hung on the abbey gates as a warning to other recalcitrant Catholics.

Had William had those memories in mind when he sent Mary here? Elizabeth would not put it past her brother to layer message upon message. A royal abbey, dissolved by royal command and given into the hands of a committed Protestant, now housing the most devoted Catholic in England.

John Dudley, Earl of Warwick, waited for them in the echoing hall, the floor laid with glazed tiles of green and blue, patterned in swirls like moving water. Six years older than Robert, he looked more like their sturdy and rough-edged father than did his younger brother. But there was a certain similarity in his expressions and turn of speech that reminded Elizabeth of Robert.

John greeted Elizabeth and Minuette courteously and briefly, managing to convey his regrets that they would not be guests at Syon House without touching on Guildford's crimes or his father's current precarious position. Then he escorted them directly to Mary in the wing of Syon House set aside for her use.

Elizabeth thought that her sister could hardly complain at being ill-used in her house arrest, considering the lavish appointments of her chambers. As Syon House was considerably newer than most royal palaces, the rooms were bright and airy, high windows giving on to views of the lavish gardens just beginning to show spangled hints of colour from early blooming crocus and daffodils.

The fact remained that, however opulently gilded, Syon House was a prison, with the Earl of Warwick on guard to ensure Mary did not slip away into rebellious hands or receive any visitors who might be looking to stir up trouble. But how was that significantly different from anywhere Mary lived? She was always at William's mercy. This was just a particularly stark reminder of that fact.

As the elder sister, Mary did not deign to rise when Elizabeth and Minuette entered. Seated in an intricately carved chair before a blazing fire, Mary Tudor did not look like a figurehead for rebellion. Though elegantly dressed and impeccable in her manner and bearing, Mary was aging rapidly. Thirty-eight this year, Elizabeth mused, and wearing that somber dark brown overdress and starched hood, looking even older. Her dark red hair was still thick, but her high, broad forehead showed new lines. The once-sharp jawline that narrowed to a pointed chin was growing soft and blurred.

One thing that never changed was the surety of Mary's birth and position. She still held a grudge against the younger sister who had usurped her title as Princess of Wales so many years ago. Never mind that William had come along soon after and supplanted them both—it was Elizabeth whom Mary had always disliked.

Not that she would betray it in words. "Welcome, sister," Mary said. "I am grateful to be remembered by my family."

"Have you been comfortable?" Elizabeth asked politely. Of course she had; William would never allow less.

Mary sniffed. "I would prefer to be allowed to go home. I do not see why I cannot stay at Beaulieu."

"Do you not? I would have thought events at Framlingham were self-evident. The Crown cannot risk a foreign power interfering in your life."

Mary's hands moved restlessly on the arms of her chair, her jeweled rings sending flashes of blue and red and green into the shadows. "I have answered the king's questions—if they were truly his. More likely it is my enemies who conspire to blacken me to the king. If the Duke of Norfolk was involved in a plot against the king, I had no knowledge of it and so I have stated. Is my word not good enough?"

Talking to Mary was always an exercise in patience. She was intelligent and educated, but she had little sense of irony and none at all of humour. And always she would be blinded by her obsession with what she saw as England's heresy.

Which meant Elizabeth could run rings around her when she chose. But today she wasn't here for entertainment; she was here for information. She damped down her normal impulse to dazzle Mary with her youth and beauty, and aimed for honesty rather than cleverness.

"Tell me, dear sister: if the Duke of Norfolk had said, 'There are Spanish ships waiting to take you to the emperor, you need only ride out a few miles . . .' would you not have gone? You came so close five years ago."

In 1550, Mary had indeed come close to escaping England in that very way—a ride to the east coast and Spanish ships waiting for her. In the end it had been her own indecision that cost her the chance. She had simply waited too long trying to divine what God meant her to do.

"And that is why I am punished now," Mary said flatly. "Kept in this house of that heretic, Northumberland. It is insulting, and now you are come to mock."

Minuette intervened. "No, my lady, never to mock. The king's affections will always be inclined to leniency, but you cannot allow yourself to be used by those of evil intent."

Elizabeth sat back and watched her sister and her friend regard each other. Mary had no cause to love Minuette after what had happened at Framlingham, but there was something gentle about Minuette that could disarm the most suspicious. Today she looked like an angel in her pale blue gown and white underskirt, a bright counterpoint of hope to Mary's dark and fading appearance.

"I might give the same advice to my brother," Mary challenged Minuette. "He should take care to whom he listens, for heretics will never counsel honestly."

"We are not here to debate religion."

"And clearly you are not here for affection's sake, so why are you here?" Mary flung this question at her sister.

Elizabeth grudgingly admired Mary's bluntness and replied in kind. "Do you believe that Norfolk intended open rebellion against the king?"

This time Mary didn't respond immediately. After a considered pause, she said, "If he did, I had no knowledge, and that, I think, makes it unlikely. The duke would have needed me for such a move, and it is unlikely he could have kept it secret from me for so long. I had heard nothing of rebellion."

"What had you heard?"

"That there might exist a document of interest to the Catholic cause."

The Penitent's Confession. Elizabeth would have to speak cautiously here. "And had you heard that such a document was in Norfolk's hands?"

"No." Mary spoke definitely. "He did not have whatever he thought this document was. He was searching for it, tracking rumours and gossip that always turned to nothing in the end."

Until Minuette had found it in the very heart of Framlingham, hidden in the altar of the lady chapel. Elizabeth searched Mary's face, and could not find deception there. Was this one of those things that had Rochford so worried—that he could not believe Mary would not have known if Norfolk had the inflammatory Penitent's Confession in his hands? And if she had not known, did that mean Norfolk himself had no idea that the forged document was concealed in his house? If that were true, it indeed meant someone else had planted it to bring down the Howard family.

And that someone remained undiscovered. Elizabeth sighed.

Mary was no fool. "Was that the wrong answer?" she asked.

"Not if it is true."

"I do not lie, sister. Say whatever else you like about me, but you know that I do not lie."

Not even to make her own life easier. No, Mary was inflexible and fanatic and damned irritating, but she was not a liar.

Mary went on, cannily enough. "You will not be staying here at Syon House, now that Northumberland has overreached with his son's marriage. Does that mean the king will release me from this pretense of confinement?"

"That is for the king to say," Elizabeth said bluntly.

"I hear he will join you at Richmond shortly. Do you think . . ." Mary hesitated. Elizabeth knew how it pained her to plead. "Will you ask William to see me when he arrives? And if he will not see me, at least ask him if I may return to Beaulieu."

Elizabeth said nothing for a long moment, then she nodded curtly. "I will ask."

What else could she do? Mary, however reluctantly and acrimoniously, was her sister. Though Henry's three children might have wildly different temperaments, they shared a certain turn of mind that was instantly recognizable—the call of blood, perhaps.

When they had bade Mary goodbye, they found John Dudley waiting for them a courteous distance down the corridor—close enough to keep an eye on the doorway, but not close enough to eavesdrop. That was a courtesy afforded because of Elizabeth's status. If Mary were to have less exalted visitors, John Dudley would ensure he knew every word that was spoken. As he walked them out of Syon House, they were joined by another of Northumberland's sons, Ambrose. Though Elizabeth did not usually deal privately with Robert's family—only when their interests impinged on wider affairs—she knew that Ambrose was Robert's favorite amongst his brothers.

It was Ambrose who spoke first. "I understand you have met my father's newest scholar, Dr. Dee."

"Yes, we met him at Christmas at court. He is quite . . . knowledgeable." And disconcerting, Elizabeth thought.

"John and I have just had word that Dr. Dee will be coming to Syon House with Robert the day after tomorrow. It would be an honour if the two of you would join us for dinner while they are in residence." He nodded politely to Minuette, including her.

How much of that was planned solely to tempt her? Elizabeth

wondered. She had expected Robert would find his way to her before the rest of the court caught up, but she hadn't thought it would be quite this quick.

Still, though Northumberland was out of favour, and Elizabeth slightly out of temper with Robert because of Guildford's stupidity, she had no wish to decline. "It would be our pleasure."

17 March 1555
Richmond Palace

I was quite right that we would not be spending much time with Mary. I don't blame Elizabeth, for her sister is not the easiest of company. And I find myself uncomfortably reminded of Framlingham whenever I am with the Lady Mary. I feel as though I should apologize to her for the violence that ended in her confinement, although Giles's death had nothing to do with Mary and, apparently, nothing to do with the Penitent's Confession, either. I was so certain last fall that I had solved that puzzle! So certain that I could lay Alyce's pregnancy—and her death—at the feet of Giles Howard. I wish I still could, for the belief that I was avenging my friend kept my guilt at bay. Now I have only the memory of his violence and my own, and it is vastly less comfortable.

But I cannot lie to myself simply for comfort. The evidence against Giles—and perhaps all of the Howards—has vanished like smoke and I am left with only Alyce herself to guide me. I have been tracking down the women we both served within Queen Anne's household, but I had guessed before I began that it would be pointless. Alyce kept to herself, and if she didn't let secrets slip with me, it's not likely they slipped at all. Not at court, at least.

And as I have heard nothing from my stepfather about his investigations, I have been quite at a loss. Until yesterday's visit to Syon

House, when I found out that Dr. Dee is arriving with Robert. Now I have an idea: an unorthodox one, to say the least. We shall see if Elizabeth will give me permission.

At first Elizabeth resisted Minuette's plan. As she said pointedly, "Alyce de Clare is dead and buried and you cannot change that. And we already know the why of it—she was a spy who got herself with child and tumbled down a staircase."

But Minuette refused to give up, and she had learned stubbornness from Elizabeth's own mother. "She didn't get herself with child alone! And I'm not convinced she simply fell down that staircase. Either way, her spying on Queen Anne was done at someone else's command. If it wasn't on behalf of the Howard family, then whoever wanted to plaster those broadsides about your mother's past around court has never been exposed. Wouldn't you like to discover the man who defamed your brother's birth?"

And so at last Elizabeth agreed to summon Dr. Dee to see them at Richmond after his arrival with Robert at Syon House. Their dinner with the Dudley sons had been somewhat stilted, to say the least. With Mary present as well, and the Dudley sons' father still banished from court—not to mention Guildford's continuing absence and Margaret Clifford's confinement to the Tower—there were topics aplenty to be avoided.

Elizabeth's permission to Minuette was conditional on her own presence at the meeting. So when Dr. Dee arrived at Richmond, Minuette stood back and waited while Elizabeth greeted their guest.

"Dr. Dee," Elizabeth said, "thank you for coming to see us."

"Of course, Your Highness. It is I who am flattered by your invitation."

Minuette was impressed with his confidence; if Dee was at all concerned about why he'd been summoned to a private audience with royalty, he didn't show it. He just stood there looking from Elizabeth to Minuette with an inscrutable expression on that somewhat ageless face. As though he knew plenty of things that he did not care to express.

Elizabeth waved him to a chair. "Please," she said, then indicated that Minuette should begin.

"Dr. Dee," Minuette said, "we're wondering what you might be able to tell us about a political plot."

"Is that not a matter for an intelligencer?"

"The trouble with intelligencers is that they all interpret information according to who is paying them. We are looking rather for the truth."

"The truth . . ." Dee smiled and looked all at once every bit the young man he was. "That is a rare commodity. What particular truth are you seeking?"

"A young woman who served the late Queen Anne died quite suddenly two years ago at court. She was with child at the time, and embroiled in a plot to discredit the king. We want to know the truth of her death. I was wondering if you could chart her stars. Perhaps the heavens might point the way to those who used her."

Dee looked intrigued. "To chart the stars of the dead is not a usual practice. But if you can tell me what I need to know of her birth, then yes, I can give you a chart. Whether it will be useful . . ." He shrugged.

"More to the point," Elizabeth intervened sharply, "I am interested in knowing who used this woman and plotted against my brother."

"Was that not the late Duke of Norfolk, Your Highness? He was being held in the Tower at the time of his death."

"The evidence against the duke is, shall we say, less than compelling. Clearly Norfolk had motive, Catholic devotee that he was, but I would not condemn a man or his family based solely on motive."

"That is wise, Your Highness. We all have motives that are less than pure. But we do not all act on them."

Why did Minuette feel that he was speaking straight to her? What exactly had he seen in her stars at Christmas? she wondered anew. Did John Dee know she was in love with Dominic? Did he know the lies she was telling to William and Elizabeth? She had told herself the secrecy was for William's own good . . . *We all have motives that are less than pure.*

But John Dee wasn't even looking at her; he gave a thin, enigmatic smile to Elizabeth and asked, "Are you asking me to decipher your brother's stars more fully?"

"Can you tell me if he's still in danger?"

Minuette held her breath, for there was an almost tangible tension between Elizabeth and John Dee, as though each was attempting to divine the other's thoughts. It was the unspoken conversation of two people who have known each other for years.

Dee broke the connection first. "Your brother will always be in danger, Your Highness. He is a young king in a divided land and he will never be free of enemies. The stars do not speak of an immediate physical danger, if that is what you seek to know. But there are plots within plots swirling around him. I do not think you have unraveled them fully just yet."

"I don't suppose you care to tell me what I will find when all is unraveled?"

"No." Leaving open the question of whether he was capable of doing so, Minuette realized wryly. Though the topic had wandered rather far afield from Alyce, she held her tongue. She would get Alyce's star chart; Elizabeth could ask whatever else she desired.

"Any suggestions on where to begin my unraveling, Dr. Dee?"

"I do not think, Your Highness, that you need me to teach you how to unravel plots. You are your father's daughter; trust your instincts."

Robert did not especially like Syon House. He preferred the luxury and convenience of Ely Place in London or the home where he'd done most of his growing up, Dudley Castle in the West Midlands. His father had only started building Syon House eight years ago, after it had been Crown property for a decade. Not that it had done much good for the Crown: Henry VIII's body had rested here one night on its way to Windsor for burial, and people claimed his coffin had burst in the night and dogs were found licking the king's remains.

And with Mary presently confined here, like a dour black raven in her wing of Syon House, Robert wished he were elsewhere. But this was the nearest he could get to Richmond; once William and the court arrived next week, Robert would be free to take up residence there as well. Until then, his brothers were good enough company.

More or less. Ambrose flung a pair of hose at his head when Robert walked into his bedchamber. "Stop strewing your clothes around my room," Ambrose complained. "How does your wife put up with your mess?"

"Amy," Robert retorted sharply, "is accommodating."

Ambrose raised a knowing eyebrow. "But not quite so accommodating as you would like, is she? Or else you would have a divorce already."

Although he loved his brothers, there were some subjects

Robert would not discuss with them. Elizabeth was one; his wife was another.

He twisted the subject away from his own flaws. "How long is Guildford going to hide away?"

"Until Father tells him to show himself. I think he hopes the king's temper will blow over."

"Guildford may believe that, fool that he is, but Father should know better. He's made the mistake of the old men at court—assuming that because William is young he is changeable. The king may have Henry's rages, but he has Anne's memory for slights."

Ambrose shrugged. "I wouldn't worry. Father knows what he's doing."

Robert hoped so. Because if he didn't—if Northumberland continued to err in his relationship with the Crown—then the whole family would be dragged into the mess. Robert was not slow to advance his own ambitions, but his family would always call to his first loyalty.

A point he remembered when Lord Rochford showed up at Syon House the next day. John, as the one charged with Mary's confinement, met with the Lord Chancellor at once, closeted alone with him for orders or reports or whatever had to be communicated between London and its royal half prisoner.

Robert lingered around the park, guessing that Rochford would want to speak to him as well and reluctant to be sent for like a servant. Sure enough, when Rochford and John came out of doors, Rochford said, "I will take a turn in the park with your brother, Warwick. He will see me on my way."

John shot one troubled look at Robert—as though he could see the tangled nature of the ties between him and Rochford—but naturally he acquiesced. "Of course, Your Grace."

As he and Rochford strolled amongst the neatly divided flower beds, Robert said, "I didn't think you were allowed to speak to me outside the shadows of dank cellars or empty outbuildings."

"You flatter yourself," Rochford replied smoothly. "Who would think you important enough to catch my eye for more than the most casual conversation?"

"What do you want?" Usually Robert only spoke bluntly to Rochford when he'd been drinking, but he was unnerved having the Lord Chancellor in his home and among his family. It was a reminder of the perilous secrets he was keeping from them.

"You have been reticent with your reports on Mistress Wyatt. As you have seen her quite recently here, away from the court, I wondered what you might have to tell me."

"Very little." The truth was, Robert found it hard to concentrate on any woman but Elizabeth, and he was uncomfortable about spying on Elizabeth's friend. So he fell back on generalities. "Mistress Wyatt is beautiful, she is the princess's closest confidante, she is well-liked by everyone who knows her."

Rochford came close to rolling his eyes. "I see I shall have to be specific. Does she continue to pry into Alyce de Clare's death?"

"Not that I'm aware. She appears to be doing nothing more taxing than dealing with Elizabeth's correspondence and enjoying herself. Why are you so concerned about her?"

"Because she is an anomaly," Rochford answered promptly. "I think the time has come to settle the girl's future. I'm sure I can find her a suitable husband who will occupy her time and leave her less . . . influential in my niece's life. Pity none of your brothers are available at the moment."

Robert tried—and failed—to imagine Minuette married to one of his brothers. John was far too humourless; Guildford too young and thoughtless. Perhaps Henry or Ambrose would have done, were they not both married at the moment, but truthfully, when Robert thought of Minuette, there were only two men who seemed to belong with her: William and Dominic.

They had turned back to the house and nearly reached Rochford's horse when the Lord Chancellor remarked in a manner that would have passed for casual in any other man, "By the way, William intends to elevate two men at Easter. He's going to allow Surrey to become Duke of Norfolk. And the second man . . ."

Rochford paused meaningfully, and, despite his own studied air of disinterest, Robert felt his pulse twitch. Was he at last going to be given a title of his own, more than just the mere courtesy "lord" afforded him by his father's title? Was this the beginning of his vaguely promised reward for doing Rochford's bidding, the beginning of making him eligible in title and wealth to seek Elizabeth, if only his marriage were dissolved?

As though he knew precisely the hopes he was dashing, Rochford finished bluntly, "Dominic Courtenay will be named Duke of Exeter."

29 March 1555
Richmond Palace

John Dee came to see me yesterday with Alyce's chart. I cannot deny that he is a man who unsettles me. I feel as though he knows all my secrets . . . but does he know Alyce's? He didn't name the gentleman for me—I hadn't really expected him to—but he did tell me more of Alyce. That behind her reserve lay a passionate nature. That she was so tightly wound that she was likely to come undone when in love and behave recklessly. That she was fierce in her independence and prickly in her friendships. All of which I knew, to some degree, but at the end Dr. Dee said one very illuminating thing: "She was not a woman to take her secrets to the grave. She would want to be known, and understood. She was a woman to leave a record."

I remembered the letters she entrusted to me at her death, and her book of Petrarch's poetry that had contained a cipher. I wonder what happened to them after we searched through them? I shall have to ask Dominic.

Just before he left me, Dr. Dee made an intriguing request: he asked me to speak for him to Elizabeth. His exact words were—"I think Her Highness and I would work well together." When I asked him if he contemplated leaving the Dudley household, he smiled enigmatically and said only, "The stars are in motion, mistress. Who knows where they might lead us all?"

Every time he speaks of stars, I think of the pendant Dominic gave me. In his story, we four are the stars, bound together. Who knows where the motion of one might lead us all?

Minuette left her diary open to allow the ink to dry while she fussed with her sleeves and kirtle. William and the rest of the court had arrived at Richmond last night, but it wasn't for him— nor even for Dominic—that she troubled about her appearance this afternoon. No, the person she was off to see was much more unpredictable, and so Minuette focused on her clothing as if that would be the deciding factor in whether Lady Rochford would speak to her or not.

She had not spoken directly to the duchess since that awful, awkward encounter in a corridor at Greenwich when she had found herself in the wrong place at the wrong time. That day, Lady Rochford had been emerging from what could only have been an improper liaison with Giles Howard, but even her husband's unexpected presence in the corridor had not shaken the duchess. She had simply smiled with all the warmth of a predatory cat and proceeded to give Minuette some rather improper and blunt advice on how to manipulate men. But despite Minuette's personal distaste for Lady Rochford, one thing John Dee had said stayed with her as she pondered Alyce's death: *We all carry with us our pasts. Who we were then informs who we are now.*

And Alyce's past lay in the household of George and Jane Boleyn, where her father had been a clerk to Lord Rochford and her mother a lady-in-waiting to his wife. Perhaps, Minuette thought, Lady Rochford might have some insight into Alyce as a child and young woman that would help her divine Alyce's secrets.

Wherever the Duchess of Rochford was, there were people; not because Jane herself was engaging, but because of her title and her position and her husband. As aunt by marriage to the King of England, it would have taken more than a bitter disposition and a sour temper to keep people away from her. Minuette did not usually involve herself in this circle, but today she forced herself to small talk and gossip. It was surprisingly easy, but then, she was known to be very dear to Elizabeth and William and so people were flattered by her attention.

At last she maneuvered herself near enough Lady Rochford that, when there was a lull in the conversation, she was able to say quietly, "Might I speak with you privately for a few minutes?"

Lady Rochford considered her with those flat eyes that very nearly made Minuette twitch. "Could it be that you are at last prepared to seek my advice?"

A woman has one power in this world. If you're wise, you learn to use it to your advantage.

"I am seeking information."

"On behalf of my niece?"

"For the peace of my own conscience." Minuette itched to be elsewhere, but she would not rush Lady Rochford. She was gambling that the woman would not be able to resist being important.

"Dear me," Lady Rochford replied. "A conscience at court—how remarkable."

She stood and beckoned Minuette to follow her to a corner somewhat secluded by several high-backed chairs. Settling into one with her back to the rest of the room, Lady Rochford waited for Minuette to sit, then said, "What is it you wish to know?"

Taking in the duchess's ostentatious gown embroidered in gold thread and the costly jewels around her neck, Minuette knew she had been wise to armour herself in a similar, if less showy, gown of intricately pleated silk. Jane Boleyn set great store by the perquisites of her position and she respected only those who could match her. Minuette settled in to ask her questions without being either pleading or condescending.

"The de Clare sisters, Alyce and Emma. I understand their parents were in the service of yourself and your husband."

"They were."

"Do you remember them?"

"Of course."

Minuette tried to hold onto her patience. "What can you tell me about them?"

Lady Rochford arched an eyebrow in a face that was remarkably smooth for her age. "That one is married, and one is dead."

So much for patience. "Why was Alyce brought to court, and not Emma? Alyce was the younger sister, after all." Minuette had met Emma de Clare, now married none too well to a gentleman farmer, and knew how much the older sister had resented the younger one her opportunities. Not that she could see what bearing any of that had on Alyce's death.

Interest sharpened Lady Rochford's unnaturally white face (everyone knew she powdered it liberally with white lead and vinegar), though she was still clearly determined to be unhelpfully brief. "I had intended to bring Emma into my household at court after her father's death. My husband objected."

"But he allowed Alyce at court."

"Not in my household."

No, that was true. Why had Alyce been placed with the queen rather than the duchess? It argued greater favour, from Lord Rochford at least. Why would he have preferred Alyce to Emma?

Lady Rochford waited as though she could see Minuette's thoughts tumbling over one another. Smiling grimly, she said, "My husband has his own criteria for appropriate women at his court."

His court, not *the king's* court. Fascinating. "What made Alyce more appropriate than Emma?"

"Precisely what you are imagining."

"Lady Rochford—"

"If I have to spell it out for you, then you should be in a convent. If they still existed in England. Everyone keeps telling me how innocent you are, how sweet, how refreshing in your directness and such a bright counterpoint to Elizabeth's intensity—everyone except my husband."

Minuette nearly shivered at the notion that people were gossiping about her, and that Lady Rochford was listening. But she couldn't resist a final question, although she wasn't at all certain she wanted the answer. "And what does your husband say about me, Your Grace?"

Lady Rochford rose. Pinning Minuette in place with her gaze, she replied, "My husband says nothing. But he watches you."

She swept away, leaving Minuette feeling as though she'd been in the clutches of a cat that had determined at the last moment not to eat the mouse. Yet.

CHAPTER SIX

15 April 1555
Richmond Palace

It has been the most wonderful day of celebration. Yesterday was Easter and a service was held in honour of the two newest titled dukes of the realm. Today was their investiture. The Earl of Surrey is now the Duke of Norfolk, and he looked so young and serious throughout the ceremony that I cannot help but believe he is truly interested in serving England. My stepfather is at court for his nephew's investiture, and I know he wishes to speak with me. But not today, for I can only think of one thing today.

Dominic Courtenay, Duke of Exeter . . . there is nothing William could do that would give me more pleasure.

Except to dance at my wedding.

Minuette spent so long getting dressed that Elizabeth actually went on to the dancing without her. She could not regret it, though, for she was conscious of how well she looked tonight. Her gown was new, made with fabrics that William had (discreetly) gifted her: a sky blue satin underskirt and bodice, with an overdress and sleeves of white embroidered in shades of blue and green. The pearls and sapphires of the necklace Dominic had given her almost two years ago complemented the dress perfectly. She matched them with pearl drop earrings borrowed from Elizabeth and a silver-gilt ribbon studded with minor gems wound through her loosely piled-up hair. Even her shoes were perfect, blue silk with a velvet bow on each.

When Carrie finished adjusting the last curl off her neck, she said softly, "You are a vision and no mistake, my lady. He will be very proud of you."

I hope so, Minuette thought, without knowing if Carrie meant William or Dominic or both. She had never spoken directly of either one to her maid, but she didn't have to. Carrie had seen her weep at Hever and shiver at Hampton Court, and Minuette had often come back to her rooms flushed and happy or thoughtful and melancholy, depending on the occasion. Sometimes she believed Carrie knew her heart better than she did.

So happy, so proud, so delighted was Minuette on this night that she could not believe her eyes when she entered the great hall and the first person she sighted was Eleanor Percy. She had not seen William's former mistress since the night of her husband's death (the night I killed her husband, she thought, then forced the memory away) and Minuette had never anticipated seeing her again at court, preening at a bemused Earl of Pembroke as though she had never been away.

Her surprise meant she didn't move quickly enough, and Eleanor seized the moment. "Mistress Wyatt," she cried. "What a pleasure! How . . . sweet you look tonight." Eleanor managed to make it sound as though Minuette were a twelve-year-old still dressed for the schoolroom.

But as always with Eleanor, Minuette knew precisely the right response. "Thank you. You are looking very . . . maternal."

Maybe not precisely the right response, for Eleanor's smile

widened and she said, "If you could only see my daughter. She is so lovely, with her red-gold hair."

The colour of the Tudors', she didn't say. She didn't have to. Everyone knew her daughter was William's and not her dead husband's. Minuette wanted nothing more than to slap her smiling face, or retort that William meant to give her a crown as well as children, but the reasonable part of her was watching it all with amusement, her mind whispering, *Why do you care? It's Dominic you love. And even as your friend, William never loved Eleanor as he loves you.*

Reasonable as that voice was, truthfully the only thing that lifted Minuette's chin was the memory of William on his knees before her, pleading with her to marry him. "I confess myself astonished to see you. But then, the king has always been kind to those in less fortunate circumstances."

"My widowhood, you mean?" Eleanor asked.

And for an instant Minuette was sickeningly ashamed of herself. Eleanor was a widow because of her. She managed to say, more gently, "I am sorry for your husband's death." More than you'll ever know, she thought.

But Eleanor was a survivor and she didn't bother to play the grieving wife for Minuette. Instead, she shrugged and said, "Life goes on, Mistress Wyatt. And life is full of opportunities."

So much for kindness; Eleanor was laying down battle lines, and so Minuette let her dislike of the woman guide her own steps straight to William. Usually they circled each other in public— William for discretion's sake, Minuette for Dominic's sake—but tonight she behaved as she'd used to when William was nothing more than her friend, and laid claim to him as Eleanor had always driven her to do.

When she slipped her hand through William's arm, he startled for a moment, distracted from his conversation with the new

Duke of Norfolk and Bishop Bonner. But he covered it quickly and conversed for another minute. Bonner looked at her thoughtfully when the two men bowed themselves away, but she ignored the bishop. It felt wonderful to look at William and say, "Wouldn't you like to dance?"

He tilted his head and she saw his other hand begin to rise, as though he meant to touch her cheek. But he refrained and said only, "What has prompted this?" Even as he asked, however, comprehension came. "Ah, I see."

"You didn't tell me she would be returning to court."

"It was a last-minute arrangement. Norfolk is her nephew by marriage and she came with the family—"

"The family whose name she quickly dropped so as not to be tainted."

"I could hardly say no to her presence tonight. I'm sorry I didn't tell you." His voice lowered. "You know that it's all over between us, don't you? I care nothing for Eleanor. I care nothing for anyone but—"

He stopped himself, aware of how very public this discussion was. That same reasonable voice prodded Minuette's conscience. *Why are you so pleased with William's declarations?*

She told that voice to be quiet as William used his hold on her hand to guide her into the opening steps of a galliard. She allowed herself to dance without thinking, enjoying movement for its own sake and also as a distraction from a conscience that kept prodding uncomfortably at her motivations.

That reasonable voice of conscience sounded disturbingly like Dominic.

She searched for him as she danced, and didn't have to look far. In his customary sober clothing only partially relieved by the ducal collar he wore for the first time, he leaned against a pillar and watched her dance with William, his expression stony. She could see why he had picked up the nickname the King's Shadow, for he seemed a darker version of Will—as though William had all the light and pleasure of his power and Dominic all the burden of it. She grew uneasy as he continued to watch them; just how angry was he?

William had seen what she did. "I believe you shall have to dance with someone else after this," he murmured. "Or Dominic will wonder what has happened to our discretion."

She didn't think it was their discretion Dominic was worried about. Although he had often been difficult to decipher, it had only grown worse in the last months. But tonight she had the distinct impression that he was jealous.

This knowledge didn't give her the same pleasure that Eleanor's jealousy did. In fact, it brought her back to earth with a thump and made her stomach turn over as she finished the dance and braced herself to speak to Dominic while William was engulfed by a crowd of other women.

I can deal with jealousy, she told herself. *All I need do is persuade him to come outside for a bit and be private and remind him whom it is I truly love.* But when she approached him, Dominic took her by the arm without waiting for her to speak and escorted her out the nearest door.

"What were you thinking?" he demanded, his dark green eyes furious. "You practically threw yourself at William."

"It was seeing Eleanor," she answered, stung by his anger. "I wasn't warned and it was a shock. You know that Eleanor has always had that effect on me, and it doesn't have anything to do with loving you. You needn't be jealous."

He stopped abruptly and released her arm. The corridor was empty except for a cursory guard, but still he kept his voice at a whisper. "This has nothing to do with jealousy. This has to do with wisdom. Do you think I was the only one to notice the two of you? The way he touched your hand? He was talking to a duke and a bishop at the time! They are neither of them stupid. And Eleanor could not take her eyes off you."

"We have always danced together. There was nothing new in that."

"There was in this dance. The two of you . . ." Dominic stopped, his jaw tense. "There was a heat to it that only a fool or a saint could have missed. And Lord Rochford is neither. I'll warrant he'll have something to say about it before long."

"What of it?" she shot back. "Perhaps that is what we need—to have it confronted so William can realize it will never come to work and he can release me."

Dominic was no longer touching her, but his eyes riveted her in place and she remembered Hampton Court two years ago and the rain falling on them as they faced off in a malodorous kitchen lane. She longed to lean into him, to close her eyes and touch the black hair that tumbled to his collar and have his hands on her . . .

"Do you want William to release you?" he whispered intensely. "Sometimes I wonder."

He turned and left her.

The moment William saw Rochford's face the morning after the ducal investitures, he knew he was in for an unpleasant conversation. No guessing needed—he knew what his uncle was going to say. Even before Rochford went to the trouble to take William into his privy garden where they could walk alone out of earshot.

Still, he said it more bluntly than William had expected. "Your Majesty, you must send Mistress Wyatt away."

"Must?" William could not keep the flash of anger out of that word, although he knew it made him sound like a petulant child.

With effort, he managed to repress the other hasty words that sprang to mind. Instead, he continued, "You oversee my government, Lord Rochford, not my court. Keep to administration and leave personal matters to me."

"There are no personal matters where kings are concerned. Particularly not a king's marriage."

"The council approved my betrothal to Elisabeth de France." William bent over and snapped off several tulips in particularly pleasing shades of cream and pink. They would look very well in Minuette's hands.

"Your betrothal is why we are preparing to receive French envoys in ten days' time. They will be here for a month, including Elisabeth de France's uncle, and they must go back to Henri convinced of your intent in this matter. You cannot hope to have Mistress Wyatt at your side every moment of every day without causing insult to the French. Even if she were no more than your mistress—"

"*If?*"

Rochford regarded him coolly. "Have you forgotten I once served your father? I know the look of the Tudors when they are still anticipating their desires. You've not had the girl yet. And she's shrewd enough to make certain you don't until she has what she wants."

"As shrewd as my mother, then."

"We are not discussing your mother."

"Aren't we? How many people lined up to say precisely the same things to my father? If he had listened to them, you would be nothing more than a country gentleman of limited means."

"And you would never have been born." Rochford waved his hand in an impatient gesture. "That is not the point. As your chancellor, I see to England's interests. Your position is not as secure as you would like, Your Majesty. That is why I support

Elisabeth de France. In spite of my distaste for the Papists, a Catholic father-in-law will be a useful tie. With any luck, useful enough to keep plotting to a minimum."

"You overestimate the appeal of the plotters. I'm popular with my people. And no one seriously wants a woman ruling England."

"You are popular," Rochford agreed in a more measured tone. "You might be able to pull it off. But not without splitting the nobility of England right down the center. The rifts your father created are still echoing. You are meant to close those rifts, not widen them."

"I will be patient and careful, Uncle. I will do nothing in haste that might injure our security. But," William added, "my marriage will be, in the end, my own choice."

"Unless you are prepared to break the treaty at once and lose what you have gained, I would advise that, for the duration of the envoys' visit, you give no cause for discontent. If you will not send Mistress Wyatt away, at least make her presence less prominent."

William turned his back on Rochford and tossed away the tulips—he had crushed the stems in his displeasure. "I'll consider it."

All through the endless afternoon of meetings and audiences that followed, William did consider it. He was skilled at listening with half his attention and even replied sensibly when necessary, while the rest of his mind churned over the conversation with his uncle. Rochford had been wise enough to disengage for the moment, but William was under no illusions that this was the end of it. They would fight this battle again.

When the last applicant for position had bowed humbly away, William returned to the privy garden and walked alone among the bravest of the spring flowers. It had rained since this morning: the ground was damp, but the sky was beginning to clear and the newness of the air eased a little of his tension.

His uncle was right. He'd known it from the moment Rochford had given his measured advice. England could not afford to break with France yet, not with the treasury depleted, the last harvests poor, and the Catholics held at bay by promises and hopes.

On the other hand, William had just spent two weeks without Minuette at court and had not liked it at all. He would not send her away, so he would simply have to grit his teeth and be as publicly indifferent to her as possible while the French were here.

It won't kill me not to touch her, he decided, as long as I can still look at her.

Two days after Dominic's investiture as Duke of Exeter, Minuette went walking with her stepfather along the river gardens at Richmond as the noon sun peeked through the clouds with a fickle promise of warmth. Fidelis accompanied her, as he nearly always did these days. Large dogs were required to remain in the stable precincts at court, but William had made an exception for Fidelis. She liked that the enormous hound gave her a measure of gravity, and it meant that few approached her rashly. Stephen Howard shook his head when he saw them together.

"Are you certain he's not a hellhound?" he asked. "He's looking at me quite suspiciously."

"Intelligent dog."

He sighed. "Must we always spar when we meet, daughter?"

"I am not your daughter."

"Temper, temper . . . do you really want to risk me leaving court without telling you what I've learned?"

Since this kind of sparring could go on for hours, Minuette surrendered. "Very well. What have you learned?"

"Precious little. Every trail seems to wander into mist as soon as it's looked at twice. For instance, I have a correspondent on the Continent who claims that the Spanish navy never set sail for England last autumn."

"But Lord Rochford said—"

"Rochford has his intelligence and I have mine. Who is to say whose is correct? It may be that his agents wanted him to believe the navy was on the move."

"Or your agents want you to believe that it wasn't," she retorted. "How is one supposed to divine fact from all this?"

He nodded. "Good girl. You have learned the first rule of politics—there is no fact, only interpretation. And that depends entirely on who is doing the interpreting."

"Well, you and I know the Penitent's Confession was a slanderous fraud. That is fact. And Alyce de Clare's death is another fact."

Howard shook his head. "I wonder, Minuette: if Alyce de Clare had been merely a nameless lady-in-waiting, if she had not been your friend, would you still be so eager to make inquiries? You will make yourself sick caring so much about others. Her family seems content to let it lie—why not you?"

Minuette told the truth with perhaps more force than necessary. "Precisely because her family—and everyone else—is content to let it lie. I failed to help Alyce when I might have. All I can offer her now is the truth."

Howard shook his head. "You are stubborn and self-righteous, rarely an attractive combination."

"Then why are you helping me?"

He paused along the path to look out at the Thames, and Minuette instinctively held her tongue as he considered. Finally, he said, "Do you know when it was I fell in love with your mother?"

"No."

"I first saw her at court in 1528. She was attending Anne at the time, just twenty-one and the loveliest, merriest girl I'd ever seen. Like most men, I suppose, I appreciated her and thought she would be pleasant in . . . well, you can imagine the thoughts of a man dutifully but not lovingly married."

"Is this supposed to make me think better of you?" Minuette asked caustically. The last thing she needed was to hear her stepfather wax poetic on her mother's physical charms.

Howard smiled wickedly in a manner that reminded her of William at his most mischievous. "Don't fear, our private encounters will remain locked in my memory. But the thing is, that's not when I loved her."

"Is there a point to this?" It seemed unfair to Minuette that her stepfather should be alive to talk about his love for her mother when she would never be able to hear her own father do the same.

"The point is, Minuette, that the day I fell in love with your mother was not the day I first fantasized about her but rather the day on which she cursed me soundly for being rude to a serving maid. The girl had spilled something on me—Wine? Fish sauce? I honestly can't remember—but I told the chit off with more cruelty than was warranted and your mother overheard. I will never forget Marie's fierceness in defending someone who was not in a position to defend herself. An instinct she most clearly bequeathed to you."

With a pensive sigh, as though relinquishing a moment he wished he could hold onto, Howard turned away from the river. He addressed Minuette briskly. "And that is why I am helping you. Yes, Alyce de Clare's mysterious death while engaged in spying on Queen Anne is definitely a fact. As is her pregnancy at the time of her death. As you have pointed out, Alyce did not get herself with child. I am working on that list of men you gave me, but people's memories are hard to pin down two years after the fact, especially when I cannot tell them why I am asking. That is not to say I do not have ideas, but I will be specific only when I have something more solid than supposition to offer."

"Thank you."

"May I ask you something?"

Warily, she nodded.

"Does anyone else know of your continuing queries into Alyce de Clare's death?"

"Yes, of course. Princess Elizabeth has been most helpful to me." No need to specify that her help had included securing something so outlandish as a star chart from John Dee.

"But not the king or his newest duke?"

"Do you mean Dominic? They are both of them far too busy with other matters. I will not bother them until I have something more solid than supposition to offer."

"Which means that you are certain they would both tell you to drop it if they knew. Well, stepdaughter, if you will not listen to your king I doubt you will listen to me, but still I must offer what advice I can. Be careful. Whoever was behind Alyce de Clare's spying has manipulated the downfall of one the most powerful men in England. My brother is dead and my nephew is only restored to his position by the grace of the king. Do you suppose such a man would rest easy if he knew you were still making inquiries into his plots?"

Tension like fingernails across her skin made Minuette shiver. But she met Howard's eyes squarely. "I know what I'm doing."

"Your mother all over again," he murmured. He left her with a kiss on the forehead and a last piece of advice. "Keep an eye on those men of yours," he warned. "Kings and dukes . . . who would have guessed the company Marie's daughter would keep? Don't let it go to your head."

No fear of that, she thought wryly, at least not in the way you mean. These days she was mostly aware of the responsibility incumbent on her to keep William happy and Dominic content with waiting. Not to mention that she still served Elizabeth first, which at times she tended to overlook. Not so today; she went off with dutiful heart to spend the afternoon dealing with a backlog of royal correspondence that needed a personal reply from a lady of the princess's household.

Only hours later, when Minuette had the righteous sense of duty done, did she snap her fingers to Fidelis, who had spent the afternoon snoring quietly against the wall of her study. Usually she returned the dog to the stables before she dressed for dinner, but tonight she decided to take him with her and have Carrie return him later. Since she couldn't spend all the hours she liked with Dominic, sometimes Fidelis had to do in his stead.

She sent a passing girl to fetch Carrie and let herself into her chamber. As she pushed open the door, Fidelis gave off a sound she had never heard from him before—a deep, warning growl that washed over her skin and left it alive with nerves.

"What is it?" she asked the dog, who had somehow frozen as though in mid-motion. She instinctively stepped back, wondering who was in her room and what was wrong, and even as she wondered Fidelis launched through the door.

For all his enormity he sprang silently, an impressive flash of muscle and intent. There was something moving in the rushes on the floor beneath her bed, something that Fidelis snapped at with deadly intent but not quite deadly accuracy. Minuette had just time enough to register the sinuous shape of a snake at Fidelis's feet before it sank its fangs into the wolfhound's leg.

She screamed, but the dog needed only that moment of the snake's bite to snap it in half with its powerful jaw. Her scream died into echoing silence as she stared at the mess of blood and colour and wrong shapes and how had this happened and she would not faint, she would not—

Carrie caught at her arm. "It's all right, milady, come away now."

"No, Fidelis, is he all right, he was bit—" Her voice came out high and tremulous.

"He'll be fine, you just come away and I'll summon the guards. If your scream hasn't already set them running."

Minuette shuddered once, then shook her head. "No guards. Dominic first."

"I'm not leaving you here. What if there are more vipers?"

"Then Fidelis would be going after them. Still, I'll close the door and stay in the corridor until you return. Quickly now."

Carrie returned with Dominic in less than ten minutes. He came with his man, Harrington, at his heels and the two of them entered the chamber first and searched thoroughly before letting the women inside and shutting the door.

Dominic's expression was so tensely blank that she thought his face might crack. He looked her over from head to toe and demanded, "Are you sure you're uninjured?"

"Quite sure. Fidelis knew—he must have smelled it, I don't know, but he knew the moment I touched the door. Is he hurt?"

Harrington had been examining the hound's leg. "He's been bitten, but he's a big dog. I wager he'll do."

"Make sure of it," Dominic ordered. "Take him to the stables and tell them he was bit by an adder, but don't tell them where. Tell them he was chasing rabbits or something."

"Right."

Minuette knelt impulsively before the wolfhound and wrapped her arms around his neck. "Thank you," she whispered into his soft, warm coat. Only now was she beginning to tremble. The big dog met her eyes with understanding, and she blinked back tears as he followed Harrington out, limping.

After that one moment of impersonal examination, Dominic hadn't looked at her again. "No more sleeping here. Get new rooms. And from now on Fidelis sleeps with you."

"Fidelis is enormous, I'm lucky to get away with having him indoors ever. No one will want him underfoot all the time—"

"William isn't no one, and he'll order it," Dominic interrupted brusquely. Carrie stood in the doorway, watching them both with an attention that perhaps accounted for his remoteness. "And if William doesn't, I will. This was no accident or mere prank, Minuette. Whoever did this meant you real harm."

She shivered, for the first time letting it settle on her. If she hadn't brought Fidelis with her, if she had returned him to the stables as she usually did before changing . . . She wondered what an adder bite felt like. It only killed uncommonly, but then how common was it to find one indoors?

Carrie, prepared as always, had brought a linen bag back with her, and she handed it to Dominic, who scooped up the remains of the dead reptile along with the bloody rushes. When he rose, he gazed at her with an intensity not at all remote, and the weight of his eyes was unbearable, confirming how serious he thought this, and she wanted him to wrap her in his arms and keep her safe and tell her everything would be all right.

But of course he didn't. Turning away—as he always seemed to be doing these days—he said, "I'll speak to Elizabeth about new rooms for you."

CHAPTER SEVEN

OR THE FIRST time in the long years of their friendship, Dominic was the one shouting at William instead of the other way round. "If you keep Minuette at court solely because you would miss her, then your selfishness will get her killed!"

The door to William's private oratory opened as he yelled, and Elizabeth slid in quietly. "I could hear you from the corridor," she remarked impassively. "And don't exaggerate, Dominic. Minuette is unharmed."

"Because she had the wolfhound with her! If she hadn't—"

Dominic stopped because he couldn't continue without giving himself away completely. Since last night, he had been balanced on a knife's edge of fury and terror, and if he lost that balance the whole world would know how he felt about Minuette. He'd never done anything harder than leaving her last night when all he'd wanted was to sweep her away into the safety of his own rooms where he could protect her at every moment. Instead he'd been sharp and cold with her; now he was angry and unreasonable with William. Because if anything happened to Minuette . . .

William had let him rant without comment, but Elizabeth was

willing to argue. "If Will sends her away again before the French delegation arrives, the gossipmongers will let loose. People will say he's sending his mistress away to keep her from French eyes. Minuette's reputation will suffer."

"To hell with her reputation," Dominic spat fiercely. "I won't let her come to harm because of what gossips will say." He wished he could pace like William usually did, but the oratory was cramped with the three of them inside. Set aside for William's personal prayers, the space was little more than an alcove with a door, and the lectern with the English Bible filled at least half of it.

"And you think William will let her come to harm? Of course she'll be guarded more thoroughly and—"

"Someone put an *adder* in her room!"

"Enough." Though he didn't raise his voice, William's tone was pure monarch—expecting and receiving instant obedience.

"In this," William continued flatly, "as in so many other things, Dominic is right. I will not risk Minuette's safety. But Elizabeth, you are also right. It will not do to give anyone a weapon to use against her in future. If I send her away from court while my sister remains, then it will be seen as a very personal move."

"What do you propose?" Dominic spoke calmly, now that he appeared to have gained his point.

William nodded to his sister. "The French arrive on May first. I need you here to greet them, but you need not remain the duration of their visit. If you withdraw to Hatfield after they arrive, you can take Minuette with you and there will be little talk of her absence."

"I thought you needed me to charm the French."

"I can contrive another opportunity that will do as well. Besides, the Protestants will claim your withdrawal as a sign of support for their opposition to the French marriage, so it's useful on more than one front."

Dominic broke in. "And until then? How do we keep Minuette safe for another ten days?"

"By all means," William said, "set your own man to guarding her. He's not one of mine, so people will pay less attention."

"Maybe we want people paying attention—or one person, at least." For Dominic didn't give a damn about the French, or diplomatic tangles. He wanted only two things: to keep Minuette safe and to find out who had set a poisonous snake loose in her room. He didn't think he would have to look far to find the culprit. "Why is Eleanor still at court?"

For the first time today, he could feel the slow burn of William's irritation. "Lady Rochford made room for her amongst her ladies. There seemed no harm in it for a few days."

"And where might Eleanor have been yesterday afternoon and evening?"

"Are you asking if *I* am her alibi? You know I am not, since we were in meetings together and then I played tennis with the Earl of Oxford."

Because he was angry, Dominic said what he might have only thought at another time. "It would simplify matters if Eleanor had been in your bed during the relevant period."

"Dominic!" Elizabeth remonstrated.

Her brother ignored her. "I'm sorry to complicate matters with my fidelity. Really, Dom, I know your opinion of me never runs very high, but do you honestly think I would revert to Eleanor the moment she returned simply because she is available? Minuette means far too much to me. How many times do I need to prove it?"

Over and over and over again and it will never matter because you cannot love her as I do . . . Stop it, Dominic commanded himself. He had to get hold of his control and his temper before everything fell apart. And still William faced him, hurt because his friend did not trust him.

Grudgingly, Dominic said, "I apologize."

"Accepted. And you're right: Eleanor cannot be wholly discounted. Although I have a hard time imagining her skulking around corridors and handling venomous snakes. She's much more direct. But by all means, question her yourself. Just be careful about it—get what information you can without giving away too much in return. The longer Eleanor remains ignorant of my true intentions for Minuette, the better. No need to give her reason to hate Minuette more than she already does."

Excused from the king's presence, Dominic went straight from the oratory to track down Eleanor, for he had never been more anxious to confront someone in his life. He knew, dimly, that he would be better served by disinterest and an open mind, but he didn't care—he needed to turn his fear and anger on someone. He had not forgotten the look in Eleanor's eyes as she had watched Minuette and William dancing the other night. From Eleanor's point of view, she had good reason to hate Minuette.

Almost as many reasons as he had to hate William—if only William weren't his best friend.

He found her strolling in the gardens with another woman from Lady Rochford's household. The duchess's women were easy to pick out, being often the most elaborately dressed and most likely to skirt the edge of protocol. Dominic might have expected a recent widow such as Eleanor to dress in a more somber fashion, but then she had never made an effort to pretend any attachment to her late husband. Today she wore a bodice and overskirt of bright cerise that highlighted her fair hair and skin; it was laced so tightly that her waist was tiny beneath her generous cleavage.

"I'd like to speak with you, Mistress Howard. Privately."

"It's Mistress Percy," she retorted, "and I'm not free at the moment."

"It's not a request."

She raised one insolent eyebrow. "Are you saying it's an order?"

Dominic forcibly ignored the other woman, who made no attempt to disguise her fascination with the drama. He cursed himself for not having approached Eleanor when no one else was present. "If you insist."

Eleanor knew when she was matched, or maybe she welcomed this confrontation. Certainly, she showed no concern as she walked off with Dominic, leaving her companion to no doubt rush to the nearest pair of ears and spread the story. Eleanor attempted to put her hand through his arm, as if they were strolling for pleasure, but he was in no mood to play.

He had little choice but to lead her to his own rooms—anywhere else would be far too public. He left Harrington in the outer reception room, as a guard against intrusion, and ushered Eleanor to his closet, where he pulled the single chair out from the table and placed it in the middle of the room. Like everywhere he lived, however briefly, the room was spare, a handful of books stacked on the table and correspondence kept tidily out of sight in a document case.

Eleanor seated herself with a flourish, letting her gown billow out in a rush of silk and embroidered gauzy underskirts. "I am not invited into your bedchamber?"

I'd sooner bed a wolf, Dominic thought. With no desire to prolong this encounter, he demanded bluntly, "Where did you find the adder—did you bribe someone to procure it for you?"

She blinked once, in what might have been genuine surprise, before her expression settled into one of bewilderment. "I haven't the least idea what you mean."

"Where were you yesterday between noon and seven in the evening?"

"I spent the afternoon in Lady Rochford's chambers, then had dinner privately with family members. Including my late husband's nephew, the new Duke of Norfolk. You remember my husband, don't you? You were the last person Giles ever saw—or almost the last. I don't suppose you were the one wearing the blood-soaked dress that was burned at Framlingham later that night."

Damn it. So Eleanor had guessed what had really happened in the lady chapel at Framlingham. Dominic had done his best to ensure Minuette's involvement was never known, and once he might have withdrawn, not wishing to provoke Eleanor further. But there was more at stake now than a widow's guess at how her attempted-rapist husband had died.

"Someone set an adder loose in Mistress Wyatt's bedchamber last night. Do you know anything about it?"

Dominic leaned against the bolted door, arms folded, watching Eleanor. She was so naturally devious that it was impossible to know if her calculating answers meant she was responsible for the reptile or that she was merely thinking quickly.

"Mistress Wyatt has enemies. Surely you are not so naïve that you are surprised by that."

"And her most conspicuous enemy is you."

"Do you think me a fool?" Eleanor leaned forward a little, giving Dominic a clear view of her breasts swelling above her square neckline.

"You've never made a secret of your loathing for Mistress Wyatt."

"Half the court loathes the other half. That does not lead to murder."

"Then what does?"

"Self-interest," Eleanor answered promptly. "You want to get to the bottom of this, look to those whose interests have been threatened by this girl." She tipped her chin up and eyed him thoughtfully. "Which, I suppose, places me on your list. But I assure you, when I want William back, I will not need violence to do it. I am skilled at tricks your precious Minuette would blush to know of. For all his recent infatuation, the king has not forgotten me."

Not knowing which was worse—her arrogance or her recognition of William's current passion—Dominic said tightly, "You may go—for now. I shall inform the king that you have been less than cooperative. If I were you, I would start packing. I believe your time at court is drawing to an end."

Eleanor rose in a silken flutter and stepped near him, until he could not move without touching her. Her smile had a distinctly intimate feel to it. "I don't know why you keep to yourself, Dominic, but I know frustration when I see it. If you ever wish to seek relief . . ."

She drew her fingertips across his cheekbone. Catching her wrist cruelly in one hand, Dominic used his other hand to unbolt and open the door.

As Dominic watched Eleanor walk away, he caught Harrington's unspoken query and shook his head. This wasn't quite what William had meant. He had not been discreet, and he had not been disinterested. In just a few days back at court, it seemed Eleanor had already divined William's passion for Minuette. Even if she did not know the depth of it, she could wreak havoc with the French if she so chose, which was one more reason to get her away from court as quickly as possible.

But even more worrying to Dominic was the thought that, if she could perceive William's love for Minuette so plainly, might she not also uncover his?

Elizabeth knew perfectly well she was being snappish and irritable and that her temper had nothing to do with those she took it out on. At least she refrained from throwing things as her mother had used to.

One source of her temper continued to be her young cousin's disastrous marriage. Margaret Clifford was a very silly girl, and so Elizabeth told her in no uncertain terms when she left Richmond one day to visit Margaret in the Tower. The girl was cowed but not entirely without spirit—Margaret was a great-niece of Henry VIII, after all—and she absolutely denied knowing Guildford Dudley's whereabouts. When Elizabeth asked the child—for she was hardly more than that, despite her obvious pregnancy, "Do you not think less of your husband for abandoning you to take the punishment?" Margaret shrewdly answered, "I may think less of him, but if I were ruled by my head I should not be in this place. Hearts are stubborn things, Your Highness."

Irritation with the whole of the Dudley family was compounded by William's clandestine infatuation—which was rapidly becoming not at all clandestine—and Dominic's mounting concern for Minuette's safety, which spilled out into tension between him and the king. Elizabeth felt as though she was surrounded on all sides by the suffocating weight of passion. She could hardly wait for the French to arrive so that she and Minuette might escape soon after and keep away from all these men.

But her next visitor of note was not a man—it was Jane Dudley, Duchess of Northumberland. John Dudley's wife and Robert's mother.

Elizabeth received the duchess in her privy chamber, curious about the nature of this unusual visit. The duchess was not often at court; she preferred to provide stability from behind the scenes of her ambitious family. But with her husband banished from court until Guildford showed himself, Jane Dudley was clearly prepared to step in.

"Your Highness," she began, sinking into an elegant curtsey. "Thank you for seeing me at such a busy time."

Elizabeth waited for her to rise, and pondered on how well Jane Dudley looked for a woman in her mid-forties who had borne thirteen children. She was still rather slender and her brown hair was richly coiled beneath the new-style French hood with the heart shape. The dip in the center of the hood accented her dark eyes, which were Robert's down to the intelligent gleam. The duchess dressed well but without ostentation, trusting to expensive fabrics and impeccable lines rather than fripperies to denote her status.

"What can I do for you?" Elizabeth asked kindly.

She expected a plea for leniency, for both Jane's husband and son, a request for Elizabeth to intervene with the king to bring an end to the matter.

Instead, the duchess answered mildly, "You can do my family the great honour of agreeing to visit our home at Dudley Castle later this year."

There was a slight change in the air of the privy chamber, as though one of Elizabeth's attendants had let out a quickly smothered gasp. She cast a forbidding look at the corner where her women sat with their needlework, to let them know she had noticed and would deal with it later. Like her mother before her, Elizabeth kept a tight rein on the women who attended her.

Elizabeth turned back to the duchess. She raised a single eyebrow, a trick she had long practiced. "I hardly think this is the most propitious time for a royal to be visiting your home." But that was why the duchess was asking, surely—to mitigate the court's displeasure in the eyes of the people. The petitioner might be Jane Dudley, but the petition had the Duke of Northumberland written all over it.

"The matter of Guildford's apology and submission will be resolved this very evening." The serenity of the duchess's voice was belied by the tightness of her posture.

"He has finally deigned to answer the king's summons?" Elizabeth asked drily.

"Of course he would not long leave his bride in the Tower. Guildford is a man of honour."

"Not honourable enough to seek permission for this marriage. A daring that shows itself rather in the father, than the son."

Jane Dudley's face darkened briefly. But then, in a move Elizabeth could never have predicted, the duchess knelt. Proud, yes, but sincerity radiating from her very stiffness. This was not a woman to abase herself purely for show—it meant something to her, if only that she loved her husband enough to do as he'd asked. Elizabeth's irritation lessened.

"Your Highness, my husband's great sin is that he loves his family. His faults will only ever be those of a father. I swear that my family would never do anything to injure your brother's throne or his dignity."

It was impossible not to believe her. Which was perhaps why Northumberland had sent his wife.

"I will beg if you wish me to, Your Highness. I swear to you as a mother—as Robert's mother—that I wish your presence in my home solely for the honour of it, and for such an honour I would be indebted to you all my life."

The mention of Robert made Elizabeth purse her lips, for Jane Dudley—like her cunning husband—clearly had more than one purpose to every move. But did not she herself also? She could match the Dudleys for playing games of power, and the truth was that she liked them. No matter how vexed she might grow with Robert, she could not imagine removing him permanently from her life. Who would stand up to her if she did? He was the only man she'd ever met—save her brother—whose will was as strong as her own.

She offered her hand to the duchess, who kissed it. "When Guildford has made his amends and the summer is over, then I will consider coming to Dudley Castle. You have my word."

Let William rage if he wanted—if he could determine to marry Minuette, then she could visit where she wished.

"He is here, Your Majesty."

William looked up from the gaming table where he and three others played dice. "Guildford?" he asked his uncle.

Rochford inclined his head once. "Shall I send him away?"

That was one way to play it—make the boy sweat by appearing at court and then being sent away again. William could drag that out for days, making Guildford wonder every night if he would be arrested before he could even see the king. As tempting as that was, the French delegation would be here in two days and it would be better to have this matter contained before then.

"Wait ten minutes, then bring him to the throne room. Make sure word spreads so that as many as wish are present to watch."

He sent a page for Dominic, rolled twice more and paid his losses amicably, then stood and stretched. He was unexpectedly tense about this encounter. It was good to see Dominic, who met him outside the presence chamber. Ignoring everyone else who walked around them, William motioned his friend to match his steps.

"Ready?" Dominic asked.

It was such a relief to communicate in brief phrases and be

fully understood. "Royally ready." Meaning his temper was under firm control and his measures today would not be impulsive.

That did not mean they would be lenient.

The throne room buzzed with more suppressed energy than normal as word leaked that Guildford Dudley had returned to court. William felt the jostling for position. Courtiers hardly waited for him to pass before they rose from their bows and curtsies. At his side he heard Dominic mutter, "Vultures," and smiled inwardly. In some things Dominic was—not naïve, but idealistic. Of course people wanted to see someone else fall. It meant they themselves were safe. For today.

It took a few minutes with his moderate pace to circle the room and feed the tension, then William took his place beneath the canopy of estate, that decorative cloth that hung above his throne, and seated himself. He was wearing a coronet of beaten gold and a collar of rubies to emphasize his authority, and although he rested his arms negligently on the throne arms, his pose was anything but casual.

There was no announcement, no warning, just Rochford throwing the far door open, then stepping aside to let Guildford Dudley enter. Northumberland was a prudent few steps behind his son, and Robert Dudley was nowhere to be seen. That didn't surprise William. Of all the Dudleys, Robert had the keenest sense of self-preservation.

It seemed to him that he could read the different silences in the hall. Gleeful, yes, for Northumberland was often abrasive and his arrogance and ambition had earned him many enemies. But there was pity, too, for a handsome young man, and something less easy to define. Wariness, perhaps.

He had to hand it to Guildford, he made a wonderful obeisance. If the boy (Guildford was actually a year older than William but he seemed a boy in every way) hadn't been so staunchly Protestant, he'd likely have prostrated himself wholly. As it was, Guildford knelt on both knees and bowed his head almost low enough to touch the floor.

William let him remain in that position. "Offering your neck so readily? I thought for certain a Dudley would have some fight in him."

"Your Majesty, I crave pardon for my error."

"Error?" William echoed softly. "Is that what you call it?"

He thought Northumberland flinched—no doubt the duke recognized the silken tone of fury that William knew was so like his father's.

Guildford prudently did not rise, but his head came up enough for him to meet William's gaze. "I call it love, Your Majesty. A sin, to be sure, but motivated by love alone."

"If you love Margaret Clifford so much, why did you hide away and let her be taken to the Tower in your stead?"

Was it his imagination that Guildford's eyes flicked to the side, toward his father? "I am young. Perhaps I listened to counselors I should not have."

William rose and gestured impatiently for Guildford to do the same. Warily, the boy stood and waited while William stepped near enough that he might have whispered if he'd wanted. Instead, he let his voice carry to every avid listener in the throne room. "I too am young, and I know what it is to have competing counsel. Do you know what the difference is between us, Dudley? I am not stupid enough to follow evil counsel straight to my own destruction."

Northumberland moved in protest as guards stepped through to seize his son by the arms.

"You will have time to ponder on the difference between

youth and stupidity while I ponder what to do with you," William said coldly.

He gestured to the guards. "Take him to the Tower—and on no account is he to see his wife." He almost spat the last word, and everyone in the room averted their eyes. Except Dominic, who watched William with that familiar hooded expression that disapproved without ever having to say a word.

William remained in the throne room after Guildford was taken away—his father went after him, to try to pick up the pieces, no doubt—mingling with the crowd to show that he was not shaken, to show that he knew what he was doing, to show that he had the pulse of his court and knew his people well. Dominic also remained, but he did not so much mingle as stand in one place and reply briefly to whoever attempted to speak with him. It would have exasperated William if he hadn't found it so amusing. Dominic had to be the most reluctant duke in English history. Where any other man would be avidly building his power base and making alliances with every breath, Dominic appeared indifferent. Was there nothing that could move that aloof temperament? William wondered. He might have to get serious about finding Dominic a woman.

And yet, as different as they were, it was a relief to leave the throne room behind and walk out with Dominic. However frustrating his friend might be as a political player, at least with Dominic one always knew exactly where one stood.

CHAPTER EIGHT

O N THE LAST day of April the English court removed from Richmond to Hampton Court just a few miles west. And on a May Day of clear but chilly blue skies, the French delegation arrived. They came in a procession of barges that stretched more than a quarter mile along the Thames, a breeze just sufficient to play out the blue banner of France with its three gold fleur-de-lis. Charles de Valois—duc d'Orléans and younger brother of King Henri—was greeted by the privy council, Lord Rochford doing the honours of first welcome. Minuette, standing with the women of Elizabeth's household, watched the Lord Chancellor and his wife step forward to greet *le duc* with a salute on each cheek and speaking fluent French.

Minuette pointedly ignored Dominic, who spent more time watching her than he did the French. Did he really think someone was going to attack her in daylight, with dozens of courtiers pressing round? When she was sure no one else was watching, she rolled her eyes at him. His lips almost quirked into a smile, but then he was swept up into the small group that would accompany Charles to greet William and Elizabeth personally. The king and princess had waited in the throne room together, manipulating the moment to give the best impression of royal protocol and position.

That was an encounter Minuette would have dearly loved to see. Just two years ago Elizabeth had been meant to marry Charles, but he had married a relative of the Holy Roman Emperor instead, and that first disintegration of an English/French marriage treaty had led irrevocably to open war. Minuette was certain Elizabeth would not regret the lost marriage—though only thirty-three, Charles's penchant for adventurous living had aged him prematurely, and even draped with all the gold and silver and expensive fabrics a French prince could command, as a man he could never compare to Robert Dudley. Not that Elizabeth had had much to do with Robert the last while. She claimed to be keeping her distance out of political necessity, what with Guildford in the Tower and his father teetering on disgrace, but Minuette knew better. Elizabeth was hurt that Robert had not warned her of Guildford's rash marriage, and she also hated being reminded that, like all his brothers now, Robert was a married man. Not that Robert was a man to give up easily. He alone of his family remained at court, wisely keeping a low profile, but present all the same.

Was there any way their love could ever come to a good end? Minuette wondered. And just for a moment she imagined pressing William for a favour, attempting to persuade him that if he meant to marry for love, he should allow his sister the same . . .

It would never work. For one thing, Minuette was not comfortable with imagining just what sort of persuasion she would have to employ, and for another, William was not likely to allow himself to be persuaded. He needed Elizabeth to make a politically smart marriage for England's sake.

"Going to remain at the river all day, Mistress Wyatt?" Lady

Rochford inquired. Minuette wondered why she had not continued inside with her husband and the French. Probably she had
not been invited—Jane Boleyn was prickly at best, not at all the
sort of woman to put men at ease.

"Good day to you, Your Grace," Minuette replied imperson-
ally. "You are looking quite well." *If one likes a woman who's all
brittleness and venom.* Even attired in a wine-coloured bodice and
cloth-of-gold underskirt, no amount of gilding could smooth
away the sharp angles of Jane Boleyn's face or the suspicious
sharpness of her gaze. And yet, Minuette knew there were men
who found their way to the duchess's cold bed—either they liked
the pale, thin, spiteful sort of woman or else they wanted to dis-
concert Rochford by bedding his wife. Minuette was fairly certain Lord Rochford didn't care.

In her precise, imperious voice, Lady Rochford answered, "I
am glad that I still look well, despite the loss to my household.
Eleanor Percy has long been such a favorite of mine, I found it
difficult to have her sent away."

Minuette knew she was being baited and steadfastly held her
tongue.

With a grudging respect, Lady Rochford added, "It appears
you have taken my advice to heart and learned to use your power
to persuade a man, else the king would never have sent Eleanor
away. I wonder how precisely you persuaded William—and how
the French would feel about it if they knew?"

That was rich, this woman who was all subterfuge and deviousness, accusing her of scheming. But because Lady Rochford
had hinted at things best left unsaid, Minuette forced a civil answer. "I can't believe the French have ever thought twice about
me. I am not nearly interesting enough for such notice."

Lady Rochford all but hissed her final piece of advice. "See that you keep it that way. Consider that counsel from my husband as well as myself."

1 May 1555
Hampton Court

I have spent the afternoon carrying dread around in my stomach. I do not trust Eleanor Percy, and Lord Rochford is alarmingly devious, but Lady Rochford is the only person I've ever met who truly frightens me. She is a woman of unstable passions and I cannot possibly predict what she might do next. She might as easily announce to the French that William is in love with me (although she cannot have proof) as she could stick a dagger in my back. Is it possible that it wasn't Eleanor who loosed that adder in my room, but Lady Rochford? I know I should tell Dominic the things she said to me today, but I am tired of always speaking of conflict and danger. And after all, it was only a warning.

For now I must let the worry seep away, because there is a banquet tonight to welcome the French and then there will be dancing . . . and when William is at his busiest being king, I will ask Dominic to slip away and meet me somewhere private. Not everything I have to tell him is unpleasant.

After an afternoon and evening spent entertaining Charles de Valois, Elizabeth was devoutly glad that she was not his wife. They would never have suited each other, for he was vulgar and outrageous when he thought he was being charming, and yet she was able to make such sly fun of him that he could not quite pin it down. She did her duty and danced with him first, and then with great relief passed him over to Jane Grey. Let Charles try to make headway against Jane's solid piety.

"Regretting your lost husband?"

At the sound of Robert's voice, Elizabeth smiled instinctively before remembering that she was still angry with him and all the Dudleys. "Not everyone takes marriage lightly," she replied, turning. Robert was looking especially handsome tonight. Black and white suited his dramatic dark colouring.

"No, not everyone." He gave her that look of being able to read every unexpressed thought, then said, "William, at least, seems happy. Perilously so."

"What could be perilous about happiness?"

Robert lowered his voice once more—not in seduction this time, but in warning. "Happiness can make men careless. People are talking, Your Highness. And not just the gossips and the jealous. The older lords are worried. They, at least, have not forgotten your mother."

"I have no idea what you mean," Elizabeth remarked, but she could not keep her eyes from straying to where Minuette was the center of a circle of young men. Her laugh was the merriest sound in the entire room.

Robert had followed her gaze. "I quite like your friend, and I would not fault the judgment of any man who fell in love with her. She'll make a charming diversion. The nobility will grant him that."

"How very generous of them." Elizabeth was dismayed, not so much at the gossip, which she had anticipated, but at how accurately the court seemed to be reading William's intentions. If the lords encouraged her brother to make Minuette his mistress, it was because they feared she might become much more.

Robert leaned closer while keeping his face turned to the crowds, as if they were discussing any matter of slight importance. "The realm is not as stable as your brother would like. The treasury's in dire straits after the French campaign and several years of drought, and William's religious moderation has not been popular with either faction. But the Catholics are always and ever the real concern. They are keenly aware that Mary remains under house arrest. If William breaks his French betrothal . . ."

He did not need to finish that thought. Elizabeth knew perfectly well the only thing keeping the Catholics at bay was the French Catholic princess who was meant to become England's queen.

Robert had one final word of advice. "You must keep him reined in, Elizabeth. And for heaven's sake try to talk some sense into him."

He offered her his hand. She allowed him to lead her out to the dancing, her eyes still on Minuette, laughing and chattering away as if she had not a care in the world.

Robert's head turned that direction as well. "Dangerous," he murmured.

Dominic reached the orchard first and braced his back against an apple tree. From there he could see the faint outline of the door in the stone walls of Hampton Court through which Minuette would come. It had been dark for an hour and he wasn't sure how long he would have to wait. Minuette needed to time her departure so as to be unnoticed, not only by William but by those at court who were beginning to pay attention to her. In the days before the French arrival, William had hardly been away from her side at all; though the king had publicly managed to maintain the illusion of friendship, the whispers were beginning to strengthen. At tonight's welcoming banquet, Dominic had caught the French ambassador watching William and Minuette together and had itched to strike the smug look of approval from his face. Being French, the ambassador would have no problem with William having such an appealing mistress.

The shadows shifted, black to gray, as the door opened and a cloaked figure slipped through. The concealing cloak did not quite cover the silver glimmer of her gown, and the jewels round her neck and in her hair were like little sparks of moonlight. Or stars, caught fast to the woman who was like a star herself . . .

Dominic reached for her hand as she neared and pulled her wordlessly forward, deeper into the concealment of an orchard just beginning to bud. Only when the walls and windows of Hampton Court were out of sight did he stop.

She was in his arms at once, and he felt his shoulders relax. This feeling of relief surprised him every time; he never realized how tense he was until they were entirely alone and he could let it go.

"I've missed you, my lord duke," she murmured.

"Don't call me that."

"Why not? It was a such wonderful thing for William to do." So Minuette had been saying ever since his investiture.

"William does many wonderful things." Could she hear the knife-edge of jealousy in his voice?

Whether she could or not, she did precisely the right thing, bringing her mouth up to his in an unhesitating movement. He let his mind empty of everything, aware only of the texture and taste of her lips and, briefly, her tongue. He spent so much of his time not letting himself think about touching her that it took an effort of will to drop that restraint and allow his body to guide him.

Much too soon, she stepped out of the kiss. "William does nothing so wonderful as that," she said lightly, though Dominic could hear the shiver beneath her words.

They sat at the base of a tree, Dominic's back against the trunk and Minuette carefully arranging her skirts and cloak before leaning against his side. He put his arm around her, and her head came to rest on his shoulder.

As pleasant as it was to sit in silence and peace, this time would not last and Dominic had things to say. "Elizabeth leaves court the day after tomorrow."

"She does."

"I will miss you." Which was always the truth, no matter the relief of knowing she would be somewhere safer.

And then Minuette said the unexpected. "I'm not going with her. I have told William no."

Dominic shifted so he could look at her face. In the moonlit shadows filtering through the trees, she appeared absolutely serious. With a steady voice that cost him an effort, he replied, "You cannot stay at court, Minuette." Why did she even want to? Because she couldn't bear to be parted from him? Or was it William who had persuaded her to stay?

Again, uncannily, she spoke straight to his worst instincts. "This isn't about William! Honestly, Dominic, can you not see that part of him will be glad to have me gone? You miss the strain in him. He is warm-blooded. And though he has no wish to offer insult to my face, I imagine he will welcome the opportunity to seek relief."

Dominic gave a strangled laugh at Minuette's cool assessment of the nature of William's strain—and its remedy. "If you aren't going with Elizabeth, then where?"

He heard the laughter beneath her words. "The new Duke of Exeter has not been paying attention to the right kinds of gossip. You should be listening to the women, Dominic, then you would guess what is coming."

He let himself answer in kind. "Be as superior as you like, my love, but at least tell me straight out what I have missed."

"On the last day of the French delegation's visit, it will be publicly announced that Lady Rochford is going to return the favour. She will go to Paris, bringing with her several young ladies who will remain to serve in Elisabeth de France's household until she grows up enough to marry William. He has asked me to go as well."

"Not to remain?" Elisabeth de France was not even ten years old yet, surely William didn't mean to send Minuette away for so long . . . not that William meant to marry Elisabeth in any case. He was finding it hard to follow all the twisted pathways of secrets.

"Of course I won't stay for more than a few weeks," she replied. "I'll return when Lady Rochford does. But that's not the important part."

Minuette going overseas, an ocean between them—how could that not be the important part? Dominic's heart couldn't decide whether to stutter or stop all together.

"I have asked William if, rather than going to Hatfield with Elizabeth, I might go to Wynfield until it is time to leave for France. I told him I wished a little time to myself away from the pressures of publicity and travel. He has given me permission."

She bit her lip, and when she spoke again her voice was husky. "And if I am at Wynfield . . ."

She did not finish. She did not need to. Dominic felt his blood quicken at the thought of Minuette away from court, away from prying eyes and sharp tongues, away from Elizabeth and, especially, William. He could visit Wynfield. Indeed, William might even ask it of him, as he had asked him numerous times since November to dance with Minuette or sit with her at pageants or otherwise keep her occupied when the king was busy.

She ran her fingers along the line of his jaw, making his heart

stutter in quite another manner. He could see only the pale shim-
mer of her face as she whispered, "You will come to Wynfield,
won't you?"

He answered her with his lips and his hands. She moved
against him, and the tree trunk dug into his back and the ground
was hard but he didn't care, he would have stayed there all night
if he could, with the warmth of her lips and the softness of her
throat and the elusive curves of her figure beneath the stiff bodice.

Reluctantly they parted at last and Dominic pressed his lips to
her hair, waiting for his breathing—and hers—to even. Then he
led her back to the orchard's edge, where she would slip away
first. She lifted her head, and for one moment Dominic thought
she would kiss him once more. He should have known better, for
the walls of Hampton Court rose before them and they were ever
careful to minimize their betrayal.

Only after she vanished through the outer door that would
lead her through the back lanes of the kitchens did Dominic let
his mind wander to the possibilities of Wynfield and the pleasures of being alone with Minuette in a house not owned by
William.

On her last day at court before retreating to Hatfield, Elizabeth
went hawking with William and the French, after which, when
she and William were alone, growing irritation with her brother
spilled out into a blazing row.

The catalyst was William's casual announcement to the French
and various English court members that Prince Erik of Sweden
would be sending his brother to pay court to Elizabeth on his
behalf. But the seeds of the argument had been planted long
before—from the moment months ago when William had told

her he meant to marry Minuette. If he married for love, then her chance of doing so vanished. Though she accepted that, she was human enough to fiercely resent it.

"I don't want him here," she told William flatly once they were behind closed doors. "You can just send straight back to Erik and tell him his brother is not welcome in England."

"No, I can't. It's a reasonable request, and politically wise at this point. Erik expects I would like to balance the effects of my expected French marriage with a staunchly Protestant husband for you."

"And what does he gain?"

"You. This isn't political for Erik. The man is genuinely en-amoured of you."

"The man has never met me."

"Which is why he's enamoured of you." His tone was some-where between irritation and amusement.

Elizabeth struggled to keep her voice level. "I won't do it. I won't meet with an envoy from a prince whose suit you have no intention of granting."

"What do you mean?"

"If you were truly going to marry Elisabeth de France, then Erik might indeed be a serious prospect for me. But you are going to marry Minuette. And when you do, all hell will break loose with the Catholics. That's where I come in."

"Go on."

He must have known she would figure it out; she felt a burst of resentment that he was humouring her. "When you break the French treaty, you'll need Spain on your side. What better way to achieve that than to marry me off to Philip?"

Heir to the Spanish throne and a large part of the Netherlands, nephew of the Holy Roman Emperor—yes, Philip Hapsburg would be a far more powerful alliance than the passive Swedes. Elizabeth waited for her brother to refute it.

He did not refute, or confirm. "Allowing Erik to send an envoy can do no harm. We'll entertain him, show him the best of the English court, and send him home with a carefully equivocal response. It will serve its purpose."

"That purpose being to distract attention from your own behavior?"

William was beginning to lose his temper—she could see it in his darkening cheeks and hear it in his too-precise enunciation. "I will inform Prince Erik we will gladly receive his brother at our court this autumn. And you will look to your own behavior while he is here."

"Meaning?"

"Meaning you'd best keep away from Robert Dudley."

She longed to scream at him, or slam her way out of the room, or even throw something. But an idea struck her at the very moment she opened her mouth. Instead of an angry retort, she found herself saying, "I'll agree to behave precisely as you want on one condition."

He narrowed his eyes. "I don't do conditions."

"You do with me."

"What is it?"

"I want to go to France with Lady Rochford."

He gave a bark of astonished laughter. "Absolutely not."

"Why not?"

"You are my heir. I cannot risk sending you out of England as long as that is true."

"You are king and you left England last year. To fight a war, as I recall. I will be doing nothing so risky."

He shook his head, but she knew she was every bit as stubborn as her brother. "Let me do this, Will. I am a much better representative than our aunt anyway. And if you want to impress the French with your devotion to their princess, then who better to send than your own dear sister?"

Then she delivered the final blow. "Besides, you are sending Minuette. Won't you feel better having me there to protect her from any amorous French gentlemen?"

He narrowed his eyes. "If I agree, you will be gracious to Prince Erik's representatives?"

She smiled sweetly. "As gracious as ever a woman was."

In her head, she heard an echo of a voice from a wintry night, John Dee saying, *Before another year passes, you will be your brother's voice in a foreign land.*

As if he were reading her mind, William said, "Do you suppose this was fated to happen? Or are you merely taking advantage of John Dee's words?"

"Does it matter?" she answered lightly.

He shook his head, ruefully this time, and grinned down at her. "I should know better than to fight with you, Sister. I never win."

CHAPTER NINE

*I confess to a pang of envy when I read Elizabeth's letters from
Hatfield. Even removed from the court, her household is always in the
heart of things. As she plans for her first visit abroad, she is deep in
study and correspondence. Trust Elizabeth to put all her energy into
being perfectly prepared.*

*Though Wynfield is more remote than Hatfield, both physically and
culturally, I have myself been busy from morning till night. I begin each
day in consultation with Mistress Holly, who has kept the interior of
Wynfield spotless all these long years. She is almost giddy now that she
has someone to actually serve. And the presence of an actual duke in the
house . . . frankly, I am surprised Dominic hasn't yet given her a fit.*

*In the afternoons, while Dominic is busy with treasury business, I
ride out with Asherton. I have now visited every tenant farm and
cottage on the estate. There are only twelve in all, but I quite delight in
the pretty households and the healthy faces of my people. My father was
born at Wynfield and I can judge the respect in which he was held by
the reverent manner in which he is spoken of to me.*

*My only concern is Carrie. It cannot be easy for her, returning to
Wynfield where her husband and children are buried. If only she would*

talk about it, I would be easier in mind. But she has become withdrawn and speaks only when asked a direct question—and then only if the answer cannot be conveyed by a nod or shake of the head. I shall have to do something about her.

15 May 1555
Wynfield Mote

I have walked out with Carrie every morning for the past five days, hoping that a less formal setting would induce her to talk. It has, little by little. She has shown me the cottage where her children were born and the creekside path they would run along. With each mention of them, the shadows in her eyes have rolled back a little more, until she can speak almost easily of her lost family. Ben, her husband, did the blacksmithing work on the estate and had a marvelous touch with horses. The little boy, named for his father, was an adventuresome lad who walked at nine months and climbed his first tree when he was not quite two. And her daughter—I never knew that her daughter was named Marie for my mother.

18 May 1555
Wynfield Mote

Not all is as perfect on my estate as I had thought. Today I came upon two little girls at the entrance to the kitchens. Both bobbed when they saw me and scurried away before I could speak to them. As I wondered, perplexed, what I had done to frighten them, the cook came out with a basket filled with food. She, too, bobbed an uncertain curtsey and would have fled if I had not stopped her.

When she told me that the food was for a widow and her family, I told her to deliver it herself and then went to find Asherton to demand why I had not been told of such need in my own household.

The father of the family was one of my tenant farmers, Asherton told me, who died from the sweating sickness last summer, along with his two oldest sons. Now there is only his widow, the two small girls, and a twelve-year-old boy who is doing his best to fill his father's shoes.

"I know I should have told you," Asherton said, voluble in defense. "It's your decision what to do with a farm that has no one to run it. You're within your rights to find another farmer and turn off the family—"

As if I would! I was shocked he would think such a thing of me, and told him so in no uncertain terms. I also told him that the boy is to be given whatever laboring help he needs from my own gardeners and servants, and that of course the family must be fed in the meantime.

I visited the widow and her children tonight. It pained me to see their hollowed cheeks and even more to hear their effusive thanks. I have done as close to nothing as anyone could, and for the first time the words I've heard around court have taken on personal meaning: drought, crop failures, starvation.

I will not let that happen to anyone in my care, so far as it is in my power!

22 May 1555
Wynfield Mote

I have been here nearly three weeks now and still I have found reasons to put off visiting Alyce's sister. Emma Hadley was so unpleasant to me last year that I do not relish being alone with her again. But unpleasantness aside, I need her. I know that Alyce's personal belongings were sent to Emma after her death, and if there is anything to be discovered about the man who Alyce loved, it will be somewhere amongst her clothes and books and mementoes.

I shall send Harrington with a message today, asking if I may call on her the day after tomorrow.

As expected, Emma Hadley's permission was instantly granted. She might envy and dislike Minuette—at least that had been the impression she'd given last year—but that same envy meant she would never turn down a personal visit from someone so closely connected to the court. Minuette prepared to grit her teeth and pretend Emma was just another annoying foreign dignitary who had to be flattered.

She decided to take Fidelis with her. The wolfhound, as predicted, had recovered quickly from the adder bite, and she gladly brought him with her to Wynfield. He loved the country and was at her side whenever she rode out or walked. She was glad to have him as steadfast ballast when she rode to Emma Hadley's home.

Harrington rode with her. Minuette had refused to allow Dominic to come—she could imagine how unbearable Emma would be if the Duke of Exeter showed up at her house—and Dominic refused to allow her to go alone, so Harrington was the compromise. Though Minuette had never spoken more than a few words to Harrington (she wasn't sure anyone ever spoke more than a few words to Harrington), she was glad of his solid presence.

As the Hadley farm and manor house came into sight, Harrington said suddenly, "I knew her, back when she was Emma de Clare."

Minuette startled noticeably, and Winterfall shied under her. Reining the horse back in, she said, "You knew Emma de Clare?" But of course, Harrington came from Rochford's household. She should have remembered that.

"A little. She and her sister."

Harrington was full of surprises, Minuette thought. "And what did you think of Alyce de Clare?"

"A woman always searching for the next thing. Ambitious, but not cruel with it."

"Did you like her?"

He shrugged. "She wasn't the sort of lady I could know well enough to either like or dislike. But I'll tell you who did like her—Lord Rochford."

Which squared with what Lady Rochford had hinted—that at one point Alyce had been more than a clerk's daughter to Rochford himself. Of course, he wouldn't be the man who'd fathered her child while ordering her to undermine his sister and nephew, but it was interesting. If Lord Rochford was the sort of man Alyce liked, then who else might fit the role of ambitious, proud, charismatic, the kind of man to blind her to danger until too late?

"Well, Harrington," Minuette said as they reined up in front of the Hadley manor house, "now I'm wondering what sort of lady you could know enough to either like or dislike."

She meant it to tease him, as she would have teased Dominic, but instead he answered gravely, without even looking at her, "I like you."

All in all, Minuette was rather flustered as she was welcomed into the Hadley home and shown into the same stuffy parlour as on her previous visit. But within minutes she was ready to broach her true purpose. Sideways, of course, for she could hardly let Emma know that the court still had doubts about the nature of her sister's untimely death.

"Mistress Hadley, I understand that Alyce's belongings were sent to you after her death. It was such a time of shock to those of us who knew and liked her that it is only now I am beginning to feel the loss of her. I wrote her a few letters over the time we served together in the queen's household, and I wondered if I might look through her things for them. It would be a great kindness."

The look Emma gave her was half simpering, half curious. No doubt the woman thought Minuette wanted to remove any possible sources of gossip. But she dared not refuse. "I cannot say that I recall any letters from you amongst her things, but I did not search overclosely. Too painful, as you said."

"Then I might look myself?"

"Of course. Whenever is convenient for you."

"It is convenient now." She would not give Emma time to go through her sister's effects once more, with Emma's suspicion sharpened by her request. If there was anything of use, she needed to remove it today.

Though Emma herself was plump and careworn, she kept an impeccably neat household. Alyce's few belongings were stored in a small chest in Emma's own bedroom. She politely, though no doubt grudgingly, left Minuette to examine its contents alone.

There was no clothing, which was not surprising. Surely the practical Emma had made use of the rich fabrics and jewelry of her sister's court wardrobe. The dresses would have had to be shortened and considerably let out, Minuette thought uncharitably.

She and Alyce had shared a chamber almost constantly for two years, so she knew the spines of the few books in her friend's possession. A Tyndale Bible, *In Praise of Folly* by Erasmus, More's *Utopia* . . . all in English save for a single volume of Petrarch's poems. It was that last volume that had contained a cipher key. Dominic had used the key gleaned from its pages to decipher the coded letters sent to Alyce in which she had been ordered to spy on Queen Anne. Surely the man who had given her that book had also been her unknown lover. Minuette would not believe that Alyce had been embroiled in two clandestine affairs at the same time.

She set the books aside and leafed through the personal letters that made up what remained of Alyce's possessions. There were actually two from Minuette, brief notes rather than letters, and she was touched that Alyce had kept them. The remainder was a motley collection of stilted missives from Emma containing domestic news, a few from other women at court, and one from Queen Anne herself. Minuette gathered these up, though she doubted there were any obvious clues, and returned them to the silver casket that had held them. She remembered that casket well; for many months it had stood near her own smaller case in the various rooms the two girls had shared.

She found Emma and showed her the books and the casket with its letters. "Might I borrow these for a time?" she asked, making it clear from her tone that it was not a request.

Greed warred with Emma's desire to be useful. "The casket belonged to my mother, and I would like the books to go to my son," she said finally. "If you will take care to return them."

"Of course. I also wondered, did you keep the letters Alyce wrote to you?"

She didn't have high hopes that Alyce would have spilled her indiscretions to her sister, but one never knew what information might have slipped through unexpectedly.

Emma brought them to Minuette, several inches thick and bound with a lavender ribbon. Touched by that evidence of sentiment, Minuette said sincerely, "I do thank you, Mistress Hadley. I liked Alyce very much and I still grieve for her death. I promise to return everything to you in good order."

Emma nodded, then ruined the moment by adding, "I hear that the new Duke of Exeter is staying at Wynfield with you. Is that quite proper?"

Minuette smiled frostily. "Do you think that I would do anything at all improper?"

As she rode away, however, she couldn't ignore her own conscience. It uncomfortably concurred with Emma's question. *Seeing as how I feel about Dominic, being alone with him in a private house isn't proper at all.*

After three weeks at Wynfield, Dominic was still marveling at how Minuette had changed upon her arrival. She had lost none of her brightness and spirit, but the nervous energy that had driven her for months had spun itself out. At Wynfield she had gained serenity, a sense of belonging to a world entirely her own.

Dominic's own nerves had quieted since his arrival. To look at Minuette without fear or guilt, to not have to watch every word or movement, and, above all, to be entirely free of jealousy, was intoxicatingly liberating. They were not indiscreet, not even in Wynfield's relative safety, but at least they need not jump every time someone came into view.

Riding next to him, Minuette urged her horse forward a little and cocked her head at Dominic in invitation. But he shook his head, in no hurry today. Tomorrow he would ride out early, back to London and the grinding business of paring down court expenditures, while Minuette prepared for departure to France in two weeks. She had suggested a long outing for this last day, to somewhere she would not name. She wanted it to be a surprise, she said. She had even convinced him to leave Harrington behind, persuading Dominic that the two of them would be perfectly safe together. Also, Fidelis loped along beside the horses, and Dominic was persuaded that gentle as the hound was with Minuette, he would make a formidable weapon if needed. It gave him more pride than he dared admit to see the wolfhound alongside the Spanish horse William had given to Minuette on her seventeenth birthday. She seemed to love both equally.

"There it is," Minuette said proudly as they reached the crest of a gentle hill.

Following her gaze, Dominic looked down to a small structure, nestled in a stand of beeches that shivered in the light wind, their leaves tossing from green to gold and back again. A round Saxon tower rose at one end of the stone structure.

"It's a church," he said. Unnecessarily, for even if Minuette had not known where she was bringing him, it could never have been mistaken for anything else.

She let her breath out impatiently. "An *ancient* church," she said, as if that explained everything. She clicked to her horse and moved ahead without another word.

When they reached the copse and the church, Minuette allowed Dominic to help her down, but she kept her chin lifted and did not speak all the while he helped her prepare—shaking out a tapestried coverlet on the grass, unpacking the saddlebags filled with food, tethering the horses. Fidelis watched it all with supreme indifference, as though he caught and mirrored his mistress's every mood.

When all was readied, Dominic extended his hand to help her sit, but she ignored it. Instead, she sank gracefully down with her dark blue riding skirts spread around her and her back straight and high. She was not truly offended—if she had been, she would be spitting words of fire at him—but he could not figure out quite what she was.

At last he ventured a question. "Am I to be allowed to eat?"

"Not until you apologize."

"For what?"

She looked at him with perfect gravity. "Mocking my church."

"You can't be serious . . ."

It was her eyes that gave her away, shining with an expression he couldn't place at first, though it was enough to make him pause. And then her lips curved in a smile, and he knew it for what it was. Minuette was flirting with him.

He felt his heart turn over and let himself enjoy the feel of it. Something so innocent and natural. Something they could never do openly away from this place.

Bowing his head, he matched her grave tone. "I apologize. It's a perfectly lovely church, though do you not fear we shall offend God by picnicking on his very doorstep?"

She laughed, and Dominic marveled at the effect of it on her face and his pulse. Suddenly, he realized that her laughter in public always had a hint of calculation running beneath it, as if she never stopped thinking and was always aware of the multiple lives tangled up in her heart.

"You needn't worry," she replied, handing him a loaf of new-baked bread. "This church is no longer consecrated. It was Catholic . . . of course it was Catholic, they were *all* Catholic. But it had not been used for years, so Carrie says, and after the break with Rome it was left empty by the reformers."

As they ate warm bread and fresh cheese and candied orange peel, Minuette told him a little of the history of the church, garnered from Carrie and Mistress Holly. Dominic didn't take any of it in, but he enjoyed the sound of her voice rising and falling, the animation in her face and hands as she talked.

When they finished eating, she asked, "Would you care to see inside?"

She allowed him to take her hand and help her up. Any other time and place, he would have moved to offer her his arm, but today he kept her hand. He could feel everything, from her linen blackwork sleeves brushing his wrist to each individual finger wound through his.

The interior of the church was surprisingly attractive, with heraldic windows pouring dusky-hued light into the well-proportioned Norman nave. The altar and a stone font remained, but the rest of the building was stripped of furnishings or decoration. Dominic felt a pang at this evidence of Henry VIII's ruthless plunder of so many churches.

"Carrie's mother was married here, even though the church had been long empty by then," Minuette told him. "Not that it needed to be a church, but I suppose she felt that even an empty church would lend a little grace to the event."

"I don't follow."

"It was a *di praesenti* marriage." Minuette's voice had altered, curiously intense as she spoke with a rapidity that betrayed her nerves. "Not that Carrie knew the Latin term, certainly her parents didn't, but they understood the principle well enough. As long as they each, of their own will, said 'I marry thee,' then the marriage was binding in the eyes of the Church. Carrie's mother was being pressed to marry someone else, someone her parents favoured. So she simply avoided the fuss of parents and priests and came here with the man she wanted. They made their present vows and that was that. No matter how displeased her family, she was married and it could not be undone."

An uneasy pause followed, in which Dominic could almost hear the beat of Minuette's heart, quick and uncertain. She said nothing more.

He let go of her hand and stepped away, turning slowly, taking in every corner of the church from ceiling to floor and back again. Without looking at her, he said, "You and I are not tenant farmers, Minuette. We live by different rules."

"I thought the court lived by its own rules. Dominic, don't you ever wish—"

He had to cut her off before she could name any of the many things he wished. "Not like that, my love. I will not take you in secret. I will marry you when William gives his consent and not a moment before."

It was harsh, because it had to be harsh.

Though he had reveled in being alone with Minuette, there were perils in it as well. One night the first week they had stayed up late playing chess. Dominic was not nearly as good a player as William or Minuette, but the attraction had not really been the game but the chance to sit across from her and watch her breathing and the way the tip of her tongue stuck out when she concentrated. By the time Dominic had lost his fourth game to her, he didn't care about discretion any longer.

They had kissed in the firelit solitude of the medieval hall until he couldn't think of anything but the feel of her and how badly he wanted his hands on her skin and not the fabric of her dress, and then Minuette had broken away and said, "The hall is not especially private. Perhaps not the wisest place to . . ."

She had trailed off and though he thought she meant it invitingly, he couldn't allow himself to follow that thought or the possible invitation. He had turned away so she might not see how she'd aroused him and said shakily, "Not wise at all. Goodnight, Minuette."

He had put a chair in front of his own door that night, so that if he tried to go to her, he would be reminded that he shouldn't. Couldn't.

They had taken care not to stay up so late again.

But as they rode back to Wynfield from her perfect little abandoned church, he found himself thinking, Tonight is our last night. Perhaps I can allow myself to slip just a little.

A hope that was dashed the moment he saw the royal standard flying from the courtyard of Minuette's home.

William met them in the hall, springing up from his sprawled position in a chair to hug Minuette fiercely.

"What are you doing here?" she asked, sounding not nearly as rattled as Dominic felt.

"I missed you," he said into her hair and, after much too long, released her. "The French left two days ago and I couldn't stay away. Thank goodness Dom is here, for needing to meet urgently with my closest councilor is excellent cover."

Dominic felt his shutters come down hard and fast. "An urgent treasury affair? Does anyone even pretend to believe that?"

"I didn't say it was a treasury affair. And yes, it is urgent. I wouldn't want you to miss the ship to France."

Minuette stilled and so did Dominic, not daring to hope, as she said to William, "France? Do you mean—"

"Do you think I would send my most precious treasure to France without an appropriate guard? Of course Dom must go with you."

Dominic swallowed, trying to gain control before speaking. "Nothing like leaving things to the last minute."

"I like to keep my kingdom guessing. It keeps plotting to a minimum." William stretched contentedly and looked around the hall. "This is a very pleasant house, Minuette. I approve."

"Thank you. I must speak to Mistress Holly about dinner and an appropriate guest chamber. She will be a little overwrought and need soothing. Your men will mostly have to sleep in the outbuildings, I'm afraid. It won't be elaborate, I hope you don't mind."

The king caught her hand and raised it to his lips. "I would be content to dine with you in a stable, sweetling."

William could not remember ever being so happy as he was that night, eating simple food in a simple room with only Dominic and Minuette for company. He should remember this feeling, he decided—perhaps when he married Minuette they could make this house their retreat. Of course it would need to be expanded and modernized. New kitchens and bedchambers for those who would need to attend him. Perhaps a tennis court or a maze or both. He would speak to someone about it and then he could present the plans to Minuette later. For Christmas?

He was so content, that it was a pity Dominic insisted on discussing court matters. Although Dominic was now, rankwise, the equal of Rochford, he had not lost his habit of corresponding with his former guardian, and thus he knew all about the competing sermons that had been preached in London the first Sunday of the French visit.

"I hear Latimer greatly offended the French with his opinions of marriage," Dominic remarked. "Namely, that you should not marry in respect of alliance."

"Oh, yes, Latimer was quite eloquent on that matter." William tore off a piece of bread with restless hands. "Truly, it was as though he spoke straight to my own wishes: 'for God's love beware where you marry; choose your wife in a faithful stock.' I cannot quarrel with that." He grinned at Minuette, then went on, "Though I'll admit his timing could have been better."

"And Bonner spoke in favour of the French marriage."

"Rather more than that," William replied wryly. "As no doubt my uncle wrote you. Bonner was careful in his wording, but the bishop left little doubt that he hopes a Catholic wife will lead to Catholic children and thus England might be returned to the so-called true faith."

"Why do you let Bishop Bonner continue preaching?" Minuette wanted to know. "He's going to get himself into trouble."

William shot a glance at Dominic and read there his knowledge of the trouble that had already come. "He has," Dominic answered tersely. "Bonner was arrested the day after that sermon."

Minuette looked to William. "What will happen to him?"

William caressed her cheek. "You need not worry about it, sweetling. Politics and religion are not only troublesome but boring. We will speak of other things."

Dominic did not miss the mutinous expression that briefly crossed Minuette's face, but she did not argue. For the duration of dinner they spoke of Minuette's farms and of the visiting Frenchman who had passed out, dead drunk, in the middle of a state dinner and other trivia until she at last excused herself.

Left alone with Dominic, William stretched out his legs and contemplated his friend. After a long moment, right when expected, Dominic asked, "Why are you sending me to France?" He raised a hand when William opened his mouth. "And don't tell me it's solely for Minuette. I know what Bonner really preached. You have need of me here."

It was true that Bishop Bonner had finally crossed the line from religious disagreement to state treason. His sermon had centered on Mary, still confined at Syon House (for her own protection, William thought of it, keeping her away from those who would use her), but Bonner had inflamed sentiment in favour of his half sister, and with the French marriage not precisely what Catholics hoped for . . .

"I could easily have Bonner tried for heresy for comparing Mary to the Virgin, but as he's given us so many other ways to attack?" William shook his head. "He'll end up executed, Dominic. Latimer intends no mercy. And why should he? Bonner was quick enough to torture and burn Anne Askew at the end of my father's reign."

It was true that Bonner had plenty of crimes to account for, but Dominic approached the issue practically. "Can you afford to antagonize the Catholics so openly? They might start imagining that they themselves are not safe in their beliefs."

"As long as the French betrothal holds, the Catholics will bite their tongues. It means no hope of getting out of it this year, but I never really expected to marry Minuette for at least another two years. Also, I have Northumberland's son in prison and the duke himself banished from court at the moment, so there's some measure of balance."

"But to see to the future balance—that is why I'm going to France."

"I have an assignment for you while there. Besides Minuette, I mean. I need you to speak with the Spanish ambassador in Paris." There wasn't currently one in England, the last having been expelled during the Norfolk debacle.

He could have bet Dominic would figure it out. "Elizabeth," his friend said simply.

"Elizabeth," William agreed.

"A marriage to Prince Philip."

"Right."

"To appease the Catholics when you spurn the French and marry Minuette."

"Can we quit stating the obvious and talk about how you need to approach this?"

"I know how to approach it," Dominic said flatly. "I worked for Rochford, remember? Does he know? About Minuette, I mean."

"My uncle knows I need to marry Elizabeth strategically. He is not opposed."

Dominic stood. "May I?" he asked. William waved his permission, and Dominic began to pace. "If Elizabeth marries Philip, she'll leave England to become the future Queen of Spain. You'll be choosing a rather permanent alliance."

"I'll need it," William remarked wryly.

"Why don't you want Minuette to know?"

William shifted uncomfortably and reached for his wine goblet. "Because Elizabeth is not happy about it. I don't need dramatics from Minuette as well."

"Why not? You've never minded Minuette arguing with you before."

"But now I need her support!" He jumped up, and once again it was familiar, William pacing in agitation while Dominic stood motionless and watched. "I need her, Dom. She is my center, my still calm in a stormy sea. She keeps *me* balanced and that is good for England. You are my right hand, Dom—but Minuette is my soul. I need you both. You can see that, can't you?"

Dominic, after a weighted pause, answered tonelessly, "Yes, I see that. Of course I'll do what you ask."

"Thank you, my friend. And remember—the Spanish ambassador is secondary. Keeping Minuette safe is always your first mission."

"I won't forget."

They talked together for another hour, politics and treasury and military—nothing pressing, just the easy conversation of two young men who inhabited the same world. When they separated for the night, William waited five minutes, then made his way to Minuette's room. He knocked softly, hoping she was expecting him, and sure enough she opened the door to him herself. William grinned, sweeping her into a kiss and closing the door behind him with his foot.

Dominic did not sleep. He had heard William go to Minuette's room, and he had counted every minute that the two were together. He had promised himself that if it were any longer than thirty minutes, he would get Carrie to intervene, but after twenty minutes he heard William's footsteps return and his door close firmly. It had stayed that way the rest of the night.

So it was partly fatigue and partly jealousy and partly exasperation that sent him to William's door at dawn. He knocked once and let himself in, seeing as William was not accustomed to being entirely alone and probably wouldn't know how to open a door himself.

The king was still in bed, but awake enough to scowl. "What are you doing?"

"We'd best get an early start." Even to himself he sounded clipped and angry.

Yawning, William sat up and swung his legs out of bed. He had been given the nicest chamber in the house, which had once been that of Minuette's parents. Dominic thought it quite pleasant with its dark wood and embroidered linens and the diamond-paned windows that overlooked the rose garden.

It did not suit William at all—he looked like a Barbary horse kept incongruously in a farmer's field. "Why do I think I'm about to get a lecture?"

"Do you deserve one?"

With a roll of his eyes, William replied, "Just get it over with, Dom. It's about last night, isn't it? You're going to tell me I shouldn't have been in her chambers."

"No, you shouldn't. Court gossip is one thing—but this is Minuette's home. It's not fair to put her in the position of either refusing you or losing her people's respect."

"Nothing happened. You know that, don't you? She doesn't have to refuse me, because I'm not asking anything wrong of her. Even you can't see anything inappropriate in spending twenty minutes alone with the woman I love. It's not nearly what I want, but it's the most I can have, so yes, if I can steal a private moment in a private house to kiss her, I will."

Dominic snatched up the nearest linen shirt and tossed it at William. "Get dressed," he said.

"Don't be so self-righteous," William grumbled. "Just try to put yourself in my place—loving a woman you can't openly touch. Do you know how long it's been since I've had a woman? Surely you cannot grudge me the smallest of comforts."

Do you know how long it's been for me? Dominic wanted to shout. He hadn't had a woman since Aimée in France more than eighteen months ago. And he wouldn't, until he could have Minuette.

William pulled on his shirt and said thoughtfully, "You know, Dom, I wasn't going to bring this up until after France, but I think it's time you and I had a serious discussion about your own marriage."

Feeling as though he might choke, Dominic said, "I don't need you to marry me off."

"But you will eventually need my permission. Not only are you a duke, but you also have royal blood through your grandmother. Honestly, can you not see how the women are angling for you these days? You're going to have to choose soon. And as to that choice . . . I would like you to seriously consider Jane Grey."

Dominic had no patience for this conversation. All he could think of was William and Minuette alone last night, kissing (And more than kissing? he wondered savagely. Where do Will's hands wander when he's alone with her?), and he had to force himself to respond.

"I don't think Jane Grey likes me," was all he could manage.

"Jane likes you fine. And her mother definitely likes your title. If they can't have me, they'll settle for you."

"How flattering," Dominic muttered.

"Look, I know that whoever this one beautiful woman is that John Dee claimed is in your future, it isn't Jane Grey. But it would be an outstanding marriage for both of you. And she's a nice, sweet girl. She'll make a pleasant home for you, give you lots of children, and not be unduly difficult when you find your beautiful woman."

"Can we not have this conversation right now?" Dominic asked. Because if it went on much longer, he was going to have to think seriously about hitting his friend in order to shut him up.

William sighed. "Just think about it, all right? We'll talk it over at the end of the summer." He hesitated, then said, "I do hope . . . that is, if you are already in love, Dom . . . I don't know if you are, but if so, clearly it's with someone unsuitable or you would tell me about her. And if you are . . ."

Dominic thought his heartbeat must be audible not only to his king but to the entire household. "If I am? Say what you mean, William."

"I do hope it's not Elizabeth."

After a long, blank moment, Dominic laughed aloud. William at first looked affronted, but then joined in. "I take it that's a no," he said merrily.

Dominic shook his head. "I am not in love with Elizabeth. I like her very much, but that is all."

"I'm glad. Not that I don't think you good enough for my sister, but there are always political complications."

"Always."

"And truly, Dom, if you are going to love just one woman, I want it to be a woman who will love you as you deserve. Perhaps it won't be the woman you marry, but I suppose we'll see."

The laughter died. "I suppose we will."

CHAPTER TEN

D OMINIC'S FIRST VISIT to France had been as a poorly concealed spy for Lord Rochford in 1553. He had been greeted courteously, treated generously, and watched endlessly. His second visit had been with the English army in the summer of 1554, and that had entailed more than four bloody months of sieges and battles and their aftermath.

This third visit in three years was by far the most dangerous. Dominic was the senior peer escorting a gaggle of females ranging from Elizabeth and Lady Rochford to six young girls, none of them older than fifteen, who would be taken into Elisabeth de France's household for the foreseeable future. All of them came with their own maids and attendants, and between seasickness and feminine sniping, Dominic figured his most difficult task was simply getting all of them from England to the French court. Without tossing one of them overboard or making more than three of them cry in any given day.

He could swear that every time he saw her, Minuette was laughing at him.

After the voyage from Dover to Le Havre—conquered and garrisoned by the English armies last year—it took nearly a week to get them to Paris by river. They were accompanied by officials from the French king's household, supervised by Cardinal de Guise, and treated to every courtesy and comfort along the way.

The French court itself welcomed them exuberantly at the great royal château of Fontainebleau. The present King Henri's father had expanded and decorated it extensively, and Henri was continuing that work. Dominic, usually indifferent to style and décor, had to admit to awe at the Salle des Fêtes, newly completed in the Italian Mannerist style (or so he was told—he didn't know Mannerist from Gothic). The gallery was flooded with light from the tall windows, the better to appreciate the frescoes between the windows and the paintings that filled every wall. The geometric design of the ceiling was highlighted in gold gilding. It was the most impressive single room Dominic had ever seen, and a stunning setting for the elegant, languid grace of the French court. The royals themselves did not attend this opening reception—Elizabeth was dining privately with King Henri II, Queen Catherine de Medici, and William's betrothed princess. But everyone else of importance was in the Salle des Fêtes on this late afternoon in June, and once Dominic got his bearings, he amused himself with watching Lady Rochford, who stood out amongst the others like a crow in the midst of peacocks.

Minuette detached herself from two of the young ladies-in-waiting who had come from England and moved to Dominic's side. "Lady Rochford does look as though she cannot decide whether to allow herself to be dazzled or if it would be better to behave as though all this is nothing to her."

"Which do you think it is, really?"

"Envy," Minuette decided, after a considering moment. "If she didn't frighten me so much—and if she wasn't so relentlessly offensive—I would feel sorry for her. She is always seeking to make people pay attention. It can't be easy to be married to someone who spends so much of his time in other women's beds."

Why did their every conversation turn to marriage? Dominic said abruptly, "Have you met Madame de Poitiers yet?"

"No. Is she here?" Minuette craned to try to see Europe's most famous courtesan.

Oh, she was here. Dominic had felt her keen gaze the moment he'd entered the room. He'd had only one private conversation with the French king's mistress during his last visit, but a rather memorable one. He was quite sure Diane de Poitiers would want to speak to him, so he might as well get it over with. In public, where perhaps she would not be so bold.

Or perhaps she would be so bold. Her first words, as Dominic bowed, were, "Could this possibly be the young lady we once discussed?"

He felt his face begin to flame and wished he could openly curse a woman. Or at least tell her to keep her mouth shut. "*Madame,* this is Mademoiselle Genevieve Wyatt. She is the principal lady to our own fair Princess Elizabeth."

As Minuette curtsied, Dominic wondered what her impression would be of King Henri's notorious mistress. In her mid-fifties now, Diane had the figure and vigor of a much younger woman and her skin was still radiantly fair and lovely. She knew how to turn every gift to an advantage, from her beautiful shoulders and bosom to the styling of her dark hair to the exquisite detailed embroidery done in threads of gold along the lower skirts of her brocade dress. But it was not her looks alone that had kept the much younger French king at her side for twenty years. She was a brilliant advisor and administrator who was known to sign state papers with the joint names *HenriDiane.*

Also, Dominic had seen the royal initials everywhere represented in the Salle des Fêtes, and Henri's bold H was not joined to his wife's C, but twined with his mistress's voluptuous D. That was the action of a man truly in love.

Diane de Poitiers had expressions that could hold entire conversations on their own. Now she favoured Dominic with one that said *I see straight through you but perhaps I'll humour you for the young lady's sake.*

"Genevieve." She rolled the word. "A good French name."

"My mother was French, *madame la duchesse.* She was a companion to the late Queen Anne and went to England in her service."

"Ah, how charming your French is! Not quite native, but not pure English, either. Very good, mademoiselle. I shall look forward to speaking with you more during your sojourn here."

"Merci, madame."

Diane turned her focused gaze to Dominic. "And you, *le duc nouveau,* I shall quite look forward to continuing our last conversation when we can be . . . more private." She leaned forward and said in a conspiratorial aside, "I should beware Aimée, however. She has not forgotten your last visit and may wish to redress matters."

With a gracious goodbye, Diane de Poitiers drifted off, leaving Dominic completely stunned. Minuette looked at him sidelong and said, "Aimée?"

"No one. Just one of her ladies, I believe." And please don't ask me more, he thought. He did not want to explain about a woman who was furious with him for having too soon ended a careless affair he should never have started. He didn't imagine Minuette thought him unfamiliar with women, should he say?—but nor did he want to have any conversation with her about specifics.

It was a great relief to hear a man hailing him. He would have seized on anyone at the moment, but Renaud LeClerc was much more than just anyone. Despite the fact that they'd last met on the battlefield a year ago, they remained fast friends, two soldiers who understood one another.

"Dominic!" Renaud took him by the shoulders in an awkward hug. "I did not think to have so soon the pleasure of meeting again. I am glad your king sent you, though honestly—guarding women? Is that really a soldier's job?"

"A soldier's job is whatever he is ordered," Dominic replied with an honest grin. Renaud was so straightforward, so unlike nobles and kings and sly mistresses. "How is your wife, my friend?"

"Ah, you can soon see for yourself for Nicole is coming to court. She wishes to meet the English ladies and to thank you for sending me home safely to her. She will be here next week. Now," Renaud turned to Minuette, "we are both being inexcusable. Will you introduce me to this charming *jolie fille*?"

"Mademoiselle Genevieve Wyatt," Dominic said, "I present le Vicomte Renaud LeClerc, Marshall of France and commander of His Majesty King Henri's armies."

Renaud bent to kiss Minuette's hand, then regarded her with the naked appraisal that only the French could get away with. He definitely approved, but then who wouldn't? In this gathering of experienced, elegant, jaded women, Minuette had the freshness and splendor of an English rose amidst exotic and heavily scented bouquets. Dominic felt a rush of possessive pride that he struggled to conceal.

"A true English beauty," Renaud murmured. "It is an honour, Mademoiselle Wyatt."

"The honour is mine, *monsieur le comte*. I have heard many wonderful things about your family from Dominic."

Renaud straightened and said, almost to himself, "She is who she is, *n'est-ce pas*? And as she is . . ."

He met Dominic's eyes then, and Dominic knew the Frenchman remembered sitting by the fire with him at his own home and saying, of his wife, *Nicole, as she is, was the only one for me.*

If anyone could guess his heart, it was probably Renaud. That should worry him, but for a moment he relished being in the company of someone who understood him clearly and without judgment.

On their second day at Fontainebleau, the Englishwomen were formally introduced to Elisabeth de France's household. The young princess, just ten years old, held court with as much dignity as though she were twice that age, dressed in a stiff French gown of cloth-of-gold and crimson to emphasize her future position as England's queen. Minuette was the last introduced, after Elizabeth and the Duchess of Rochford and her six young charges from good English noble families, who would remain in France in Elisabeth's service.

Lady Rochford introduced Minuette flawlessly enough ("a lady of our own Princess Elizabeth"), but there was a sting to her tone that even the child appeared to notice. Though there were, of course, French adults in the room—from governess to priest to the French princess's own ladies-in-waiting—Elisabeth was the seat of authority at the moment, and she took her duties seriously.

"You are most welcome, mademoiselle," Elisabeth de France said gravely. It was a royal's rebuke to an ungracious woman more than four times her age. "I am happy to be acquainted with any friend of my future *belle-soeur,* and I have been told you are also well known to the king, God save him."

Minuette rose from her curtsey. "I am, Your Highness," she answered with matching gravity, her heart touched by the sweet, high voice of childhood. "The king has instructed me to observe carefully that I might bring him reports of your interests and beauty."

In truth, William had said nothing at all about his betrothed to her, and probably not to anyone outside his council members. Why did that suddenly bother her? Why, in the presence of this wide-eyed, glittering child, did she feel profoundly guilty, struck by the urge to apologize and confess. *I did not mean to steal Will's love,* she wanted to say, *and I promise to do all I can to turn him to you.*

It might have been amusing if it weren't all so complicated.

She said as much to Dominic as he escorted her to the grand welcome banquet that night. When she told him of Elisabeth de France's eager questions about William, about her request that Minuette attend her in the coming days to speak of England and her future husband, Dominic shrugged it off. "She's a girl raised to please. It's all new to her. No doubt, by her third or fourth betrothal, she'll be much more sanguine."

"Like our own Elizabeth?" Minuette snapped. "It's cruel, what is done to royal women. She's just a little girl, and she thinks William a mythical prince who will make every dream come true. It's not fair to her."

"That is not your fault," he said, more gently. "If it was not William, it would—and will—be another prince. It's what the girl was born to."

"Then I am delighted not to be royal!"

"Not royal, no," Dominic murmured. "But are you any more free?"

She remembered something Elizabeth had said to her last year, referring to Anne Boleyn and her Henry. *I think she loved him as well as she was able, considering she had no choice in the matter.*

Being loved by William, she had to admit, was beginning to feel like a cage. Highly gilded and widely coveted—but a cage nonetheless.

———

"Elizabeth, *la plus belle princesse* . . ." She could quite get used to this. In England, she was always one step behind William. And though she knew intellectually that this extravagant welcome and praise from the French was mostly due to their desire to impress her brother, she let herself be flattered and dream a little of what it might be like to be adored solely for herself.

The opening grand banquet, given the second day after their arrival, was exquisite in both food and ritual. Although much of the elaborate solemnity amused Elizabeth, it also delighted her. For the first time in months she gave herself up solely to the pleasures of the moment—one of which was upstaging her cousin, Mary of Scotland. Mary might be Queen Regnant of Scotland and the future Queen of France, but Elizabeth was the honoured guest tonight, and thus had pride of place at the high table next to King Henri. She admitted, grudgingly, that her cousin was lovely—unusually tall for her age and with the distinct red-gold hair of her Tudor grandmother—but at twelve, Mary was little more than a girl with a promise of beauty. Elizabeth held every advantage at this dinner and she reveled in it.

To be fair, Mary was gracious and professed herself ecstatic to meet Elizabeth. "It is my greatest wish, cousin, to be united with England in both faith and friendship."

United faith would never happen, not with the Scots queen's ardent Catholicism. And though friendship looked possible just now with both she and William intending matrimonial ties with the French, that also would be shattered the moment William broke the treaty. But whatever else might happen, Mary Stuart had been Scotland's queen since she was six days old, and her actions in future might make all the difference to England's precarious security. The entire point of her being at the French court, being groomed as France's future queen, was to make permanent the *auld alliance* of France and Scotland. England would be under enormous pressure when the French king could claim to rule part of their own island.

The dancing that followed the banquet was elaborate, but Elizabeth was beginning to see beneath the surface to the universal similarities of royal courts. Fontainebleau was impressive, but tone down the dazzle just a bit and it was not much different from Greenwich or Richmond or Whitehall. Look beneath the fabulous jewels and the ostentatious fashions that made the men like peacocks and the women like statues, and the types were ones Elizabeth had known all her life: the hangers-on, the empty-headed, the flatterers, and the rare possessors of true ability.

She danced with King Henri and with his son, the dauphin (who, at eleven years old, was highly impressed by his own dignity). She danced with handsome, charming men of Valois and Navarre and Orléans, flirted brilliantly with the Admiral of France, and finally found herself dancing with a man she'd heard about from both her brother and Dominic: Vicomte Renaud LeClerc.

"It is a great pleasure to meet you, Your Highness," he began, in very good English.

She answered him in French. "The pleasure is mine, as my brother's representative. I am glad to be a symbol of honourable peace between us."

"Do you think all peace honourable?"

"Do you?" Elizabeth shot back.

He smiled with delight. "It depends on the peace, Your Highness, and on the fight. Honour can be found in almost any circumstance."

"Now that does sound like someone I know. No wonder Lord Exeter speaks so highly of you."

LeClerc chuckled. "Dominic is a good man, though perhaps a trifle serious for one his age."

"I know exactly what you mean."

"So serious in fact that I wonder, Your Highness, if our dear friend *le duc* chafes at being charged with—though honourable—such a light duty."

She could read his subtext as clearly as if he'd shouted it. *What else is he here for?* LeClerc was asking. Although Elizabeth had the same question, she refused to dwell on it. She could guess why Dominic was in France.

LeClerc continued with a seemingly unrelated question. "Now that your royal brother's matrimonial future is secure, he will be looking to secure your own happiness next, *non?*"

Elizabeth found herself looking for Dominic and, finding him deep in conversation with the Duc de Guise, suppressed a sigh. Who else might Dominic be tasked with speaking to on this trip? And what choices would she be presented with when they returned to England? She knew as well as her brother that the Spanish kept an ambassador at the French court.

For one painful second the thought of Robert pierced through her, but then she walled it off. Between Dominic's probable charge to approach her future Spanish husband and the royal hopes and plans of both Mary Stuart and Elisabeth de France, she could not afford to be sidetracked into thinking about Robert.

Her resolve lasted less than twelve hours. For when Minuette joined her for a late breakfast the next day, Elizabeth had just received a missive from Robert Dudley.

Minuette watched her read, then asked, "What does Robert have to say?"

"That being on progress with William is remarkably similar to a battlefield: uncomfortable lodgings, indifferent food, and surprise ambushes from aggressive females who are more trouble than even enemy soldiers." Elizabeth tossed the letter onto the table, amidst the plated gold dishes. "Although Robert is not precise about whether the aggressive females confine their ambushes solely to my brother."

Minuette correctly sensed Elizabeth's mood. She said quietly, "Robert doesn't trouble to write solely to tease. Which is all that is, you know."

"I do know," Elizabeth said. "But does it not bother *you*? Knowing that William is constantly besieged by women who want whatever they can have of him?"

Two years ago Elizabeth would have wagered that she could name any one of Minuette's thoughts simply by reading her expressions. But that had changed, and now she could only go by Minuette's words. "I don't dwell upon it, Elizabeth. I assure you, I do not spend my days eaten up with jealousy over William."

Elizabeth meant to probe deeper, but Minuette said quickly, "So why else did Robert write?"

"Oh, he had a message for me from John Dee." Elizabeth picked the letter back up and read from it. " 'Dr. Dee has many friends in Europe, men of intelligence and experience. He mentioned that one of them might be coming to see you, with a letter of introduction from Lord Burghley.' "

"Lord Burghley? From the privy council?"

"The same. I confess, I find myself intrigued to meet someone who commands the interest of men as different as John Dee and William Cecil. Let the attendants know that I am to be notified at once if this man comes calling. His name is Francis Walsingham."

After bidding farewell to his sister and Minuette in Dover, William had set off on his annual summer progress. This year's carefully calculated itinerary included stays with both the Earl of

Pembroke and William Cecil, Lord Burghley, as well as a tour of royal castles in Wales. The timing of the various visits and delegations and embassies meant that, for the first time in his life, he celebrated his birthday alone. He was not even at Hampton Court, but at Conwy Castle in North Wales, an imposing but cheerless military structure that made him all the more restless for missing Minuette. And not just her—Elizabeth was as much a part of his life as breathing, and Dominic was always and ever his most trusted voice. William had plenty of hangers-on for this progress, but no one he trusted half as much as Dominic.

Except, from time to time, his uncle.

Today he needed to trust someone, for he had before him a royal execution warrant awaiting his signature. William studied the single sheet, though he knew it by heart. It ordered the death by burning of Edmund Bonner, once Bishop of London, convicted now of heresy and treason.

"Why not the axe?" William asked his uncle once more. "The heresy charge only matters because of the treason attached to it. I am no pedant, insisting on the uniformity of private conscience."

"But many of your people do so insist, including some of your chief advisors," Rochford answered grimly. "At least insofar as such private conscience is expressed in words. The axe is not as fearsome as the fire, Your Majesty. You should begin as you mean to go on, and Bonner's death at the stake will set a bar for dissent that the Catholics will know they cannot cross."

William stared at the signatures already on the warrant— every member of the privy council except one. He was glad Dominic was in France, for he was not absolutely certain that his friend would have signed. But Dom is not king, he thought, and with that he scrawled *Henry Rex* in bold letters at the bottom of the warrant.

"See to it," he told his uncle, handing it over. "And while you are burning Bonner, I will head east and visit my sister, Mary, at Beaulieu. I would not have her hear of this by report, but from my own conviction."

"That is wise, Your Majesty. Afterward, you will continue on to Kenninghall?"

"Might as well get all the Catholic wrath over with at once. And remind the Howards that I continue to hold their fortunes in my hand."

"And . . . the child?" Rochford asked delicately.

For all of the Howards were at Kenninghall awaiting the royal visit, including Eleanor and the little girl born last year who was almost certainly his child. William was uneasy about seeing Eleanor again after the unresolved incident with the adder in Minuette's room, but it seemed only right to at least set eyes on the child. He wondered who she looked like, and if he would feel anything for her.

But his uncle didn't need to know that. "I'm going to Kenninghall to intimidate the new Duke of Norfolk. My personal affairs are not part of it."

"So you say. Perhaps one day you will learn better."

"Don't," William warned.

"It is my duty to advise you, and I will do so no matter how unpleasant the task. A king has no personal affairs. Everything you do affects England."

"I never forget that. Nor do I ever forget that, by God's will, I *am* king."

"By God's will, and your grandfather's battles."

"Choose your words carefully, Uncle."

"Edward IV thought it God's will that he be king, and so did his bloody brother, Richard. But their personal affairs undid them, allowing your grandfather the opportunity to claim the throne."

"The throne that was his by right."

"Rights do not always enter into it, William." Rochford rarely called him by name. "Thrones are won and held by many means. The Catholics believe your throne is Mary's by right. By our rights, the Scots throne is legally yours, but has thus far required more force than we can muster to hold it. Ireland you hold by force alone. Those with power will always trump those with mere right on their side."

"I know this, Uncle. I have listened to you over the years, despite what you may think. Just because I don't always take your advice—"

"This isn't all about you!"

William rocked back in his seat, staring at Rochford's furious face. Part of him was instantly ten years old, cowed and desperate to please. That part wanted Elizabeth or Dominic to stand up for him, wanted to run away with Minuette to make him laugh and remind him he was king.

That part vanished in a wave of icy rage.

"Do tell, Lord Rochford: if being king isn't about me, then whom is it about?"

"Do you have any idea what your mother went through to get you where you are today? What it cost her in pride and security? The price my family paid?" His uncle did not back down, pressing his point, and William wondered how long he'd been wanting to say these things.

"The price you paid to be the most powerful family in England?" William let his voice cut through in the very way he'd learned from Rochford. "Tell me, Uncle, what exactly is it you think the King of England owes you?"

Something not fear, not surprise, not anything he could name, flashed in his uncle's eyes. "To remember who you are and who you have always been meant to be. Your Majesty."

"My father's son," William answered, biting off each word.

"That's what I'm afraid of."

"Go back to London. I will not need you again on this progress."

His temper lasted through Rochford's obedient if resentful departure the next morning, up until a courier brought letters from France. When William saw Minuette's distinctive handwriting, he dismissed his attendants with a sullen wave. Tossing the other dozen letters the courier had brought onto a table, he broke the seal of Minuette's and read.

25 June 1555
Fontainebleau Palace

William,

Are you enjoying Wales? Dominic, for one, is envious of your travels there. He cannot stop speaking of the wild beauty of the mountains. I think he is just trying to forget how much he despises having to flatter the French.

And then you will go on to Kenninghall! I have always heard it spoken of as one of the finest manors in northern England. To be sure, I believe it was the Howards who spoke of it as such, so perhaps I should not give too much credence to the praise.

I fear I am not missing England as much as I should. It has been such sweet pleasure to not have to guard every word and gesture, knowing that I am not being watched at every moment. You must feel something of the same relief.

Elizabeth is, naturally, a wonderful success. I have heard only the highest praises for her beauty and her learning and her wit. She is extremely good at representing England—you would be so proud of her. Dominic is the same as ever—watchful and serious and so much fun to tease. And your little French princess is quite sweet. She has asked me to tell her stories of you as a boy. Do not worry—I have kept your reputation as a glorious king intact. It would not do to disillusion her.

The days are passing away rapidly. It will not be long before we return. Until then,

Minuette

William smiled as he read, for he could almost hear Minuette's lilting voice speaking the words she had written. Brief as the letter was, its effect was enough to ease the pain in his shoulders and neck and remind him that he had at least one pleasant thing in a life otherwise burdened by duty and treachery.

He stretched his long legs out before him and stared unseeing at the tapestry draped across the far wall. This summer progress had not been nearly as relaxing as earlier ones. These few months were supposed to be a time of relief for a king, with nothing more pressing than the next day's hunt or the next night's feast.

The truth was, his council was becoming more recalcitrant with every week that passed. Not Dominic, of course, but many of those who composed the privy council thought nothing of opposing even his slightest plan. And it was impossible to get through anything these days without being reminded of England's rising debt. If he had hoped this progress would help him escape from the pressures of ruling, William had been disappointed. Those councilors who were not with him in person wrote lengthy letters detailing plague in London and flooding in

Anglia. And, with unrelenting regularity, protests and clashes over religion.

He thanked God daily for Minuette. If he had not her image with him always—perfect and uncomplicated—he'd have run mad before now.

Slipping her letter inside his doublet, William briefly considered the unread messages confronting him critically from where he'd tossed them. He'd deal with them later. What he needed now was a change of scene. Pausing long enough for a cup of wine, he escaped to the quiet garden that had been set aside for his use. There, he spied Robert Dudley slouching elegantly against a tree and waved him over. He had allowed him on this progress, despite his brother's disgrace, because the man was an excellent rider, a superb dice player, and an amusing wit. Without anyone else around to entertain him, he might as well have Robert.

"Looking forward to Kenninghall? You've not been there before, I believe," William said, knowing very well he hadn't.

Robert's smile was full of mischief. "The Howards and Dudleys are civil in public, but civility does not extend to inviting the enemy into your home."

"Enemies?" William said repressively. "I dislike any of my people finding enemies amongst our own."

"The word was ill-chosen, Your Majesty." Robert Dudley was nothing if not smooth. "Enmity amongst the nobles is far more a matter of words than deeds. We will always hold together where our own interests are concerned."

"Your own interests being the same as England's, of course."

Robert didn't miss a beat. "Of course."

Wondering if the man could ever be thrown off-balance, William abruptly changed the subject. "Does not your wife miss you? You are so often gone from home."

A twitch of the eye was the only sign that Robert had his points of weakness. "I serve at your pleasure. Amy knows that. She bears with it as any wife must."

William nearly snorted at his audacity. Everyone knew that Robert had long been investigating the possibility of a divorce. Perhaps it was time to point out that, divorced or not, he would never be a suitable husband for Elizabeth. Might as well take out some of his restlessness and irritation on Robert.

"Politically speaking, who do you think is the wisest choice for my sister's husband—another French match, to further cement the ties of the treaty, or a Protestant lord at home to appease the rabid anti-Papists?"

"Being Protestant myself, you cannot expect me to recommend the princess marry a Catholic. I'm hardly an objective judge."

"Not objective at all." William infused the words with meaning.

There was a long pause, and when Robert spoke again, his voice had lost its aloof amusement. "I fear I cannot consider your sister's marriage solely in a political light, Your Majesty. I have known her too long and liked her too well to think of her only as a means of extracting you from your own folly." In a voice lowered to a whisper, he continued, "She will do whatever you ask, without demur. But you'll be sacrificing her happiness for your own."

"I would hold my tongue if I were you."

"I have no wish to incur your anger, Your Majesty. But you must know your interests have not gone unnoticed. You think me foolish in my hopes. My folly is nothing compared to yours. If you expect to break with France and place a simple girl on England's throne—"

"You will cease such idle speculation. If relations with France are damaged by malicious gossip, I will hold you and all Protestants responsible. Take care that you do not bring down disaster on your own head."

William turned on his heel and stalked away as Robert said softly, "I might counsel you the same."

CHAPTER ELEVEN

"A MAN TO see you, Your Highness."

Elizabeth turned, frowning, from appraising two gowns in decision, and said to Kat, "French? I haven't forgotten an appointment, have I?"

"As if you ever would," Kat Ashley sniffed. Even the French court could not shake the woman's imperturbable calm. "No, this man is English. Francis Walsingham, he says. He has brought a letter of introduction."

She handed it over, and Elizabeth read swiftly the words of praise and recommendation from Lord Burghley. "I'll see him in the presence chamber, Kat."

When she swept into the presence chamber set aside for her use at Fontainebleau, Elizabeth saw a tall man with a pointed beard, younger than she'd expected, dressed in the sober style of an academic. His medium-brown hair dipped into a widow's peak, accenting his frighteningly intelligent eyes. The kind of eyes ever alert to secrets, she thought. Wherever they occur.

He bowed. "Francis Walsingham, Your Highness. Thank you for seeing me."

"Lord Burghley, a man I greatly respect, wrote in his introduction that meeting with you would be worth my time. Why is that?"

"Because of what I can do for you."

"How presumptuous."

"Yes, Your Highness."

Despite herself, she laughed out loud and gestured for him to make himself comfortable. They both sat and she said, "So what can a presumptuous man do for me?"

"I can give you knowledge."

"I have studied many years to gain knowledge for myself."

"There is knowledge . . . and *knowledge,* Your Highness."

"Speak plainly, Master Walsingham."

"I am an intelligencer. The knowledge I can give you will be that found in dark streets and far-off palaces, whispers and rumours of whispers in places you could never go yourself."

She arched her eyebrow. "And I suppose such knowledge will cost me dear."

"Knowledge is never too dear."

She leaned back in her chair, attempting to intimidate him with her frank appraisal. Walsingham just looked back at her calmly. "You have worked for Lord Burghley?" she asked.

"From time to time."

"Anyone else? Anyone outside of England?"

"I am loyal, if that is what you are asking, Your Highness. Loyal to England and its tolerance. Loyal to a stable government without the fanaticism of Popery. Loyal, if you allow it, to you personally."

And that, Elizabeth knew, was the appeal. To have her own intelligencer, a man of secrets and knowledge to work for her alone. William had any number of such men working for his government—why should she not have the same?

"It should not be too difficult to tease out secret knowledge while I am in France. I will see what you can do, Master Walsingham. Impress me, and I will consider your future."

He bowed once more, but did not seem overly surprised by her challenge. "It will be my honour, Your Highness."

It was a relief to William to leave Wales behind, even on an unpleasant errand. He nearly changed his mind a dozen times on his way to Beaulieu, but whatever Dominic might claim, he had a sense of duty. Especially where family was concerned.

His own guards saluted as he rode into Beaulieu. Although he had recently allowed Mary to return to her favorite residence, he kept his half sister under guard, still wary after last year's maneuverings. Rochford might be doubtful of the late Duke of Norfolk's intention to rebel last autumn, but William could never rest easy while Mary was alive. There would always be unscrupulous, power-hungry men to use her.

He was greeted by John Dudley, Earl of Warwick. Despite Guildford's arrest and the Duke of Northumberland's continuing absence from court, William had seen no need to relieve Warwick of his position. Northumberland's oldest son had done a creditable job overseeing Mary's house arrest and should not be punished for his father's arrogance. Six years older than Robert, Warwick was much more like their father—blunt and straightforward and, most importantly, a devout Protestant who took seriously his task of keeping Mary from fomenting further rebellion.

"Your Majesty." He bowed, not quite as gracefully as Robert would have managed. "The Lady Mary is ready for you in her privy chamber."

"How is she?" William asked as they walked together through the quadrangular palace. His father had built much of it after acquiring it from his future father-in-law a decade before Henry even thought of Anne as his wife. Ironic, William often thought, that Beaulieu was Mary's favorite home. Though likely it had to do with their father's stamp on the architecture and the many remnants of his seal in various interiors.

"The heat does not agree with the Lady Mary, but then neither does the cold nor the wind nor the rain." There was a hint of his brother's humour in Warwick's voice, but he was far more respectful than Robert. "She has been low in spirits, Your Majesty. I know your visit will cheer her."

I doubt it, William thought grimly. Not with the news I bring.

He saw at once what Warwick meant when his sister curtsied to him. He raised her up and studied her face. Though she had gained weight in the last few years, her cheeks today were gaunt and her deep-set eyes feverish. "I am sorry you have not been well," he said, truthfully.

"I will be all the better for your presence," she answered.

"Please, sit."

Mary's privy chamber was a reflection of the woman: richly decorated but somber, almost old-fashioned, in its feel. Even the air felt heavy in here. William did not wonder that his sister was often ill if she spent so much time brooding in this chamber. It was a shrine to crucifixes and representations of martyrdom, and he thought cynically that if all the Reformation had done was remove this depressing décor from England, it had been worth it. They were alone today, at William's politely worded command, for he wanted only to deliver his news and be done with it.

When they were both seated—Mary in a cushioned chair nicely judged to be almost but not quite the equal of the king's—William said, "I do apologize that I have not been to see you before. It has been a busy time, particularly with the prolonged visit from the French."

"And now our sister returns the favour with a tour of France," Mary replied with a thin smile. "I am certain Elizabeth is enjoying herself."

"Elizabeth is my personal representative to the French court. She is tasked with ensuring an appropriate respect for England and our current peace treaty."

"The treaty that will tie you to the French king's daughter." Mary spoke neutrally, but that in itself was damning.

"How can you not approve of my betrothal to Elisabeth de France? She is Catholic."

"And if that was why you chose her, I would rejoice, brother. But the girl is too young to hold out against you. Your council will force her to raise your children in heresy and thus damn their souls before they are even born."

William drew a breath to steady himself. He did not enjoy fighting with women. "That is not the point of this visit, Mary. I have some news for you, news that I fear you will find unpleasant."

She tilted her head in query, one hand restlessly fingering the rosary she wore at her waist. The expression on her face might have been patience but was more likely stubbornness.

"Edmund Bonner has been convicted of treason. He will die at the stake two days from now."

She blinked once, the only betrayal of her feelings. "Burning at the stake is not the penalty for treason."

"He was also convicted of heresy."

"Oh, William." Now there was true emotion in her voice, a plea of anger and sorrow. "How can a follower of the True Church commit heresy? It is not for you to say—"

"It *is* for me to say. I am Supreme Head of the Church, Mary. That is never going to change. We will never return to Rome and their corrupted popes. I allow you to worship as gives you comfort, but do not press me. My leniency is not unlimited."

"I must speak as my conscience demands—"

"And that is why you are, and will remain, under house arrest. I will not allow your conscience to endanger my people or my throne. I am sorry for you, Mary, but this is the life you have chosen. As long as you cling to the past, you will remain locked away. But remember—that is your choice. I do not make it for you."

She paused, breathing heavily, and William was smitten by the reminder of her poor health. At last, she said simply, "I will pray for you, brother, as I never cease to do."

"And I welcome your prayers as coming from my own dear sister. Rest well, Mary."

William was so anxious to get away from her cloying religious devotion that he did not even stay the night.

After their dispute in Wales, Robert Dudley was not surprised when William told him he was not welcome to accompany him for the rest of the king's progress. He was not the only one; Rochford, too, had been sent packing. *One by one William's picking us off,* Robert thought, and grimaced. He wished uneasily that Dominic were in the country. The new duke might be humourless and inflexible, but those very qualities made him a good ballast for William's mercurial moods.

For about three minutes he considered going to Dudley Castle and seeing his father; for less time even than that he considered visiting his own home—and wife. Instead, Robert returned to London and Ely Place. He expected the town house to be empty of his family, but to his surprise he found his mother in residence.

"What are you doing here?" he asked, after the filial kisses had been bestowed. "London is never pleasant in July."

"Edmund Bonner will be executed tomorrow." His mother might be dressed as a woman of the court in her dark gray silk and diamond earrings, but she spoke with an inflexible purpose.

Alarmed, Robert said, "Surely you don't mean to attend! A burning is not a fit spectacle for any woman."

"That didn't stop Bishop Bonner from inflicting it upon Anne Askew."

How could he have overlooked his mother's championship of the Protestant martyr? Bonner had had Anne Askew tortured to the point that she'd had to be carried to her own burning in a chair, unable to even walk to her death. His mother had a most active conscience, and she had never forgiven the Catholic bishop for his torment of Askew. But even so, there was no way Robert could let her anywhere near the raw brutality of Bonner's death. If for no other reason than that his father would kill him if he didn't stop her.

"Mother, be reasonable. If you won't be swayed by propriety, then at least consider the matter politically. If the Duchess of Northumberland were to be found at the execution of a recalcitrant Catholic bishop, it would be seen as gloating. His death may be necessary, but inflaming the religious divide is not."

"And how would it be seen if one of the duchess's younger sons were to be found at the execution?"

Robert pressed his lips tight to keep from swearing. Had he just been neatly maneuvered into attending Bonner's burning? He wouldn't put it past his astute mother to have orchestrated the entire thing—including even his argument with William—just to get him to London and to the execution. It was true that he would not be a controversial spectator—in the midst of the crowds avid to watch the spectacle, he could much more easily blend in than his mother. And even if he were noticed, he was, as Rochford kept telling him, not important enough to cause more than a ripple of interest.

"Fine," he answered. "I will watch Bonner burn and tell you all about it, but then you must leave London. No doubt Father is missing you." Unlike too many marriages—his own, for example—that was not mere politeness. His parents were fiercely devoted to each other.

With his acquiescence, his mother's stern expression softened. "I miss your father," she agreed. "But Bonner is not the only thing that keeps me in London. I have one son here who is not at liberty to leave. You have not forgotten Guildford, have you?"

"I have not. But just because the king is on progress doesn't mean you're going to get into the Tower to see Guildford. Rochford has returned to Whitehall, and I promise that the guards' orders are strict. None of us will see Guildford until the king is ready to let us do so. And the worst way to get the king's permission is to maneuver behind his back."

She favoured him with a smile of approval. It made her look much younger than any mother of thirteen had the right to look, Robert thought. "It is easy to overlook your intelligence in the midst of your charm," his mother said. "After Bonner's death, I will return to Dudley Castle and await word from the princess on our invitation. Do you suppose she will come?"

Robert shrugged. "I suppose Elizabeth will do precisely what she pleases."

Having placated his mother, he did as she'd asked and attended the execution of Edmund Bonner, Bishop of London. It took place at West Smithfield, a large grassy space just outside the city walls. Robert had seen men die by hanging—and of course on the battlefield—but this was something else entirely. Bonner stood in an empty tar barrel, bound to a stake, and faggots were heaped high about him. Sometimes, Robert knew, those condemned to burning were strangled first but there was no such mercy for heretics. There was a priest to pray for Bonner, but no one tried to plead with him to recant. Only the Catholics cared enough to save a man's soul at the end, Robert thought cynically, or perhaps they were enamoured of their own righteousness. The Protestants were more pragmatic and there were no wasted words or time; the faggots were simply lit.

As long as he lived, Robert hoped to never see anything half so terrible again. It took Bonner a long time to fall unconscious from the smoke, long enough for him to scream from the pain of the flames. It was a sickening death, and so Robert reported to his mother when he returned to Ely Place.

"That is why Mary must never be allowed near the throne," his mother said firmly, looking up from her needlework, her face very pale. "How long do you think it would take the Catholics to import the Inquisition to England?"

"And so we fight fire with fire," Robert answered ironically.

"And so we do what we must."

She left for Dudley Castle the following morning. As Robert waved farewell, he kept thinking that his mother had sounded awfully like Lord Rochford. He was beginning to be wary of people who were so inflexibly certain. It made him wonder what his father was doing at Dudley Castle this summer. He was pretty sure it was more than just wait for Elizabeth's answer to their invitation. He was also pretty sure that he didn't want to know about it.

After almost a month at Fontainebleau, Dominic was more than ready to leave the French court behind. It was even worse than England, where at least he knew the courtiers and politicians and lawyers, and where the peculiarly English character was familiar. The French court made England's look like child's play. Everything here was byzantine and circular so that one step led not to the next but to an entirely different path that bore no relation to where you actually thought you were going.

He had not spoken directly to the Spanish ambassador, as

would have been his choice. The man had a French servant deliver a message from a Spanish servant to the effect that discretion was in order. *I will send you word of time and place,* the ambassador had written. *Be prepared to disguise yourself sufficiently not to be followed.*

Who would want to follow me? was Dominic's first thought. But he was not stupid enough to fail to recognize that as William's friend and now a duke in his own right he would indeed be followed and watched. Friendship with kings is always one-sided, he thought sourly, and Renaud seemed to see the same thing in him.

"Still playing diplomatic games against your nature?" the Frenchman asked as the two of them sparred comfortably in an empty practice yard. "I think it keeps you sleepless, *mon ami* . . . or perhaps there is a more pleasant reason for your look of tiredness?"

Dominic met the insinuation with less grace. "There is no woman, Renaud, so keep your thoughts to yourself."

Renaud laughed. "I was not implying what you think. If you are sleepless over a woman—and let us not pretend, we both know that I have met this most particular woman—it is because she is *not* in your bed at night. Why not marry the *très belle fille* and remedy the situation?"

"If you mean Mistress Wyatt, she is the especial friend of the king and his sister and was raised a royal ward. Her marriage will not be a simple matter. And also," Dominic struck furiously at Renaud's blade, forcing him to step back a pace, "I don't know what you're talking about."

Renaud parried. "*Bon.* Of course. But if you *did* know what I was talking about . . . are you not also an especial friend of your king? I would think a marriage would not be that complicated."

"No more, Renaud," Dominic said sharply, disengaging his

sword at the same moment. "I will discuss many things with you, but marriage is personal."

Renaud regarded him thoughtfully. "Acknowledged. But you should remember, Dominic, that matters of life and death can depend on a marriage. Such as that of your king and my royal princess. That, you will want to remember."

"I remember it every day," Dominic retorted. "And I desire the peace it ensures between our countries. I have no wish to clash with you in the field again."

"Nor I. After all, the last time I ended up your prisoner."

Dominic could not shake the suspicion that there had been more than one point to Renaud's conversation; he just wasn't sure he had followed them all. It worried him, even as he watched Minuette charm the French right and left. She was as lovely here as in England, but her spontaneity and freshness were even more noticeable in the mannered court. Of course, next to some of the Frenchwomen, even Elizabeth looked positively impulsive.

But Elizabeth was here for a political purpose, and her position kept her to a strict round of carefully orchestrated public events: hawking with King Henri and the dauphin, afternoon visits to nearby noble homes, attending a Catholic mass with Queen Catherine de Medici and the young Princess Elisabeth. Minuette could move more freely. One morning might be spent walking in the classical gardens with Elisabeth and Mary of Scotland, the two royal girls chattering with Minuette as though they had known her all their lives while dogs of various sizes played around them. Another day Minuette received a private tour of Saint Denis, the magnificent church raised by Abbot Suger in the twelfth century and burial place of French kings. As Dominic made it his business to always know her whereabouts (and ensure Harrington was with her if he could not be), he received many assurances of her interest in and enthusiasm for France.

The promised word from the Spanish ambassador came just three days before their scheduled departure from Fontainebleau. It was smuggled to Dominic in code, amidst a sheaf of innocuous dispatches from home. Deciphered, it gave him directions to a meeting place at midnight (why is it always midnight? Dominic wondered) and instructed him, *Come alone and do not dress the gentleman.*

That last order was considerably easier than the first. Dominic only dressed as a duke when forced into it; by choice his clothing, though well made and of expensive fabric, was unadorned and somber and easy enough to conceal him in the dark. But *come alone* meant leaving Harrington out of it, and the big, silent man had a sixth sense for trouble. He plainly did not believe Dominic when he said he was tired and would not need him again that evening, but he respected Dominic and left when finally ordered. Dominic couldn't swear that Harrington wouldn't stand watch for his return, however.

The directions led him to an unsavory section of Paris that, beneath its seediness, held the outlines of old glamour. London had places like this, where the nobility could go slumming without actually delving into the worst of poverty and apathy. Dominic had been to such places a handful of times, though never for pleasure. It was, he admitted, perfectly suited to a clandestine meeting of gentlemen, for they would not stand out as long as they adapted the slightly furtive air of men looking for a hard drink and an easy woman.

There was an abundance of both drinks and women in the front room of the indicated public house, but as directed Dominic went straight through, up the rickety stairs, and knocked once on the second door on the right of the unlit landing.

It was opened noiselessly by the Spanish ambassador himself. Simon Renard was in his early forties, with darkish hair and a lighter, red-tinged beard. Dominic knew of him, from his earlier studies for Rochford, and he knew the man was highly intelligent and, like all good spies, innately suspicious. Renard looked past him into the shadows of the corridor, to ensure he had come alone.

Without a greeting, he let Dominic enter and shut the door before saying a word. "Shall it be Monsieur Courtenay tonight?" he asked in accented but clear French. "We would not want titles thrown about freely. I understand this meeting will never have taken place."

Dominic pointedly sat down on the only chair in the room, a rather precarious cane-bottomed seat, leaving Renard to choose between standing or perching on the bed that no doubt usually saw quite other activities. Renard chose to lean against the door, in a pose Dominic recognized. It was usually his own.

There was no point in waiting for the ambassador to begin things; as Renard had said, this meeting was William's idea. And though he no doubt knew the topic—or guessed shrewdly—it was still Dominic's job to state it aloud.

"My king is interested in Prince Philip and his matrimonial intentions."

"*Vraiment,* I had heard you are no diplomat, but still . . ." He shrugged. Clearly Renard had not expected him to state it with such bluntness. "If it is plain speaking you want—then tell me, does your king truly think he can marry a French princess on one hand and send his sister to Spain on the other hand? It would be the strangest of marriage beds all around."

Dominic could not be blunt about the next part; he had to hint without revealing anything. "My king respects Spain and recognizes her great power. To wed his own dearest sister to Spain would be an honour beyond measure. There is no tie greater than that of blood. Where his sister goes, the king's heart will follow."

The Spaniard's eyes narrowed. "I thought your king's heart was to be found here, with the little princess at the French court. Can a heart be split?"

"The love for a bride may grow cold—but the love for a sister is forever."

"And does your king's love grow cold?"

"It may be that winter is coming for certain loves."

The ambassador's expression was thoughtful, and discerning. Dominic was as satisfied as he could be that he'd been understood. Elizabeth to Spain, in exchange for an alliance when William withdrew from his French marriage plans.

With a single nod, Renard said abruptly, "The message will reach my prince, you may be assured. Perhaps a reply may be brought to England itself?"

"It is likely." In other words, another ambassador would soon be allowed in London.

"Then perhaps you and I will meet again, Monsieur Courtenay. I have always wished to see England."

With his hand on the door to let Dominic out, Renard paused at the last minute. "Winter is coming for certain loves, you say. Is it possible that a new love has withered the old?"

Dominic met his gaze without blinking. "You would have to ask my king."

He left the public house at once, not at all tempted to linger for a drink. It was a relief to have that done, and now he could focus on getting the women back to England. Returning Minuette to William, true, but also one step closer to ending the French game, one step closer to the decision point.

Distraction cost him dearly. He only heard the footsteps at the last moment, just quick enough to half deflect the blow from behind. The cudgel glanced off the side of his head rather than landing full on. He stumbled and his attacker moved in once more. But Dominic was paying full attention now and stepped into the attack, which threw off the other man's balance and allowed Dominic to slam his palm into his attacker's nose. A crunch and a gush of blood, and then the man ran. Dominic began to give chase, but his steps were not entirely steady and he had not gone far before another man swung out of a doorway and seized his arm.

Dominic braced and prepared to elbow him in the face when a familiar voice shouted, "Don't be a fool, Dominic!"

Only one man pronounced his name in that fashion, with the long vowels. Dominic lowered his arm and said, "Why in the devil's name are you following me, Renaud?"

CHAPTER TWELVE

R ENAUD WOULD NOT answer him until they had returned
to the court. They did not go to Dominic's more public
guest chamber, but to Renaud's own small room attached to the
barracks. It was a soldier's room: ordered, precise, and, if not
quite bare, certainly not domestic. Here, Renaud brought water
and a cloth and began to clean the blood from Dominic's hair.

He winced at the pressure, gentle as it was. The blow had
caught him above the right ear and felt as though it had left a
small crater behind.

"It is clean," Renaud assured him. "It was not meant to kill."

Dominic was forced to agree. He'd been distracted enough—
more shame to him—that even with his last-second movement a
killing blow would have done far more damage to his skull.
"Why try only to knock me out?" he wondered aloud. "Rob-
bery?"

Renaud rinsed the cloth in the water, red bleeding into the
bowl, then sighed and took a seat across the small table from
Dominic. "He followed you from the tavern. A tavern well-
known as a gathering place for men of the Spanish embassy."

"Which returns us to the pressing question—why were *you*
following me?"

"Isn't the pressing question why a Spaniard would strike you down after you'd met with his ambassador?"

Dominic debated denying the charge, but what was the point? Renaud had clearly figured it out. "We can both guess the answer to that: the ambassador wanted my meeting to become public without spreading the news himself. Hit me, leave me unconscious, and have me 'discovered' in the streets, leading the French to wonder why I was found in a notorious meeting place of the Spanish."

"Someone does not trust England's intentions." Renaud shook his head, his expression deeply wary. "Dominic, what is it your king has asked of you?"

Dominic chose to meet the question with silence, knowing Renaud did not expect him to answer. Indeed, the Frenchman went on almost immediately.

"I know, you cannot answer. And I will not force your secrets into the open. But if I can be suspicious, then others are ten times more so. Even here, I have heard rumours that your king is enamoured of a young woman. There is . . . disquiet at the news. If only you English were not so prudish! I suppose he will not make her his mistress, and so means to upset all of Europe just as his father did."

Dominic stood up a little more forcefully than intended, dizziness reminding him of his head wound. "Thank you for your aid tonight. I must go."

Renaud also stood, and gripped Dominic's arm. "Let us speak for a moment not as adversaries, but as friends. The name of this young woman has also been spoken in some circles, and it is she whom I have seen you watching at our court. You are correct— a marriage between you would be extremely complicated. But if she truly is your Nicole, my friend—"

"What?" Dominic said roughly. "What if she is?"

He almost hoped that the older man would tell him what to do, or at least point a path. Instead, Renaud said, "If she is, then you have my understanding and my sympathy. And as much reason as I to wish your king well married to my own princess. Perhaps he will listen to you."

"William hears what he wants to hear." It was the most damning statement Dominic could make, and as close to treasonous as he'd ever been.

"If he will not hear, then you must. I am your friend, Dominic, but my country comes first. Always. I do not want war, but where France goes, I must follow. Do you understand?"

France is suspicious and we will not let ourselves be taken by surprise. "I understand perfectly."

He pulled out of Renaud's grip and walked out, sick from much more than being struck in the head.

23 July 1555
Fontainebleau Palace

After just more than five weeks at the French court, tomorrow is our final day. I cannot decide if I am more excited about returning home or about tomorrow night's closing festivities. Probably tomorrow, since returning to England means more than just home—it means a return to secrecy on all sides and my lingering doubts about Alyce's death and the plots behind it.

Not that there aren't secrets and plots aplenty in France! After my initial introduction to Diane de Poitiers, I thought her merely being polite when she hinted that she would speak to me at more length during our stay. But I begin to believe she never does anything for mere politeness. Three days ago I received a gold-edged invitation to a private meeting in La Duchesse's chambers at Fontainebleau. With more than a little trepidation, I went. Even Elizabeth was surprised—she herself has not been so favoured. But then, she is here to represent England officially and it would not do to offend Queen Catherine by meeting in private with her rival.

It was a most . . . disconcerting encounter. Like Queen Anne, Madame de Poitiers has the trick of looking through one as though she knows all one's secrets and is privately amused by them. I was not surprised that she asked me about William—everyone here knows I am close to both the Tudor siblings—but I was surprised when she next turned her inquisitiveness to the subject of Dominic.

What does the new duke make of his estates? she asked. Does he continue to prefer the soldier's life to that of the court? How does he deal with the ambitious females who flatter him for his rank and his person? That last question was asked in a most impertinent manner, and with a flick of her eyes, Madame de Poitiers indicated one of her women who sat nearby ostensibly reading but mostly just listening to us.

"Aimée was quite inconsolable with his coldness. I tried to tell her that the English are not like our men—that refusing to enjoy a woman's particular . . . skills . . . does not mean the woman herself is not worth it."

I did not at all like the look of Aimée. She is dark and voluptuous, and the smug air of experience about her reminds me of Eleanor. And I remembered what Madame de Poitiers had said to Dominic at the beginning of our stay—that he should beware Aimée.

Looking at the woman, who met my gaze with a knowing smile, I do not believe this Aimée possesses a heart. If Dominic injured her at all, it can only have been to her pride. And I do not feel sorry for her.

Minuette stayed awake long after Carrie left her that night in her elaborate, overornamented bedchamber. Some hours after midnight, still sleepless, she considered rising and writing more in her diary simply for something to do, but at last she found herself drifting into a pleasant state of half daydreams that revolved around Dominic and the abandoned church near Wynfield and, in the distance, the glimpse of two children, one fair and one dark. She had nearly put names to those shadowy children when a creak broke her focus.

It was very soft, so that she almost thought she'd imagined it, but Minuette was not imagining the slight change in the blackness where the door to her room opened. Before she could decide what to do, the door was pulled closed carefully and all was once more black. For a moment she panicked at the thought of someone shut in the room with her, but there was no feeling of another human, no change in breath or silence. But that moment held her frozen just long enough so when she did get out of bed and threw open her door, she saw nothing but an empty corridor.

And an object—irregular and disturbing in outline—on her chamber floor.

Minuette focused on essentials, refusing to study the object or let her mind jump ahead. She left the door open while she located the beeswax candle on the tabletop where she'd left her jewelry casket. She had to step into the corridor—avoiding the unknown object—to light it from one of the torches that was kept burning at distant intervals, and she was cross when she realized she was shaking. Candle lit, she returned to her chamber and shut the door. Only then did she allow herself to take a good look at what her unknown visitor had left.

It was a dead rat, wound in velvet as though in a grotesque parody of court dress.

There was a parchment beneath it, though it took all Minuette's nerve—and the use of her chamber pot—to edge the rat aside enough to see it.

She immediately wished she hadn't bothered. The page was a parody of the broadsides that had once plastered London in protest against the despised Anne Boleyn. This was a rough but recognizable sketch of Minuette herself, bared to the waist and looming giant-sized between William on one side and Elisabeth de France on the other. Beneath her feet lay a dove, symbol of peace. One of Minuette's heels smashed its head.

She sat down abruptly on the edge of her bed, staring dizzily at the rat as though the dead creature might come to life any second and bite her. She almost wished it would, for this was more twisted and disturbing than the straightforward threat of the adder that Fidelis had killed. So much for removing me from England to keep me safe, she thought numbly.

At least one question had been answered: her enemy was not Eleanor. Or at least, not this particular enemy—seeing as an ocean presently divided them.

There was no way she could sleep with that dead rat in her bedroom and the vulgar paper would have to be destroyed before anyone at the French court saw it, not to mention dealing with the uncomfortable knowledge that someone had opened her door only minutes ago. The culprit had no doubt thought her sound asleep and would not expect an outcry until morning. She could call for Carrie, but even as Minuette threw on a bed robe over her nightgown, she knew that wasn't the help she wanted.

She left the candle burning in the room and, gingerly pulling it free from the rat's body, brought the broadside with her to show Dominic.

He'll be in bed, she thought. If he didn't hear her knock, would she dare enter his chambers and wake him herself? The thought made her stomach clench, not unpleasantly, as she imagined leaning over him, touching his shoulder or even his face as he slept.

Think about the rat, she commanded herself, not the image of Dominic in bed, looking up at her with those dark green eyes that pulled her into recklessness. What did he wear to bed? And if he wanted to kiss her . . .

Veering between desire and discipline, Minuette came to the corridor where Dominic was quartered. His door was at the far end of the right-hand side—he had made sure she'd known that in case she needed him for just such an emergency. She had just started toward it when his door was pulled open from the inside.

Minuette froze as a woman came into the corridor, a woman who almost at once turned and embraced the man behind her.

Though she had never seen him naked, there was no mistaking Dominic for anyone else, not even with his face obscured while he kissed the woman clinging to him.

Dominic resisted sleep for a long time, but he finally fell into fitful dreams. Faces drifted before him, melting into one another: William to Renaud to the Spanish ambassador; Elizabeth to Anne Boleyn to his own mother. And finally, as a reward, Minuette herself. In his dream she was dressed for sleep, the loose gown bewitchingly light and suggestive of her shape beneath. Her hair hung over her shoulders and down her back and felt warm and heavy when he buried his hands in it. She let him pull her to him, and he could feel the outlines of her body pressed against his and the warmth of her breath on his mouth, and then she was kissing him . . .

He wasn't dreaming. Long, loose hair hung around his face, a woman next to him in bed, her mouth teasing at his. "Minuette?" he said, disbelieving.

He was right to disbelieve. The woman pulled back, her face illuminated by the moonlight that came through his window. He knew every plane and angle of Minuette's face and this one was rounder, plumper, and yet familiar. But groggy with sleep and injury-addled, it took him a heartbeat to place her.

Aimée. Who was his mistress for a brief time during the winter of 1553 and had been miffed when she was dismissed. *I should beware Aimée,* Diane de Poitiers had warned him two weeks ago. *She . . . may wish to redress matters.*

So it appeared. Aimée's smile was hungry with intimacy. Her chemise had slipped off one shoulder, leaving it bare and much more appealing to him than it should be. "All this time wasted, monsieur, but tonight I will have what I want," she whispered. "Is it not what you want also? I can feel that it is."

He swallowed, trying to pull together his scattered wits. Did he want her? Undoubtedly. His body had wishes of its own and was presently making them rather strongly known.

But he had never let his body rule him where Minuette was concerned, and he would not start with someone else. He escaped the bed with as much dignity as he could muster naked, and said, "I regret that you have presumed too far."

She hesitated between coyness and anger. Then, with a shrug, she scrambled off the bed as well. "If you do not want me, then put me out," she challenged.

She meant it literally. He had to pick up the bed robe she'd discarded and put it around her shoulders. She would not help him at all, only letting her body press back against him as he turned her around. She did not resist, but she did not fight him, either, for which he gave devout thanks. All she'd have to do was scream and a diplomatic incident of catastrophic proportions would erupt.

Only when he'd pushed her out the door and begun to close it did Aimée move. She whirled round and kissed him, so fiercely and thoroughly that desire shot through his hungry body. He would stop her, he told himself, he would not let her back in, but for just this moment it was such pleasure to not think about anything or anyone but himself, and his hands knew where all her curves were and she was skilled and familiar and it had been so long . . .

She drew back delicately and murmured, "*Au revoir,* Dominic."

He shut the door and shoved a chair in front of it. It wouldn't keep anyone out, but it would at least give him warning. This was the second time in one night that he'd been caught unawares—he didn't want it happening again.

Elizabeth received Walsingham privately in the afternoon of their final day at Fontainebleau. He bowed with that air of casual respect that she was beginning to suspect she liked. Once he had been seated at her invitation, she asked, "You have news?"

"Lord Exeter left court alone last night, quite late. He went to a tavern that is known to cater to the Emperor's men. He met with someone in a private room upstairs. I cannot swear to the identity of the person he was meeting, but the public rooms were filled with Spanish soldiers."

"The ambassador?" she guessed.

He inclined his head. "Most likely."

"Interesting." She didn't know Walsingham yet, so she would not speak openly of William's plans for the Spanish. Not that he wasn't intelligent enough to guess.

"Your Highness, there was an interesting development afterward."

She looked at him expectantly. "Yes?"

"When Exeter left the tavern, he was followed by a Spanish soldier and attacked. One blow only, and Exeter sent his attacker running quite neatly. And then another man appeared. This second man took Exeter off with him, all the way back to court."

"Another Spanish soldier?"

"No. It was Renaud LeClerc."

Elizabeth narrowed her eyes, pondering. That was strange indeed. LeClerc was Dominic's friend, as far as two nationalities could be friends. How had he known about Dominic's meeting with the Spanish ambassador? More crucially, what would he tell the French king about it?

"Your Highness," Walsingham said, "there are rumours about the young lady in attendance upon you. Mistress Wyatt is whispered to be a favorite of your brother. A favorite in all its shades of meanings. Is there a reason for the French to wonder about the marriage contract?"

"Do you think I would tell you if there were?"

He gave a private, approving smile. "I think that your brother could benefit from your subtlety. Unfounded or not, rumours that England is looking to the Emperor could stir trouble. Until your brother is safely married elsewhere, the French king will always be uneasy about his intentions toward Mary of Scotland. It would be a disaster for the Continent to have England and Scotland united, even in a forced union."

"Mary Stuart is safely in the French king's hands."

"But Mary Stuart's kingdom is on England's doorstep. War can be put to many uses, Your Highness."

Don't worry about Mary Stuart, Elizabeth nearly told him. *My brother's hopes are quite elsewhere.* "And what has Mary of Scotland to do with rumours about Mistress Wyatt?"

"Rumours don't require one neat path of logic. They are able to twist every incident into a weapon. If this young woman is truly favoured by the king, then she can be used against him. I would keep a watchful eye on her, if I were you."

"Thank you for your advice," she said drily.

"There is one more thing, Your Highness. You know that I am acquainted with John Dee; indeed, we have been correspondents for some time. He has written to me from England because he is . . . *concerned* about the current tenor of the Duke of Northumberland's household."

Elizabeth had asked him to impress her; clearly Walsingham had taken that to mean going beyond his immediate surroundings in searching out intelligence. And it went right to the heart of the things she needed—but didn't necessarily wish—to know. "What is the current tenor of the duke's household?"

"Self-contained, even more so than usual. The Dudleys have always been an insular family, but Northumberland has not even attempted to return to court since the king arrested Guildford three months ago. For a man of his ambition, that is in itself unusual."

"Perhaps he is merely showing an unexpected degree of common sense in allowing my brother's anger to cool."

Walsingham inclined his head in acknowledgment, but not agreement. "Dr. Dee writes that the household has played host this summer to a number of radical Protestant gentlemen. Gentlemen who have the ability to raise armed men if need be."

"Are you telling me that the Duke of Northumberland is preparing to raise an army against the king?" This confirmed all her worst fears. Why would Northumberland resort to soldiers if his only crime, as he claimed, was being too lenient with his son, Guildford? This level of preparation and paranoia argued for his involvement in having brought down Norfolk.

Walsingham watched her neutrally, which goaded her into asking, "Do you have an opinion of this intelligence? Do I take the written statement of a single man as proof of Northumberland's intentions? I will not be one of those women who trembles at every shadow of a possibility!"

"There is less danger in fearing too much than too little."

Elizabeth studied Walsingham. Already she felt comfortable with him, to a degree she rarely did with most men. His dark eyes seemed a window to his fervent desire to serve England and, more specifically, herself. Waiting now for her to speak, Walsingham sat in perfect composure, his body still but giving the impression that he was ready to spring to action any moment—whatever action might be necessary.

She had made her decision almost upon meeting him; the information he'd provided, as well as his calm demeanor in doing so, only confirmed it. "Return to England with me. My household could use a man of your talents. England may not be as varied in culture and experience as the Continent, but I assure you we have any number of conspiracies, quite enough to keep you busy for years to come."

Walsingham paused just long enough to give the appearance of thought. "It would be an honour and a pleasure to serve you, Your Highness."

"Make your arrangements and be ready to leave with us tomorrow."

"I will. And if I might make a suggestion—there is little you can do about Northumberland tonight. But you can keep a careful eye on your young Mistress Wyatt. I am certain many others will be watching her tonight as well. Perhaps even one who should not be watching her in quite the manner that he is."

He did not elaborate, but Elizabeth carried that enigmatic warning with her throughout the evening. Surely it was one of the French royals—probably the king himself—Walsingham had meant. Though Henri was known to be devoted to his mistress, Madame de Poitiers, she was not the only woman he had betrayed his marriage with and surely he could appreciate another beautiful young woman. And if he suspected that William found Minuette alluring, the enticement would be even greater. But it was their final night at court, so how much trouble could the French king lead her into?

It proved easy to watch Minuette that night, for she was as brilliant and dazzling as Elizabeth had ever seen her. Although Elizabeth herself was dressed in cloth-of-silver with a fortune in diamonds and pearls in her hair and around her neck and sewn to her gown, she knew that for once she did not match her friend for brilliance. Minuette was like a flame, in a gown of crimson and ivory velvet and her hair caught back from her face with a fillet of gold. She was beautiful and charming and, as Elizabeth watched her with increasing concern, pitch perfect in every movement.

It had to be an act, Elizabeth judged. Minuette was never that studied. Everything she did tonight appeared to aim at an effect, from flirting with the French king to drinking cup after cup of wine brought to her by eager young (and not-so-young) men. What on earth could have made Minuette put so much energy into this performance? Was she aware of the swirling rumours about her relationship with William? Although if that were it, Elizabeth would have expected her to act with more decorum, not less. Minuette's behavior tonight could only reinforce the opinion that she was all but William's mistress. And after all, perhaps that was the right effect to aim for. If the French believed her to be the king's mistress, they would not think to worry about her as an impediment to the French marriage.

Elizabeth might have intervened, just to make certain Minuette was behaving with political deliberation, but she saw that Dominic was watching Minuette just as closely. From his expression, he liked what he saw as little as Elizabeth did. Let him deal with it, she thought. Dealing with things is what he does best. Elizabeth returned her attention to the Cardinal of Lorraine and allowed herself to be lulled by outrageous French compliments.

Minuette had never drunk so much at one time in her life. She found the experience quite heady. The wine blurred the edges of her painful emotions—most of them. She could not think of the half-dressed woman leaving Dominic's room without wanting to hide away and never see anyone again. Especially Dominic.

But the catch was that even alone all she could see was him. His hair tousled from sleep (or not), his body bare (and beautiful, her treacherous mind whispered), the play of torchlight and shadow on the muscles beneath his skin as he passionately kissed the woman who had clearly just come from his bed . . . the woman it had taken Minuette only a moment to identify as Madame de Poitiers's lady, Aimée.

Minuette was not an innocent. She knew men took women to their beds whom they would never take anywhere else. One had only to meet Eleanor Percy to know that. It wasn't as though she herself was sleeping with Dominic, so why should he not seek release elsewhere? A woman at the French court was ideal in many ways—a momentary thing, a woman he would not see again nor probably even wish to. Just because Dominic took most things far more seriously than William, that didn't mean bedding a woman was one of them. No doubt he did that as casually as most men.

But she could not bear the thought of any woman touching him, kissing him, being undressed by him . . . He said he could wait for me! she raged.

She was silent as Carrie dressed her for the closing banquet and dancing. The maid tried to engage her in conversation multiple times, but Minuette deliberately ignored her. If she once admitted what had happened last night, the hurt of it might overwhelm the anger. And she needed to remain angry. It was anger that had fueled her so well last night that she had flung the dead rat out of her window by its tail (after removing the velvet shroud) without flinching. The broadside she had burnt. At some point she should let Dominic know about it. But not tonight. Tonight she was going to make Dominic regret with all his heart that he hadn't waited for her.

Drinking definitely helped fuel her anger—and her recklessness. It also seemed to make her plenty desirable, since she could hardly choose with whom to dance. Even the French king partnered her in a galliard, and she smiled headily and laughed at all his witticisms, most of which she did not understand.

At each moment her every breath alerted her to Dominic. She had never felt so sensitive to his presence. Tonight she wanted him to watch her. Tonight she wanted him to want her.

A tiny whisper of a conscience (this time sounding like Elizabeth) kept up a commentary of sarcasm beneath all her actions. *Oh yes, this is the final impression you wish to leave on the French court—that you are tipsy and wanton.* But another, deeper voice, echoed beneath that one, Dominic's whispered words at Framlingham: *Wanton is not always wicked.*

She didn't think he would say that to her tonight. She didn't have to look at him to feel the force of his disapproval from across the ostentatious, overly decorated Salle des Fêtes. You don't like this, she thought, sipping wine and giggling inanely at a gentleman whose name she hadn't bothered to learn. Well, isn't that too bad. At least I have all my clothes on.

The worst moment was when she found herself accidentally face-to-face with Aimée. From the rich waves of her hair and the insolent way she held herself, she might as well have been wearing only the thin gown she'd worn last night. Minuette turned abruptly away, and heard the lilt of Aimée's laughter and a phrase spoken with mock pity: *la pauvre vierge anglaise!*

Poor English virgin.

Conversations began to wane in and out of her attention. She wasn't interested in talking—she moved from dance to dance and from man to obliging man. The French were nothing if not obliging. So obliging that Minuette often found herself having to step out of a too-intimate embrace or pretending not to understand the coyly worded invitations to join a man somewhere more private.

Only one man reached through her recklessness. Renaud LeClerc danced with her quite late in the evening and warned softly, "In my experience, mademoiselle, arguments are better settled with either words or a sword than with wine."

"You think I need a sword?" Maybe she did at that.

"I think directness is always preferable to games, mademoiselle."

She tilted her head in unthinking flirtation. "I thought the French liked games."

He leaned in closer. "But Dominic is not French. And you are only bewildering him."

He drew back and held her eyes with his, until her heart pounded in her ears.

"Did you ever think that perhaps Dominic is the one bewildering me?" she whispered.

"Yes, talking things over is not Dominic's strong suit. All the more need for you to take the lead."

He bowed and kissed her hand, then squeezed it before leaving her on the edge of the room with her head swimming and eyes stinging with tears she dare not shed. What was she doing? He was right. It was Dominic she should be dancing with, not these men whose names she did not know and whose faces she would never see again.

Time to remedy that.

———

Being hit on the head and then surprised by the wrong woman in his bed was not conducive to being well rested. It wasn't so much Dominic's head that ached as it was his entire being. He was sore and sick at heart and eager to return to England's cleaner, sharper air. If last night's encounter with Aimée had done anything (besides frustrate him), it had made him ponder how much longer he could endure pretending not to love Minuette. He was loyal and he was disciplined—but he was also a man. Something had to give sooner rather than later. If he could make her understand how he felt, how desperately he wanted her and how achingly difficult it was not to throw himself at her every time they were alone, then maybe she would agree to tell William the truth.

At the banquet they were separated, all of the English scattered amongst the bright plumage of the French royals and nobles: Lady Rochford next to the dauphin (she didn't look pleased at being paired with a boy, no matter his title); Elizabeth with King Henri; and Minuette with the Cardinal de Guise. Dominic himself was seated between Elisabeth de France and William's cousin, Mary Stuart. The need to be gracious to two royal ladies, however young, kept his attention diverted when all he wanted was to catch Minuette's eye.

When the banquet was finished and the dancing began in the Salle des Fêtes, Dominic drew a breath of relief at being finally free. He would dance with Minuette—perhaps a seductive *volta*—and begin to let his armour slip. Just enough for her to glimpse the passion he kept well-buried.

But he could not get near enough to Minuette to even ask her to dance. She passed from Frenchman to Frenchman without so much as a glance his way. The only time she stopped flirting or dancing was to drink from the abundant wine offerings. Did she not know how she was tormenting him?

He was unconscious of staring until Renaud murmured in his ear, "What has the young lady done to make you scowl so?"

Dominic shook his head and immediately regretted it as the pain flashed sharp. "Am I scowling? I thought that was how I always look."

"Near enough, *mon ami*. So come and dance with my Nicole. She will make you cheerful."

She very nearly did, for Renaud's wife was one of the most peaceful women Dominic had ever met. Short, slightly plump, dressed neatly but unexceptionally in dove gray silk, Nicole seemed wrapped in contentment whether here at the heart of court or in her Loire Valley home. As they danced a pavane, she smiled up at him and said, "I wish to thank you, *monsieur le duc,* for your care of my husband last summer. Although defeat is never easy for a soldier, I know you treated him with great kindness. I am grateful that you sent him home to me so quickly and unharmed."

"It was my honour, madame," Dominic replied truthfully. "And how is your new daughter?"

Her smile widened, lighting her face with beauty. "Six months old and already Renaud claims that he will have to kill many men in future to protect her virtue. He dotes upon her."

"And your sons?" They had two, sturdy boys.

"Both are well and growing so fast! I am glad that there is now peace between our countries, monsieur, for this is the first summer in many that my husband has not been at war somewhere. He will return home with me soon and that is all I ever want."

Studying Nicole LeClerc's glowing face—a woman serenely in love with her husband and children and home, so glad to be at peace that her husband might be safe—Dominic realized just how many people William had it in his power to injure. When the king broke the French marriage contract, it wasn't just Elisabeth de France who would be affected, nor even her royal father. Their pride would suffer, but if it came to war again many men and women stood to lose much more.

He has to marry Elisabeth, Dominic realized, and not just because I want Minuette. It is wise, and it has always been my job to tell him what is wise. Had not William often said he relied on Dominic to be honest when no one else would be?

Sustained by the righteousness of that thought, Dominic bid Nicole a heartfelt farewell and determined to pin down Minuette tonight if it was the last thing he did. He felt the need to apologize to her—though he wasn't stupid enough to tell her about Aimée, he still felt guilty—and to discover why she was so unreachable tonight.

Dominic wound his way through the Salle des Fêtes, slowed by the increasingly volatile Frenchmen whose tongues and tempers were loosened by drink (not to mention the Frenchwomen whose boldness increased as the evening wore on) and by the necessity to behave courteously. He had to change directions once to avoid Aimée, and finally caught sight of Minuette, burning bright in her crimson gown. She stood against one of the frescoed walls speaking to Renaud.

Or rather, Renaud was speaking to her, leaning in close, and when he straightened, Minuette looked directly at Dominic as though she had known precisely where he was. Renaud stepped away. Dominic could almost see Minuette's indecision and the moment when she steadied herself before coming to him.

He allowed himself to watch her, exquisite in her crimson gown and lit up like a torch so that no man could ignore her. His desire roused as it always was in her presence; it wasn't until she asked, "Will you dance, Dominic?" that he smelled the wine on her breath. He had seen her drink more than usual at dinner and afterward, but he had not realized that she was drunk.

Minuette's expression was all seduction as she took his hand and put it on her waist. "Don't you want to dance with me?" She stepped into him, and instinctively he led her into the opening of an allemande.

But the second time she fumbled a step, he couldn't pretend any longer that all was well. Grasping her by the upper arm, he towed her off the dance floor into a window embrasure that gave the illusion of privacy.

"You're drunk," he said flatly. "Care to tell me why?"

She opened her mouth, then a shadow of obstinacy crossed her face and he knew they were going to argue. "No."

"I'm taking you back to your room."

Her laugh was tipsy, and wrong. "And will you stay?"

"Long enough to find Carrie. You need to sleep this off."

"I don't want to sleep."

"Too bad."

She jerked her arm out of his grasp and hissed, "Don't tell me what to do. If I want to dance, I'll stay and dance. If I want to drink, then I will."

"What is wrong with you?"

"And if I want to kiss you . . ." She tipped her face up to him and her lips parted.

He stepped back hastily. "Not here, Minuette. People will talk."

Fury darkened her face, for a moment making her look disconcertingly like William in a temper. "And heaven forbid anyone should talk about *you*." The scathing words spilled out of her, almost tumbling over each other. "It's your job to be perfect and remote and never give rise to a single rumour."

"I don't know why you're upset, but can we please talk about it elsewhere?" Already, those nearest to their alcove were turning curious heads at the commotion.

Minuette didn't move. "In your chambers perhaps? Except no, it would not be wise to take me to your bed. You reserve that for a French whore!"

Even while his sickened mind took in the fact that, somehow, Minuette knew about Aimée last night, Dominic knew he had to get her out of this far too public place—and fast. He reached for her hand, desperate to get somewhere private, muttering, "Minuette, please—"

She struck as rapidly as a snake, her palm connecting with his left cheek so hard that it rattled clear through his already aching skull. His vision clouded for a handful of breaths, and when it cleared he could see that she was nearly as shocked as he was, as though her moment of violence had released all her pent-up emotions. When he said, "Please, let me take you to Carrie," she dipped her head and let him escort her out without a word. A trail of glances followed in their wake—including Aimée herself, who looked so satisfied that Dominic wanted to follow Minuette's example and slap her.

Minuette did not speak another word, and Dominic could not choose where to begin. How to explain what had happened last night? How to assure her she had no reason for jealousy? (*But doesn't she?* his conscience whispered. *That last kiss in the corridor was as much you as Aimée.*) Words were never his strong suit, and besides, Minuette was wilting fast from the unaccustomed effects of too much wine.

When they reached her chambers, Dominic said shortly, "Have Carrie bring you some water. You're going to be sick, and we have a long journey home."

And this, he thought blackly, is a perfect end to another stay in France. He hoped devoutly he would never lay eyes on this wretched country again.

CHAPTER THIRTEEN

GETTING THE WOMEN out of France was even worse than getting them there in the first place. They were fewer than half in number: only Lady Rochford, Elizabeth, Minuette, and their attendants. The young girls remained at the French court to serve in Elisabeth de France's household. But the women who departed were all of them difficult. Lady Rochford was restless and discontented at leaving the French court (or perhaps at having to return to her husband), and Elizabeth was at her most exacting and capricious.

Minuette refused to speak to him at all, which he did not find surprising, for when they left Fontainebleau she was wretched from the aftereffects of immoderate drinking. Good, Dominic thought. She will not make that mistake again. So he had let her alone, and letting her alone became easier the farther they traveled and the quieter she remained. She rode in a carriage with Lady Rochford until they reached the Seine, not once joining Elizabeth on horseback, and on the river she always contrived to be in a different barge than he was.

They spent one night in Harfleur, Dominic rounding the garrison and making notes on their readiness against possible French incursions in future. Harfleur, Le Havre, and Calais were all that remained of England's once vast holdings in France, and Dominic did not mean to lose them through any oversight of his. They took ship at Le Havre and Minuette went below before they'd even lost sight of the coast. He stared after her bleakly, wondering if she ever meant to speak to him again, wondering how he was supposed to apologize for a most private matter when they were always in public.

Elizabeth came noiselessly beside him and, with her characteristic insight, observed, "You'll have to settle this before we return to court. William will want to know why you two are quarreling. I know you don't want to tell him she got drunk and slapped you."

"You don't think someone else will report it?" Dominic said savagely. "Lady Rochford is no friend of Minuette, and surely your uncle has informants in France."

She shrugged, steady on her feet despite the rolling of the ship's deck. "My brother can ignore everyone but you. Fix it, Dominic. Otherwise, he will be displeased."

At the moment, he didn't particularly care if William were displeased. In fact, he was tired of everything being about William all the time. But for his own sake he desperately wanted this fixed, so he went below and knocked on Minuette's door.

Carrie opened it. "May I speak with her?" he asked.

"I'm sorry, my lord, she is resting and does not wish to be disturbed."

She smiled helplessly, as though in sympathy with him but bound to follow her mistress's orders. Dominic swore under his breath as she closed the door in his face.

Elizabeth must have appreciated his attempt—or at least recognized he was out of his depth—because she took the matter out of his hands once they landed at Dover. There were royal men and horses at Dover Castle prepared to ride on with them the next morning, but Elizabeth took Dominic aside. "My aunt and I will be quite all right now. I thought you might like to visit your mother, since we are somewhat near Maidstone. Take Minuette with you."

He would have protested, but in a move remarkably like William, she simply walked away. Knowing the folly of arguing with a Tudor, Dominic set his jaw and had Harrington arrange horses for a separate small party.

Minuette, however, was prepared to argue with the princess. The next morning, when Dominic approached them in the courtyard of Dover Castle, he heard her say sharply, "I do not need to be sent off like a child because you think I'm in a temper."

"Then prove you're not a child and do what I ask." Elizabeth's reply had the ring of royal steel in it. "I will make it an order if I must."

Minuette whirled so suddenly that she stumbled into Dominic. He put a hand out to steady her. It was the closest they'd been since that last night at Fontainebleau, and her eyes held more than anger and disdain—though those were present. But there were also tears, like a deep well that has been troubled by a stone and not yet come to rest.

"Minuette," he said beseechingly, and his tone must have warned her of his wish to take her in his arms right here, princess and royal guards be damned.

"Not here, Dominic." She lifted her chin and her eyes blazed with fury. "People will talk."

And so they rode together to his mother's home, Dominic not sure which fears to focus on: his mad mother, his need to set things straight with Minuette, his duty to return to William and persuade him of the importance of the French marriage . . .

He'd once worried about his mother burning the house down around him. Tonight he would almost welcome it. At least it would be a distraction.

In preparation for dinner, Carrie brought Minuette a simple gown of moss green with embroidered cream flowers. Minuette shook her head. "I need something more . . . elaborate." As armour, she meant.

"I'm sorry, mistress, it's what there is. Most of your things went on to court with the princess."

She searched Carrie's guileless face and knew that her maid wanted her vulnerable tonight. Fine, she would prove that she could hold her own without finery and jewels. And since when do I need to hold my own against Dominic? she thought, a little forlornly.

Of course Carrie was right, for more reasons than one. When Minuette joined the table, she knew that she would have been wildly inappropriate dressed as a court lady. Dominic's mother, Philippa, wore a simple dress of midnight blue and no jewelry except a rosary that her son tactfully ignored. It had a familiar look to it, and Minuette wondered if, like her mother's, it had been a gift from the late Queen Anne. Philippa Boleyn Courtenay had been Anne's cousin, and as young girls they had been very close. Before Philippa's unhappy marriage and Anne's turn to Henry and Protestantism.

There was also a clerk at dinner, a man named Michael, dressed with equal soberness. A skillful conversationalist, he had traveled extensively in Europe and entertained them with stories of scholars and sailors. Dominic, as usual, spoke little and seemed absorbed in watching his mother. Philippa appeared a little distracted and unworldly but not dangerous.

Until she brought up a dangerous subject. "I see you took care to be out of the country when your king burned a saint," she said to her son.

Bonner was dead? Minuette opened her mouth in surprise, but Dominic cut her off. "Bonner was no saint, Mother. He preached treason, and would gladly have practiced it at any opportunity."

"Men aren't burned for treason, but for heresy. How could God not strike down your king for this? William is the heretic! Denying the presence of Christ, daring to take on himself the power of God. Your king—"

"He is your king as well, Mother. He's the one who allows you this home, the clothes you wear, the food you eat. You would do well to remember that."

"I would be damned if I acknowledge him as my king. Mary should have the throne. And she will when the world is set right."

"Do you have anything to say to this?" Dominic demanded of Michael, who had listened with a closed-off expression.

He looked at Dominic mildly enough, but something in his eyes shook Minuette, and suddenly she realized what she should have seen before—Michael was no clerk. "The wicked take the truth to be hard," the priest—for that he surely was—murmured.

"You will watch your words, and ensure my mother watches hers, or I will see to it that you are put out of England for good."

Michael almost smiled. "You are not hard enough for the quarrels of religion, Lord Exeter. You have not studied your king so well to learn that."

Philippa rose abruptly. Leaning down to take Minuette's face in her hands, she rasped urgently, "My son *is* hard, though, child. Don't you mistake it. The Courtenay men are all of them hard. His love will crush the life right out of you." Her eyes glittered unnervingly.

"Mother!"

The priest intervened. "I'll take her to her chambers. Come along, Philippa."

He led her away and suddenly it was just Minuette and Dominic, and she knew the moment had come for confrontation. Trembling, she braced herself for his recriminations about her drinking and her appalling behavior that last night at the French court. She also braced herself to be angry about Aimée coming from his bed, but she was unprepared for what Dominic said first, or how he said it.

"My mother is right, you know. You have ample cause to regret that I fell in love with you."

At once, her anger dissolved into bewilderment and hurt. "Do you mean that you are regretting having fallen in love with me?"

"Unlike you, Minuette, I mean exactly what I say."

Oh, here came anger again. With a vengeance. "What are you implying?"

"I have watched you with William, and I have heard him speak of you, and I know that he has not the slightest doubt you love him. And I honestly don't know if that is a result of his own delusions, or a measure of your ability to dissemble, or the simple fact that you are truly in love with him."

"So this is my fault," she said, feeling a stab of pain behind her right eye. "You think I'm a liar—to William or to you or perhaps both. That would be convenient for you because, if I am false, then what does it matter whom you take to bed?"

He flinched and she was savagely glad of it. "I did not take Aimée to bed."

"Really? So it is only in public corridors that you kiss a woman while completely naked?"

"I did not sleep with her," he said stubbornly. "She caught me unawares while I was asleep and I put her out at once."

"It didn't look like you were putting her out. It looked like you were enjoying yourself quite thoroughly." She was almost frightened by the savagery in her voice.

Dominic's cheeks darkened. "I swear to you by all that is holy, I did not sleep with her that night. We had a brief . . . liaison when I was last at the French court two years ago. She wished to take advantage of that. And think of me what you like, Minuette, but I have the desires and weaknesses of all men. I should not have kissed her as I did. But that was the whole of it, I swear. And you are avoiding my question."

"I don't believe you actually asked me anything." With every patient statement Dominic made, she wanted more than ever to break his infuriating control. If that smug French girl could shake him so that he acted on impulse, why couldn't she?

She wanted to hurt him as she'd been hurt, so she said the worst thing she could think of. "Will touches me, you know. When we are alone. You did not imagine we spend all that time playing chess, did you? His control is not as good as yours—or is it that he desires me more? He is careful, of course, of my honour. I am virgin still, if it matters to you. But I have spent much time with my eyes closed and his hands and mouth on me, and do you know what I see then? Always you."

"Don't."

"Don't what? Be honest? I know a woman is not supposed to feel this way, or at least a *lady* isn't. But it is the truth. When I saw you kissing that woman, I wanted to be her. I wanted to be the one coming from you half dressed and wanton. I want *you,* Dominic, in every way. I think it is you who must regret loving me, for you have scarcely come near me for months."

Her eyes were stinging and she struggled with all her might not to cry. She had meant to hurt him, not humiliate herself. She hadn't even known how deeply his coldness had damaged her until it spilled out.

Dominic moved so swiftly that she just had time to breathe in before he pulled her against him. His kiss was not gentle, not sensitive and careful like he usually was. It was demanding and brutal, and Minuette met it with equal passion. Her hands wound into his hair, seeking to tug him closer. His arms dropped to her hips and tightened, holding her fixed against him. At some point she felt herself back into the table's edge. Dominic released her just long enough to shove a spot clear of dishes and food and then she pulled him with her as he laid her down on the wooden surface.

"You think I do not want you?" His voice was rougher than she'd ever heard it when he pulled away. "If I did not love you so much, I would show you this moment that my desire is the equal of any man's. Do you imagine I have not thought of the possibilities? A *di future* marriage—we have made our future vows. I dream every night of cementing that promise with my body. And if we were anyone else, I would. But to do it right, Minuette, to marry with a priest and witnesses, so that it cannot be undone—that is worth waiting for."

"So your honour will always be greater than your desire," she snapped, shoving against his chest until he moved and let her up. She hated that he could be so reasonable when she seemed to be all blood and breath and warm skin.

"Do you want me to take you on a table?" he yelled. "Get you with child and make a hasty marriage after? The last court couple who tried that are both in the Tower!"

"Stop it!"

"I will not take you in secret. Give me the word, and I'll go straight to William myself and tell him the truth."

"We can't just throw this in his face. He's not ready to hear it."

"He'll never be ready, Minuette. I know you don't want to hurt him. But he isn't a child, and he wouldn't thank you for treating him as such."

"Don't tell me how to deal with William!"

He shook his head. "I can't do this anymore." His voice was controlled now, and his expression. But his eyes were deep with sorrow. "You won't confess, and I won't lie."

Her skin that had burned so hot flushed with cold. She knew that implacable tone—it meant that Dominic would not be moved. "So where does that leave us?"

"I won't force the issue against your will. But I can't be alone with you until this is settled. When we return to court, I will ask the king to give me leave. I should spend some time at Tiverton now that I am its master. When you have made your choice, you let me know."

This isn't happening, she thought. She stared after him blankly, bewildered and heartsick as he turned away. Before vanishing through the door, he stopped and said, "I am glad to know you are virgin still. If you were not, I should have to kill him."

Elizabeth was reunited with William at their father's lavish but still unfinished Nonsuch Palace. The fortified north side was medieval in appearance, but the south side had all the splendor of octagonal towers and decorative elements. Her brother greeted her with a kiss on both cheeks in the inner courtyard with its high-relief stucco panels, then led her into one of the towers for a private dinner.

Truly private, for he dismissed the attendants curtly and, the moment they were alone, snapped about her decision not to bring Minuette with her. "She'll be as anxious to see me as I am to see her. Why did you send her on to Dominic's mother?"

"As a courtesy. They have long been correspondents."

"A courtesy the woman will not remember. Her mind is gone."

"She is mad only now and again. Surely you can spare Minuette for a few days longer? Besides, this will help settle rumours of your affections, which you must know have already spread to the French court."

What else could she say? Tell him that Minuette and Dominic had been quarreling (as much as one could quarrel with a maddeningly reserved man like Dominic), that Minuette had behaved erratically that last night in France, flirting outrageously and drinking far too much for her own good? She couldn't say any of that. Nor could she explain the uneasy feeling that had settled in her stomach as she'd watched Minuette and Dominic at odds with other during the journey home.

One who should not be watching her in quite the manner that he is, Walsingham had warned her. Surely he hadn't meant Dominic. And yet . . .

Since she couldn't say any of that, she parried. "Have you and Robert quarreled?"

"Why, because I did not bring him along to our private celebration tonight?" he asked sarcastically. "I thought his absence might settle the rumours of your affections, Sister."

She blinked. William was often imperious, but almost never rude. Not to her.

And she knew that they had fought. Robert had written to her often during her sojourn in France, and the things he had not said were even more revealing than the things he had.

She opened her mouth to be biting, and realized that William wasn't really speaking to her. His temperament was all about who wasn't here: he was taut, almost frantic, with his impatience to see Minuette.

So she changed her sentence to, "How was your visit to Kenninghall? Did the Howards behave themselves?"

"Impeccably."

"Including Eleanor?"

"Indeed. I think you would not know her now. She has . . . softened. Grown up. Motherhood suits her." William spoke casually, as if he thought nothing of it, but she did not miss the strained set of his shoulders or the way his eyes darted without settling on her.

Elizabeth was more inclined to believe that widowhood suited Eleanor Percy. "And the child?"

"She is healthy, active. Only sixteen months and already she can speak intelligibly."

"What does she look like?" she asked, meaning, *Who does she look like?*

He met Elizabeth's eyes at last. "Her hair is red-gold and curls naturally."

Like my own, she thought painfully.

"She is called Anne," William added.

To keep from showing that any of this had shaken her, Elizabeth said, "Presumptuous of Eleanor, giving her child that name."

"*My* child. She is mine, Elizabeth. I am taking steps to recognize her formally. And Eleanor will return to Lady Rochford's household at court. It was her only request."

Because of that red-gold hair, she thought. Being invited to court is Eleanor's reward for having living proof of my brother's virility.

"Be careful, Will. I'm not sure who will be less pleased—Dominic or Minuette."

He laughed, clearly relieved that she didn't intend to lecture. "Minuette, no doubt about it. But she will have to learn to trust me. Now, tell me about this new man you've retained. Walton something?"

"Walsingham."

"Another scholar, like John Dee?"

"Walsingham knows Dee, but his talents are . . . varied. Lord Burghley also knows him; it was his letter of introduction that got him to me in France. He is an intelligent man with a wide acquaintance. I shall certainly find him something useful to do."

Like keep an eye on you, she decided. For some reason, she didn't want to tell William that Walsingham had tracked Dominic for her to the Spanish ambassador. Better if she had her own sources of intelligence and kept them private. Even she never knew everything that William might think of.

But some secrets she could not in good conscience keep. "He had a letter from John Dee while we were in France. It seems Dee is concerned about the Duke of Northumberland. The duke has been receiving guests while he has remained away from court—men of radical disposition and the will to enforce it with arms."

"So I've heard," William replied, snatching away her momentary triumph. "Rochford's keeping an eye on them. He thinks it's mostly Northumberland busying himself while waiting to see what I do about Guildford."

"What are you going to do?"

"Wait for the child to be born. If Guildford is lucky, it will be a girl, and if he is wise, he will accept an annulment of the marriage, humble himself to the dust, and vow never to lay eyes on Margaret Clifford again."

"And if he is neither lucky nor wise?"

"Then we shall see." He gave her a look that spoke of confidences kept, of so many things he knew and never told.

It made her feel less guilty about keeping her own counsel.

Two could play this game, and no one better than Henry's children.

The nearer they drew to Nonsuch, the more Dominic felt Minuette closing herself off. He couldn't fault her, for he was withdrawing, too. Their honest—if angry—passion at his mother's house could not last, and already they were barricaded behind their secrets. How can it be otherwise? he thought miserably. As long as we are lying, we will never have peace. But he did not regret what he had said to her. Between breaking his heart and breaking his loyalty, it would have to be his heart that suffered. He realized wretchedly that part of him was already preparing to say goodbye to Minuette.

That resignation strengthened when they reached the court. The royal banners streamed from the walls and towers of Nonsuch Palace, and William himself stood waiting in the courtyard. He greeted Dominic first, warmly, but with all his being yearning for Minuette. It was obvious to Dominic—he worried how obvious it might be to the others. Elizabeth was quick to take possession of her lady, but not before William had swept Minuette into an embrace that lasted too long to be merely friendly. Dominic saw Rochford watching them and almost rejoiced. From his expression, the Lord Chancellor clearly knew about William's intentions, and just as clearly was dead set against it. Good—Rochford had long practice in enforcing his will on a kingdom. William would be hard pressed to oppose his uncle. And though it stung Dominic to speak about Minuette at all with William, he knew he would have to begin persuading him. Put aside his own reticence and argue for England's sake. Right before he asked to leave court.

He began as soon as he was alone with William. When the

women withdrew from the courtyard, he and the king walked in Nonsuch Great Park with only four guards ahead and behind for privacy.

"Tell me about Simon Renard," William said.

"Like all ambassadors," Dominic answered. "He speaks in maybes and perhaps and what-ifs."

"Must have driven you crazy."

Dominic shrugged. "Only when I have to play the same game. I didn't bother with Renard. When I told him you wished to approach Prince Philip, he grasped at once that you intend to set aside the French."

"Did he grasp why?"

"I don't think so. He didn't mention any particular woman, at least. I would say that he suspects you of wishing to solidify your position with a Protestant marriage. Jane Grey, probably." Dominic slid lightly over her name, hoping William would not renew their earlier conversation about her.

"Good." William sounded satisfied. "What will Renard do next?"

"He promised to approach his prince, and intimated he would prefer to return you an answer in person."

"If he brings me the right answer, he is welcome at my court as long as he wishes. Did he seem amenable?"

"He didn't seem displeased. But when it comes to a decision— I don't know. Elizabeth is a prize, no doubt of it, but an alliance means more than just a marriage. Will it be to Spain's benefit to ally themselves militarily with us? That likely depends on circumstances at the time of any alliance."

"And you think we cannot compete with France."

"I think that we have to try harder to prove our strength, seeing as France shares the Continent with Spain and we do not.

Your victory last year has helped tremendously. But we must hold what we took and, maybe, fight once more. Which no doubt we will have to do when you discard Elisabeth de France."

"Why Dominic, you do not sound as though you like that plan. Aren't you the soldier? I expect a bit more enthusiasm for battle from you."

He thought of Renaud LeClerc and of Nicole, who was so glad to have her husband home. He thought of the little princess in France who yearned desperately to know how to please her betrothed. And he thought of William, moving them all around as though they were chess pieces to be picked up and cast aside at his whim.

"As a soldier, I anticipate necessary battles, not those fought for sport. We have bought peace, Your Majesty, at a dear price. Why be in a rush to throw that away?"

Dominic knew it was his use of William's title, as much as his tone, that narrowed the king's eyes as he answered. "If I were in a rush to throw away peace, then Minuette would already be carrying my son. Don't lecture me about patience."

"I only meant that, more than any other man, your decisions cannot be based solely on your own preferences."

"Do you think I don't know that?" William's shout carried, and Dominic knew he had gone too far. "Everyone is so keen to remind me that my choices matter to England. What everyone seems to forget is this: I *am* England. I have been from the moment my father drew his last breath. And as I would do nothing to injure myself, I am incapable of injuring England."

"It's only that . . . with Minuette—" Fortunately, he didn't have to think how to continue, because William cut in.

"England needs me as king, and I need Minuette as my queen. She will be good for *England* because she is good for *me*. Don't argue my uncle's side for him, Dom. He does it quite thoroughly on his own."

"What if I am arguing my own side?"

William's brow furrowed. "I would expect you, of all people, to approve of Minuette. Others may look only at her birth, or her less than wealthy circumstances, or her youth. But you know better. You know her goodness, her generosity, her kindness to all, her understanding of human nature, her charm and poise and diplomatic skill . . . you know my people will love her. Look me in the eyes and tell me that Minuette will not make a glorious queen."

It had been months since Dominic had been able to look his friend in the eyes. "Not everyone sees her as you do."

"They will. And on the day she gives me a royal son and England falls at her feet, I will remind you that I was right and you were wrong."

"Until that day," Dominic warned, "tread carefully. The French are wary."

"You just keep me apprised of your friend's thoughts. I expect if French wariness turns into French aggression, Renaud LeClerc will know of it first."

Wonderful, Dominic thought. Not only have I failed to persuade William to reconsider Minuette, now he intends to use my friendships against me. "Yes, Your Majesty."

CHAPTER FOURTEEN

THE NIGHT THAT Minuette returned to court, William summoned her to play chess after dinner. Elizabeth watched her go with a troubled expression; Dominic was nowhere to be seen. As long as they played in sight of William's guards and gentlemen in the presence chamber, Minuette was easy enough. But all too soon William escorted her into his privy chamber and shut the door on the two of them alone.

"I missed you so much." He pulled her onto his lap and momentarily buried his face in her hair. "As hard as it is to be near you and restrain myself, it's infinitely harder to not have you here at all."

"This is restraint?" Minuette teased, to cover the fact that her heart thumped irregularly.

He grinned wickedly. "I promise—when I am no longer restrained, sweetling, you shall know the difference at once." He traced the neckline of her dress with one finger, and despite herself she shivered—and hated herself for it. How could she be so furiously jealous with Dominic for kissing a woman who meant nothing to him when William, who meant so very much to her, could rouse her body even while her mind remained disengaged?

The damning truth was that she responded to William's touch.

How was she to stop it? Her mind, at least, always remained detached and ironic, making sarcastic comments about her behavior and William's indiscretion.

But when Dominic touched her, she was incapable of thinking at all. *And that's your difference, Dominic. When you touch me there is nothing else in my world but you.*

Tonight, as William trailed kisses where his finger had traced, Minuette attempted to distract him with a genuine question. "Why didn't you tell me about Bishop Bonner's execution?"

"There was no need. You would hear of it when it happened—no need to distress you beforehand."

"You never used to trouble about distressing me. You used to tell me everything—well, nearly everything. I am not a china figurine, Will. You needn't worry about breaking me."

"Oh, I'm not," he said huskily, and captured her mouth with his. His arms tightened until she found it hard to breathe, but still her mind worked.

"I mean it," she insisted when he stopped to draw breath. "I wish you would talk to me like you used to. Or do you not trust me anymore?"

That startled him into releasing his hold on her. With creased brow, he said, "You know I do. You, Dom, Elizabeth—you are the only three I trust."

"Then tell me the truth—who pressed for Bonner's burning?"

"Look, the man committed treason in everything but the final action, he didn't trouble to deny it at the end. He wanted me off the throne and Mary on it."

"And you could have had his head for that. Why burn him at the stake?"

"A well-placed blow to heresy carries a long reach. I spared the young Thomas Howard, allowed him to be made Duke of Norfolk, and still the Catholics are discontented. And with the Dudleys behaving badly and out of favour, the Protestants are also restless and want to ensure that I remain firmly on their side. Bonner was trouble. I did what had to be done."

She studied him intently, then nodded. "I just don't want you to be taken advantage of."

He threw his head back and laughed. "No one takes advantage of me, sweetling. That's my prerogative."

"Is it? Then why is Eleanor Percy serving in Lady Rochford's household once more?"

His jaw tightened. "She is nothing to do with you, Minuette. Eleanor is under strict instructions to leave you alone."

"That's as good as throwing fuel on a fire, Will. If she thinks you are trying to shield me—"

None too gently, William removed her from his lap and stood. "That's enough, Minuette. Eleanor is my concern. But since you are so curious about knowing things, I will tell you that I have formally recognized Anne Howard as my daughter."

Minuette thought of this little girl, not even two years old, caught in political and emotional forces that could so easily destroy her. "Did you like her?" she asked.

"Did I like who?"

"Your daughter. When you saw her at Kenninghall. Did you like her?"

William's face twisted and he sighed. "I loved her, the moment I saw her. The child reminds me of Elizabeth."

And of course clever Eleanor had used that resemblance to her advantage, Minuette thought cynically. But William was right—Eleanor had given him a child and he owed her certain things. And it wasn't as though she herself was truly afraid of Eleanor Percy. Although she'd wanted to believe that Eleanor had orchestrated the incident of the adder in her bedchamber, she'd never been convinced of it, and the dead rat in France was more evidence of Eleanor's innocence. She could hardly have left a rodent and a nasty broadside in Minuette's chamber in France while she'd been at Kenninghall in the north of England.

William wrapped his arms around her and said softly, "Eleanor is in the past, my darling. You know that, don't you? I am sorry to cause you pain in anything. It is never done intentionally."

Something about the urgency in his voice and the way he held her more in appeal than passion . . . all at once Minuette could see what had happened at Kenninghall as clearly as if she'd been there. William had met his daughter, had been instantly smitten by her, and Eleanor seized the moment. No doubt William had been easy to persuade. Probably Eleanor knew how to touch him just so, how to encourage him to slip. Unlike Dominic, William did not make a habit out of saying no to himself.

He had gone to bed with Eleanor at Kenninghall, and now Eleanor was back at court. Right where she'd always intended to be.

Could this be Minuette's moment to tell the truth?

She imagined opening her mouth and pouring out to William her love for Dominic. And she knew instantly that she wouldn't, without exactly knowing why. Because of the dangerous, royal fury that had sent Guildford Dudley and his bride to the Tower? Because William had listened to Rochford and allowed a man to burn to death?

No. Politics had nothing to do with her silence. She had kept this secret for months now, locked away so deep that even Dominic could hardly find it in her any longer, for the sole reason that it would hurt William. More than just wound his pride or damage his ego. *You are the only three I trust.* And with her confession, that number would be down to one. No matter if William forgave them—he would never trust either her or Dominic again.

I can't do that to him, she realized bleakly. Something has to break elsewhere.

His breathing ragged, William whispered, "I wish we could be alone tonight."

"We can't."

"I know. Will you come hawking tomorrow? I'm taking the French ambassador out, but you can ride along with Elizabeth and no one will think twice."

She shook her head. "Not tomorrow. It will be better for us both if I'm not there."

He groaned and nuzzled her neck. "You are so good, Minuette. So good for me. What would I do without you?"

I honestly don't know. And that's why I'm lying to you and breaking my own heart as I do so.

"Courtenay, I'd like a word with you."

Rochford's voice was unmistakable, and Dominic stopped in his tracks. He'd been stalking through the corridors of Nonsuch, attempting to remember where he'd been quartered, while trying to ignore the fact that William and Minuette had disappeared after dinner.

The last thing he wanted was to spar with the Lord Chancellor just now. "Can it wait?" he asked, more abruptly than he'd ever spoken to Rochford before.

"If it could wait, I would not have asked."

Dominic folded his arms. "If it's to do with France, the privy council is scheduled to meet in two days. I'll report then."

Apparently more amused than irritated, Rochford replied, "It is to do with Mistress Wyatt."

Dominic waited for more. It was never wise to anticipate what Rochford might be going to say; better to be certain of the specifics first.

Rochford obliged. "What did the French make of her?"

"The French find every female charming."

"You know what I mean."

Dominic sighed. He wanted to run his hands through his hair in frustration but wouldn't allow Rochford that sign of discomfort. "As far as I could tell, the French are content with the English respect offered their princess and expect her marriage to William to be celebrated in due course." He left out Renaud's hints about Minuette; he was not going to stand here and debate with Rochford the nuances of French opinion on Minuette as William's mistress.

"What do you expect?" Rochford asked.

"Why are you asking me?"

"Because you are the only man who might have some idea of how to stop the king from his disastrous plans."

Dominic laughed bitterly. "If I knew how to stop William doing as he chooses, we wouldn't be having this conversation. I know England needs the French princess. Do you think I haven't told him that?"

Rochford tipped his head thoughtfully, as though he'd heard something more in Dominic's tone. "Tell me honestly, Courtenay—despite your personal friendship for the Wyatt girl, would you rejoice to see her crowned queen?"

Dominic met Rochford's unblinking eyes and, as he'd been bid, answered honestly. "No."

"Then I suggest you find a way to make William listen to you. The king has a brilliant mind and his father's instincts for political survival. But he also has his father's stubbornness. Of all his advisors, you are the only one to whom he might listen. You must remind him, as many times as necessary, that he is meant to look to England's interests."

Rochford nodded once, as though setting a seal on his orders, then strolled away. Dominic would have sworn after his retreating back, but he couldn't summon the strength.

Definitely time to leave court. Tomorrow he would ask William for permission.

As summoned, Robert Dudley arrived at Nonsuch Palace the morning of August 15. He had been summoned by Rochford, not William, and as he was led to the Lord Chancellor's private apartments, Robert wondered what the king would have to say about his return. At least he would have the chance to see Elizabeth—he had missed her desperately the last six weeks.

Lord Rochford was not alone when Robert was shown into his privy chamber. The room itself was dominated by a square desk of English oak and, as always, there were clerks and attendants coming in and out with papers to be signed, reports to be made, and orders to be issued. But unusually, Lady Rochford was also there, turning her hard, assessing gaze on Robert from the seat across the desk from her husband.

With a flick of his hand at his wife, Rochford said, "You must excuse us, my dear."

"Of course." She rose and offered her hand to Robert, who kissed it. "Lord Robert, you are looking very well."

"Thank you, my lady." But don't think your position is enough to entice me into an affair, he thought. You'll have to find another young man to absorb your jealous fury at your husband. Not that Jane Boleyn was unattractive—her pale skin remained smooth, her hair thick, her figure untouched by childbearing—but there was a restlessness behind her tightly held control that made Robert wary.

As if she could sense his reservations, Lady Rochford withdrew her hand and gave him a rather chilly farewell. When she left the privy chamber, Rochford indicated that Robert should take the seat she had vacated.

A public conversation, Robert thought with interest. That's new. The Lord Chancellor's men were well-trained, of course; not one came near enough the desk to be a serious threat to privacy as long as they kept their voices down.

"I'm afraid," Rochford began, "that the young lady about whom I have been concerned is more of a threat than I first thought."

"Yes?" Robert said neutrally. Playing politics with the Catholic powers was one thing—meddling with a king's affections was far more dangerous. Besides, he rather liked Minuette.

"I need you to speak directly to the young lady. Make it clear that she is on treacherous ground. I do not particularly wish her ill, but I will not let England be ruined by a simple girl of no particular talent or ability."

And how many men said the same of your sister? Robert wanted to ask. But he knew better than to attract Rochford's displeasure. Also, he had a favour to ask.

"I'll speak to her," he agreed. "In return, might I be allowed to visit my brother, Guildford, in the Tower? It would ease my mother's heart to know I have seen him."

"That may not be in my power. You would better ask the king."

"Surely a word from his Lord Chancellor will go a long ways in predisposing the king to such a request."

Rochford's hooded eyes didn't waver. "I will consider if such a request is in the country's best interests."

Which could mean anything from, *Do what I want and I'll take care of it* to *What makes you think you have the right to ask anything?*

With effortful politeness, Robert said, "Thank you."

"You'd best deal with the issue of the young lady at once. I believe she did not go hawking with the court this morning." Rochford waved over a clerk, pointedly dismissing Robert.

Only when he had left the Lord Chancellor's apartments did Robert think seriously about what to say to Minuette. She was almost as willful as Elizabeth, more likely to persist in a course simply because someone told her not to. But he did not like that she was in Rochford's sights. It was in her best interests to remain inconspicuous and stay away from William.

And as Rochford had said, might as well get it over with. He was looking for someone to direct him to Minuette's chambers when Eleanor Percy intercepted him.

"May I be of service, Lord Robert?" she purred in that throaty voice that could make any man stop in his tracks.

"Back at court?" Robert asked. "I wonder if you'll manage to remain this time."

Her smile promised tangled bedsheets and skillful hands and eagerness. So that's the way of it, he thought. She's got her claws into William once more. One more reason to warn Minuette off.

But might as well make use of her. "Could you locate Mistress Wyatt for me?" he asked abruptly. "Tell her I'd like to speak with her. I'll be in the map room."

She curtsied. "I am at your service, my lord."

I doubt that, he thought uneasily. The only one you've ever served is yourself.

As Eleanor walked away, Robert dismissed her from his mind and concentrated on finding the right words with which to warn off Minuette.

Minuette had tossed and turned all night, her conscience conflicted and restless. The next morning, with most of the court out hawking, she picked up a veil she'd begun embroidering before she went to France, and put it down somewhere else a minute later. She considered pulling out her diary, but knew she would never be able to focus enough to write anything. At last, she sat down long enough to reread the letter that had been waiting for her at Nonsuch.

Genevieve, her stepfather had written, *I have reached the end of the list of names you handed me earlier this year. I do not like what I am left with. There are only four names that cannot be absolutely ruled out, but almost a dozen more that are alibis for one another. Can we trust for certain that the Earl of Sussex was with his wife that important month when your friend fell pregnant when it is his brother-in-law, also on your list, who is his sole alibi? You must see the issues there. Men will lie for many reasons, and covering another man's infidelities is one of them. I would tell you where my own suspicions lie, but likely you already have guessed and would think me merely prejudiced. Perhaps I am. That does not mean I am wrong.*

She could guess, all right. Two of the men who had alibied each other on that list of Alyce's possible lovers were the Duke of Northumberland and his son, Robert Dudley. Minuette did not especially want to think about that just now, but it worried away at her.

After the fourth circuit of her suite—William had insisted she have more space, so now she had a small reception chamber as well as a bedchamber and a tiny room for Carrie—Minuette's attention fell on the silver casket she had taken from Emma Hadley's home back in May.

It had been amongst the possessions sent from Wynfield to Nonsuch for her return. She wished Fidelis had also been returned to her, but the wolfhound remained at Wynfield. She would have to speak to William about having him brought to court again. In the meantime, she needed to dispatch Alyce's personal items back to her sister. Might as well look them over one last time before having Carrie see to their return.

Minuette forced herself to reread every letter contained in the casket, including the ones Alyce had written to her sister. But no matter how hard she tried to find something unusual, some sign of a code or clue about the man in the dead woman's life, she could find nothing. After nearly two hours of staring at the single letters of each word on each page, she laid them aside and rubbed her temples.

Now what? She could hear John Dee's voice, saying with surety of Alyce: *She was a woman to leave a record.*

But where? The orders from her lover had been openly ciphered, so that anyone seeing them would know they contained secrets. Nothing Minuette had found showed any sign of being anything other than what it was. Where else could she look?

As she pondered, she stared at the casket that had held the letters and now stood empty. It was silver, perhaps a foot wide and high, with ornate fretwork details on the sides. On the curved top were cinquefoils, the five-pointed flowers enameled in yellow and red. Minuette knew the casket had belonged to Alyce's mother and that her friend had always had it with her at court.

She ran her fingers carefully along every surface, recalling the hidden altar piece at Framlingham that had once concealed a precious document. She detected nothing unusual. Next, she opened the casket. The interior was lined entirely with brown velvet that was shiny in several spots, no doubt from age. Considering, Minuette used her fingertips to trace the edges of the velvet. The bottom yielded nothing to her touch. But when she moved to the rounded top, almost at once her fingers caught at a corner where the fabric did not quite align.

Holding her breath, she pried loose one corner and then along one edge to another corner. The fabric pulled loose where it had merely been tucked in and she could hear the rustle of pages before she pulled them loose. She let her breath out in relief.

Here at last was Alyce's accounting of her actions.

He danced with me tonight, twice . . . I should not be moved by him, but he makes me laugh . . . he is dangerous but that is part of the allure, I could never fall in love with a commonplace man . . . I know I am not the only woman in his life, but he makes me feel that I am . . . he's asked me to spend a month with him, and though I know it is reckless to the point of lunacy, I will go . . . I told him about my condition today and he could not even be bothered to be angry—worse, he was indifferent . . . I am finished doing as he bids—rather risk the king's wrath now than later . . . I will tell him what I mean to do, for I owe him that much . . .

Nothing as useful as a name, of course. But from the descriptions alone, the words convincingly ruled out the late Giles Howard. Even the most besotted woman could never have described him as alluring.

Minuette considered the pages before her and the letter from her stepfather. In that tangle of information, she knew one thing for certain: she needed to talk to Dominic.

She didn't think he had gone hawking with William and Elizabeth—more likely he was working somewhere in the palace. She penned a brief message, asking him if they might meet later today to discuss "a matter of the past." Let him interpret that as he wished.

When Minuette handed the message to Carrie and asked her to deliver it to Dominic, Carrie frowned and suggested she leave the suite as well. "You could walk in the galleries. It will do you good to look at something other than your own walls. And with the court out hawking, the galleries will be empty. You will not have to watch yourself so closely. I will find you when I have Lord Exeter's reply."

Minuette wondered, not for the first time, how much Carrie guessed of her dilemma. She had the uncomfortable feeling that her maid knew the innermost workings of her heart as well as she knew the linen underclothes she wore. Well, whatever Carrie might know or guess, Minuette could not speak freely. Not in the very heart of William's palace.

As Carrie had advised, the long galleries were as empty as they could ever be. With William hawking, there was little need for hopeful courtiers to stand around waiting for him to pass through the corridors to plead whatever causes they had to plead. Those whom Minuette passed this morning seemed as anxious for solitude as she, and no one spoke to her.

Except the one person she least wanted to see.

She was standing in the gallery, gazing blindly at a tapestry of an idyllic country retreat complete with swans on a lake and a hunting dog pursuing ducks, when Eleanor Percy found her. "Mistress Wyatt."

It was the first time she had seen Eleanor since the adder incident, and it was the politest voice Eleanor had ever used with her. Minuette inclined her head in the barest acknowledgment and waited for the other woman to pass on. But Eleanor, it seemed, had been in search of her, though the tight lacing of her bodice showed rather an interest in looking for men than for a woman. "Lord Robert Dudley would like to speak with you privately."

Whatever for? she nearly asked. It was almost as though Robert knew what she had just read in her stepfather's letter. "And why would he send you to find me?"

Eleanor gleamed in that particular way of hers, designed to make men stop thinking and women roll their eyes. "I was conveniently nearby. He's in the map room just now. I believe this is a conversation you would prefer to have out of sight of the royals. Will you come?"

It seemed Eleanor meant to lead her there. Minuette tried to politely refuse, then less politely, but Eleanor said, "I wouldn't want you to slip away. Lord Robert was quite specific."

Something in the way she said his name . . . could Eleanor have moved on in her choice of men? Surely not, at least not with Robert. He had an eye for women, but he had a sharper eye for his own preservation. And bedding the king's former mistress in the king's own palace was sure to jeopardize one's future. Especially when one was in love with the king's sister.

Warily she followed Eleanor through the empty corridors to the map room, so-called because of the frescoed map of Europe that covered one entire wall. It was mostly used for exchequer business, but today there was only Robert sitting at a table with a ledger open before him. He shut it as the women entered and rose. "Thank you for coming, Minuette."

To Eleanor, who waited at her side, he said, "You may go." There was nothing, not even a flicker, to betray the slightest personal interest in her. Perhaps she had merely been convenient, at that. Minuette was just glad to see her go.

"Please," Robert said, and they sat across from each other. She had seen him in this mood only once before, solemn and serious, when he had come to Framlingham last fall to tell her that the Spanish navy was on the move and she'd best hurry and find the Penitent's Confession she'd been sent to locate. Robert serious was very serious indeed.

As though he could read her mind, he asked, "Do you remember the night Giles Howard died?"

I might have enjoyed you willing, but I will revel in you fighting. Giles upon her, sword in one hand, the other hand digging into her arm, dragging her up . . . pushing her against the wall . . .

246 · LAURA ANDERSEN

then he was falling and there was blood on her hands and wet across her face and her dress and spurting across the stones of the floor.

"I remember."

"I know it was you, Minuette."

"You know what was me?"

"You are the one who killed Giles Howard, not Dominic. I saw Dominic that night, not ten minutes afterward, in the clothes he was wearing in that lady chapel, and he had only smears and streaks of blood on him. You, however . . . your gown was so soaked in blood that your maid burnt it."

She met his gaze steadily, but her thoughts raced as swiftly as her heart. It wasn't as though she regretted killing Giles, considering what he'd meant to do to her. It just wasn't something she wanted to remember. Or anyone else to know.

"Why are you bringing this to my attention now?" she asked softly. Robert Dudley was always a hard man to read, but never more so than when he was serious.

"Because you are in a precarious position, Minuette, and I would like you to take my advice."

"By threatening me?"

"By proving to you that I have your best interests at heart. If I did not, I would have spread this news, for there are many at court who would pay to know anything that might discredit you. I am not interested in injuring you."

"What are you interested in, Lord Robert?"

"Protecting England. You have to walk away from William."

How to play this? Innocent? Outraged? Or as Robert was playing it—matter-of-fact and straightforward?

"Assuming that I know what you are talking about, why would I do that?" Was she always to be in the position of defending a match she didn't even desire? Life would be so much easier if she could just tell everyone—anyone—the truth: *I have no intention of marrying William ever.* "And why are you the one to give me this advice?"

"Because no one else will," he retorted. "At least, no one you want to tangle with. Would you rather be discussing this with my father? Or the Lord Chancellor? Or why not bring the new Duke of Norfolk into it—surely he'd have an opinion as to whether the king should marry the woman who murdered his nephew."

She rose, pleased that her body responded gracefully even though panic was lurking deep. "I will not be threatened by you."

Robert stood as well and leaned toward her, his palms flat against the table, speaking fast and low. "Look, I am as close to the holy quartet as anyone can be who isn't part of it. You, Dominic, William, Elizabeth—I know how the dynamics work. William thinks he runs things, but that is only because he is king. It has always been the two of you together doing what you want and leaving the others to clear up after. Dominic won't speak to you of this because . . . well, because Dominic never speaks and because he cannot see beyond his loyalty to Will. And Elizabeth, for all her brains and wit, has a blind spot where her brother is concerned. She may not believe that everything the king does must be right, but damned if she'll let anyone else accuse him of it."

He stepped around the table, urgency threading his voice. "You're the one with all the power here. You must walk away from William. If you don't—"

"Who put you up to this? I know this isn't coming from you. Is it your father who's warning me off? What exactly does the Duke of Northumberland threaten if I do not walk away?"

His face darkened. "You are in over your head. That is my

warning, no one else's. If you don't walk away from William, someone might ensure that you are forced to."

She would not give him the satisfaction of knowing he had shaken her. With a contemptuous turn of her shoulder, she walked out straight-backed and unflinching. But so unnerved was she inside that she flinched when Eleanor fell into step with her in the corridor.

"Here to escort me elsewhere?" Minuette asked.

This time Eleanor did not trouble with politeness. "You grow increasingly troublesome with each day that passes."

"Troublesome to whom? You? Forgive me for not caring."

"Don't be a fool. I don't like you, but I am beginning to feel sorry for you. You're no match for the king. William will have what he wants, and if you don't play it right, you'll end up with nothing."

"I know what I'm doing." Minuette nearly laughed aloud at the breathtaking folly of the situation—proclaiming her ability to end as William's wife to his former mistress. Never mind that she wasn't at all interested in being queen.

Eleanor studied her intently, eyes glittering, then shook her head. "You did me a favour, ridding me of Giles. So I will say it plainly one last time: you have enemies you've never dreamed of. And their tactics are not confined to innuendo and court gossip. You think the Catholics make bad enemies? They are as nothing to the hard hearts of the Protestants."

Minuette stared as Eleanor swept away. What was she implying—that Minuette was in actual peril? That was absurd. Beyond Elizabeth and Dominic, no one knew for certain that William wished to marry her. Minuette shook her head and went back to her rooms, convincing herself as she went that Eleanor's words had been nothing more than an attempt to rattle her.

Robert's words, though, had been meant to do more than

that. Combined with her stepfather's insinuations and her own increasing uneasiness with the Dudley men's alibis, how could she not perceive it as a threat? But how could she believe that Robert, a man she'd known since childhood, actually meant her harm?

Carrie met her at the door to her chamber with a note in Dominic's familiar handwriting. He wrote that he would meet her in the gardens as soon as she could be there. Though there had been tension between them since his mother's house, just the thought of seeing him lightened her mood. Compared to the murky depths of court politics, Dominic was like a refreshing dose of clear water. She would tell him everything and welcome his opinion.

She briefly considered changing clothes, but she didn't want to waste the time. At the last moment her gaze fell on the star pendant lying neatly on the dressing table. She hadn't worn it since leaving the French court, and had laid it away in the small, locked casket that kept her few valuable pieces. Carrie must have pulled it out for some reason. Perhaps it was a hint from her discreet maid. Well, she would take the hint.

It took her three tries to catch the clasp blindly, but at last it settled into place, the filigreed star nestling into the hollow of her throat. With footsteps as light as her heart, Minuette went down the stairs, through the courtyards, and into the gardens.

She saw Dominic, dark and watchful near the fountains, and increased her pace.

At the last moment Elizabeth decided it was too hot to go hawking with William and the French ambassador. She was practicing with her lute master when Robert Dudley appeared in her presence chamber. Although she was still annoyed with him in proxy for his family, it was hard to remember that when she saw him. He was such a familiar presence—both comforting and arousing—a reminder of herself as Elizabeth first and a princess second. She finished the lute arrangement of her father's song, "Pastyme with Good Company," then waved Robert to join her near the window while the lute master took her instrument and bowed himself away.

"You're looking terrifyingly solemn," she remarked. "What dreadful crisis has brought you to that?"

He hesitated, as though deciding which flippant response to give. Then he settled on truth. "I expect to be an uncle within a fortnight."

"I know." Margaret Clifford was hugely pregnant. She remained confined to the Tower, as was Guildford Dudley, though the two of them were kept strictly apart. She didn't need Robert to elaborate on the solemnity—if Margaret's child was a son, it would be the first boy born in the royal line since William. A Protestant boy, thus less dangerous than a Catholic one, but no doubt there would be treacherous whispers about moving him up in the line of succession. At the least, a boy would give Northumberland, as the child's grandfather, a good deal too much power.

Elizabeth added, "You know William has moved to annul the marriage."

"And you know that isn't always an answer. Your father kept Mary in the line of succession despite the dissolution of his marriage to Catherine."

"That's not going to happen here," she warned. "If it's a boy, the council will ensure he has no legal claim at all."

Robert shrugged and leaned back, but there was an underlying anxiety to his movements. "That's not really my concern. I am not interested in maneuvering five steps from the throne for a shadow of a possibility that will never come to pass. Your brother will marry and produce any number of sons. And I will be glad of it, for your sake."

"You do not think I could rule England if called upon?" she demanded, piqued.

There was his lightning-quick grin. "You could rule England better than any twenty men I know. But is that the life you would choose—always answering to others? Never doing something merely because you wish it?"

"William does any number of things merely because he wishes it."

"William is a king, and you, my dear, would be a queen. A ruling queen, but a woman nonetheless. You know the expectations would be vastly different."

"And entirely theoretical. As you point out, no doubt William will have sons and to spare."

But would he? Their father, virile and powerful as he'd been, hadn't. William had already fathered one daughter. And she remembered John Dee, studying her palm last winter, promising something that she'd been afraid to grasp at, afraid to know, so that she'd snatched her hand away at the last moment rather than see it . . .

"Truly, Your Highness, I did not come to discuss our brothers, at least not directly. My mother has written and asked me to remind you that you promised to consider visiting Dudley Castle this autumn. It would please her greatly if you consented."

"Please *her*?" she asked archly.

And now his other smile, the intimate, private one that Elizabeth hoped she alone ever saw. Surely he didn't smile at his wife this way? "Do I need to tell you how it would please me?" he whispered. "There are so many ways . . ." He leaned in, until she could feel his breath on her cheek. "Perhaps you will let me enumerate them one at a time when you are in my home."

William won't want me to go, she thought. Not with the crisis looming over Guildford and Margaret. But I've done any number of things I don't want to please him.

"I'll come," she said softly. "But don't tell the king. I'll work it out myself."

She closed her eyes as lips brushed her cheek. Just as she shivered, there was a tumult across the room. Her eyes flew open as Robert drew back and shot to his feet. Dominic was pushing his way through the door, carrying someone in his arms and his voice strained beyond recognition. "She needs a physician. *Now*."

When Elizabeth saw the bright gold hair spilling over Dominic's arm, her heart turned over in fear.

Dominic paced the length of Elizabeth's presence chamber for the agonizingly long minutes until the physician's arrival. The man was taken straight through to the princess's bedchamber, where Minuette lay with labored breath and slowing heart. Dominic could still feel each beat of it as he'd rested his palm against her chest . . .

It had taken him agonizing moments to realize something was wrong. When she approached him in the gardens, he'd seen only what he always saw—her hair shining in the patchy sunlight, the lightness of her walk, and the star pendant circling her long, white neck. But when she drew near enough, he saw the crease between her eyebrows, as if she were worried or in pain.

"Are you hurt?" He reached instinctively to touch her, but stopped.

"No, I . . ." She put a hand to her chest. "I'm just having a hard time catching my breath."

Dominic led her to the nearest bench and made her sit. He knelt before her and studied her face. "Are you ill?"

"No, it's just a momentary weakness. It will pass."

Minuette had never suffered a momentary weakness in her life. Dominic was debating whether to get her inside when she gave a breathless little cry. "I feel odd, like tingling in my chest. But my skin is numb. I can't feel my throat."

Heedless of decorum, Dominic put his palm to her bare skin, between her throat and the neckline of her gown. He felt her heartbeat, and his fear grew. It was slow—too slow. What was wrong with her? There'd been no recent cases of sweating sickness or plague and he couldn't think of another illness that could come on this fast.

Through his worry he could feel his mind trying to tell him something. Something not right. As he pulled his hand away, he realized that the tips of his fingers were tingling. Minuette had said her chest was tingling. *I can't feel my throat.*

This was no illness.

"Oh, God," he prayed. Poison, it must be poison. And if it had gotten on his fingers, it must be on her somehow, absorbing through the skin.

The pendant. He had brushed against the pendant when he put his hand to her chest—he remembered the feel of the star against his fingertips.

He wrenched the pendant off her in one sharp movement. Dropping it to the ground, Dominic swung her up into his arms. She was awake and aware, but she was focused only on breathing, on the effort needed to draw in breath after breath.

"Where is she?" Carrie's voice pulled him back to his surroundings. Carrie looked as though she had run to Elizabeth's chambers. Her normally neat presence was betrayed by red cheeks and the locks of hair that had slipped from beneath her linen coif.

"She's in the princess's bed. The physician is with her."

When Carrie had vanished within, Dominic forced himself to

think. He should retrieve the pendant. Before whoever had poisoned it had a chance to get rid of it.

It lay where he had dropped it, sparkling pretty and harmless on the cobblestone path. Picking it up by the broken clasp, Dominic dropped it into a leather pouch and pulled the lacing tight. His fingertips were numb where he had touched it earlier. He wasn't worried about himself—he was bigger and stronger by far than Minuette, and he had brushed only briefly against the jewels. But she had worn them against her bare skin for . . . what? Five, ten minutes? Longer? How much poison had her body absorbed?

Though his hands were steady, he felt as though he were shaking to pieces from the inside out. Dominic closed his eyes, hoping that would help, but it only increased his sense of instability. And in the darkness of his mind, all he could see was Minuette swaying into his arms.

He opened his eyes and returned to Elizabeth's rooms, where the physician was waiting for him. The man sniffed the pendant delicately, then touched one finger to the star before returning it to the pouch.

"Can you tell what poison it is?" Dominic demanded.

"Given her symptoms, likely monkshood. You're right, it's on the pendant itself. Monkshood is just as deadly when absorbed through the skin as when ingested."

"Will she . . ."

He could not finish the question. The physician shrugged. "I'll see if she can tell me how long she was wearing that. But there's no way to know how much was on there. She's young and healthy. If the absorption was small enough . . ."

"How long before we know?"

The physician was equally blunt. "If she's going to die, she won't last the night."

There was movement behind the physician and Dominic looked over the man's shoulder to where Elizabeth stood in the doorway, her face white but perfectly composed. Dropping the leather pouch and its dangerous contents on the nearest table, the physician returned to his vigil within.

"What can I do?" Dominic asked Elizabeth.

"Find William. If he hasn't returned from hawking, go after him. If we do not alert him at once, he'll never forgive us."

He'd forgotten about the king. Yes, he must be told—and discreetly. This story must not be spread abroad. Not until they had an ending to it, and could put a name to the person responsible.

Dominic went straight to the stables to commandeer a horse, but the hawking party was just riding back in. William and the French ambassador were telling each other vulgar jokes and laughing uproariously. Dominic tried to catch William's eye, but when that failed he interrupted. "A word, Your Majesty?"

His tone must have alerted William, for he smoothly excused himself from the ambassador and the other members of the party. When Dominic whispered the news in his ear, William went noticeably pale. He motioned a page to them and said, "Report to Lord Rochford that I will be unavailable for the remainder of the day. He is to see to the comfort of the French ambassador and deal with any matters that might arise before tomorrow."

William didn't say another word as they paced quickly back to Elizabeth's chambers. That suited Dominic. He could not have spoken more than the necessities if his life depended on it.

Elizabeth's privy chamber was empty. Without pausing, William let himself into the sickroom and shut the door behind him.

After staring at that closed door for what felt like an hour, Dominic retrieved the leather pouch that held Minuette's treacherous pendant and escaped. If he was not to be allowed into the sickroom—and why should he be? It was the province of women, whatever liberties the king might take—he preferred to shut himself up in his own rooms. There were many things he could be doing—helping Rochford with the French or beginning inquiries into how this had happened. Who had got into Minuette's rooms and when? Where had they found monkshood? And above all, why?

But none of that mattered at the moment. Nothing mattered but that Minuette's heart continue to beat.

It was the longest night of Dominic's life. When he wasn't pacing like a caged lion, he sagged to the floor with his back against the wall, arms braced on his bent knees. At first he knew time was passing because of the changes in the light coming through his window. But when darkness fell, he sat unmoving, as though he'd been suspended in a bubble where time did not exist. Almost, he envied his mother her surety of faith; at the least, a rosary would have given occupation to his hands while he waited. He almost got up then, for he knew Minuette kept her own mother's rosary hidden in the false bottom of her jewelry casket. But he could not face her empty chamber, not until he knew whether she would return to it.

In the dark, dead hours of the night, Dominic felt his hope flicker and go out. If the end neared, he thought desperately, surely Elizabeth would summon him. She would not let Minuette go without allowing him to tell her goodbye. Even as simply her friend, he deserved that. But no one came.

When finally there was a knock on his door, he had to blink himself into reality. Lifting his head from his hands, he saw that the first faint grey of dawn had come.

The second knock was louder, and Dominic had to swallow past the terror in his throat to answer. "Who is it?"

"Harrington."

Through his mingled hope and dread, Dominic called sharply, "What do you want?"

"I've a woman wants to see you."

In the time it took him to cross the room and open the door, Dominic imagined several scenarios. Elizabeth, grieved and shaking. One of the ladies-in-waiting, summoning him at Minuette's request. It was dawn. Had she lived through the night?

Carrie stood at Harrington's side, looking exhausted and ill herself. But her face lit in an angelic smile when she saw Dominic. "She's come through it, my lord. She's tired and very weak, but her heart is beating normal and she can breathe easy now. Physician said himself that she'll do."

Dominic had spent so many hours preparing himself for the worst that he wasn't ready for this. He gaped at Carrie for several moments, long enough for her smile to falter and her eyes to grow quizzical. Plainly she was wondering if he'd understood.

Finally, he found the only words that meant anything. "Thank God."

Her smile returned. "Yes, my lord. I must get back. She's sleeping peaceful for now and Her Highness has asked that she be kept quiet for the day. No visitors."

"Of course." He could wait. Minuette would live.

"My lord." Carrie hesitated. "Is there anything you'd like me to tell her?"

It wasn't the question so much as the look she gave him, as if she could see into the dark hours of his vigil. Her expression reminded him of Diane de Poitiers—though the two women were poles apart in appearance and dress and comportment, Carrie had the same piercing look of understanding more than she told. Did Carrie know? If she did, it was by her own intuition, for Dominic knew Minuette had not revealed their secret even to her maid. Just as he had not told Harrington—though, come to think of it, Harrington seemed to have a hint of sympathy in his own grave eyes.

Dominic thought of all the things he'd like to say to Minuette at this moment, and knew that he must say none of them. It was harder than he'd imagined, trying to think of innocent words that would raise no one's suspicions but would convey what he wanted to Minuette herself.

And then he thought of the pendant, his gift that had been turned against her, and sighed. "Tell her she is still the sweetest and merriest star of all."

CHAPTER FIFTEEN

AFTER A FEW hours of snatched sleep, Elizabeth met with her brother and Dominic in her privy chamber. It had been an awful night, reminiscent of Hever last summer when it had been her mother struggling to breathe on her deathbed while Minuette had held her hand. There had been no one to hold Elizabeth's hand last night. William stayed just long enough to ensure that Minuette was being cared for, then locked himself away in his own rooms. Elizabeth suspected he'd spent much of that time drinking. She didn't know what Dominic had been doing, but when he appeared he looked no more rested than her brother.

In spite of the lack of sleep, Elizabeth had managed to behave as normal for public eyes, dismissing Minuette's illness as a severe headache. The physician and Carrie were sworn to secrecy and Minuette had been returned to her own chambers just after dawn. But Elizabeth saw more than one thoughtful expression amongst her women as her story made the rounds, and she felt, with a sinking heart, that they were now in a different kind of trouble. When a woman was as near to a man as Minuette was to William, any illness would be credited to one cause.

It was a point she tried to make when the three shut themselves away in privacy. Dominic was in no mood to hear it. As he had once before, he wanted Minuette sent away from court at the earliest possible moment. And as she had once before, Elizabeth argued. She pointed out that speculation was no doubt already bubbling that Minuette was pregnant, that the only way to refute such rumours was to keep her here and show her off as much as possible. Let the court see that she did not continue ill, or swell with child. Send her away, and tongues would wag that she was going to bear William's child in secret.

But William was entirely on Dominic's side. "Someone meant to kill her. Monkshood is not playing. Minuette must go until we know who that person is and have dealt with him—or her."

He knew it meant further weeks of separation. He knew that rumours of an illicit pregnancy would further impede his marriage plans. It was the first time Elizabeth had seen her brother do something truly disinterested, and she realized with a bittersweet pang that his love for Minuette did go beyond desire.

"This time, she doesn't go to Wynfield," William ordered. "Sending adequate royal guards with her would only spark more gossip. You must take her to Hatfield, Elizabeth. No one will blink twice if I increase your protection."

Elizabeth had hoped for that solution, for she had a plan of her own. First was to get Minuette well. A week or two, the physician thought, and she would be strong enough to travel. They would travel to Hatfield, right enough, but from there it wouldn't be hard to persuade Minuette to travel to Dudley Castle with her. Even William would have to approve that plan, for she would have a chaperone around Robert—if Elizabeth had meant to tell him. Which she didn't—at least not in advance. But when he found out later, she would be able to point out that she'd known very well that, as a Howard widow, Eleanor Percy would never show her face in such a Protestant household as the Dudleys. For surely Eleanor must be considered the most likely assassin.

That was for William and Dominic to discover—how to deal with the matter of poison. And poisoner.

For the first time in their friendship, William found himself trying to restrain Dominic from too hasty action. No, not the first time, he corrected himself. As William watched his friend pace the perimeter of his private closet, he could almost see Dominic's knife once more at Giles Howard's throat. And just look how that had ended.

William was no less angry. But he knew how to use his anger, how to let white-hot emotion cool into deadly resolve. It was something he had learned, ironically enough, from Dominic—*think before you act*. There were too many traps here, possibilities and consequences that must be considered. He would take his time and act when he was ready. If only he could keep Dominic reined in.

"Why have you not put Eleanor under arrest?" Dominic growled for the fourth time that hour.

And, for the fourth time, William gave the same reply. "We have no evidence."

"She hates Minuette, she always has. Do you think she'd balk at killing? You said it yourself once—the woman's only virtue is devotion to her own interests. No doubt Eleanor believes that with Minuette dead, you'd turn back to her."

"I've given her no cause to think so."

"You met her daughter this summer. That alone would have given Eleanor cause to hope. And then you invited her to return here to court."

"Even you cannot fault my behavior since her return."

"And before her return?" Dominic asked brusquely.

William forced himself not to blink. Dominic did not listen to gossip—if there had been gossip, which was unlikely. They had been extremely discreet at Kenninghall.

If there was any act of his life William wished undone, it was admitting Eleanor to his chambers that summer night two months ago. He had first met Eleanor's daughter that day. *His* daughter, William was sure of it. The girl looked like Elizabeth, and had an air about her disconcertingly like their mother. He'd been disarmed by the child and by the emotions she'd raised. And Eleanor had been . . . familiar. Tempting. She knew him well, and no doubt she played the moment for all it was worth, but he had let her. He had argued against his conscience ever since, certain that Minuette would not expect complete celibacy from him, that she would know what men need and understand that his love for her was completely different than an hour's dalliance with another woman . . .

But if he learned that Eleanor had deliberately harmed Minuette after he had allowed her to return to court, he would never forgive himself. And he would do more than throw Eleanor in the Tower.

"I'm not disagreeing with you," he said. "I don't trust Eleanor, and I'm quite willing to see her punished. But I'm nowhere near convinced she could do this alone. It was planned, Dominic. One doesn't keep monkshood on one's person merely in hopes that an opportunity of using it will arise." William wasn't quite sure if that was really what he believed or if he was just grasping for an answer that made his own failure less.

For the first time today, Dominic stopped and listened to him. "If not Eleanor alone . . . whom do you suspect, Will?"

"Eleanor must be questioned—but I don't want her arrested, not yet. That sets off too many alarms. Bully her if you like, but don't spread it widely. If there's more to this than her jealousy of Minuette, I don't want us missing anything from prejudice."

Dominic could have sent a page after Eleanor, but he could not be still. It wasn't anger or fear driving him—just a clarity of purpose that had narrowed to one objective. Find Minuette's enemy.

It took him nearly an hour to track down Eleanor, playing the virginals in one of the medieval galleries in the older section of the palace. She was surrounded by a crowd of appreciative men. Most of them seemed more appreciative of her attributes than her musical talent.

"I'd like to speak with you, Mistress Percy. Privately."

She smiled at him, as smooth and bland as cream. "It will be my pleasure, Lord Exeter."

Leaving the disappointed and envious men behind, Dominic did not take her to his own rooms this time. Instead, he led her into the empty chapel.

"How religious," she remarked.

Dominic launched straight to the heart of the matter. "Where did you keep the monkshood?"

She blinked. "I haven't the least idea what you mean."

"If it was ever in your possession, we'll find evidence of it. You can't have got rid of every trace." Dominic was bluffing. William might not think much of Eleanor's planning abilities, but even she would have disposed of whatever had contained the monkshood poison. She need only have thrown it in the river.

"Has someone been poisoned?" She was such a practiced performer that Dominic could not tell if her studied shock was false. He had the impression she was never less than studied.

"Where were you yesterday in the early afternoon hours?"

"Are you accusing me of something?" Her voice trembled, but she met his eyes squarely, and Dominic was almost certain he saw a flicker of triumph in them.

"Yesterday someone slipped into Mistress Wyatt's rooms, painted a solution of monkshood on the back of one of her pendants, and left it for her to wear."

He knew he was supposed to keep it quiet, but he would have bet anything that Eleanor already knew. And he was too angry to be careful.

Eleanor narrowed her eyes. "I believe I warned you some months ago that she has enemies. It seems one of them is growing desperate."

"Mistress Wyatt poses no threat to anyone of importance."

"Of course she does. A blind man could see how William follows after her like a lapdog. Rumour has it she'll not give in for anything less than marriage. Trying Anne's tricks on Anne's son—it's quite cunning really. But she's no match for Will. He'll have her yet, and when he has, the allure of her innocence will quickly pall. Still, some might believe she poses a serious threat to the French marriage. And that might be a matter for poison."

Too furious to be calm, and afraid he might hurt Eleanor if this continued, Dominic said, "You may go—for now. The king will order further questioning as he deems fit."

"You have no evidence."

"Since when is that an obstacle?"

Her face darkened, and Dominic caught a glimpse of the hard, obsessive woman behind the practiced mask. She stood in one disdainful movement. "William will never harm me based solely on one man's opinion. Not when evidence exists against the true culprits."

"If you know of evidence, and you do not disclose it, you'll be arrested as an accessory."

She appeared to consider his words, then shrugged. "To prove that I don't hold a grudge, I'll tell you this. Did you know that yesterday afternoon Minuette had a private conversation with Lord Robert Dudley? He sent me to fetch her to him and told me to make certain she was not followed. Ask yourself why Robert Dudley would want her away from her rooms at that moment. Very convenient timing for the poisoner. And before you jump at the fact that I was the one to convey the message, and thus undoubtedly knew of the arrangement, remember whose son Robert Dudley is. With one son in prison, the Duke of Northumberland is desperate to regain influence with the king. He doesn't want William wedding a French princess, but still less does he want the king tying himself to a silly girl of uncertain religious temperament. And Black Jack Dudley has a history of getting what he wants."

25 August 1555
Hatfield

I have been asked over and over what I remember of the day I was poisoned. But only Dominic has asked me what I remember of the night itself.

I remember the paralyzing numbness that spread from my throat down my body. I remember the terror of believing each breath might be my last. I remember my vision fading to a yellow-green haze. I remember Carrie's fierce face, determined to pull me through by sheer force of will; Elizabeth, calm and reassuring despite the tightness of her lips.

I remember wanting Dominic, and panicking because he was not there. I don't ever want to feel that again.

5 September 1555
Hatfield

I lost my temper with Elizabeth today. She has been nothing but sweet and solicitous and I could not bear it a moment longer. I'm not a child, I reminded her. I know what's going on. Someone—likely Eleanor Percy—wants me removed. Permanently. I'll agree not to make it easy for her, to leave court and allow William and Dominic to gather their evidence, to keep out of harm's way until the threat is removed . . . but I will do those things because they are logical, not because I am ordered to.

And if I am acting on logic, then I must admit that the poisoner may not be Eleanor after all. It may not be jealousy that prompted the attempt on my life, but fear. Because, whatever men might think, I am more than just a pretty face that a king desires.

I am Alyce de Clare's friend, the only one who still wants to know who used her and discarded her when she was no longer convenient.

Perhaps I am drawing near to my answer—an answer someone would kill to keep.

When we left court for Hatfield, I gave Dominic the silver casket with Alyce's concealed notes about her love affair. I also told him of my stepfather's insinuations and the problem of a father and son being one another's alibis for the period in which Alyce fell pregnant.

I have not told Elizabeth any of it, because of where the threads are leading me. Because of whom I may be closing in on. I have not forgotten that my pendant was left out on my dressing table during my private meeting with Robert Dudley.

If it is Northumberland who set up Norfolk last year, who arranged the charade of treason to bring down the Catholic powers, then Elizabeth is the last person I can tell.

Especially since we leave tomorrow for Dudley Castle.

Clearly, Elizabeth's primary concerns on this journey were speed and stealth. Minuette had to persuade her friend that she was capable of riding thirty miles a day in order not to be left behind. There was no way she was letting Elizabeth go to Northumberland's home without her, and so she didn't blanch when she realized that they would travel in a small group of mounted knights and the two women only. No maids, no carts except one to come along as fast as it could, and packhorses to carry the finery the women would need until the cart caught up to them. This isn't right, Minuette thought anxiously as they left Hatfield before dawn.

Clearly Elizabeth meant to get them to Dudley Castle before William could find out and intervene. She had given orders to her household that, in her absence, no one was to leave Hatfield. Minuette had expected as much, and she glanced ruefully at Carrie as they left. She had told her maid to try to get word to Dominic at court, but the chances didn't look good. She didn't even have Fidelis to keep her company; the wolfhound was still at Wynfield Mote.

But she said nothing, not even when her strength began to flag late on the second day. She had thought herself recovered from the effects of the poison, but clearly she had been more weakened than she knew. She gritted her teeth and rode on. At their pace, they would reach Northumberland's home sometime on the fourth day.

On the morning of day four they left the small inn where Minuette and Elizabeth had shared a room (the innkeepers had been shocked nearly senseless at the appearance of two women dressed as they were, even though Elizabeth had instructed the men to call her only "milady"), and had ridden just two miles when a party of horsemen appeared coming toward them. Minuette recognized the green and gold colours of Northumberland's badge, and Elizabeth said softly, "Robert."

Sure enough, Robert led the horsemen, looking as smoothly elegant as ever as he swung off his mount and knelt in the road at the side of Elizabeth's horse. "Your Highness. Our family could have no greater honour than your presence in our home."

"Then best lead the way, Lord Robert," Elizabeth replied tartly, "so that I might reach your home. It has been a dusty journey."

He grinned and swung back onto his horse. Minuette rode behind them, watching thoughtfully the two heads—bright and dark—close together as they laughed and teased and entertained each other.

She had never so hoped that she was wrong in her suspicions.

It was early afternoon when Dudley Castle came into view. The twelfth-century keep towered high on an ancient earthen motte, surveying the lush countryside around it. As they approached the perimeter wall near the base of the hill, they passed a succession of deserted buildings.

"St. James Priory," one of the Dudley guards answered, when she asked about it. "Clunaic monks until the late king brought down their wickedness." He spat in satisfaction.

She must remember that she was in the heart of Protestant country here—it made her nearly as uncomfortable as when she'd been in Lady Mary's Catholic household last year. Fanaticism of all kinds unnerved her.

The moat had been filled in, and they rode up to an intriguing triple-arch entry. She heard Robert describing it to Elizabeth as her horse drew nearer. "The Triple Gate," he said. "The Suttons added the extra gatehouse two hundred years ago. About the same time as the chapel and undercroft. But don't worry, we live much more modern. Wait until you see the work my father had done ten years ago. He brought in Sharrington to construct an entire wing of domestic quarters. You'll be quite comfortable."

The guards fell back as Robert, Elizabeth, and Minuette rode through the Triple Gate and passed into the open space atop the motte. The high earthwork mound on which Dudley Castle stood was flat at the top and quite spacious. She studied the Sharrington range—it really was beautiful, all pale stone and pointed rooflines and narrow windows—while Robert helped Elizabeth dismount. Then he was at Minuette's horse, and she let him help her down. She stumbled, her body all at once feeling the fatigue of this rapid journey. "Are you all right, Mistress Wyatt?" Robert asked.

She responded with the same distant politeness. "Perfectly all right."

His eyes narrowed and she thought he might press her, but then Elizabeth said sharply, "Robert? Why is there a royal messenger here?"

He swung round and both he and Minuette caught sight of the royal colours on another horse. She blinked. Had William really caught his sister this fast?

"Out of sight," Robert whispered, and whisked both women into the nearest doorway, which was at the base of the old keep. "Stay here, and I'll see what's going on."

This is ridiculous, Minuette thought, and opened her mouth to say so. Elizabeth did not lurk in secret. She was a princess of England and she was not afraid of her brother.

But Elizabeth held her hand up in warning and Minuette subsided. She might be here to protect Elizabeth from her worst instincts, but Minuette was still in her service.

Robert returned in minutes. "The rider has gone," he reported, "and it had nothing to do with you."

"Then what's wrong?" Elizabeth asked. Robert's face had changed, the mischief subdued beneath worry.

"He brought word that Margaret Clifford has been safely delivered of a son."

Minuette drew in breath. Oh dear. William must be angry.

But Robert had further news. "Guildford and Margaret's marriage has been annulled. And my brother has been charged with treason."

For a second Minuette hoped that Elizabeth would see reason and leave at once. How could she stay when her brother was going to try Robert's brother for treason? But Robert anticipated her. "Please, Elizabeth, we need you now more than ever. It may not be the most festive reception, but please stay."

She looked at him as though leaving had never crossed her mind. "Of course I'll stay. I didn't ride four days to simply turn around. I understand that the welcome must be . . . moderated. But I am quite as anxious to speak to your father as he is to speak with me."

Minuette sighed deeply. This was even worse than being at Framlingham last autumn, for there at least she'd had Carrie to keep her grounded. And Robert had been there as well, ironically, in case the situation got out of hand. Here, he was much more likely to be the one who pushed the situation out of hand. What she wouldn't give for a contingent of royal troops at her command just now.

Elizabeth entered Dudley Castle on the thrill of enthusiasm and the satisfaction of getting away with something. It made the inconveniences of being without her own maids and only the barest possible wardrobe worth it. For dinner that first night she made do with one of the Dudley maids to dress her, but then she sent the fluttering, stammering girl away and had Minuette do her hair and the finishing touches. Her friend looked drawn, but when Elizabeth asked if she wished to skip dinner tonight and rest, she answered, "On no account. I didn't ride all this way to miss the sparks."

"You think there will be sparks?"

"There are always sparks when you and Robert collide. But I was thinking more of the delicate timing. The duke and duchess must be worried for Guildford. They will wonder if you can tell them what William means to do."

"I wish I knew," Elizabeth said. "Surely the trial is just a message. A warning, to offset the baby boy. Likely he'll keep Guildford locked up for some time to come, but William cannot mean to harm the boy for an unwise marriage."

Minuette shrugged. "If unwise is the whole of it."

"What else could it be? Guildford is hardly a mastermind of treasonable activity—he is simply a fool who acts long before he ever thinks. He might have relished snatching at a forbidden royal girl, but no more than that."

"I agree, Guildford is a fool. His father is not."

Elizabeth waited until Minuette inserted the last jeweled pin into her hair, then twisted away to look at her friend. "What are you saying? That Northumberland set it up?"

"Do I need to say it? It's what you've been thinking for months now."

Elizabeth held her eyes, laughing softly and not entirely with amusement. "So you've learned to read my secrets."

"I learned long ago that if I were thinking something, you were sure to have thought of it ages before I did. You're here to find evidence of Northumberland's guilt and present it to William."

"I am here to find evidence of guilt *or* innocence. I have not rushed to judgment, Minuette."

"But you are suspicious. I know you are. Everyone is—William, Lord Rochford—they suspect that Northumberland manipulated Norfolk's downfall and then pressed the advantage for his own family's sake."

When had Minuette become so insightful, and so hard? Elizabeth instinctively argued the opposite side. "By a secret, illegal marriage to a royal? If Northumberland wanted to play that game, it would be for higher stakes." *It would be me he aimed at,* Elizabeth meant, *me and Robert.* Northumberland had hinted as much last year, before Norfolk's downfall.

"Possibly Guildford got ahead of himself, getting Margaret with child before Northumberland could lay the ground for William's permission. Possibly Northumberland has had to make the best of an imperfect situation."

"Possibly, yes. And possibly no. Just because my brother has taught you how to be suspicious doesn't mean this comes to you naturally, Minuette. Deviousness is not your strong suit. Let me survey the field before you rush to attack."

Dinner was a family affair, although with the number of living children the Duchess of Northumberland had borne her husband, that didn't make it a small gathering. All of their offspring were present, save Guildford and the eldest son, John, who remained at Beaulieu with Mary to enforce her house arrest. Several spouses were in attendance as well, including Anne, the daughter of Edward Seymour who was married to John and was thus the Countess of Warwick. Elizabeth knew Lady Warwick better than any of the other women, for Robert's mother usually kept away from court, preferring her private life at home. Elizabeth was also acquainted with Mary Sidney, Robert's sister, who had borne her first son less than a year previous. As Mary Sidney spoke of the infant with her mother, Elizabeth felt a piercing sense of loss that her own mother would never know any grandchildren.

Elizabeth watched Robert's parents at table, looking for signs of their fabled attachment. She found it not in elaborate gestures or fulsome caresses, but in their easy understanding of each other and the comfortable level of their talk—but with all that, there was also a spark between them. The kind of spark that Minuette claimed Elizabeth and Robert had.

No one spoke of Guildford at dinner, but Northumberland did ask for the pleasure of a private audience with Elizabeth in the morning. "Of course," she replied. "I imagine there is much we have to discuss."

They had reached the final course, an array of sugared fruits and candied ginger, when a newcomer entered the dining hall. She was not a servant, that much was clear from her brocaded green dress, but Elizabeth could not easily place her in the family.

Silence descended, broken by Northumberland, who, after a sigh that Elizabeth heard distinctly, said, "We did not know you were coming."

"I did not know I would not be welcome."

"Of course you are always welcome. Come, make your recognition to the Princess of Wales."

Elizabeth felt all eyes on her, except for Robert's. He had gone dead white and was staring at the woman as though she was a particularly unpleasant ghost. Elizabeth remained seated as the woman—who seemed much of an age with her, with round cheeks and fair hair, not uncomely—approached the table and sank into a low curtsey. "Your Highness," she said, something in her tone at odds with her outward submission. "I have waited a long time to meet you."

"And you are?" Since no one, not even Northumberland, seemed eager to give the woman a name.

From her curtsey, the woman raised her eyes and said slyly, "I am Amy Dudley. Lord Robert's wife."

CHAPTER SIXTEEN

ONCE THE WOMEN were safely ensconced at Hatfield, William closeted himself with Dominic and asked for his friend's assessment of the situation. As Dominic outlined Eleanor's claim that Robert Dudley had deliberately detained Minuette while her necklace was poisoned, William paced with slow steps, hands behind his back.

"I assume you've eliminated Eleanor as a suspect?" he asked.

"While Minuette was with Robert Dudley, Eleanor spent the time speaking with her brother in the corridor outside the map room. And unlike his sister, Jonathan Percy is rigidly honest. He would not lie for her."

Especially not to absolve Eleanor of trying to kill Minuette—for Jonathan Percy had once been in love with her. He had even asked William for permission to marry her before the war in France, though Minuette had had the good sense to decline.

"That leaves us with the Duke of Northumberland," William mused aloud, and met Dominic's eyes. His friend looked deeply unhappy.

As for himself, William wasn't sure what he was feeling. Not surprised—no, definitely not surprised. The thought had been lurking in the back of his mind for months, ever since the late Duke of Norfolk's death and the unraveling of any but the slightest circumstantial evidence against him. He had even allowed the new Duke of Norfolk to be racked in the Tower, and the man had confessed nothing. Perhaps because there was nothing to confess. Perhaps Norfolk had not intended treason after all—at least not in the detailed manner implied by Minuette's discovery of the Penitent's Confession.

"Do you think Northumberland could be behind it all?" he asked Dominic now.

"He could be. He has a sincere and burning personal hatred of the Catholics and he'd not balk at bringing down Norfolk. And it's true that Guildford's marriage occurred only after you released the younger Howard from the Tower."

"Retaliation?" William snorted. "Why? Northumberland must have known that would come back on him."

Dominic shrugged. "Of all your nobles, Northumberland is the most likely to act in anger. He lashes out first and considers much later. Maybe he simply gambled on having a tie, however unfortunate, to the royal family."

"On the theory that I would be less likely to punish? He lost that gamble. Guildford stands trial tomorrow. There is little doubt that he is guilty, and the sentence for his crime is death. I think he shall have to be an example to his father." He studied Dominic closely. "If I ask you to attend his execution, will you?"

The answer was not as long in coming as he'd feared. "Yes. But I would prefer to have more evidence of his father's crimes."

"Have at it. The Dudleys are all away from London just now, aren't they?"

"They are."

"Then search their London house. Top to bottom, cracks and

crevices. Interrogate the servants and the neighbors. I want to know everything that's gone on there in the last two years. Just you, though, no one else in this search yet. If you find something . . . well, then we'll see."

When Dominic hesitated, William snapped impatiently, "What?"

"This could be no more than an attempt on Eleanor's part to divert suspicion. She would not hesitate to throw someone else to the wolves in order to distract attention from her own deeds."

"Don't let your personal dislike colour your judgment, Dom. Follow the evidence, wherever it leads. This is about more than a single poisoning and a jealous mistress."

William spent the next hour with his secretary signing letters. He could not have said to whom they were going or what issues they addressed—for all he knew, he was signing away English possession of Calais—because he was consumed with wondering what Dominic might uncover. It was almost a relief when his uncle appeared, asking for a moment of his time in private.

Rochford waited until they were alone before speaking. "I know that you've kept Mistress Wyatt's illness as quiet as possible. I understand why. However, I've discovered some information, from a person who might know what caused the young lady's sudden collapse."

Was this just Rochford trying to guess at secrets? To get him to admit Minuette had been poisoned? William couldn't take the chance and deny it. "Who?"

"A lady in my wife's household."

"Tell me."

"Apparently this young woman has been slipping out at night to meet a man. She came to my wife this morning and confessed— her conscience has been troubled by things this man's been saying. Dropping hints about services rendered to powerful courtiers, and boasting about the promotions he will soon receive. And he's had an unusual amount of ready money. When she asked him about it, he winked and told her gold came easy for a man with the right skills and the discretion not to talk about them."

"And?" William prompted his uncle, who seemed reluctant to continue.

"She saw this man the day of Mistress Wyatt's illness. In the corridor outside her bedchamber. He was coming out of another woman's room and she was jealous for a little, until he told her he was merely delivering a message to the young lady from his patron."

"And do we know who that patron might be?"

"He is a minor functionary in the Duke of Northumberland's London household."

A message—not in writing, but in poison. Here was proof to satisfy even Dominic: the attempt on Minuette's life had indeed been masterminded by Northumberland.

William drew a deep breath and let it out. "If the clerk's tongue is loose enough to hint to his mistress, he should have any number of things to tell us once he's in the Tower."

Rochford nodded in agreement. "Shall I have him arrested?"

"Discreetly. Absolutely no one must know that he has any connection, however tenuous, to Mistress Wyatt. Do I make myself clear?"

"Eminently, Your Majesty. I will see to it." He paused. "Is there anything else you would like me to see to before Guildford Dudley's trial tomorrow?"

"I have it in hand, thank you."

"As you say."

He's getting better at this, William thought, offering counsel without telling me what to do. It pleased him that his uncle was beginning to respect his authority.

Now pray God Dominic found something damning to wrap it up neatly before word leaked to any of Northumberland's supporters.

Dominic returned to Whitehall well after midnight, only to be informed by Harrington that the king had left orders for him to report no matter what hour he returned. He took a few minutes to change his shirt, dusty and creased from hours of prying through wardrobes and checking loose floorboards, then gathered up what he had found.

He was shown to William's private oratory, a small space somewhat plainer than of old but still beautiful with its gilded and carved screens and the lectern upon which rested the pride of William's reign, the Tyndale Bible in English. It was open to the book of Luke and, as William beckoned him in, he said, "Chapter twenty-one—'for these be the days of vengeance.' Even you will agree with that when I tell you what I learned from my uncle this afternoon."

"Which was?"

William glanced at the sheaf of papers Dominic held, but continued with his own news. "I have a man in the Tower being questioned. He was seen in Minuette's rooms the day she was poisoned. He claimed to be delivering a message from his employer, the Duke of Northumberland."

Dominic was seized by an urge to question the man himself—or perhaps not so much question as inflict pain upon.

"Tell me you found something," William added.

"You're not going to like it."

William visibly restrained himself from reaching for the papers Dominic held. "I won't like what?"

For a moment, Dominic hesitated. He knew what would follow from this and he almost did not want to go on. Let the nobility tear itself to pieces, what did he care?

But he cared very much when Minuette was a target. "You know Northumberland hasn't been at his London house for months, not since you sent him away from court. There was little to raise any suspicions, but he left so hastily I suppose he overlooked a few things. I would call them suggestive, rather than conclusive."

William swiped his hand impatiently. "Such as?"

"A partial accounting of monies paid out to individuals indicated only by their initials. Some foreign coins, including French and Dutch. And a vial—an empty vial."

"A vial that could have held monkshood? Where is it?"

"With Harrington. I'll take it to an apothecary tomorrow and see what they can tell me."

"Is that all?"

Dominic sighed. "And a partial letter, begun but never sent."

He handed over the pages and William studied the first one. "This is your handwriting," the king pointed out.

"The original is beneath. A letter in Northumberland's hand, in cipher."

He watched William read, guessing at the emotions his friend was experiencing, the disappointment and fury that Dominic had passed through in the last hours. He had thought himself prepared for whatever his search of Ely Place turned up. He had not been prepared for this: incontrovertible evidence of state treason. Unlike the suspicions against Norfolk last year, this could not be mistaken for anything else.

The letter, as Dominic had said, was only partially complete. It had been addressed to one of the principal ministers in the strongly Protestant Low Countries and it was clearly not the first letter Northumberland had sent.

The duke referenced previous communications throughout the letter, and addressed specific issues that the minister must have raised. Some of it was innocent enough and might occasion no more than a raised eyebrow and a reminder that some phrases could be interpreted in more than one way. But when discussion had turned to Minuette, Northumberland's language became seditious.

> *The girl is a nuisance, nothing more. The king is young, and young men often intend impulsive things. She seeks to take advantage of his infatuation, but I assure you, she has not the late queen's abilities. William need only be persuaded that he can fulfill both his duty and his desire—let him take her to his bed, give her children if he must, but I swear to you, she will never be queen.*
>
> *If all else fails, I will not see England drawn into war over a mistress with pretensions. Better a queen who will be ruled by wisdom than a king who seeks only his own desires.*

William read the last sentence aloud, dropping the words like coals heaped on Northumberland's head. Then he looked at Dominic and said, "He would never countenance Mary on the throne. He may seek to use the Catholics, but he would not turn England back to Rome. Not even to gain a pliable ruler."

"He didn't mean Mary," Dominic countered, staring at his friend's outraged face. "He meant Elizabeth."

"He cannot imagine Elizabeth would usurp my place under any circumstances!"

"If you were dead, and it was between your sisters . . . of course Elizabeth would take the throne."

William let out his breath in a furious hiss. "Doubtless with his own son, Robert, beside her."

"Quite possibly that is his thought."

"Which means Robert is as guilty as his father."

"Possibly." Dominic was always cautious, and he knew that Robert was less prone to wild overreactions than his father. But he held in his mind the image of Robert distracting Minuette during the very hour someone smeared a lethal solution of monkshood on her star pendant.

William flung the damning pages to the floor of his oratory. His face was implacable. "Tomorrow Guildford will be tried and sentenced. He will be executed the day after. As soon as you have seen him die, take a contingent of soldiers. March to Dudley Castle to arrest the Duke of Northumberland and Lord Robert Dudley. I'll have my uncle see to Eleanor's arrest as well. This time, she's not coming out of the Tower until I'm satisfied that she will never again be a threat to Minuette."

Better and better, Dominic thought with satisfaction. And hated himself for relishing Eleanor's downfall.

"I'm just glad the women are well out of it at Hatfield," William mused. "I can only imagine the fireworks that will erupt when Elizabeth learns of Robert's perfidy."

Elizabeth did not sleep at all for fury. She counted it to her credit that she had managed to eke out a few meaningless words to Amy Dudley last night before Robert had escorted his wife out of the hall, more or less commanding her that "you must be weary after your journey—you should not have troubled yourself."

Oh, it was no trouble, Elizabeth knew, watching the way Amy

slipped her hand through Robert's stiff arm. Amy had been awaiting her opportunity for a good many years.

Elizabeth had excused herself almost immediately afterward and spoken to no one, not even Minuette. Her friend was wise enough not to murmur more than, "Well, that was awkward," in a manifestly dry-toned understatement.

It wasn't as though Amy came as any surprise. Elizabeth was well aware of Robert's marriage. In fact, William had attended it five years ago as a fourteen-year-old regented king. Elizabeth herself had been invited, but had been staying with her mother at Blickling Hall at the time. Robert had been only eighteen at his marriage, Amy not even quite that. Elizabeth, no matter how hard she'd tried since, had never been able to forget Lord Burghley's cynical statement that theirs was "a carnal marriage." True, Amy was the only child of a wealthy gentleman. True, she would inherit a fortune and lands when both her parents died. But considering how ambitious Northumberland was for all of his multitude of children, Robert must have pressed hard to marry Amy for nothing more than love alone. Or at least lust. Elizabeth didn't know which of the two motives she preferred.

Not that Robert seemed particularly attached to Amy any longer. In the last three years he had hardly been away from court, and Elizabeth had heard that Amy often resided with her parents rather than at the rented manor she had once shared with her husband. And in five years of marriage, there had not been even a hint of a pregnancy. Whether because Amy was barren or because Robert could not be bothered to try (Elizabeth rather hoped it was that) or, most likely, because he had learned greater ambitions and knew that annulling or divorcing a wife who had given him children would complicate matters.

None of that matters, Elizabeth told herself. *Not any longer.* It was one thing to know about Amy Dudley in abstract—it was quite another to meet her in the flesh. She was not as elegant as Elizabeth, not as clever or learned, not as wealthy, not as privileged, nowhere near as desirable as herself in any way . . . but she was real from the top of her blond head to the tips of her squared-off fingers and little feet. And in the eyes of God, this very real woman was Robert's *wife*.

If Elizabeth could have stormed out of Dudley Castle, she would have. But she would not be driven from any house by a mere gentlewoman married to a fifth son. She was the royal guest here. It was for Amy Dudley to leave.

Which point she made clear when she found Robert leaning against the wall across from her chamber door. He looked as though he'd been there for some time.

"Don't," Elizabeth snapped. "I have a meeting with your father. You are not welcome."

"I didn't tell her you would be here. I swear it."

"Clearly she has learned the Dudley gift for scavenging information."

"Elizabeth—"

"If she's here to meet me, she has done so. I will not see her again. If that is her aim, she may as well be on her way at once."

"I've told her to be ready to depart at noon."

"You go with her."

She turned to walk away but Robert gripped her arm and swung her around.

"How dare you?" She slapped his hand away.

"Don't do this, Elizabeth." More gently, he let his fingers rest on her cheek. "Please."

"How can you think to touch me with your wife in the same house?"

"Because I have no wife in any sense that matters. I was a fool to marry Amy—I was young and hot-blooded and a damned idiot, and every hour since then I have regretted it. I touch you because you are the only woman in the world who matters to me. You know that."

"How long since you've been in her bed?" How she hated herself for needing to know.

"More than two years. And I will not go back, not ever. Not while I live and love you, Elizabeth."

"If you love me, you will do as I ask. Take your wife away from here. When I want to see you again, I will send for you. Until then, you would be wise not to press me." She hated herself for softening, but damn Robert! He could always do that to her.

Robert knew when he had won. He dropped his hand and kissed hers. "I am, as ever, yours to command."

She hoped his father would be as accommodating, but she doubted it. If Robert resembled a stream, slipping swiftly and noiselessly around any obstacle in its path, then Northumberland was a mountain, looming and unmovable.

At least Amy Dudley's unexpected appearance had given her the upper hand. Northumberland began apologizing the moment the two of them were alone in his study. The paneled space was cozily hung with tapestries, and rich rugs covered the plank floor. Elizabeth was surprised at the number of books in view—though she knew Northumberland had gone to great lengths to educate his children in humanist principles, she had always thought of the duke as less interested. A reminder that one cannot always judge by the exterior.

"My daughter-in-law should have known better," Northumberland said gruffly. "But like most women, Amy has more temper than sense."

"Most women?" Elizabeth asked, thinking it was an apt description of Northumberland himself.

"Your Highness, of course, is a model of all that is wise and measured."

"I am not here to discuss your son's wife—at least, not this particular wife. I am rather more interested in Guildford and my cousin, Margaret. Did you introduce them intending an assault on royal privilege?"

He shook his head. "It wasn't like that, Your Highness. I did ensure they met, and yes, I had it in mind that perhaps Guildford would make the girl a good husband. But she was only fourteen! I thought I had plenty of time to speak to the king."

"Youthful passion," Elizabeth remarked drily.

"My sons are not always temperate in their loves."

She would not let him turn this back on her, nor discomfit her with sly allusions to Robert. "When one threatens royal pre-rogative, one must pay the price. If you expect me to plead for him to my brother, I am not particularly inclined to do so. Guild-ford was entirely in the wrong."

Northumberland flushed; he was not adept at hiding his feel-ings. "What harm could it do? Guildford is no threat to the king or the succession. He's had the marriage annulled and the baby declared a bastard."

"If that were an unshakable answer, then the Catholics would not be constantly threatening us with my half sister, Mary."

"This isn't about religion!" Moderating his voice, the duke said, "Your Highness, you love your brother. What would you do to protect him from the consequences of his own follies?"

"Are you implying that your king is foolish?"

"No man is perfect—certainly not a man in love."

Elizabeth stood up in a swirl of silken outrage. "You would be wise to keep your opinions of my brother to yourself. As to other matters—I did not come here to discuss Guildford. I am interested in larger concerns. We will meet again when you have had a chance to grow calm and consider your future. I would ponder deeply on any actions from your past that you might wish to confess. Actions having to do with the Howard family, perhaps."

"Norfolk?" Northumberland regarded her suspiciously. "You can't imagine I was part of that Catholic plot, Your Highness!"

"No. But I can imagine very easily that you could manufacture a Catholic plot in order to destroy your enemies."

She could not tell if his blank expression was surprise or calculation. Perhaps he had learned something from Robert. With a false and flattering smile, Elizabeth added, "I plan to remain at Dudley Castle for a week at least. We will speak again when you are prepared to be honest."

If she managed to bring Northumberland to confession, perhaps the sting of Amy Dudley would ease. And perhaps William would not be so furious with her when he found out where she had gone.

It had been a long time since anything had taken Minuette's mind off her own knot of troubles, but the eruption of Robert's wife on the scene had done just that. For a woman of middling height and no outstanding beauty, Amy Dudley had commanded the eye and the attention of every person in the hall last night— none more so than Elizabeth. Minuette had never seen her friend so miserably fixed on a single human being in her life. It was as though a demon had walked into the room.

She had known better than to make Elizabeth talk about it, though she did desperately wish that Carrie was here so she could talk it over with someone. When Minuette rose the next morning, she let herself gossip a little with the Dudley maid who came to help her dress.

"Is it usual for Lord Robert's wife to accompany him to Dudley Castle?"

"No, miss," the girl said as she laced one of Minuette's periwinkle sleeves to her overdress. "She's more likely to be here when he isn't. 'Course, Lord Robert is hardly ever here hisself."

Because he's at court, making certain Elizabeth doesn't have occasion to forget him, Minuette thought cynically. She'd always been a bit cynical where Robert was concerned. Not because she doubted his regard for Elizabeth, but because she doubted its purity. Would he have been anywhere near as enamoured if Elizabeth were not a princess royal of England? For certain he would not be as patiently loyal. He liked women too well, in all the shaded meanings of that term.

"What is she like, Lord Robert's wife?" Minuette asked curiously. It wasn't as though she expected to ever be in Northumberland's household again—it wouldn't harm her to get a reputation for nosiness.

The maid was happy to reply. "She don't put on airs, but it's her as has the money, and she don't let Lord Robert forget it. To be sure, I remember when she first came here, after the wedding— very sweet, they were, he liked quoting foreign poetry to her. Italian, I think. I daresay she's had no poetry from him for ages now."

The maid stepped back and adjusted a creased seam on Minuette's blue velvet stomacher. "Certainly no poetry last night," the maid sniffed. "I weren't serving in that wing, but they do say you could hear them yelling a long ways off."

"Where is their wing?"

"The family's in the first section of Sharrington range. But if it's her you want to see, best hurry. Lord Robert's taking her home straightaway."

Is he indeed? Minuette thought. I think I shall have to simply barge in and introduce myself to Amy Dudley.

Because the maid's phrase about Italian poetry was fluttering in her skull like a nervous butterfly.

It was easy enough to find the chamber Amy Dudley had been assigned to (and which, incidentally, it appeared she had slept in alone—there were no signs of a man's presence), for there was a banging and general noise level that Minuette was long familiar with from serving the late Queen Anne. It meant the woman in question was out of temper and letting it show.

Minuette knocked on the frame of the half-open door. "May I be of some assistance?" she asked. Doing what, she wasn't sure. Her talents ran more to flirting for information and writing flattering letters that appeared to promise without actually promising. She supposed she could pack dresses if forced to do so.

Amy whirled and eyed her carefully. "You're with *her,* aren't you? No one bothered to give me your name last night."

"Genevieve Wyatt," she supplied, ignoring Amy's impertinent reference to Elizabeth. *She is Robert's wife, after all,* Minuette reminded herself. And it must have taken all Amy Dudley's nerve to walk into that room last night and face down the Tudor princess who had ensnared her husband's heart. "I simply wished to introduce myself and ask if there was anything you needed."

"Yes, there is something I need." Amy snapped at the two maids packing, "You may go." When they had gone, Amy shut the door behind them and said to Minuette, "I need to know how far things have gone between Robert and her."

The way she avoided saying Elizabeth's name reminded Minuette forcibly of Mary Tudor. She had spent some weeks with her last year and even after all these years Mary still referred to Anne Boleyn as "the person" or "the woman."

"I assure you, your husband has not compromised your honour." Which wasn't precisely true. To be precisely true, Minuette would have had to answer, *Robert hasn't slept with Elizabeth and never will, because she is far too smart to allow that to happen. But no doubt he's slept with any number of more willing women, and he would bed Elizabeth this very minute if she allowed it.*

Sometimes it was best not to be precisely honest.

Amy's lips tightened, as though she had heard every unspoken version of Minuette's thoughts, and she sniffed. "He'll never get out of this marriage. My family will see to it. My father is quite an important landowner."

Minuette thought pityingly, *And Elizabeth's brother is the King of England. Care to wager who would win if they went against each other?* But she let Amy rant, as surely the woman had come here to Dudley Castle to do. As she couldn't do it to Elizabeth's face, she might as well spill it all to Elizabeth's dear friend.

"She thinks he's so faithful, so undyingly loyal to the romance of loving a woman he cannot have. That's how little she knows Robert. He could not be faithful if his life depended on it. He confined himself to my bed alone for no more than a month after our marriage before he required other women as well. Does she believe she is different?"

No, Minuette thought, *but she manages not to think about that part. And Robert is careful not to flaunt his women before her. As apparently he has not been with you.*

"They're not all serving women, either," Amy challenged. "There was a court woman, he was quite infatuated with her for a time. He even brought her into our home."

Minuette startled, and Amy laughed bitterly. "No, he's not quite that wretched, he didn't know I would be there. I mostly live near my parents, so give him his due, when he came waltzing into Kenilworth with his court whore, he was quite as shocked to see me as I was to see them. Not that it prevented him from sending me away without even pretending to be kind. The servants say Robert kept this woman with him a whole month. I wonder what he told your mistress about where he was while he played house with a woman neither his wife nor his precious princess."

The same butterflies that had alarmed at the phrase "Italian poetry" were winging madly now in Minuette's skull. I don't want to know this, she thought, but she also knew it was too late to back out now.

"Did you see this woman?" Minuette's voice sounded distant and flat in her own ears.

"I saw her. Proud, she was, though dressed no better than me. Dark colours for a dark countenance, I remember that."

"How old was she? What did she look like?"

Amy paused. "Don't tell me you're one of his conquests! If you're the jealous type, then you should keep well away from Robert."

Summoning up her most imperious tone, Minuette said, "I am not jealous, and I have never looked twice at your husband in that manner. But it is of great importance that you tell me details of this woman's appearance."

Cowed, Amy muttered, "She was younger than me. Eighteen or nineteen, maybe? Dark, like I said. Not as dark as Robert, but nothing like the princess either. Brown eyes, she had, and straight brown hair to her waist. Shorter than you, and more generous in her figure."

Minuette longed to close her eyes and curse, but she had one more question. "When did Robert spend that month with her at Kenilworth?"

"Late winter two years ago. Almost spring—March, I think it was."

She did close her eyes then, though she kept her swearing silent. Alyce de Clare had spent four weeks away from court in March of 1553—Alyce, with brown eyes and brown hair to her waist—and less than four months later she had been with child at the time of her sudden death.

Robert was the man she'd been searching for. The man who'd gotten Alyce with child. The man who'd used her to spy on Queen Anne—using a cipher contained in an Italian poetry book. The man—the link—to the fraudulent Penitent's Confession and the subsequent downfall of the late Duke of Norfolk.

Robert was the traitor.

CHAPTER SEVENTEEN

"S HE'S SAFELY IN the Tower?" William asked his uncle. Rochford had just returned from arresting Eleanor on undefined charges. It would, in fact, be a tricky business charging her, as William did not want to make widely known the attack on Minuette. Probably Eleanor would end up being charged with treason. If she was connected to Northumberland in any way, that charge would stick.

"She's there," Rochford answered. "Did not take it well."

William snorted. "She wouldn't. Eleanor is the original example of an utterly selfish point of view. She sees things only as they affect her."

"Rather like a king, in fact." Rochford spoke so drily that William had to puzzle out whether it was a jest. His uncle didn't often joke, but this time he quirked his lips in a grin.

"Unless Eleanor has a government and an army to back up her wishes, then her wishes will never reign supreme." William paced the length of the privy chamber and back again. "No word from Dominic yet?"

"He only left yesterday, Your Majesty. Even riding hard, he won't reach Dudley Castle until sometime tomorrow."

"I know. I just hate sitting here while others do my work for me."

"No one can do your work for you—that's rather the point of being king. But I know it can be chafing to feel as though others are running around and you are sitting still. Believe me, sitting still can often be the hardest work of all. It all depends on the men you have doing the running around."

What William really wanted to do was ride to Hatfield— ostensibly to tell Elizabeth in person about the Dudleys' perfidy, actually to put his arms around Minuette and assure her that she was safe now. But he knew that would have to wait until Dominic had the Dudley men safely under arrest. William could not risk Elizabeth doing something rash and finding a way to warn Robert of what was coming.

Could it be that he didn't trust his own sister?

Not where her heart was concerned, he realized uneasily. Elizabeth might convince herself that she knew better than the evidence, and then heaven only knew what action she would take to prove it.

The door was flung wide and Rochford exclaimed, "What are you doing!" before even William could protest. His guards had their weapons drawn in an instant but William recognized the man, breathing heavily as he bowed behind them.

"Let him through," he commanded, wondering what on earth had brought John Dee to court in this state.

"Your Majesty." Dee bowed. "I've come straight from Dudley Castle and there's something you need to know."

"What?"

Dee was blunt. "Princess Elizabeth arrived at Dudley Castle four days ago with her friend, Mistress Wyatt. I do not think it wise for them to remain there."

Caught completely off guard, William couldn't decide whether to laugh in disbelief or swear. "Then why in heaven's name did you leave them there and come away yourself, Doctor?"

"Have you ever tried to persuade Her Highness to a course she did not wish? Princess Elizabeth declined to leave at my suggestion, and I could hardly force her to do so. But when I realized that you did not know of her visit to Dudley Castle, I thought it prudent to alert you as quickly as possible."

William looked at his uncle, who seemed—for once—utterly at a loss for words. "Lord Rochford, we shall have to send an army after Dominic. Raise five thousand men as quickly as you can and send them after me."

"Where are you going?"

"To Dudley Castle." William turned back to John Dee. "You did well, Doctor. Perhaps now would be a good time for you to terminate your connection to the Dudley family and come to my court instead."

"Perhaps it would. But the first matter is retrieving your women." Dee said it as though he knew that William's urgency concerned Minuette even more than his sister.

Not that he wouldn't make Northumberland pay for his insolence with Elizabeth. No one touched a Tudor and lived to tell about it.

Dominic pressed hard on the ride from London and made Dudley Castle late on the third day. Reining up outside the village, he studied the castle looming on its medieval motte above, the fading daylight and damp mist lending it a desolate air. The castle had a perimeter wall, quite low, and the moat had been filled in, but this was no longer a defensible structure so much as it was a family home. Why was he thinking such things anyway? He had only five men in his immediate party, including Harrington, and though he expected anger at his news, he certainly did not anticipate violence.

Still, he kept a wary eye out as they rode up the motte. Men bearing the Northumberland badge with its azure lion greeted them a fair distance before the entrance. They spoke politely, no doubt recognizing Dominic's standard—gold with lions similar to Northumberland, and also the crimson discs distinctive to the Courtenays—but recognition did not buy them easy entrance.

"We have orders," the spokesman told Dominic. "You are welcome, my lord duke, but the others will have to wait here."

Dominic shrugged and dismounted. "Fair enough."

Before Harrington could protest—whatever that might look like in a man so taciturn—Dominic added, "But my own man, at least, comes with me."

The guard, relieved not to have had more of an argument, readily acquiesced. Harrington strode a pace behind, his eyes roaming constantly. Something was definitely odd in the Dudley household. Dominic wasn't surprised that the duke knew he was coming—he hadn't traveled in secrecy and had ridden straight through the heart of Northumberland's power base—but he was troubled at Northumberland's attempts to control the number of men coming into his home.

Still, he was allowed to retain his sword and dagger, and Harrington's size alone made him a formidable weapon in his own right. And Northumberland was not so stupid as to offer real harm to the king's closest friend.

The duke himself met them in the inner courtyard. Dominic could see the powerful figure waiting for them as they crossed beneath the Triple Gate. Even from a distance Northumberland radiated tension. He stood alone—no wife or family to soften his greeting. *I don't think I'll be asked to stay,* Dominic thought wryly.

"Exeter," Northumberland said gruffly when they were in

speaking distance. Dominic stopped a good ten feet away from the duke, and inclined his head in greeting. "What news do you bring?"

"Would you prefer to withdraw somewhere more private?" Dominic asked. Though there was no family about, the courtyard held plenty of servants and more than a handful of armed men bearing Dudley badges.

"I would prefer to hear your news on my feet and at this moment."

Dominic delivered his news, more or less truthfully. "Guildford has been found guilty of felonious treason against the king's own body. He has been sentenced to death."

Actually, Guildford was already dead. Dominic had attended his execution the day before he left London. In his memory he held a picture of Guildford's body, being borne away with his severed head. But William and Rochford had decided it would be wiser that Northumberland not know of his son's execution just yet, in order to reduce the likelihood of his resistance to arrest. Assuming one of the duke's own sources in London hadn't already brought the news.

A muscle along his jawline twitched, but Northumberland did not move otherwise. "I suppose the king wants me to beg before he'll commute the sentence."

"The king will not commute the sentence, Your Grace. I'm here to take you to London to answer charges laid against you personally."

"You plan to take me with half a dozen men?" Northumberland huffed a bitter laugh. "You've grown as arrogant as the boy king, Exeter, if you think you can bring me in on your own."

"I have a half a dozen men outside your gates—but another half a hundred two miles off. Surely you know that."

"I know it."

"Your Grace, if you will submit yourself and your son Robert to my custody, the king will be inclined to deal generously with the rest of your family."

"Robert?" Northumberland's brow creased. "What has he to do with this?"

"I have a warrant for Robert as well as for you. The charges will be explained in London."

The duke snorted. "Too bad for you that Robert isn't here. My son rode off to Kenilworth ten days ago. Afraid you've missed him."

Damn it. "Not for long. Don't make this harder than it needs to be. You have no position from which to bargain, Your Grace. We have hard evidence. You must come to London and answer it."

"I don't know what evidence you think you have, you jumped-up son of a traitor, but you are dead wrong when you claim that I have no bargaining position." Northumberland no longer bothered to pretend politeness. "I really thought you must have known, I thought even that arrogant young brat of a king couldn't be so careless as to mislay something precious to him. But neither of you have any idea, do you?"

"No idea of what?" Dominic's tension increased. He did not like surprises.

Northumberland barked an order at a guard. "Fetch the younger one."

Dominic's training as a soldier stood him in good stead, allowing him to control his tumultuous thoughts by focusing on the physical details of the courtyard. As though taking notes of enemy positions, he assessed the layout of the domestic wings and outbuildings. His uneasiness increased as he realized that, just as the family were not to be seen, neither were any female servants. Only men were visible, many with the hard faces and powerful figures of fighting men.

First thing he'd do when he got back to his camp was send out scouts to discover if Northumberland had troops within twenty miles of here. Fifty royal guards would not be enough to bring in the duke if he were prepared to resist in battle.

Dominic tried not to let curiosity about what—or who—the young one might be, but he recognized that his body was taut with uncertainty. He was a soldier first, and he couldn't fight what he didn't understand. Still, he had come here to arrest Northumberland, and he wouldn't leave until he'd done so.

That surety sustained him right up to the moment when the guard reappeared escorting the person he'd been sent to fetch. Young. Golden-haired. Female.

Minuette.

Dominic only realized he'd stopped breathing when his chest began to hurt. He took a series of quick sharp breaths—as much to control his fury as to fill his lungs—and said, "What do you think you are doing?" He wasn't sure if he was speaking to Northumberland or Minuette herself. How the hell had she gotten from Hatfield to Dudley Castle?

"What do you think she's doing here?" Northumberland jeered, jerking his head to the guard, who brought Minuette to stand next to the duke. "This girl goes nowhere alone."

God and all the angels in heaven . . . "You are holding Princess Elizabeth hostage?" Dominic asked in disbelief. How had Northumberland tricked the princess here from Hatfield? What was Minuette thinking, riding across country after nearly dying from poison? Dominic didn't know if he wanted to hug her or shake her. He would have done either gladly so long as he could reach her.

But though no weapons had been drawn, they didn't need to be. Northumberland had made his stand. Misguided, impulsive, rashly hotheaded, and ultimately suicidal, but a stand nonetheless.

"The princess came willingly at my request. Well, let's not mince words, she came for Robert and to spite her brother. Elizabeth's got Henry's stubbornness and Anne's willfulness, and she wanted to show that she is her own mistress. And now she is my bargaining point."

"You'll die for this, Dudley. And threatening the king's sister will only ensure that you take your family down with you."

"I won't bargain with you." Northumberland was dismissive. "Go back to your half a hundred men and don't return without the king. I will deal only with William."

Dominic flicked his eyes over Minuette in assessment. She appeared unharmed and not at all frightened—more irritated than anything. She nodded at his unspoken query and said, "Elizabeth is perfectly well. You needn't worry about us. Except for the inconvenience of not being allowed to leave, we have been treated with the utmost courtesy." Her words were laden with sarcasm, and Dominic almost smiled. He could imagine Elizabeth's temper. He hoped she was taking her fury out on everyone inside.

"I'll be back," he promised Minuette. Then, repeated, to Northumberland as a warning. "I will be back."

"I count on it."

Harrington didn't speak until they were remounting their horses outside the gates. "Send to the king?"

"As fast as a man can ride."

Minuette watched Elizabeth pace, reminding her of William in her controlled agitation. The simple cut of the princess's dark green overdress and the lack of any jewels save a single ruby ring on her right hand enhanced the unreal nature of the situation. Elizabeth looked almost as though she were dressed for battle, and the impression was heightened by the intensity of her voice. "Tell me again what they said. Every word."

She had already gone over it three times, but Minuette complied. "Northumberland said you are his bargaining point. He told Dominic not to return until he had William with him, that the king is the only one with whom he'll bargain."

"But what is he bargaining for? If he wanted to avoid arrest, using me to bargain with is a wretchedly bad decision."

"He's bargaining for Guildford's life, I imagine. Whatever we may think of Northumberland, he loves his family. If he's going down, he will want to save them."

Elizabeth shook her head. "Who could have guessed it would come to this? A royal guest, guarded by Englishmen and not allowed to even leave this room unless one of my brother's peers permits it."

Minuette agreed it was disconcerting. They had gone to bed last night in adjoining chambers as favoured guests, accorded all the courtesies of such, and then awakened this morning to a softly spoken guard who had barred the outer doors and forbade them from leaving. Elizabeth had laughed in disbelief and moved forward regardless—until the man drew his sword. He pointed it not at her (Northumberland's men were loyal but not suicidal) but at Minuette.

Elizabeth had laughed at that a little as they dressed and waited for Northumberland to tell them what was happening. "They think of you as disposable, valuable only insofar as I would not want you hurt. If they knew what William would do to the man who pointed a sword at you!"

Now Elizabeth let out a frustrated sigh and whirled around,

skirts swirling. "This is maddening! Why doesn't Northumberland tell us something? I suppose I'm glad I sent Robert away before he got caught up in this, but if he were here, he would make sure I was kept informed."

Minuette had said nothing yet of what she'd learned from Amy. But perhaps it was time. "Elizabeth, will you sit down? There's something I need to tell you."

"What?"

"Please, sit down."

"Oh, all right." Elizabeth dropped elegantly into a chair. "What is it?" Her expression was quizzical, curious, but not alarmed. Minuette heard the patter of rain on the mullioned windows and for a moment considered not saying anything at all. But she owed Elizabeth more than that.

"The day I was poisoned, Robert asked Eleanor to fetch me to a private conversation with him. It was . . . well, it was very odd. He knows—or at least guesses well—about William's intentions toward me. Robert warned me off, Elizabeth. He told me to walk away from William, or that someone might see to it that I had to."

"Robert has superb political instincts," Elizabeth said dismissively. "He's only telling you what my uncle would like to say. No doubt Robert doesn't want to see you hurt by less scrupulous men."

"Are you certain that Robert is any more scrupulous?"

Elizabeth's eyes narrowed unpleasantly. "What are you implying?"

"I spoke to Amy Dudley before Robert took her away." Minuette hesitated, unsure exactly how much to tell Elizabeth. But her friend was not a fool.

"Women?"

"Yes."

"Do you think I do not know that Robert has women, Minuette? It means nothing. All men have women. William had Eleanor, Dominic . . . well, he keeps his own counsel but I guarantee he's had his women."

Aimée kissing him passionately in a darkened corridor in France— "That's not the point, Elizabeth. Not the pertinent point. Robert has had one particular woman. Amy met her, by accident, when Robert brought her to Kenilworth thinking the house was empty. Robert sent Amy away and kept this woman there for a month. 'Playing house,' as Amy put it. He didn't even trouble to lie to his wife about it."

Elizabeth's face was set and furious. Probably as furious with Minuette as with Robert. Too bad. This she had to hear all the way through.

"It was Alyce de Clare. Amy described her perfectly—brown eyes, waist-length brown hair, impertinent face. And the month that Robert had this woman at Kenilworth is the same month Alyce was got with child."

Elizabeth stared at her, and Minuette suddenly realized her friend wasn't shocked. Hurt, yes. Betrayed and disappointed. But not shocked. "You're saying Robert was behind the Penitent's Confession." It was not a question.

"I did not find it until after he showed up at Framlingham. He asked me where I thought it might be, he pressed me to think . . . and I told him precisely where to hide it by telling him where I was looking next. He knew, Elizabeth. I don't know why, what possible motivation he could have had, but Robert is the one who used Alyce to spy and spread the rumours about your brother's birth."

"Robert is devoted to the Protestant cause. He would never have orchestrated a Catholic rebellion."

"He wasn't creating a Catholic rebellion. He was creating the *illusion* of one, in order to crush the Howards and the rest of the Catholics. But surely he was not in it alone."

Elizabeth laughed bitterly. "His father. Yes, this has Northumberland's brutal touch to it. Everyone knows he would do anything for his family . . . it appears Robert feels the same way."

Minuette went to her friend and knelt so she could look into her eyes. "Are you all right?"

Elizabeth's expression was bleak, but her eyes were dry and her voice, when she answered, dispassionate. "Perfectly all right. I only wish we didn't have to wait the week or so it will take William to show up here in order to get this sorted. I am anxious to discover what Northumberland and his son will have to say from the confines of the Tower."

Torn between wanting to spend every moment watching Dudley Castle—as though his attention alone would ensure Minuette and Elizabeth were kept safe—and needing to do something, Dominic's desire for movement won out. His men could watch the castle as well as he could. Besides, he had to get to Robert Dudley before Robert could go to ground. And he didn't want to face William without having at least one member of the Dudley family under arrest.

He left Harrington behind to be his eyes and ears and voice with the armed men under his command and took a dozen men with him to Kenilworth. It was a long day of riding made harder by slashing autumn rain, and, with the shortening days, they would have to wait until tomorrow to make the return ride to Dudley Castle. Which meant spending a night in the same room with Robert Dudley, for there was no chance he would let Robert out of his sight.

Kenilworth was calm when they arrived and Dominic announced himself to a steward. The household looked a bit slap-dash on the surface, and he suspected the servants were underpaid and lived more on promises of Robert's connections than actual loyalty.

He was escorted into a solar paneled in dark wood and furnished pleasantly, where a woman rose to greet him. "Lord Exeter, it's an honour. My husband didn't tell me we'd be having guests."

So this was Amy Dudley. Dominic's immediate thought was to wonder what on earth had possessed Robert to marry her. She didn't seem the sort of woman who would interest the quick-witted, devilishly clever, sarcastic-tongued Robert Dudley—which meant she didn't appear to be anything like Elizabeth Tudor. Amy Dudley was rather short, dressed well if a bit showily in yellow brocade, with fair hair and penetrating eyes that seemed locked into a permanent suspicious gaze. Though he could hardly blame her for that. Any woman married to Robert Dudley who wasn't suspicious was an idiot.

He bowed in greeting. "I had hoped to speak to your husband alone."

He heard Robert clattering down the stairs through the open doorway and speaking even as he entered the solar. "What's wrong, Courtenay? I know better than to think you're here for a courtesy visit."

Amy looked between them, and Dominic repeated, "It would be best if we spoke privately."

"Why?" Amy asked. "Do you bring news from the princess?"

"Amy," Robert said warningly.

"I do not," Dominic answered. "This is a political matter."

Was that fear in Amy's eyes? In that instant, Dominic realized that she was more than just a jealous wife, touchy about her honour and position. She was truly, desperately, in love with her husband.

"Go on, Amy," Robert said. She went without protest, but shot one, troubled glance back at Dominic before closing the door.

"What's going on, Courtenay?"

"I have a warrant for your arrest, signed by the king himself. My orders are to return you to London at once to answer the charges laid against you."

"What charges are those?"

"They will be read out to you in London."

"In the Tower, you mean."

"Yes."

"So you don't mind arresting a man without knowing the details."

"I know the details. I am not at liberty to speak of them." He would not let Robert goad him into an argument. For all he knew, Amy Dudley was listening at the door.

Robert rubbed his hands through his hair, obviously thinking. "Well then, I suppose I'd best pack for London."

"My men will do that for you. You are not to leave my sight. Which means, I'm afraid, you will not be going directly to London."

"Why not?"

Could it be Robert had not known of his father's plans for Elizabeth? Impossible to tell. Dominic would wager Robert's feelings for Elizabeth—however complicated by politics and ambition—were genuine, and it was hard to credit a man in love with an act that threatened her safety.

"I came here from Dudley Castle, where I was sent to arrest your father."

"I suppose he didn't accept that easily."

"He didn't accept it at all. Your father is holding hostages: Elizabeth and Minuette. He has said he will bargain for their release, but only directly with William. So you and I are returning to Dudley Castle to talk some sense into your father. If, that is, you are concerned with Elizabeth's situation."

Robert had gone very still, and Dominic was as sure as he could be that it was the stillness of shock. So one—minor—point in his favour. "What the hell is he thinking?"

"Your brother, Guildford, has been found guilty of treason and sentenced to death. I imagine your father is thinking of bargaining for his life. He should know better." And not only because Guildford was already dead. Dominic took a step, forcing Robert to face him directly. "If you do not want a summary conviction of your own, you will come to Dudley Castle and help us get the women out of there without harm."

A most unusual expression crossed Robert's face. He looked as though he were about to protest something Dominic had said. But then a ghost of his usual mocking grin replaced the more serious look. "The women, yes. I'll wager my father has no idea that Elizabeth is not the truest prize. Detaining his sister will rouse William's ego, no doubt—but it's Minuette he will kill to protect."

"If she is so much as scratched—" Dominic could not go on calmly.

"Elizabeth will see to it she isn't," Robert said dismissively. "Frankly, Courtenay, I'm not so worried about the women as I am about my father. He has badly underestimated his hostages. It's much more likely that Elizabeth will find a way to gut him than that he will be able to use her to his own advantage. And because he is my father—" His lips twisted. "I would rather he not be gutted, so yes—I will ride with you to Dudley Castle and do my best to talk sense into him."

"You'll be in my custody," Dominic warned.

"I understand. When all this is over, there are any number of questions that need answers. I'll gladly spill my knowledge once we're in London."

Under arrest, under threat of torture and charges of treason, and still Robert made Dominic feel that he was the one pulling all the strings. Would he never get a handle on the enigma of this man?

CHAPTER EIGHTEEN

Dᴏᴍɪɴɪᴄ ᴀɴᴅ Rᴏʙᴇʀᴛ were still five miles from Dudley Castle when they were met by Harrington, riding alone and clearly relieved to see Dominic.

"Damn it," Dominic said softly, and spurred ahead to talk without being overheard. "What's happened?"

"Northumberland had troops in hold to the northwest. They swept down as soon as you had ridden out yesterday and pushed us back. No fighting, but they're standing their ground around the castle."

"How many?"

"Three thousand, give or take. They're setting up camp in a ring around the base of the motte."

Damn, damn, and damn. He should have anticipated this. Not that it would have changed his decisions—he'd needed to go after Robert, and his fifty men would have been outnumbered and forced to withdraw whether he were in command or not.

"You've sent more riders to the king? He'll need to muster troops."

"I did."

"Then let's make an encampment of our own and wait." Which he hated with every bone in his soldier's body.

Fortunately, the wait was nowhere near as long as he'd antici-pated. Before they'd been in their small, makeshift camp an hour—Robert in a tent alone, with four men guarding it—he heard the sound of hooves drumming the earth at the same moment his outer scout shouted, "Riders! Bearing the royal standard!"

Dominic was prepared to disbelieve it, although he was on his feet and running to the scout. Though the last of the day's light was nearly gone, within seconds he spotted the standard for himself—crimson and azure, lions and lilies—and wondered how the hell William had gotten here so fast.

William swung down from his horse before it had stopped moving and jerked his head to Dominic to walk. He wore a brigandine of leather, riveted to small sections of plate inside, to protect his torso. Clearly he had known he was riding into openly hostile territory. Dominic followed him away from the chaos of what looked to be at least four hundred mounted men until they could speak without shouting.

"Situation?" William demanded.

"Robert Dudley is under arrest and held under guard in the camp. He had left Dudley Castle before I arrived; I arrested him at Kenilworth. William, you should know—"

"Northumberland has the women," he cut in grimly. "I know."

"How?"

"John Dee got himself away from Dudley Castle as soon as they appeared and came to warn me. Not two hours later I had another warning. You met that man my sister picked up in France—Walsingham?"

Dominic nodded. William continued, "He was at Hatfield when Elizabeth left. He was already suspicious, and then Minu-ette's maid came to him and confessed their destination. I'm glad she at least has the sense God granted her."

It was unclear whether he meant Minuette or Carrie, but it was manifestly clear that William was furious with his sister. "They're untouched, Will," Dominic said. "I saw Minuette less than forty-eight hours ago. She swore Elizabeth is perfectly all right. Northumberland threatens, but he would never harm women."

"Do you think so?" William looked at him with a flat but dangerous expression, a gleam in his blue eyes that made Dominic wary. "I have a man in the Tower who has confessed to daubing monkshood on Minuette's pendant. This man is from Northumberland's household."

Dominic went still, and realized that despite his wish for vengeance, he had not wanted it to be Northumberland. He rather liked Robert Dudley.

"What does Northumberland ask?" William continued.

"To speak to you. He was unwilling to bargain with me."

"Bargain?" William gave a shout of not at all humourous laughter. "Oh, I'll bargain. Come to London so I can have his head, or wait for me to raze his castle—and his family—to the ground. That's the bargain he'll get from me."

Just what he needed—Dominic thought—two hotheaded and impulsive men to control. "Northumberland's castle is ringed by at least three thousand men, Will."

"I ordered Rochford to muster five thousand to march behind me. It shouldn't take more than a week to get them here. But I would prefer to end this before then, so let's go."

"Now?"

"My sister and my beloved are being kept from me, Dom. Can you think of a better time to go?"

Yes, Dominic wanted to say, *when there's more light than just a quarter moon in the sky.* But Dudley Castle was only two miles away on a straight road. He sighed. "I'll get you a fresh horse."

"And bring Robert. I want all my enemies where I can see them tonight."

William set a hard pace to Dudley Castle, leading Dominic and Robert and two dozen armed guards. Dominic had argued for more, but William merely looked at Robert and said, "Do you think it likely your father will try to kill me at first sight?"

"No, Your Majesty."

"Nor do I. If he kills me, he has no one to barter with."

Dominic had shaken his head, but kept his mouth shut after William said he would continue to wear the brigandine. That should stop an errant arrow, at least.

The party slowed as an outrider approached them from the encampment. The man had the hardened face of a professional soldier. "Your Majesty," he called. "If it please you, you are to be granted safe passage through the camp. At the base of the motte, you will dismount and walk on foot to the Triple Gate. The duke will meet with you there."

William wished he were an Old Testament ruler just now so he could smite the man for his impudence. Forcing conditions upon the king? But he knew when to channel his fury into something more useful. "Lead the way," he snapped.

He and Dominic and Robert dismounted at the base of the motte, leaving their horses and their guards surrounded by Northumberland men. Dominic kept a warning grip on Robert's arm, but Robert didn't appear ready to bolt. He looked like he was ready to negotiate, but then the Dudleys always had that look.

Northumberland waited for them under the outermost arch of the Triple Gate. He stood alone, torchlight alternately revealing and then concealing his face. His eyes flicked over his son, ignored Dominic completely, and focused on William.

"Your Majesty."

"What do you want, Northumberland?"

"No wasting time in pleasantries, I respect that. I want Guildford out of the Tower. Banish him to the Continent—I'll ensure he keeps far away from the Clifford girl and their babe."

"And in return?"

"I'll submit myself to answer any questions you care to put to me. Other than love my son, I swear I have done nothing against Your Majesty's honour or the kingdom's safety."

"You don't count it against my honour to hold my sister against her will?" William allowed his voice to be deceptively mild.

"A desperate action by a desperate father. I had to ensure you would listen to me."

"You make no plea for your other son?"

Northumberland faltered. "Robert is nothing to do with this. Any of it."

"What will you give me for Robert?"

Dominic moved in protest, but William raised a hand to keep him silent. He knew what he was doing.

"You want the two women, Your Majesty. I will exchange—your sister for my son."

"And Mistress Wyatt?" Dominic intervened sharply.

William nearly cursed him for breaking the intensity of the exchange. "It's a deal," he said. "We'll wait here while you fetch the princess to me."

Dominic waited just long enough for Northumberland to disappear before breaking into a furious whisper. "What are you thinking, leaving Minuette in there alone? The duke cares nothing for her, he's only keeping her as a threat and he's much more likely to harm her than he ever would be to touch Elizabeth—"

"Breathe, Dominic." It was Robert's half-mocking voice that

interrupted the tirade. "Our gracious majesty is about to propose a deal, if only you will shut up long enough for him to speak."

For his impudence, William struck Robert once with the back of his hand. Then he said, "Your father is going to die a traitor's death, Robert Dudley. Nothing can stop that now. If you would like to live long enough to speak for your own life at a fair and open trial, you will do one of two things. You will either persuade your father to surrender unconditionally or you will smuggle Minuette out safely. Lord Rochford is less than a week behind me with a muster of five thousand men. You have until then. Once my troops arrive, I attack the castle and, when it falls, your entire family—women and children included—will be locked in the Tower at my pleasure."

He gripped Robert's close-fitting jerkin and pulled him close. "Do we have a deal?"

Robert held very still in his grasp, and William felt a moment's satisfaction at having wiped the smug smile off his face.

"I thought royalty didn't strike deals," Robert said softly.

"Would you like me to rescind the offer and kill you now?"

With a bitter huff of laughter, Robert said, "I'll take the deal."

The look Dominic gave him assured William that he would hear plenty from his friend later, but he held his tongue for the endless minutes they waited until Northumberland returned with Elizabeth at his side. William swept his eyes across his sister. She wore a wool gown dyed deep amber gold that brought out her brown eyes and made her red hair gleam deeply. The simplicity of her hairstyle, a single plait pinned in a coil at the back of her head, made her look younger than William could remember seeing her for a long time. Her composure was the same— elegant and reserved—until she saw Robert. Her steps faltered for one moment.

William nodded to Dominic to let Robert step forward. He and Elizabeth walked toward each other. When she drew near enough, Elizabeth slapped him, on the same cheek William had struck minutes earlier.

Robert rocked back and stared at her. "I had nothing to do with this," he told her. "If I had known what my father intended—"

"That was for Alyce de Clare," Elizabeth hissed.

She stepped around Robert and walked on to William. "Shall we go?" she asked. "I am eager to hear your plans for smashing the Dudley family to pieces."

Minuette had never been confined to one suite of rooms for so long in her life, and she found herself pacing in sympathy with Elizabeth and William's tendencies. Did they pace because they always felt so confined? Of course, in their cases, confinement came because of who they were, not the size of the room they were in.

She cursed herself for not having forced Elizabeth to let her bring Carrie along. She would have been good company and even better counsel. If she had to depend on anyone she knew for counsel, it would be Dominic first, followed closely by Carrie. Of course, Carrie had given her counsel before she had left Hatfield. She'd said, "Don't go."

But she had gone—and Minuette still failed to see how she could have in good conscience not come with Elizabeth—so there was no point dwelling on the past. The urgency now lay in figuring out where Northumberland had taken Elizabeth and what her own next move should be. Pretend to be ill? Faint? Throw a tantrum? She had lots of memories of Queen Anne, and figured she could throw a royal-class tantrum if she had to.

But she hadn't gotten further than examining the breakables

in the room to determine what to start throwing first when the door swung open. She turned, hoping for Elizabeth's return, or possibly Northumberland with an explanation.

She did not expect Robert.

"Going to chuck that at my head?" As always, he had words at the ready. He indicated the candelabra she held in her right hand. "You won't be the first today."

"I can see that." His left cheek bore faint marks that looked as though they might turn into a bruise. "So you've seen Elizabeth. I'm surprised she didn't scratch your eyes out."

"The princess is too well-bred for something so vulgar."

"I'm not," Minuette warned. But she lowered the candelabra and studied him. "Why is it that every time I'm somewhere I don't want to be, caught in the midst of forces I don't entirely understand, you unexpectedly appear?"

"Just lucky, I guess."

Minuette returned the candelabra to its place and sat. Robert perched on the edge of a facing seat. "Where's Elizabeth?" she asked after a moment.

"On her way back to William's camp."

"And William just let you in here?"

"In exchange for his sister, yes. Don't fret yourself, I am well and truly arrested, Minuette. Dominic saw to that. I am only here on sufferance, to persuade my father to surrender and to get you out of here untouched."

"How do you plan to do that?"

He grinned, but his heart wasn't in it. There was real strain in his eyes. "This is my home, remember? Getting you out won't be the problem. Persuading my father to surrender will be."

"How has it come to this, Robert? I know you love your family, but betraying Elizabeth and William—"

He turned sharp in an instant. "Don't play at politics, Minuette. You're not as clever as you think you are. All you need to know is to be ready to trust me when the moment arises. I will get you safely back to your men."

"Trust you? Why should I trust a man who meant to kill me?"

"I don't . . . What the devil are you talking about?"

If she didn't know better, she would have thought he was genuinely confused. "While you lectured me about William, your confederate smeared monkshood on my pendant. If it weren't for Dominic's quick thinking, I would be dead. And you wouldn't have to trouble about getting me out of here."

Robert dropped his head into his hands. She let the silence stretch between them, and began to doubt. That doubt intensified when he raised his face to hers once more. His expression was stripped bare, and for once, Minuette saw straight through the cultivated mask of intelligence and amusement and remembered the boy she had known since she was a child: bright and irrepressible and, always, generous of heart. "I did not know, Minuette. I had nothing to do with poison. If I'd had any idea . . . you were ill, that was all anyone said. I would never have plotted to harm you."

"You harmed Alyce de Clare quick enough."

Seriousness flared into forbidding. "I told you to stay out of political games. I meant it."

"You know what I think? I think you, too, are not as clever at this game as you thought. Perhaps you are a masterful deceiver . . . or perhaps you are in dangerously over your head. What foolishness have you committed merely because your father asked it of you?"

He stood, eyes blazing and arrogance returned. "I'll come for you after dark. If my father is feeling particularly trusting, tonight. If not, then tomorrow night. Be ready."

It wasn't that night, or the next night, either. Only on the third night did Robert Dudley come for her, long after midnight. She didn't know exactly what "be ready" meant, but she'd gone to bed in her dress and heard the murmur of voices outside her door moments before Robert slipped inside. "Put those on," he commanded, tossing her a bundle.

It was women's clothing of the lowest classes: a none-too-clean smock and a square-necked kirtle that was muddy brown in colour. The sleeves were pinned rather than tied to the bodice, and there was a heavy shawl to wrap around it all. "Where did you get these?" she asked dubiously.

"I've a gift for talking women out of their clothes."

Minuette ducked behind the bed curtains, fumbling to get out of her more elaborate dress and into the simpler shapes. She could hear Robert's impatience. "Do you need help?"

"No," she snapped. "How did you get rid of the guard?"

"I told him I wished to be private with you and no one need overhear what we were up to."

"Lovely." That's what she needed—Dudley servants speculating about how loud she and Robert might become in an intimate encounter.

"He won't expect me to take all night about it, so hurry up."

She stepped out from the privacy of the curtains. "Will I do?" The skirts were meant for a fuller figure and were several inches too short, but in the dark she should be able to pass.

"Put this on." Robert handed her a linen coif, beneath which she inexpertly bundled up her hair. Only royalty and single women at court were allowed to wear their hair loose and Minuette didn't like the confinement of the coif.

"It will have to do," Robert said critically. "Keep your head down and don't say a word. Pretend you're poor and oppressed."

"I am poor." But then she remembered the pinched and hungry faces of those on her estate farms and the beggars she passed in the London streets and felt a pang of guilt. Poor was relative.

Irritation with Robert wasn't enough to keep away fear, and her heart pounded in her ears as she followed him through parts of Dudley Castle she hadn't seen during her too brief time as a guest. He couldn't take her out through the Triple Gate, of course, so they wound past the chapel to a postern gate in the outer wall. Once through it, a narrow path circled the motte tightly against the castle. He led her down this treacherous path with remarkable speed, the lantern he carried almost the only illumination. The moon was a quarter, waning into wistfulness. And it was bitterly cold, winds hinting at the winter to come. Minuette shivered but kept her head down, looking only at Robert's feet, until she heard the sounds of sleeping men looming.

"This is the tricky part," Robert whispered into her ear. "But only if a soldier decides they want a few moments alone with you. They'll take any woman at this point, but for heaven's sake don't let them look at your face or I'll never get you out of there."

Her heart ready to leap out of her mouth, Minuette realized wryly that she was far more terrified now that at any point during her imprisonment. It was as though only on the brink of freedom could she allow herself to feel the tension of the last three days in an enemy's house without even Elizabeth for company. She'd told herself that Northumberland would be a fool to harm her—but that hadn't stopped him arranging for someone to poison her in the very heart of William's court. What might he do when she was alone and completely at his mercy?

Robert passed easily through the camp, though not quite without comment. The encampment was orderly and sentries were posted to challenge. Robert got them through it all, making vulgar comments about camp women and laundry maids.

They slid sideways through the camp to the least populated area, where the tents and men thinned out and the sentries were far between. Robert pulled her close and murmured, "Now I go back, rather loudly and possibly drunkenly, while you slip into the night. Follow the edge of the village until you can't see the lights from this camp any longer, then you'll find the road leading out from between the old priory ruins. William's camp is two miles east of here. Once you're safely out of sight, take that coif off your head so William's guards can see your hair. He'd be miffed if his own men shot you on your way to him."

"Do you have a message for the king?"

"Of surrender, you mean? Tell him that if I have not brought my father to open surrender by nightfall tomorrow, I will leave Dudley badges in the priory ruins that will get him and Dominic and a handful of others through the camp the way we just came. I will leave the postern door unbarred to them if I must."

"I'll tell him."

He nodded and turned away.

"Robert," she called softly. "Have you any message for Elizabeth?"

"I think the time has long passed for that, don't you? Get on your way, Minuette."

It took forever to creep her way along the edges of the village and then to find the road. She gladly discarded the coif as soon as she could, hoping Robert was right and the wan moonlight would be enough to gleam on her bright hair. She was starting to panic, almost certain that she had gotten turned round and headed off on some other road (perhaps leading to Wales) when she heard the whicker of horses before her.

The first sentries were upon her before she knew it. They were wary, of course, for what were they to make of a solitary woman wandering into the king's camp? She gladly gave herself into the charge of one of them, who escorted her the remainder of the way. They passed a dozen more sentries before she saw firelight illuminating the gold lions on William's standard.

Before they could pass her along the chain of command, to more men who might not know her, she said, "My name is Genevieve Wyatt. If you could wake Lord Exeter, he will confirm my identity."

The sentry shot her a sharp look, but one of the guards outside William's tent intervened. "I'll watch her," he told the sentry. "Fetch Lord Exeter."

She was glad no one wanted to question her just yet, and equally glad they didn't insist on waking William first. And when she saw Dominic break into a run when he saw her, she was glad she had the excuse of being a weak female escaped from a horrid situation so that she might break down in tears and let him enfold her in his arms.

Robert was prepared for nearly anything when he slipped back into Dudley Castle through the postern door: from the best case, in which the guard had taken advantage of Robert's dismissal and was still absent from Minuette's now empty room, to the worst case, in which the Sharrington range was ablaze with lights and men searching top to bottom for their missing prisoner.

As with most things in life, the truth was somewhere in the middle. Robert went directly to his father's study and was not surprised to find his father waiting for him.

"You let her go," his father said. Robert *was* surprised at the lack of anger in his father's voice; if anything, he sounded sorrowful. "What else have you promised the king you would do?"

"Get you to surrender."

Northumberland snorted, but Robert could not miss the new hollows in his cheeks and the dark smudges beneath his eyes. The study was icy despite the blazing fire, and the Duke of Northumberland resembled a warhorse approaching the limit of his strength. "I suppose you think surrender is the only option left now that my last hostage is flown."

He had been trying to persuade his father to reason for three days without success. Now Robert would have to be blunt. "No hostage could have given you what you wished, Father. I had word at Kenilworth just before Lord Exeter arrested me—Guildford is dead. He was executed the day after the trial."

Robert knew he was often careless of other people's feelings—women, especially—but he had never been deliberately cruel. As he watched the light go out of his father's eyes, he wished he could get his hands on the man behind all this pain. His father had been reckless and angry and intemperate—but George Boleyn had taken every careless act by the Duke of Northumberland and twisted it back upon him fourfold.

If he hadn't thought it would break what little remained of his father's heart, Robert would have told him all that he himself had done at Lord Rochford's bidding. But though Robert had disappointed his father before this, he could not damn himself fully.

The best he could do was get his father to surrender into the king's hands without bloodshed. As long as Dominic stood with William, there would be someone with wisdom and balance to get at the whole truth. Robert would not let his father condemn himself utterly without at least attempting to ease the blow.

His father slumped at his desk in silence, staring at his clasped hands. Robert held his tongue for as long he dared before saying, "Father, you have other sons—and daughters, as well. Do you want us all tainted? Will you ride into battle and make yourself a rebel while Mother weeps at your death?"

What most people missed about John Dudley, Robert thought, was his humility. He had it—though it wasn't often in evidence—

but one had only to see him with his family to know that his love for them was far greater than his ambition. Robert knew he had won; now he was just waiting for his father to speak.

At long last his father raised his head. "Send your mother to me. At first light I will tell the troops to disperse and deliver myself to the king."

There were many things Robert wanted to say—*I'm sorry for Guildford, I'll do everything I can to see you redeemed, forgive me*—but through the sudden tightness in his throat all he could manage was, "Trust me, Father. I'll do everything in my power to return you home soon."

Even if he had to bring down the Chancellor of England in the bargain.

CHAPTER NINETEEN

DOMINIC COULDN'T TAKE his eyes off Minuette. Dressed in peasant clothing and with a bruised look about her eyes as though she'd been sleepless for days, she was the most beautiful creature he'd ever seen.

After that first startled moment of being woken in the dead of night, followed by the sweet relief of holding her close, Dominic had himself woken William and sent for Elizabeth to join them. She was still in the camp because she had doggedly refused to leave. "Not until Minuette is safe," she had insisted, and no one dared defy her. Now the four of them sat together in William's tent as Minuette related her story.

William held her hand, stroking it as she told them of how Robert had led her out of the castle and through the encampment surrounding the motte.

"Did they strike you as men ready to fight?" Dominic asked.

"They struck me as men I didn't want to see my face," she replied. "I don't know what a force ready to fight looks like."

"What about Robert?" William interrupted. "What did he say about his father?"

"He said that if he has not brought Northumberland to surrender by nightfall tomorrow, he will leave the postern gate I came through unbarred and Dudley badges cached to get a handful of you through the camp."

Dominic and William shared a considering glance. That was further than Dominic had thought Robert would take it. Persuading his father to wisdom was one thing—opening a back door to an enemy force was pure betrayal. "Were we wrong about Robert's involvement in his father's plots?" Dominic asked.

"When I spoke with him, Robert all but admitted to Alyce de Clare. Although . . ." Minuette hesitated. "He did seem genuinely surprised to find that someone tried to poison me."

"It's irrelevant," Elizabeth broke in. "All that matters is getting Northumberland out of that castle without bloodshed. If Robert can bring that about, then he's useful. For now."

Dominic wondered how much that apparent indifference cost her. She had left court in the latter part of August and he had not seen her again until one month later, when Northumberland released her. In those weeks, Elizabeth had aged; though her beauty was untouched, her spirit was darker. But then again, it had always been Robert who had brought out the lighthearted side of her.

"Right." William nodded. "Elizabeth, take Minuette to your tent. As soon as the sun rises, the two of you will ride out."

"No," Elizabeth said. "Not until it's over."

"It is over. You are both safe now."

"I'm not leaving until Northumberland is in your hands."

"This is nothing to do with you. If you hadn't been so stubborn and secretive, you'd never have been caught in this mess at all!"

"And that's why I'm staying!" Elizabeth shouted back. The siblings were on their feet, glaring at each other. Dominic felt the brush of Minuette's fingertips against his. He nearly grasped her hand, but William's distraction wouldn't last forever.

Elizabeth's voice cracked once before she got it under control. "Northumberland might never have taken this stand if I hadn't made it easy for him. There are women and children in that castle who do not deserve to be caught between the two of you. I am staying until the innocent are safe and Northumberland is in your hands."

"Are you sure you're not staying to plead for Robert?"

"I am finished pleading for Robert Dudley."

William scowled and shook his head, but said grudgingly, "Fine. But only because I expect the rest of my troops tomorrow. The morning after the soldiers arrive, you and Minuette are on your way no matter how matters at the castle stand."

But as dawn broke just a few hours later, ushering in a misty, chilly morning, one of William's sentries intercepted a rider from Dudley Castle, carrying a white banner of surrender.

William and Dominic rode to the castle with an impressive contingent of royal guards and heavy cavalry. More out of respect for Northumberland's dignity than to intimidate him, Dominic thought. William had his father's gift for merciful symbolism once he'd established his authority. Northumberland waited outside the Triple Gate surrounded by three of his sons: Robert, Ambrose, and Henry. The duke knelt before William. In a clear, carrying voice, he submitted himself to "the sovereign it is my good pleasure to serve in the name of God and my own conscience."

Northumberland and his sons were arrested. The women and children were allowed to remain at Dudley Castle under royal control. William had named the Earl of Arundel temporary governor of Northumberland's estates. Very temporary, Dominic thought. He didn't know if William was looking forward more to executing the duke or confiscating his lands and wealth.

Robert, uncharacteristically, was completely silent save for one question. "Is Lord Rochford marching with your troops or does he remain in London?"

William studied him for a minute before replying. "Rochford's in London. As Lord Chancellor, he will oversee your reception at the Tower."

And just like that, it was over. Dominic spurred his horse ahead of the rest, to see Elizabeth and Minuette on their way before the prisoners were brought into camp.

Both women were dressed for riding in the princess's clothing that Northumberland had sent to the camp upon Elizabeth's release. Meant for riding and hunting, the gowns were less elaborate than the typical court wardrobe: dressed so similarly, Elizabeth in red and Minuette in blue, they almost looked as though they could be sisters.

"It's done," Dominic informed them tersely. "William wants you away before the prisoners get here."

Elizabeth nodded once in acknowledgment, then turned away to mount her horse. The women had an escort of one hundred armed men—no chance of being waylaid or changing their minds along the way. Elizabeth was returning to court. But Minuette had persuaded William to let her go to Wynfield.

As Dominic moved to help her mount, she asked appealingly, "You will come, won't you?"

"It's not wise."

"I don't want to be wise any longer. I want to be honest. Come to Wynfield and we'll decide how to tell William the truth."

The truth . . . "I'll come."

Minuette tried to persuade Elizabeth to stay at Wynfield with her for at least one night. But Elizabeth declined. She was not in a companionable mood, and as gentle and perceptive as her friend was, Elizabeth was far too raw to even touch on the subject of Robert. They rode next to each other in heavy silence the last hour before their roads would separate, and finally Elizabeth asked the question that had weighed on her. "Did he kill Alyce?"

Elizabeth had not been able to get the dead woman's face out of her head for a week now. Although she'd hardly paid any attention to Alyce de Clare while the woman was alive, they had crossed paths on the very night of Alyce's death. I should have seen it then, Elizabeth thought heavily. *The way she looked at Robert, her insolence in acknowledging me, the hint of pity in her voice . . . I should have known she'd been Robert's mistress.*

And on that very night, Alyce had been found at the bottom of a staircase with a broken neck. Accident—or deadly intent?

Minuette said decisively, "I'm sure it was an accident. I suspect Alyce confronted him, no doubt they argued. But I do not believe Robert would intentionally kill a woman."

Neither did Elizabeth believe it, but she was beginning to see that she was not the best judge of anything where Robert Dudley was concerned.

What had John Dee warned her? *Even the clearest eyes cannot see straight into the sun.* Robert had been her sun, and she had been blind. Never again.

They reached the branching of the road where a third of the guards would continue with Minuette to her home near Stratford-upon-Avon. Elizabeth and the remaining guards would take the road to Oxford.

Minuette reined up next to Elizabeth. She looked smaller than usual, as though the captivity had diminished her. For one moment, Elizabeth felt that she was looking at a stranger and her friend's remoteness smote her conscience.

"Are you sure you want to go to Wynfield?" Elizabeth asked. "Perhaps it is not ideal for you to be alone just now."

"It will be good for me." Minutte smiled, and the familiar vivacity of it eased Elizabeth's heart. "There are things I must put in order at home. I won't stay away long."

"William won't let you." Elizabeth laughed softly.

Minuette's smile was sad. "Goodbye, Elizabeth."

It sounded like more of a farewell than it should have.

William and Dominic were on the road two days later. It was the last day of September and the skies hung low with sullen clouds. Northumberland and his sons were somewhere ahead of them on the road to London, under the personal guard of the Earl of Sussex. Dominic was glad to be riding freely with William rather than guarding prisoners.

He was unsure how to broach the subject of Minuette and Wynfield Mote. They passed the branching road to her home the first day, but Dominic still said nothing, afraid that if he proposed going immediately, William would seize the same opportunity. And figuring out how to tell William the truth didn't mean throwing it in his face at the first opportunity. Minuette had always been right that it would need to be tactfully and carefully done. So Dominic rode on to Oxford with the king, reaching the university town just before dusk on a sullenly wet evening that gave full promise of a bitter winter to come.

They were quartered at King's College, in plain but adequate rooms that quickly filled up with tapestries and furniture for the king's overnight stay. William insisted on visiting the fellows and students at dinner, moving amongst them in a way that almost made Dominic jealous. What would it be like to have the gift of easy conversation? he wondered. And was it a gift, or just very good training for a king who had to be popular with his people?

The first sign they had of trouble was the exhausted horse, lathered in sweat, quivering in the courtyard of the college as they returned to their quarters. Someone had ridden here at great speed.

Dominic followed William up the stairs two at a time. They met Harrington on his way down to find them. He told them what little he knew while leading them to the solarium where the rider waited. "It's one of Norfolk's men, he'd ridden to London and Rochford sent him on here. I gather there's been violence along the border, but he didn't say much. He was ordered to report directly to you."

The rider was young and possessed of northern sturdiness, though his face was tinged with gray. He looked as though he hadn't slept for days, a fact he soon confirmed. "Lord Norfolk ordered speed. I've ridden straight through from London and Carlisle before that."

"Tell me," William ordered.

"It was bloody," the young man said wretchedly, looking younger by the minute. "We'd heard of raids, so his lordship sent us across the border, as a warning, like. We weren't expecting trouble, just a band of reivers, but they were waiting for us. A full army. They swept through us like grain. And they didn't take hostages, either, just killed everyone they could reach. We lost three hundred men before we could get back to Carlisle. They didn't follow us, thank God, or we'd all have been lost."

William shared a swift look with Dominic and it seemed they had the same thought. *Bloody Scots—always meddling at the worst possible moment.* "What's Norfolk doing?" the king asked.

"He's mustering to Carlisle, with scouts posted along a twenty-mile stretch of the border. They hadn't crossed it when I left." The rider reached inside his doublet and pulled out a creased and sweat-stained letter. "He ordered me to put this into your hands alone."

William broke the seal and read, then raised his head. He

studied the young man before him. "Do you know what this says?"

"No, Your Majesty. But I can guess."

"How?"

"Because I was there, and Lord Norfolk wasn't. I'm the one who told him about the banners that rode with the army."

"What banners?" Dominic asked.

"A sable leopard and battle-axe on a field of scarlet," William answered neutrally. "Renaud LeClerc's banner. It was LeClerc who led the Scots."

Dominic stilled and in that moment felt something close to a premonition. This was not going to end well. "I don't believe that."

"Of course you do. You've said it yourself, how many times? LeClerc is the best commander Henri has. The French king's put him where he wants him—on my border. Whether it's because Henri knows what I intend, or merely because he's hoping to provoke me, it doesn't matter."

"Your Majesty." Dominic looked at Norfolk's messenger, young and exhausted and clearly not meant to overhear this politically charged conversation. With a wave of his hand, William dismissed the messenger and Dominic told Harrington to find the young man a bed.

When he and William were alone, Dominic said bluntly, "What will you do?"

"Henri seems to want war, or maybe he just wants to see how far he can push me. I thought I had taught him that lesson already. It seems he didn't learn it."

"Norfolk will need additional men if he's going to cross the border to fight."

"Is that what you would do—cross the border?"

"It's what Henri expects. He wouldn't put Renaud there if he didn't think he'd be needed for a series of full-scale battles. But you beat Henri last time by doing what he did not expect."

"Why not just bring it to open war now? I've got five thousand men nearby who can march at speed," William argued. "And if France is seen to break the treaty, then I'm no longer locked into marrying Henri's daughter. Outrage against foreign Catholics will run so high that I need not delay marrying Minuette."

"I think you overestimate the backlash. France is Catholic, but the Scots themselves are Protestant. I don't think you benefit one way or the other at this point, for it's not only the religious issue at stake. There will be many who will protest your marriage to Minuette on purely political grounds. And border wars are bloody affairs. It's the North that will pay, and it's the North that is most precariously held. Push them into war, and you may regret it. Also, it will soon be winter and any violence will have to be suspended."

"So talk to me about the unexpected."

"Negotiate," Dominic said tersely. "Keep this from blowing out of control. It saves crops and homes, not to mention lives, and it earns you a reputation as a peacemaker. It will tie Henri's hands. He doesn't want to be the warmonger to your more balanced and humane approach. And once you've restrained yourself so far in the face of blatant provocation, Henri will be caught completely off guard when the time comes for you to throw his treaty and his daughter back in his face."

That wasn't exactly pushing William into the French marriage, but Dominic did not want war. Even less did he want William using this as an excuse to marry Minuette immediately. *Please agree,* he begged silently.

William frowned, and picked up the map showing the Scots border in detail. His expression was inscrutable: he might be considering the difficulty of a late autumn battle, or he might be gauging where to send his soldiers pouring across. Dominic didn't move, afraid to tip the balance the wrong way.

Replacing the map on the table, William nodded. "Good. I'll send a rider to Norfolk, ordering him to keep his muster in Carlisle and not to engage unless the Scots cross the border first. And I'll tell him to expect you."

"Me?"

"Who better to negotiate than Renaud LeClerc's English friend? You are the one thing the Frenchman and I have in common."

"Fair enough. I'm sure Renaud and I can come to an accommodation."

Something of his relief must have showed, because William added, "I've missed you, Dom. It's my fault, I know, I've been so busy trying to know and do everything myself that I've not used you as I should. There is no one else who would have counseled me this wisely." Clapping him on the shoulder, he continued, "Every king should have at least one advisor who is honest rather than prudent. I'm glad you're mine."

The first warning Minuette had was Carrie's announcement that there was a gentleman below to see her. She had been working on a tapestry in the upper-floor solarium, and in her absorption had not even heard the sound of hooves. She asked Carrie who it was, but her maid retreated as if she had not heard the question. Fidelis raised his head and looked at her with a knowledgeable gaze. She had kept him at her side since her return. His warmth and size were comforting against the memories of her brief imprisonment.

"Do you think it's him?" she asked. The wolfhound answered by quirking an ear.

Dominic was in the hall, standing with his back to her. She

contented herself for a moment drinking in the way he stood and the way his dark hair curled against the neckline of his doublet. She realized she was trembling with the urge to run her fingers through his hair.

She must have made some sound, or perhaps Dominic sensed her, for he turned suddenly. "Might I trouble you for a bed for the night?"

Their eyes caught and his cheeks darkened. "I mean—"

"I know what you mean. Of course. I didn't think you would be able to come so soon."

"I can't stay. I'm headed north for some business along the border."

"You'll be here only one night?" She tried not to sound disappointed.

"I must be away at dawn. Truthfully, I should have pressed farther than Wynfield today."

Indeed, the afternoon light was holding and he could have ridden some ways more. Grateful that he hadn't, Minuette moved forward and took his hand in hers.

Despite his relatively early arrival, the evening wasn't nearly long enough for Minuette. They spent every minute together. In the softening twilight they walked to the nearest cottages and Minuette introduced him to several families, including the widow woman and her children who were embarrassingly effusive in their thanks for the help provided bringing in their harvest. They toured the rose garden, looking the worse for autumn wear, and she sought Dominic's opinion on remodeling the old-fashioned solar.

Mistress Holly provided a bountiful meal of roast partridge, rabbit pie, dried fish with mustard, leeks and parsnips, warm wholemeal bread, and a pastry shaped like a Tudor rose. She and Dominic ate all they could and still sent back more than three-quarters of the food; the servants would dine just as well as they had.

They sat in the hall after the meal, sipping spiced wine and saying little. Minuette kept expecting Dominic to bring up the issue of William, but he seemed content merely to sit with her. At last, when the shadows of night had long closed in, she said tentatively, "If you're away at dawn, we should retire now."

As Dominic had earlier, she blushed when she realized how that last phrase could be taken. Her blush deepened when he did not brush aside her awkward words. Rather, he leaned across the chessboard where her black queen stood triumphant and looked at her intently. His eyes seemed to trace every inch of her face and throat, and she felt his gaze as though it were fingertips running over her skin.

She had forgotten how it felt—not that she was unfamiliar with that sort of look. It was the only way William looked at her anymore, but he did not rouse in her this feeling of breathlessness, this sensitivity of her body heightening until she thought she'd burst into flame if Dominic were to touch her.

He leaned back in his chair, somehow releasing her from his gaze without taking his eyes off her. "I can ride tired."

Composing herself to stillness, Minuette suggested, "Another game, then?"

"I always lose." He smiled gently. "I thought you wanted to talk. About telling William."

"Let's talk."

He shook his head. "I want to hear you."

Only fair—she'd been the one dragging her feet for months. Still, she had made her decision at Dudley Castle. "I mean to ask William to remain at Wynfield until Christmas. No doubt he will wish me to return to court for that."

"No doubt."

"When I return to court, I will speak to Elizabeth."

Dominic nodded thoughtfully. "Break it to her first?"

"Yes."

"And what precisely will you tell her—simply that you have no intention of marrying William? Or do you mean to go so far as to tell her why?"

"I will tell her everything."

"So that she can tell William in your stead?"

Why was he interrogating her? "I thought this was what you wanted, Dominic. No more secrets, no more lies. No more twisting of our loyalties. But that doesn't mean we must be cruel. I thought you loved William, too. Do you want me to humiliate him?"

He sighed and rubbed his hand across his forehead. It was one of those rare moments when he looked as though he didn't have all the answers. "I just want to make sure this is what you want, that you're not doing it simply to appease me."

She choked out a laugh. "To appease you?" All this time, and he still did not know what she wanted. Perhaps she would have to show him.

She moved from her chair to Dominic's lap. Twining her arms around his neck, she brushed his cheek with her lips. "This is what I want," she said, then kissed his other cheek before letting her tongue flicker lightly across his lips. She felt rather than heard him groan softly, and she whispered, "You are what I want, Dominic. Must I prove it? We are alone enough here at Wynfield. I will prove it this very night if you wish. It doesn't have to be on a table."

His hands curved between her waist and her hips and his own laugh was strangled in his throat. "Don't tempt me, Minuette."

"My lord Duke of Exeter," she murmured into his ear, "I did not know you were capable of being tempted."

He stopped her words by kissing her hard and long. When she was well and truly breathless, he said, "I am tempted by you every moment of every day, Mistress Wyatt, and even more when I am in my bed at night. And if I don't leave this room now, I will be more than tempted."

He set her on her feet and found his own. Putting his hands on her shoulders to hold her just barely away from him, Dominic said, "I want you as my wife, Minuette. And now that we're close—now that we have a plan and a time—I can wait. I will let the temptation be a pleasure until the night we are wed."

"Well then, we shall have to tell William at Christmas, because I don't think I can wait much longer." She was only half teasing.

"Christmas," he agreed solemnly, and her heart quickened. "Now, tell me you've put me in a room with a door that locks on both sides."

CHAPTER TWENTY

Dispatches from Dominic Courtenay, Duke of Exeter, personal to Henry IX, King of England:

> *12 October 1555*
> *Carlisle*
>
> *The border is quiet. Norfolk's scouts report only occasional movement, probing here and there, but no sign of anything more serious. It seems they're waiting for us to make the next move. Norfolk has put me in touch with a Carlisle man who has family over the border. He'll slip across tomorrow with my message. Then we wait.*

> *17 October 1555*
> *Carlisle*
>
> *I've had a reply—a cautious acknowledgment from Renaud that he is there. But from what Norfolk's messenger has reported, I think his command is more than we'd thought. The French are encamped separately, and you know what the Scots are like— fractious and fragmented and they dislike taking orders from anyone, even when it's in their own best interests.*
>
> *Renaud will hold his troops across the border. I'm not so sure of the Scots. You must make certain Norfolk is in no doubt of his own orders. If a Scots patrol crosses the border, we must respond*

with restraint. Renaud will negotiate. We can't let that be
wrecked by a restless soldier or two.

22 October 1555
Carlisle

I shall meet you in Newcastle-on-Tyne the day after tomorrow.

Dominic and the Duke of Norfolk made a quiet entry into
Newcastle just before sundown on October 24. They wore no
symbolic colours and flew no banners, for they did not want it
widely known that they had left Carlisle. Although William's
visit here had been only hastily planned, the streets were swarm-
ing with men. Armed men, Dominic realized, his heart sinking
at the sight of so much steel this far north. Had William changed
his mind about negotiating?

Less than forty miles from the border, Newcastle was pro-
tected by massive stone towers built into a city wall. Once
through the walls, Dominic and Norfolk still had to gain entrance through the Black Gate, the barbican added by Henry III
more than three centuries before. The castle was eighty years
older than even that, and only the square Norman keep was still
habitable. But what the grim castle lacked in structure it made up
for in current guards—it took far longer for two members of the
privy council to get inside and be announced to their king than
Dominic would have guessed.

When at last he and Norfolk were with William, Dominic
said carefully, "Your Majesty, you appear to be raising an army."

William wore a simply cut doublet of black wool over a linen
shirt. His sober clothing was matched by the plainness of the
square chamber at the top of the keep, furnished with table,

chairs, and an abundance of maps. The last time Dominic had seen William studying maps like that was during the battles in France.

"The army had already been raised, against Northumberland," William answered. "Might as well put it to use. I must appear to be doing the expected if we are to gain full value from negotiation. Let the French think I'm ready to march across the border—it will add weight to your words."

Norfolk moved slightly, drawing William's attention. "You disagree, my Lord Norfolk?" the king challenged.

The duke took his time, weighing his words, and Dominic thought that, despite Norfolk's youth, he was a man who would approach every choice with clear-eyed dispassion. He would not damn himself with vengeance and sentiment like Northumberland had. "If I were in your position, Your Majesty, I would do the same. But in *my* position, I'm in two minds. I'm born and bred in the North, and I know the Scots as no southerner can. They will be at our throats every moment that they're not at one anothers'. Force is the only language they understand, and so part of me longs to take this ready army and march into their lands, doubling and tripling the destruction they have wreaked on us for too long."

"But?"

"But I am also an Englishman, and I do not relish war. If it were the Scots alone, I'd say march and burn and to hell with everything else. But the French are in this, and you need their princess. No one knows that better than I do."

It was a not-so-subtle reminder that Norfolk was a power broker in the Catholic faction. Dominic kept silent while William, with narrowed eyes and dangerously soft voice, asked, "And what is it, precisely, that you know so well?"

Norfolk was not easily intimidated, although he was also not stupid. He managed both to flatter and to warn. "You are a king men will follow, but feelings run high where religion is concerned. A French Catholic queen is the most politic decision you have ever made. It would be folly to throw that away for revenge."

"Your orders are unchanged—hold the peace along the border while Dominic slips across and negotiates the withdrawal of French troops. I'm sending a contingent of my personal guards back to Carlisle with you. That will give the spies something to debate about."

As the door closed behind Norfolk, William sighed and shook his head. "He wants that French marriage. When I throw it off, what do you think he's likely to do?"

"I think he's too clever to damn himself in rebellion. But he's a man capable of anything, so long as he's persuaded it's in his best interests."

William sighed again and ran his hands through his hair, a gesture that made him look young and vulnerable. "You know what to do."

"Wait two days for Norfolk to return to Carlisle. Then I'll send Harrington across to Renaud with the meeting place."

"Where?"

"There's a cairn at the peak of Windy Gyle in the Cheviots. The border cuts straight through the summit, a mile west of Hexpethgate crossing. It was one of several suggestions by Norfolk, and he assures me it's lonely enough. I'll take only Harrington with me, and not even Norfolk will know which spot I have chosen."

"When?"

"Five days from now."

William drummed his fingers restlessly against his thigh.

"LeClerc might suspect a trap, or a delay, or a feint to draw attention away from battle plans. He might not come."

"He'll come."

Dominic could almost feel the temperature drop as he neared the Scots border, and he cursed the French king for making this move so close to November. It was his first time in the North. Taken in all, he thought, looking around at the forbidding landscape, he preferred Wales.

Though it was clear, the wind was biting and cold and he hoped there wasn't snow in that threat. He and Harrington had ridden to the market town of Rothbury the day before and spent the night in a soot-heavy inn with bad food and worse beds. It was eighteen miles from Rothbury to Windy Gyle peak, and they moved warily through the unwelcoming terrain. He and Harrington were both dressed plainly and wore no armour. But his trust did not extend to traveling unarmed. Not even a merchant would do that in this country.

Harrington was a comfortable companion in silence. Dominic knew that the big man was scanning the horizon as well, eyes roaming ceaselessly over the hills with their folds and deceptive cuts. The Salter Road that they were on was a common trade route, but they saw no one. Not even a sheep or cow.

They approached the cairn from the south, the horses picking their way slowly up the treeless slope. After a careful circuit of the tumbled stone, Dominic was satisfied they had arrived before Renaud. He set Harrington to watch the south and west, and walked his own horse to the north, from where Renaud would arrive. He was already beginning to regret choosing this spot, for Windy Gyle more than lived up to its name; the gusts seemed to come from nowhere, a cold bite to the wind that spoke not only of winter but of violence.

It was a testament to Renaud's skill that he got closer than anyone else would have before Dominic saw him. He, too, had a single companion with him, and they appeared out of one of the folds in the hills just close enough for Dominic to recognize the horsemen. Renaud had started up the last push to the summit, his man riding behind, when he raised one hand to Dominic in greeting.

That was the moment the arrow flew.

It struck Renaud in the back, with enough force to throw him sideways off his horse. Dominic was off his own mount in an instant, scrambling headlong down the steep slope, without ever pausing to wonder if more arrows were on their way. Out of the corner of his eye he saw movement—another horseman fleeing back into the Cheviot Hills.

Renaud lay on his side, the arrow—with deadly accuracy—driven through his cloak and into his leather jerkin. Before Dominic could kneel and see the damage, he found himself at the end of a sword.

The steel blade wavered slightly in the hand of Renaud's squire. Dominic stood absolutely still and looked into the young man's face—equal parts outraged and terrified.

With exaggerated care, Dominic spread his hands wide and raised them. "It wasn't us."

"Where's your companion?"

"Coming down the slope." Dominic could hear Harrington behind him. "The arrow came from below; I saw the movement of a horseman who is no doubt getting away as we speak. Let Harrington go after him."

The boy—for he could not be more than sixteen—licked his lips, looking from Dominic to his fallen commander. He nodded once and Harrington was gone in an instant. Then the squire lowered his sword and said, his voice trembling, "Is he . . ."

Dominic was on his knees, frantically loosening the cloak and jerkin. What he saw beneath made him breathe out in relief. Beneath his unobtrusive clothing, Renaud wore a breastplate of plate armour.

Renaud had been stunned by the fall, but now he swore loudly and inventively in both French and English as Dominic helped him sit up. They disentangled the arrow from the fabric it had gone through and Renaud studied it closely. "Recognize it?" he asked.

Dominic didn't expect to. This bore all the hallmarks of an assassination, which meant anonymity.

Renaud's face was the grimmest Dominic had ever seen. "Is this why you asked me to come?" he asked accusingly. "Because you meant violence?"

"You know me better than that."

"Do I?" Renaud got to his feet, grimacing at what would no doubt be a wicked bruise. "At least I know negotiating is not on the table."

"Apparently not."

They were still standing there, glaring at each other, two soldiers trying to work out the lethal labyrinth of politics behind each one of them, when Harrington returned. Renaud's squire raised his sword in reflex, but Renaud stopped him.

"Any luck?" Dominic asked.

Harrington shook his head. "Whoever's out there knows his business. He could go to ground in any one of a dozen small valleys. If we had twenty men, we could flush him out. But the four of us alone—and one of us the target—it would take a stroke of luck to stumble over him without getting killed in the process."

Dominic studied the furrows and crinkles of the Cheviot Hills, considering. Though part of him was straining like a greyhound, desperate to lay hands on the man who had torn through

Renaud's cloak with one expert arrow, he knew Harrington was right. They might never find the assailant. And as much as Dominic wanted the archer, he wanted the man who had sent him even more. He had the beginnings of an idea, a faint churning in his chest that he was desperate to disprove.

"You'd better go," he said abruptly to Renaud. "I think you'll be let through to your men, now that we are both on guard."

"I think so, too. Are you sure, Dominic, that I was the only target today?"

He wasn't sure of anything, except that he had some burning questions to pose once he got back across the border.

Renaud shrugged. "At the least I can give you my message. We French don't want war, at least not this winter. The battle with the border forces was meant as a warning. Word leaked of your meeting with the Spanish ambassador this summer, and my king was extremely displeased with the implications. Go back to your own king and tell him that our treaty holds—for now. But he should be wary of provoking further displeasure."

"I will return that message to my king."

Renaud remounted. His squire, clearly well-trained to obey, did so as well. Renaud shook his head ruefully. "Poor Dominic, always carrying messages he does not want to know. I pray I will not see you again anytime soon, *mon ami*."

Dominic watched the two Frenchmen ride back the way they'd come, waiting for sudden movement. But it seemed they would indeed be let through. The assassin was probably under orders not to be found out, and shooting again might give something away.

Eyeing him aslant, Harrington said noncommittally, "It was Norfolk suggested this spot."

"One of several. He didn't know which I'd chosen."

He swung up onto his horse and kicked it into a gallop. The need for secrecy was gone, blown to bits by the arrow and its target. But even speed could not keep Dominic from thinking. He kept replaying bits and pieces of conversations and seeing half-forgotten images, all twining into one slender skein of fact.

They made a brief stop at Morpeth and Dominic forced himself to eat and wait two hours to rest the horses before remounting and riding the remainder of the fifty miles to Newcastle. It was several hours after dark on an autumn night of lowering fog and relentless drizzle when they reached Newcastle, and Dominic had to use his title more than once to get them through the streets and into the keep. He left Harrington with the horses and was ushered up to the same private chamber where he and Norfolk had met with the king five days earlier. William stood across the room, hands clasped behind his back and an expression of neutrality in his guileless blue eyes.

Dominic found the words stuck in his throat. He was tired and sweat-stained and he kept seeing that arrow, flying swift and straight into Renaud's back.

In the end, William spoke first. "What happened?"

"Renaud was shot in the back." Not quite a lie; not quite the truth. The result was open to interpretation.

There wasn't a flicker of response from William, and in that moment of nonreaction, Dominic was sure. "Why, Will?"

The answer was clear and cold. "Do the unexpected. Your advice, was it not?"

"It serves no purpose."

"In one stroke I have deprived Henri of his most brilliant military mind. And I have shown that I rule this island, not he. I have given Henri the only answer he will ever respect—that of force."

Through the tearing pain in his chest, Dominic said, "You never meant to negotiate. It was a ploy—to distract the French and Scots while you brought your troops north. But you could have left it at that. You could have told me five days ago that you meant war, and left Renaud out of it altogether."

"The French will be scattered and of little use without LeClerc. Now Norfolk can sweep across and deal out vengeance for his three hundred lost men. And I'll come in behind, reinforcing primacy on our own border."

Dominic didn't know if it was exhaustion or grief that was making his eyes water and his head pound so that he could not think. He had never heard William sound so much like his father.

In the end Dominic went straight to the heart of the matter, the one betrayal he could not forgive. "You used me. You used my friendship with Renaud to lure him there—and you lied to me about it."

"I needed you unwitting so that LeClerc would be unwitting. I regret the necessity of his death. But he was a soldier, and a soldier lives every day under that threat."

"On the battlefield, yes. But there are rules, Will. You broke them all today—and you did it in my name. I cannot forget that."

For the first time, William's composure faltered and Dominic saw a hint of the boy who, when in trouble, had always looked to him for approval. "Dom, I am sorry you were there. But this is part of ruling. I cannot think of individuals—I must think of kingdoms."

Dominic turned away, taking a shaky breath to steady himself. All he could think of at the moment were individuals. It seemed that he could almost see Renaud's wife in the shadows of the room. *Nicole likes to have warning. It is superstition with her that she be always in the courtyard when I return.* If Renaud had been less lucky, the Frenchman would never have ridden into that courtyard again, never watched his sons become men or his daughter grow into a woman.

"Dominic? I ride for the border in the morning. Half the command is yours if you wish."

He never wanted to see Scotland again. He turned back to William and, in his most formal voice, answered, "I would prefer to be given leave."

"Now?" William's eyes were no longer guileless. Defensiveness turned to attack. "I have never revoked your command as lieutenant-general of my armies. You are a senior peer of my government—your place is where I order you."

Dominic felt only a crushing weariness and knew he couldn't summon the ability to soothe William tonight. He didn't even want to. "I never asked for command or titles. And I will gladly relinquish both."

"You would let my armies fight without your experience? I thought I was not capable of doing it as well as you."

The premonition Dominic had felt earlier was being amply justified. How many slights did William carry, just waiting to avenge? Dominic shook his head. "Do you really want a commander in the field who is there under duress?"

"Are you telling me that you will only serve if I command it?"

"Do you so command?" Dominic didn't know what he would do if William said yes.

William turned his back on Dominic and slammed his palms onto the table behind him. A goblet fell over and crashed to the stone pavings. Dominic did not flinch.

At long last William faced him once more, his face remote and forbidding. Dominic felt as though a veil had descended between them, altering the other's form and voice into that of a stranger. He wondered if William felt it and, if so, whether he counted it as one more cost of kingship.

Friendship with kings is always one-sided; so Renaud had once told him.

"I will not ask you to serve against your conscience," William said. "For now, I suggest you withdraw to Tiverton. I gifted you the title and the estate—perhaps you should begin to act like you are a duke. I will send for you from there."

Dominic nodded. "Yes, Your Majesty." And then he delivered the final blow. "There is one more thing. Renaud LeClerc was wearing plate armour beneath his cloak. He is sore as hell, and madder than even that, but he's not dead. You might want to consider that when you lead your troops across the border."

"He was . . ." William seemed torn between anger and respect. "Why was he wearing armour?"

"He's a cautious man. One doesn't get to be a soldier of his reputation without caution." Even furious and heartsick at William's betrayal, Dominic could not in good conscience avoid giving one last piece of advice. "You should be cautious as well. Try to balance between honest reprisal and blind vengeance."

Dominic left the king and the castle and spent the night dozing in the stables. Before dawn he and Harrington were riding south out of Newcastle-on-Tyne.

Only once did Harrington speak, and his question showed the depths to which he understood Dominic. "To Wynfield Mote?"

It had been, naturally, Dominic's first impulse. But he'd had time to think through the brief hours of the night, and now he shook his head. "Surrey. My mother's house."

Minuette was in her mother's rose garden when she heard the clatter of hooves on cobbles. Hope rose in her, wild and immediate, and she did her best to quench it by refusing to run around the house and see for herself. She gathered up the knife she'd been using to deadhead the last of the roses and laid it in the basket with the shriveled petals. Removing the leather gloves that had once been her mother's, she laid them across the shears and settled the basket on her arm. Only then did she leave the gravel paths of the garden to walk sedately around to the front of the house, Fidelis stalking silently by her side.

The beating of her heart was anything but sedate when she saw Dominic, talking to Asherton as a groom led away his horse. Harrington was with him, naturally, and another man Minuette did not immediately recognize. She had eyes only for Dominic. His expression was detached, almost icy, and she relaxed only a little when he turned to her and smiled, for even then his eyes remained unreadable.

"May I have a word with you?" He indicated the direction from which she'd come.

Asherton seemed to have everything well in hand, and neither Harrington nor the other guest—who she recognized with bewilderment as Michael, the priest from Dominic's mother's home—looked at all perturbed by Dominic's abruptness. She led him back into the midst of her mother's roses, where he stood silent.

Now that he had her alone, he seemed all at once indecisive, shifting his weight and hardly looking at her. Desperate to break the tension, Minuette behaved as any good hostess would. "Will Michael be staying long?"

"Just the one night."

Minuette said lamely, "How nice."

At last Dominic shook his head and sighed, and the smile he gave her this time was almost recognizable. "I know I'm not making much sense. I had thought the hard part was behind me, deciding . . ."

"Deciding what?"

His answer did not seem to match her question. "You know, of course, that Michael is not primarily a clerk. He's a Jesuit priest, and my mother's confessor."

"I remember. I don't understand why he's here." But she thought maybe she did, only she was afraid to be wrong, afraid to grasp at the hope in case Dominic snatched it away at the last moment.

"I've brought the priest, Minuette, and a witness. I thought you might supply the church? I know you have one convenient."

Through the spinning in her head, she snatched at one point. "I thought . . . Christmas. Didn't we agree we would tell William at Christmas?"

All at once his dark green eyes were aware and full of hurt. "I shouldn't have sprung this on you. I apologize. I was thinking only of myself."

"Dominic, what has happened?"

His eyes once again went blank. "Nothing. I'm sorry, I'm not doing this very well, but . . . Do you not want to marry me?"

The vulnerability of the question made her long to comfort him for whatever hurt had brought him here. She had known for months now that something or someone would have to break to end this painful stalemate they were locked in. She had never guessed it would be Dominic. She had never guessed Dominic *could* be broken. What had been done to him?

This was not the moment to press. She reached her hands to the back of his head, laced her fingers together through the soft, dark hair and, rising on tiptoe, kissed him. There was one moment when he was stiff and surprised, then his arms came around her with unusual force and she knew it would be all right.

She pulled her head away, just enough to whisper, "The twelfth of November: our wedding day, Dominic."

That refrain danced through Minuette's thoughts like quick-silver over the next two hours. She allowed the joy of it to over-whelm the whispers of caution within, warning that some disaster must have precipitated Dominic's abrupt action. It must be William. Something the king had said or done had tipped Dominic from prudence to recklessness.

After those few heady moments in the garden, she fled into the house, afraid to speak to anyone for fear her happiness would spill into indiscretion. After a brief meal of bread and cheese, Domi-nic went ahead with Michael to the church, leaving Harrington behind to accompany her. If they were seen together at the church, they would say that Michael, as a guest, had wished to see the estate.

Minuette was so overwrought with nerves and excitement that she barely noticed Carrie's unusual quietness, until she came out into the forecourt and found three horses, not two, standing patiently. Harrington and Carrie were already mounted.

She opened her mouth to order Carrie off, and caught Har-rington's eye. "I've already tried," he said gruffly.

"You're not leaving me behind," Carrie told her, her soft brown eyes and round cheeks looking unnaturally stern. "Not today."

It seemed Carrie knew all. Had always known, perhaps. And she was right, Minuette did not want her left behind. It would be comforting to have another woman present, especially a woman who had known her mother so well.

And two witnesses were better than one.

It was a point she had to make to Dominic, when his face darkened at the sight of one more person in on their secret. But he was too practical to debate the issue—as long as Carrie knew anyway, she might as well stay.

And it was Carrie who had the second biggest surprise of the day, wrapped in soft linen on the floor of the carved quire. She shooed the men out of the church and told them not to come near until she called.

As she undid the ties binding the fluidly bulky package, she explained to Minuette. "I knew how it would be the moment I laid eyes on the priest. Hard to mistake him, however he dresses. Anyway, I've had this ready for some months. It was only a matter of wrapping it and asking Edward to ride over here while the two gentlemen were eating."

"Edward?"

Carrie blushed, as if caught in an indiscretion. "Harrington, I mean."

Minuette looked thoughtfully at her maid. So that was the way of things, was it? But Carrie had the linen undone now, and the sight of what lay within made all other thoughts slip away.

Cloth-of-silver, gleaming in the dusty interior of the church like moonlight poured out and caught in fabric. "Not the best condition," Carrie explained, "being folded and wrapped like that, but much more suitable than a riding habit."

Minuette had seen this dress before, as a child. "Is that . . ."

"Your mother wore it for her first wedding, so she told me, and on special occasions after. She put it away when your father died, and I found it where she'd left it. Needed a little mending, but not much. And all the jewels are still there."

Indeed, the square neckline was bound an inch deep on each side with rubies and sapphires, their deep colours blazing against the silver paleness of the fabric itself. Minuette touched the bodice gently with one finger, too moved to speak.

Carrie smiled. "I know a dress is just a dress. I know his lordship would marry you in your shift and never mind it. But I thought you'd like this."

Minuette did like it. And so, to judge by his expression when he saw her, did Dominic. He stopped for a long moment in the open doorway, his eyes sweeping over her where she stood, trembling, in front of the altar.

His hand, when he grasped hers, was warm and reassuring. In a clear, sonorous Latin that made Minuette feel as though her mother were just over her shoulder somewhere, watching, Father Michael began.

"Lo, brethren, we are come here before God and His angels, in the face and presence of our mother Holy Church, for to couple and unite these two bodies together, that is to say, of this man and of this woman, that they be from this time forth but one body and two souls in the faith and law of God and Holy Church, for to deserve everlasting life, whatsoever that they have done here before."

If Dominic hadn't known better, he'd have thought he was drunk. It wasn't the single glass of wine he had with dinner, either, because he'd been feeling this way for hours—since the moment he'd seen Minuette in that silvery dress, standing in the shell of a church like a statue come to life. With coloured sunlight pouring through the windows and lighting her hair like a votive candle, he had made his vows in a state of pleasant intoxication that had not left him since.

She wore the gown at dinner. The old housekeeper commented on it innocently enough, and how much Minuette looked like her mother, but she seemed too simple to suspect anything so far-fetched as a clandestine marriage. Or perhaps, he thought, she is like all the Wynfield folk—prepared to believe that whatever Minuette does must be right. He imagined that if they told Mistress Holly of their marriage, her only response would be, "How nice. Have some more pudding."

They ate alone (Michael had generously asked to be served in his room) but were careful to sit far enough apart that touching was impossible. Dominic did not mind. Now that she was his, he could wait.

As soon as the table was cleared, Minuette dismissed the housekeeper and Carrie for the night. She beat Dominic twice at chess while they waited for the household to settle into quietness around them.

Minuette took a candle in hand and, in a voice that was almost steady, said, "I shall be in my chamber."

Dominic rose and kissed her on the top of her head. "I'll give you a few minutes."

When she had gone, he paced the length of the hall, refusing to let his mind wander past the sound of his feet on the flagstones, trying to match his breathing to his even steps.

He traversed the hall back and forth a dozen times before making his way through darkened corridors to Minuette's chamber. There was no answer when he knocked.

"Minuette?" he called softly.

Her voice came from just the other side of the door, sounding half exasperated. "I sent Carrie to bed."

Dominic paused, attempting to decipher that unexpected sentence. "I hadn't really expected her to be part of this."

"No," she sighed. Opening the door just enough for him to see her face peering around it, she said, "I can't get out of my dress."

Dominic struggled to keep a straight face, but he could not entirely suppress his laughter. She answered with a rueful laugh of her own. "It's ridiculous, I know."

"I'll fetch Carrie for you."

He was half turned away when she said, in a curiously altered voice, "You could . . . would you do it?"

All at once he could not breathe. *One body and two souls.*

His hands were not entirely steady as he unlaced the two

curving seams that ran down her back from shoulders to waist. He helped her remove the overdress, followed by the full-skirted kirtle, petticoat, and finally the stiff corset. Minuette herself seemed to gain in confidence with each item removed, until she faced him in only a linen smock that made his mouth go dry at how little it concealed even by candlelight.

"My turn," she murmured, and began to undo the laces of his sleeveless doublet. He had removed the close-fitting, long-sleeved jerkin before dinner but wished now that he hadn't, if only for the pleasure of letting her undress him. Minuette's hands moved gracefully down the black velvet until Dominic shrugged the doublet off. With only a moment's hesitation, she untied the neckline of his shirt and Dominic obliged her, pulling the linen over his head, wanting to feel her hands on his skin. But it was her mouth that touched him first, bestowing a butterfly-light kiss in the hollow at the base of his throat.

When she moved into his arms at last, he had a flash of memory—Minuette jumping to him at Hampton Court more than two years ago. The sharp awareness he'd had then of a girl grown into a woman mixed now with the vivid sweetness of holding his wife for the first time. *My wife.* She smelled of clean earth and dusky roses, and Dominic felt as he had once before when holding Minuette—that he had come home.

There was a moment when he drew back—the last moment that he could—and said breathlessly, "I don't want to hurt you, love."

Her hazel eyes were enormous and trusting. "I'm not afraid," she whispered. "I could never be afraid of you."

Hours later, in the still hush before dawn, Minuette lay in his arms and asked the question he had been both expecting and dreading since yesterday.

"What has William done?"

He told her as he'd always meant to, knowing they could not expect to have more than one night's peace at a time. He told her of Scotland and of William's lies and of an arrow in the back. When he had finished, he waited for her to defend William in her gentle, tolerant way.

She did not defend him. She did not say anything. She moved against Dominic and kissed him until he forgot everything but the moment.

CHAPTER TWENTY-ONE

13 November 1555
Wynfield Mote

*I am married. And though I know it is unwise to set it down in writing,
I don't care. I want it marked somewhere outside my own head, or in
the eyes of those who were present. Dominic and I are bound, and
though some might undo the words of the priest, nothing can undo last
night. I am Dominic's wife in body and soul. No one can change that.*
   Not even a king.

15 November 1555
Wynfield Mote

*The priest left us this morning. Before his departure, he came to say
goodbye and, I think, to wish me well. He's a most unusual man, this
Father Michael. When I thanked him for his service, he said, "No
warning from you? I suppose you trust that your husband has already
warned me as thoroughly as possible not to speak."*
   *"Why would you speak?" I asked. "There is no advantage to you
in doing so."*
   He laughed then and said, "So you are the practical half of this

marriage—trusting to my silence because it serves my own ends, and not merely because I have given my word. Trust a woman to be cynical."

I believe he meant it as a compliment.

Harrington is riding back with him to Dominic's mother in Surrey. I saw Carrie saying goodbye to Harrington and know that I was not wrong about her feelings. I am glad that she has found happiness again—being so marvelously happy myself, I wish it for all the world.

Even Emma Hadley. I will go this afternoon and return at last the silver casket and Alyce's letters. And I will tell her the truth of her sister's death.

21 November 1555
Wynfield Mote

News continues to find us here. Or find me, I should say. No one at court has yet realized that Dominic is with me, though there has been much gossip from some of my correspondents about the nature of his quarrel with William. One or two have been accurate enough to pass on the news that Dominic has been banished to his estates at Tiverton for now, but there are other rumours: that Dominic joined the French in Scotland, that he struck the king in the face, or even that Dominic has been confined to the Tower with Northumberland and his sons.

When I read out such things to Dominic, I do not see surprise or even distaste in his expression. Mostly, he just looks weary. And not because he has spent nearly two months riding back and forth across England. No, this weariness goes to his heart.

I do not know how to set it right.

Between them, William and the Duke of Norfolk scorched the border counties, burning everything in their reach from crops to abbeys. Renaud LeClerc pulled back his French troops almost as if they had never been there, and the Scots were decimated. William relished the rout, for as long as he was fighting he knew that he had been right. It was only when the fighting was done and autumn turned toward an early winter in the North that he was forced to remember the look on Dominic's face when he'd realized how he'd been used.

William's justification of *I was right* veered in the long hours of night to *Tell me I was right*. He wasn't sure whom he was pleading with. Dominic—or himself? He had been sure when he'd ordered LeClerc's assassination and the subsequent battles, but in the aftermath doubts crept in. Surely it had been too good an opportunity to miss—but what about the spring when battle season rolled back around? Was England ready to face the French in war once again? The restlessness of his mind kept him sleepless, and by the time he finally returned to London at the end of November he was achy and irritable. But kings don't have time for illness, so he faced his privy council the morning after his return.

In all his considerations he had come up with two positive items, points he was swift to hammer home when he met with Rochford and the council.

First, economics. "With Northumberland's attainder, his lands and wealth belong to the Crown," he pointed out. "He wasn't the richest duke," that would be Rochford, "but nearly so. His wealth is a substantial addition to the royal coffers. Enough to strengthen the navy and prepare our forces if need be for retaliation by the French in the spring."

"So you will wait for retaliation?" William Cecil asked.

And thus William's second point. He inclined his head. "There is a reason my troops withdrew from Scotland. We were not the aggressors; we merely responded in kind. I will not be manipulated by Henri into breaking our treaty. If he wants out of it, then he can bloody well say so."

"What are the odds he will?" The Earl of Arundel looked grim.

William turned to his uncle in unspoken query. Rochford shrugged and said, "Who can tell with the French? No doubt their own councils are meeting as we are to decide what they will risk in the spring. But the king is wise—we have the funds; let us use them to build up our forces and be as prepared as possible for a campaign next year. Until then, it waits only what Henri will do in response."

Cecil nodded thoughtfully. "As for the question of Northumberland?"

William looked briefly at his uncle, then said bluntly, "There will be no trial for John Dudley. I am calling a session of Parliament to pass an Act of Attainder against him."

Thus avoiding a trial by the duke's peers, and the messy complications that might ensue. Not only could Parliament convict Northumberland, they could also set the legal seal upon William's confiscation of his lands. And giving his people a say in the fall of this unpopular noble would help satisfy some of the pent-up Catholic protests.

No one protested, or looked more than vaguely uncomfortable. Northumberland had been too strong a personality, too successful and driven and openly ambitious, to be greatly mourned. But he had been a senior peer of the realm and his coming execution was a warning that, as William could raise a man, so could he end him.

"And his sons?" Lord Burghley wanted to know.

All four of Northumberland's living sons were in the Tower, held separately from their father and from one another: John, Ambrose, Henry, and Robert. "Let them rot for now," William answered sharply. "I will deal with them in my own time." He might even send one or two of them to hell after their father. Robert, probably—he was the one who had distracted Minuette while his father's lackey attempted murder. Robert claimed to not have known about the poison—and Minuette claimed to believe him—but William was not persuaded.

"Your Majesty." It was Cecil once again; Lord Burghley must be feeling blunt this morning, William thought wryly. "Might I raise the delicate matter of marriage? If the French do retaliate in the spring and we go to war, have you given thought to who will replace Elisabeth de France as your intended bride?"

"I have given it a great deal of thought." William avoided his uncle's eyes. "As well as I have given thought to the matrimonial future of my dear sister, the Princess Elizabeth. I have sent a private embassy to the Emperor, asking for the favour of his son, Prince Philip's, company in our court next summer. I believe the request will be looked on favourably."

It was what the newly restored Spanish ambassador to his court had intimated just yesterday. Frankly, the timing was perfect. Elizabeth was so disillusioned and bitter after her experiences at Dudley Castle that she had never been more receptive to the idea of Prince Philip. *She will make a wonderful Queen of Spain,* he thought. *And won't that bother my sister Mary no end: a Protestant queen in the heart of Catholic Europe.*

His answer hadn't entirely satisfied Burghley. "May we dare to hope, Your Majesty, that if Elisabeth de France is not in your future, that you will give serious consideration to an English bride?"

He meant Jane Grey, and every man there knew it. William's second cousin, granddaughter of Henry VIII's beloved younger sister, impeccably bred and outstandingly educated. And Protestant in every bone and breath of her body and desire of her heart.

William wondered how many of his council marked his careful choice of words in answer. "I assure you that an English bride is never far from my consideration."

Let them read that as they wished. Let Rochford glare all he wanted. William was tired of deception. He could almost bless Henri for sending Renaud LeClerc and his troops across the border, for they had made the first play to unravel the treaty, and now the next was in reach.

He was glad, though, to dismiss the privy council for today. Unusually for him, he had a headache and he clearly hadn't shaken off the effects of weeks of riding and campaigning. All he wanted to do was sleep.

By nightfall William was burning with fever.

Dominic stayed at Wynfield for three weeks. News filtered through to Minuette's home readily enough, mostly from Elizabeth but also letters from diplomats and clerics and others who found her a useful contact or else simply liked her. Through them all, Dominic followed the course of the brief Scottish campaign. He was relieved both by Renaud's diplomatic pulling back of the French troops and by William's restraint in not pressing the matter to the full. The response was bloody enough to send a message, but calculated enough to make it possible for the treaty to be preserved. William was leaving it to the French to decide what the next move would be. Which made Dominic proud, somewhere beneath his overwhelming disillusion.

After that first night, he and Minuette did not discuss William. He knew it was only a temporary reprieve, that the world would force itself upon them once more and they would have to decide together how to meet it, but for three weeks he could almost pretend that his life would always go on like this: a quiet country manor, a placid household, and an adored wife.

The pretense came to a cruel end with word that Parliament would be meeting in mid-December specifically to pass an Act of Attainder against Northumberland. Minuette read aloud Elizabeth's letter, announcing it in language so formal and stilted the princess might have been writing of someone she'd never met. Minuette sighed heavily as she laid the letter aside.

"Will you go straight to court from here?" she asked Dominic. "Or make at least a short visit to Tiverton?"

"I think I shall have to go to Tiverton, if only not to make myself an utter liar. It's where William will send for me. When he does, then I will return to court. Not before." He hesitated, then said, "I'm surprised he hasn't sent for you yet."

"Like you, I will go when he sends for me. And then . . ." She left it for him to finish.

"And then we will tell him."

She moved onto his lap and rested her head on his shoulder. "When will you leave for Tiverton?"

If he didn't go at once, he might never go. "Tomorrow," he answered.

"Then we shall make good memories tonight," she whispered, before kissing him in a way that ensured she was all he could think of.

That dizzying sense of pleasure lasted through the night. An hour after dawn he was just managing to struggle into his hose and doublet, Minuette watching him from the bed with a mischievous smile, when someone knocked loudly on the door.

"Who is it?" Minuette called. Though no doubt the household knew all about where Dominic spent his nights, they were careful to preserve the fiction by not letting anyone see them together in Minuette's chamber.

"It's Carrie," came the reply, in a tight and worried voice. "An urgent letter for you has come from Her Highness."

Minuette shared a look with Dominic, then got out of bed and threw on a night robe. She opened the door. "Thank you, Carrie."

Dominic could see the letter was short, just a couple of lines, but they were enough to make the light drain from his wife's face. "What is it?" he asked, crossing the room to her.

She thrust Elizabeth's letter at him, a simple and devastating message in untidy handwriting.

William has smallpox. His condition is grave. Come at once.

By the time Minuette and Dominic reached her at Hampton Court on December 11—more than a week since she'd sent her desperate note—Elizabeth felt as though she'd lived through months of despair and nightmares. There were moments when she could almost believe that none of this was happening, since she had not seen William for herself. After the debacle at Dudley Castle, she had returned to Hatfield and stayed there, raging over Robert's betrayal, until her uncle sent for her. Rochford had written only that William was somewhat ill—it wasn't until she'd arrived at Whitehall that she discovered how truly serious it was.

Rochford hadn't let her even enter the palace walls. When she'd remonstrated, he pulled her into a near-embrace that allowed him to whisper in her ear. "It's smallpox. The rash appeared last night. You must be kept elsewhere."

Because smallpox was contagious, as deadly as it was swift. So she had traveled on to Hampton Court and sent a rider with a message to Minuette. When Dominic appeared at Hampton Court with Minuette, she was glad of it. Although she briefly wondered how the two of them had managed to arrive together when he'd been in the west, at Tiverton.

But there were larger problems at hand. "How is he?" Minuette asked at once, even as Elizabeth greeted them.

"The sores are widespread and have begun to form larger patches."

Minuette paled. Smallpox was bad enough, but in those cases where the pustules combined into large patches, mortality was especially high.

"Is he awake?" Dominic asked roughly.

"Not from what I hear. They won't let me . . . I haven't seen him. All I know is what my uncle writes to me twice daily. He will certainly be scarred. It could hardly be otherwise."

But it could be otherwise. He could be dead. That was why they wouldn't let Elizabeth see him, why she hadn't even been allowed inside Whitehall. William was king, and she was his heir.

For days now Elizabeth had been haunted by a guilty memory: John Dee telling her last Christmas that her hand was not only a woman's hand, but a ruler's. He had held her palm in his and Elizabeth had been mesmerized by his hints of knowledge, had felt that there were promises in his eyes and a word just out of her reach—

Queen.

Dominic broke her introspective despair with practicality. "I'll go straight on to Whitehall and write you myself."

"I want to go with you," Minuette said.

"Absolutely not," Dominic said firmly. "Elizabeth needs you. And William would never forgive me for exposing you to smallpox."

"What about your exposure?"

"I am the King's Shadow. It's my job to stand by him whatever peril he is in."

He shared one last look with Minuette, the two of them seemingly having an entirely wordless conversation that left Elizabeth feeling like an intruder.

Dominic, surprisingly, hugged Elizabeth before he left. "I'll stay with him," he promised her. "Until he is better."

And if he is never better? Elizabeth thought desolately. Will you stand by me if William dies?

13 December 1555
Hampton Court

It has been two days, and the news from Whitehall continues grim. Both Rochford and Dominic say as little as possible in their dispatches to minimize the danger of the country learning how very ill William is. But people know something is wrong. Anyone with eyes can see that Elizabeth is sleepless and desperately worried. Her headaches have been unrelenting since I arrived, and I am glad I can at least be useful to her. Between me and Kat Ashley and Francis Walsingham, we have kept up the pretense that she is overwrought from her temporary imprisonment by the Duke of Northumberland. Let people imagine her prostrate because of Robert's treason—better that than panic.

I do not know what we will do if William . . . I cannot even write it. It is unthinkable. Whenever I have a moment to myself, I imagine him frightened and alone and I cannot help thinking that this is my fault. It is not logical, I know, but what if Dominic and I have brought this upon him? What if, somehow, William's body knows what his mind does not and the force of our betrayal has destroyed him?

What have we done?

Whitehall Palace had become a crypt. Dominic felt it on the rare occasions he left the sickroom, as though the very walls were anticipating the worst. The corridors were hushed and conversations were conducted in whispers and sidelong glances. Rochford might be putting out daily updates on the king's health, but everyone in the palace knew they were fictions. William was not "somewhat indisposed" or "suffering from an injury in battle."

Plainly stated, Will was dying.

Dominic had seen it immediately, shocked speechless by William's appearance. The pustules were bad enough, crowded thick and foul across the king's chest and his limbs and especially his face. He did not look like William at all—the sharp features of his handsome face submerged in oozing sores. But worse even than that had been the limp body and sunken eyes. It was as though William had already given up.

Dominic set about changing that, sitting by the bedside and keeping up an almost constant stream of chatter to his friend. It was the most words he'd ever strung together at any one time in his life, and he wished William would wake up enough to say something sarcastic. *Death makes you talkative?* perhaps, or *Can't you speak of something interesting like women?*

For endless hours Dominic ignored the many others in the bedchamber and talked about last year's battle in France and their shared childhoods in the schoolroom and the tiltyard. He talked battle tactics and history and recalled pranks that William and Minuette had inflicted on the rest of them.

The physicians did whatever they could do—which was precious little—and Rochford was a constant presence as well, watching his nephew from beneath hooded eyes. Early in the hours of December 13, as William's breath grew desperately shallow, Rochford tried to send him out.

"Go get some rest, Courtenay." Rochford in private always called him by the name he'd used since Dominic's childhood.

"I'm fine."

"There's nothing you can do. You heard the physicians—

either he will recover or he won't. We are all of us in God's hands, and I cannot believe God is ready to take William just yet. Not when we need him."

Dominic wished he could read God's intentions as well as Rochford seemed to. In any case, he shook his head. "I'm staying."

With a shrug, Rochford replied, "As you will. I'll snatch an hour's sleep myself, then."

So in the darkest hours of the night, with only two physicians and a handful of men attending to William's physical needs, Dominic finally was able to say what all his words had been leading up to.

He touched William's swollen hand and leaned over the bed. "I don't know if this is what you need to hear, William, but if it is, I say it gladly. About Renaud—about the choices you made in my name—"

Intended assassination, an arrow in the back, a wife taken in secret . . . "You are my king, but you are also my friend. And so I forgive you, Will. And I'm sorry."

And please, he added silently, *please live long enough for me to make things right. Don't let my last act in your service have been a betrayal.*

As dawn edged a chilly entrance into wintry morning, William opened his eyes.

INTERLUDE

26 December 1555

Robert Dudley was confined in Beauchamp Tower, a forbidding medieval square building that looked every bit the defensive wall for which it had been built three hundred years earlier. He wasn't sure where his brothers and father were being held, for his guards were under orders to give nothing away. Not even his charm had any effect on their reticence.

When Dominic walked into his cell, Robert raised one very dramatic eyebrow. "Either I am about to be pardoned or about to be dead," he remarked wryly. "Which is it?"

"I am here on my own account," Dominic answered. "Not the king's."

"Ah. I had thought . . . So my messages are not getting through."

"You've been sending messages?"

"Not successfully, it would seem. If they've been intercepted, I'm surprised you don't know about it."

"The court has been somewhat occupied this last month."

"William's smallpox?"

When Dominic looked surprised, Robert said, "Everyone

knows. Though perhaps not quite how bad it was?" he asked thoughtfully. That would explain why the Act of Attainder against his father hadn't come through yet. The court would not have risked Parliament meeting if the king's life was truly in danger. And if William had been seriously ill, then Elizabeth must have been frantic.

Robert couldn't stand not being near her to give whatever help he could. Which was why he had to get himself out of the Tower. He had assumed, when he was arrested, that it would be simple.

But then, he had never guessed that he was being used to bring down his own father.

But now Dominic was here, and he at least was honest. "Did you know that I have not been asked a single question during my confinement? Not one." Robert sat on the cold stone ledge beneath the cell's single window. Dominic remained on his feet in the middle of the room, not that there were many options. The cell was no more than six paces in any direction. It held only a bed, a table, and a single chair.

"I think your father has been the more immediate priority."

"No doubt. Best get him out of the way before uncomfortable questions might be posed. You don't find it revealing that the council plans to convict by attainder and not in an open trial?"

"What are you implying?"

That a trial might have exposed the flaws in my father's supposed treason. That the case against him might have fallen apart like the case against Norfolk. That there's a reason I've been locked up with no one asking me anything . . .

"I need to talk to someone," Robert replied. "I have information that the king needs to know."

"What information?" Dominic hardened his voice.

"Ask yourself this—is it not revealing that in just over a year's time, two of the finest men in this kingdom, two of England's senior peers, have been disgraced and killed?"

"Norfolk died a natural death. And your father is not dead."

"Not yet. And Norfolk's death resulted from a most unnatural arrest for an act of which he was innocent."

"Innocently set up by your father's plots. Northumberland wanted the Catholics crushed and went to great lengths to arrange the fraudulent Penitent's Confession and then have you plant it in Norfolk's home. Someone should have warned your father that playing with fire always leads to burning yourself in the end."

"Someone was playing with fire, all right, and my father made his share of rash and desperate decisions. But look around you, Dominic, and tell me: Who is left standing? What voices remain to whisper in the king's ear?"

Distaste bloomed in Dominic's eyes. "I assume you are not accusing me."

Robert laughed wholeheartedly. "As if you are capable of such deceit. No, Dominic, I am not accusing you of masterminding the downfall of two of England's most powerful families."

Robert would not say the name aloud, but let it hang in the air between them—*Rochford*.

He knew he had been understood when Dominic said slowly, "A man accused will say anything—and a man as clever as you will say it convincingly."

"A man as clever as me will also have evidence."

"Tell me."

After a long, considering pause, Robert shook his head. "Not you."

"There's no way the king will speak to you in person."

"I don't want to speak to the king. I want to speak to Elizabeth."

It was Dominic's turn to laugh. "Never."

Robert leaned forward, as serious as he'd ever been. "If you do not want William and his kingdom at the mercy of a liar, you will make it happen. Bring me Elizabeth—and I will deliver you a traitor."

ACKNOWLEDGMENTS

This book was written in the immediate aftermath of a two-thousand-mile cross-country move. When not immersed in fictional Tudor worlds, I was drowning in boxes and school registration forms and impossibly winding New England roads and stark moments of homesickness for friends and family. And also the unexpected, lovely flashes of new beauties and new friends and new worlds.

Thanks to new friends who love books (we might be small, but we're opinionated!): Roz Hawk, Janelle Holt, Brenna Palkki, Patty Helsingius, Michelle McKay, Mira Pazolli. And to all my sisters from Waltham to Maynard: I know all of you by name. And you seem not to mind me too much, even if I do read trashy magazines.

A million hugs to my first and dearest new friend with an old soul: Debbie Ramsay. You (and Bill, Marina, Sasha, and Lise) are the best gift of our new lives.

Thanks to Kate Miciak: the third time's the charm, and how charmed my life is to have you as my editor! You make everything about my books inexpressibly better, even if I can't seem to add enough description the first time around.

A thousand thanks to Tamar Rydzinski, the most unflappable human being I've ever known. It's a wonderful trait in an agent, and one I wistfully admire from the depths of my high-strung temperament.

And always and ever my family: I'd like to say that all that pizza and cereal you ate contributed to this book, but we all know you'd be eating that way even if I weren't writing. Domestic I am not. But no wife and mother could love more fiercely (if at times sarcastically) than I love you.

THE BOLEYN DECEIT

Laura Andersen

A Reader's Guide

LETTER FROM ELIZABETH TUDOR TO MINUETTE WYATT

14 November 1554
Whitehall Palace

My dearest friend,

Well, Minuette, it is not often that I am taken by surprise. Before this summer, I would have hazarded that I knew you as perfectly as I know any person on earth. It is only since I came across you and William at Hever the night of my mother's death that I have begun to wonder what secrets you might be keeping. But even my imagination could not have conjured the truth.

My brother came to see me tonight, after the victory banquet from which he so conspicuously disappeared with your hand in his. When William appeared in my chambers he was at his most imperious, dismissing my attendants without pretending to wait for my orders. And when we faced each other alone across my privy chamber, he told me that you and he are betrothed.

William was shining with joy and I took my cue from that, smothering the practical questions that came effortlessly to mind. I hugged him and I congratulated him on having had the sense to fall in love with a woman worthy of everything he could offer and I let him ramble on about you for some time. As well as I know you, it was a revelation to hear you spoken of by a man in love.

But I will not lie to you, Minuette. For one thing, I may never give you this letter. I suspect I am writing solely for the solace of my own mind, to work out the tangle of hopes and emotions and ambitions within me. And so I will be honest: with each praise William sang, my concern grew. There was one moment when I thought that, if I closed my eyes, it would be my father I heard, singing my mother's praises. One would suppose that such a thought would have cheered me—for their love turned out well enough. But all I could think was that lightning does not strike twice. Though William's obstacles appear less severe than my father's—at least he has neither wife nor royal child to contend with—they are obstacles nonetheless. I do you the credit of believing you are not unaware of them.

But Minuette, what most worries me is the change in William. My ever-practical, hardheaded brother is prepared to dismiss every ambition and scrap of counsel to have you. William, who has never had any illusions where women were concerned, who carelessly married off Eleanor in order to enjoy her without complication, has made of you an angel of worship, like a saint on a pedestal.

And yet, for all my concern, perhaps that is precisely where his future wife belongs. For make no mistake, Minuette, to be a queen consort is to be a symbol more than an individual. The primary task of a consort may be straightforward—to bear a royal son—but straightforward is not the same as simple. You lived with my mother too long to believe that.

To be a king is to be born favoured of God and man and to live for one's people as much, if not more so, than for oneself. To be a queen consort is to live for one's husband and children. And until very recently, the only path to queenship has been to marry a king.

I remember the first time that point was brought home. I was quite young—only four or five—when my father joined me in a pleasure barge on the Thames as we progressed from Greenwich to Richmond. He was in a playful mood that day, and when I asked him why I had to study so many subjects, he told me about his sisters, Margaret and Mary, who had been queens of Scotland and France respectively. (Though Mary, it is well noted, was a French queen for such a brief time as to be hardly worth mentioning.)

"You are a daughter and sister of kings as they were," he noted. "And someday you will likely be a queen yourself. Where would you like to be queen of when you are grown, my sweet? France? Spain?" (I know now he was being optimistic—neither country was likely to offer for the questionably legitimate daughter of a heretic king at the time. How circumstances have changed!)

I remember perfectly what I answered, as well as I recall the play of sunlight on the water, the green of trees and grass along the riverbanks, the scent of summer flowers and sun-warmed fields. "I should like to be Queen of England," I said, in the decisive way that only a young child can manage. "For no country is greater than ours."

My father laughed, and in memory I can hear the irony in it. "I'm afraid England is out of even your reach," he said. "As God has given you a brother, He has also given England a king. Your queenship must be elsewhere."

And so, Minuette, I admit the uncomfortable truth that a part of me envies you, for you will hold the only title I covet: Queen of England. Not that I envy you the position of a king's wife. I will tell you whom I truly envy: Mary Stuart, who has it in her reach to discover the difference between being a queen by right of her husband and queen in her own right.

For Mary has been Queen Regnant of Scotland since she was six days old—though all the world struggles to understand what that truly means. For much of her life, the young queen has not even been in her kingdom but at the French court, being groomed to marry the future King of France. It seems Scotland is so eager to escape the indignities of a female ruler that they will submit to a foreign king rather than endure it. I wonder if they will ever come to regret that bargain.

Only once in English history has a woman come near to holding power as Queen Regnant, rather than a consort. Four hundred years ago lived Matilda, granddaughter of the Conqueror and herself Holy Roman Empress (through one of those advantageous marriages expected of royal daughters). She was the only surviving child of King Henry I, and that wily king brought his own feudal lords together in order to swear fealty to his daughter before his death. Do you know it is said that there was a tussle between two men over their precedence in swearing said fealty? Robert of Gloucester (bastard son of the king and thus ineligible for the throne) vied against his cousin, Stephen (nephew to the king through his mother), in order to be the first to proclaim their loyalty to Matilda's royal rights.

Ironic, for—despite his sworn vow—Stephen made a dash for the crown just after Henry's death and had himself anointed king before Matilda could cross the Channel and take her place as queen. Many years of bloody civil war ensued as Matilda and her supporters—her half brother, Robert, foremost among them—fought to force Stephen from the throne he had ungraciously and perhaps illegally seized. In the end, the matter was only settled when the aging Stephen agreed to make Matilda's son, Henry of Anjou, his heir.

And thus ended the first inglorious attempt of an English queen to rule in her own right.

Closer to home, I confess it is an issue I have been forced by my position—and yes, perhaps my temperament as well—to consider. After all, I would never have been born if my father had been content to allow his throne to pass to a daughter. Instead, Mary would hold power today and there would never have been a reformation of English religion. But the great Henry VIII could not endure the thought of his carefully crafted power being passed into a woman's hands, and so he upset popes and emperors and his own marriage in order to secure a male heir.

Though it is worth noting that, in the end, my father's will dictated that should William die before leaving a royal heir of his own, the crown was to pass to me. Henry Tudor's pride in his blood, it seems, was only slightly less than his need for a son.

And so, God forbid, if William were to die before

leaving a marriage-born child of his own, I would succeed to England's throne. You know me too well for me to waste time asserting that it is an honour I dream not of. For I have dreams, Minuette, though none of them center on the loss of a brother who has been dear to me since the moment he first curled his infant hand around my finger. But life is uncertain, and to study the history of kings is to know that preparation is never to be scoffed at.

And so two words wind through my dreams and occasionally into my waking hours: *What if?* What if I am called upon to rule England?

I do not think it arrogance to believe that I am as qualified as William. Have we not had the same education, shared the same tutors and lessons? And we all know I am by nature more suited to the intellectual demands of the position. Where does my brother outshine me?

The answer to that is stark: on the battlefield. For though I ride and hunt as well as any man, I do not wield weapons and I may not ride to war. The Great Seal of England depicts the ruler in two states: dispensing justice on one side, on the other mounted on horseback with sword unsheathed to defend the kingdom. Though an extraordinary woman may find her way to fulfill the first, how is she to perform the second? A role, by the way, that William has shown himself so perfectly fitted for on the fields of France this summer.

But his prowess in battle does not mean my brother is a perfect ruler. I feel quite certain now that I shall never send this letter, Minuette, for I am treading on dangerous ground. But I must give voice, even if only once, to my overriding concern about William's choice of bride.

Dare I write what I will not say to his face? William is

thinking of himself alone when he should be thinking of his kingdom.

Were I queen, I cannot envision a circumstance in which I would sacrifice my people's good for my own happiness, as William is so lightly doing. I love you, Minuette, as I have never loved another friend, but you are not the queen England needs. If my brother persists in his romantic obsession, I fear he will split the kingdom in two, and the rifts his birth was meant to heal will never be mended.

With that, I close this rebellious letter and will consign it to the fire. If only I could as easily wipe away my doubts and fears. For you, as well as for William, for you are nearly my sister, and I do not want you hurt as I believe you will be one way or another. And in the coming weeks I will watch my words and my expressions. It is not my place to undermine the king's will. And perhaps I am wrong. Perhaps you are precisely what William needs.

But I fear you are not. And I fear England will pay the price.

Your loving sister in all but blood,
Elizabeth

Questions and Topics for Discussion

1. In the opening chapter of the novel, Minuette writes: "William has commanded [John Dee] to give a private reading of our stars. Only the four of us—for it would not do to let our secrets, past or future, slip into wider circulation." Yet, she keeps a journal that details many of their secrets. Do you think it is dangerous for her to do so? Would you, in her place?

2. When they meet with John Dee, Minuette reflects, "We all have motives that are less than pure." Do you agree? Do you think that the nature of the court made it impossible to be anything but self-serving at heart?

3. At one point Dominic says to Minuette, "Give me the word, and I'll go straight to William myself and tell him the truth." To which Minuette responds, "We can't just throw this in his face. He's not ready to hear it." Why do you think Minuette is so set against being honest with William? Is it solely because she wishes to spare his feelings? Was there ever a moment when Minuette or Dominic could have (or should have) told William about their relationship?

4. Ironically, though she is against confessing to William, it is Minuette who proposes the *di praesenti* marriage, arguing that "the court live[s] by its own rules." Do you think she is being rational, or hopelessly naïve? What's your opinion on how they handled the situation, and how do you predict the news of their secret marriage will be met by William? By Elizabeth?

5. It is interesting that Dominic and Minuette never turn to Elizabeth for help or advice on their situation, especially given her ability to be incredibly rational and less volatile than her brother. Why do you think this is?

6. Elizabeth excuses herself for "keeping her own counsel," because she realizes that William too has "confidences kept," even from her. Each of the "holy quartet" has their reasons for keeping secrets, some trivial, some life-altering—do you think these secrets will ultimately rip them apart? Or are secrets sometimes necessary in order to keep people together?

7. Robert Dudley is an interesting character because, despite how involved he is in court life, he also does his best to keep his head down and his nose clean, unlike his father. Do you think this is wise? What do you make of his relationship with Elizabeth? With William?

8. The title of the book is *The Boleyn Deceit*. To whom or what do you think the title applies? Who are the deceivers? Who are the deceived?

9. Do you think that a true, balanced friendship can ever really exist between two people who are on vastly different

playing fields of power, as William and Dominic are? Why or why not?

10. If given a choice, would you rather be the one in power (William), or serving the one in power? Why?

11. Do you see any parallels between William and Elizabeth's relationship and that of Anne and George Boleyn?

12. How do the feelings between Dominic, Minuette, William, and Elizabeth shift over the course of the book? Compare their standing at the end of *The Boleyn Deceit* to their relationship as it was in *The Boleyn King*. Of the quartet, who do you sympathize with most?

13. During a conversation about political strategy, Will's uncle opposes him, to which William replies, "Do tell, Lord Rochford: if being king isn't about me, then whom is it about?" Do you think this is the right attitude to have? Does your opinion of William change over the course of the book?

14. There have been many books written about the Tudors, not to mention the popularity of films and television shows about this time. What do you think is so fascinating about this particular era, and this particular family (for you personally, and in more general cultural terms)?

If you were enchanted by *The Boleyn Deceit*,
you won't want to miss

THE BOLEYN RECKONING

*Laura Andersen's dazzling conclusion to the tale of
the Tudor king that never was.*

Coming soon from Ebury Press

PRELUDE

July 1536

"My lady."

Mary refused to acknowledge the greeting, for Archbishop Cranmer's avoidance of her true title was an insult to her birth and position.

"My lady Mary," the impertinent man pressed, "I bring with me a letter from the king, your father."

That she could not refuse to acknowledge. Wordlessly, she extended her hand and the heretic archbishop handed over the letter. They were alone in a small antechamber at Hatfield House, where Mary fulfilled her duty as lady-in-waiting to her tiny half sister. If Elizabeth *were* her half-sister; Mary would have liked to believe that the child was not Henry's at all. But in her heart she knew they were sisters. They shared some of the same colouring, and even at not yet three years old, the precocious Elizabeth had a fearsome will that shouted her royal parentage.

Mary's chest constricted at her father's familiar and beloved handwriting. But it was the message itself that closed off her throat and sent wings of panic fluttering through her body. *The queen is safely delivered of a son. England at last has a Prince of Wales as God intended.*

How could God have intended this? Mary wondered. How

could he have allowed her own mother—Henry's true and loyal wife—to die barren and alone while the Boleyn whore bewitched the king? How could such a woman be granted a living son when Catherine of Aragon had been denied? Mary felt for the rosary at her waist and then remembered that she was forbidden to wear it at Hatfield.

"What do you want of me?" she demanded of Cranmer. "Congratulations? I am always glad for my father's happiness, but I cannot congratulate him on a mistaken pride in a son who is not legitimate. How can he be Prince of Wales, when my father has never truly been married to that woman?"

"My lady," and despite herself, Mary recognized the kindness beneath the archbishop's inflexibility, "your honour for your mother's memory does you great credit. But your father wishes nothing more than to be reconciled with you. Why separate yourself from the comfort of the king's love and care when you need not? What he asks is so little."

"I know what he asks—that I proclaim my mother's marriage a lie, her virtue a hoax, her faith an inconvenience. The king asks me to brand myself a bastard for the sake of that woman's children."

"The king asks you to accept the inevitable. My lady, this is a fight you cannot win. Ask yourself—does God wish you to go on in defiance against your father's wishes? To live out your life in rebellion and servitude? Whatever the state of your parents' marriage, you were conceived in good faith and were born for better things."

Mary thought of how much she hated Hatfield, being in a house of Protestants who despised not only her and her mother but the Church as well. With Cranmer being so reasonable and soft-spoken, Mary asked, "What would I receive in return?"

"In return for your signature, your father will grant you the manor of Beaulieu for life. There, you will be permitted to retain a single confessor and attendants of your own choosing."

A confessor . . . Mary closed her eyes and shivered. Henry knew his women—he knew how much she longed for a household of her own again, where she could wear her rosary and pray without the sneers of heretics and be counseled by a true priest. But to sign away her rights . . . the rights her mother had died upholding . . .

"Your father is also prepared to consider the wisdom of a proper marriage, providing your behavior is acceptable."

And that was the final blow to her resistance. Though her intellect knew that "consider" was not the same thing as "arranging" or "allowing," it was considerably better than her current state. She was twenty years old and had been betrothed often in her childhood. But there was no chance she would ever be allowed to marry while she continued in defiance of the king's wishes. With each year, she would grow older. And even more than marriage, Mary wanted children.

Mother, she offered up silently, *what should I do?*

The words were so immediate and clear to her mind that Mary knew at once it was her answer. *Do what you must for now— and wait for your moment. God means you to turn England back to Him.*

Mary opened her eyes, her pride screaming but her conscience unwavering. "I will sign."

And then I will wait, she vowed silently. *And when my moment comes—I will act.*

CHAPTER ONE

18 March 1556
Richmond Palace

Today the Duke of Northumberland stands trial at Westminster Hall. Dominic traveled to London yesterday to take part, though I know he is conflicted. Robert Dudley has told him that someone other than his father is behind all the twists of treachery these last two years, but Robert will say no more to Dominic. He has asked, rather, to see Elizabeth. Dominic asked me to help persuade her, but I did not try very hard. Why should she go? Whether there is one traitor or twenty in this, it was Northumberland himself who held Elizabeth and me prisoner. And for that alone he must answer.

Besides, all Elizabeth can think of just now is William. It has been three months since the nightmare of his smallpox and the effects . . . linger.

Perhaps the resolution of Northumberland's fate will release us all from this sense that we are snared in the moment before action. The tension of waiting is almost more than I can bear.

In the absence of an Earl Marshal of England (a post which William had not filled since the death of the old Duke of Norfolk more than a year ago), the trial of John Dudley, Duke of Northumberland, was presided over by George Boleyn, Duke of Rochford and Lord Chancellor of England.

Dominic took his place with the other peers who would sit in judgment of Northumberland today, but all his attention was given to Rochford himself. Three months ago the imprisoned Robert Dudley had made an enigmatic accusation aimed at the Lord Chancellor but had thus far refused to provide any details. Robert seemed to believe that even if his father were convicted today, William would be merciful as to the sentence and so there would be time to consider the matter.

Dominic was not so certain.

The doors at the back of the hall opened and Northumberland was escorted in. The hall at Westminster was a rich backdrop to today's trial. A stage had been erected in preparation, hung with tapestries and a canopy, beneath which was a bench for Northumberland. Dominic viewed the tableau with a cynicism that he had learned from Rochford—the trappings might argue respect for the accused, but he knew all too well they were mostly meant to remind those watching how far the man had fallen.

Northumberland conducted himself with gravity, three times reverencing himself to the ground before the judges. Dominic thought wryly it was the most humility he'd ever seen from John Dudley.

The hall was crowded with spectators, including members of London City's guilds as well as diplomats and foreign merchants who would no doubt be taking careful notes and sending word of the proceedings far and wide across Europe. England had been the subject of intense Continental scrutiny for quite some time— what with her young and untried king, her inflammatory religious divide, and her highly desirable and unwed royal princess. England may not be the powerhouse that France or Spain was, but it was very often the critical piece that decided the dangerous balance of power.

And now a peer of the realm was being tried for his life. Not to mention that a mere five months ago—despite a peace treaty—a French army had engaged English troops in battle on the Scots border and since that time England's king had been mostly absent from public view. Everyone in England and Europe knew that William had been ill and some had correctly guessed at the smallpox that had driven him to seclusion. Now even his own people were beginning to grow restless. They had waited years for William to grow old enough to take his father's place as a reigning monarch. They were not content to leave the government in the hands of men like Rochford and Northumberland, rightly distrusting the motives of such powerful men. The people wanted their king.

This trial was the first step in giving them what they wanted. Northumberland was hugely unpopular—though Dominic had not been in London when the duke and his sons were paraded through the streets to the Tower, he had heard countless versions of how they had been booed and mocked, pelted with rotten fruit and even stones. With William not quite ready to return to public view yet, Northumberland's trial for high treason was a distraction.

It was also, in large part, a sham. The original plan had been to have Parliament pass an Act of Attainder against Northumberland, thus avoiding a public trial and allowing the Crown to quickly confiscate the duke's lands. Granting him a trial instead in no way meant that Northumberland stood a chance of acquittal. There could be no doubt of the verdict; this trial was for the sole purpose of placating the populace.

Rochford opened the trial with a reading of the charges, none of which Dominic could dispute: the calculated secret marriage between Northumberland's son Guildford and Margaret Clifford, a cousin to the king and thus in line to England's throne. That disastrous marriage had been annulled after Margaret had given birth to a boy, but Northumberland's impudence could not be overlooked in the matter. And then there was the damning charge of "with intent and malice aforethought confining Her Highness, Princess Elizabeth, against her will": Dominic had seen firsthand the duke's intent to keep hold of Elizabeth in his family castle until William was forced to listen to him. Related to that last was also the charge of raising troops against the king—again indisputable. For the last two charges alone, Northumberland's life was forfeit.

But Dominic was less easy about some of the other charges considered behind the scenes. That Northumberland had conspired to bring down the Howard family two years ago, that he had offered alliance with the Low Countries, even claiming in writing that Elizabeth would be a more amenable ruler than her brother . . . Dominic had been the one to find those damning letters in Northumberland's home. He just wasn't sure how much he believed in them. Papers could be forged. Letters could be planted. Witnesses could be co-opted to a certain testimony. And it hadn't escaped his attention that those particular charges were not being tried in court today.

"We'll keep it simple," Rochford had said. "Leave out the messier aspects of Northumberland's behavior."

And that was why Dominic kept a wary eye on Rochford. Because the messy aspects of this business were also the most open to other interpretations. More than eighteen months ago, the late Duke of Norfolk had died in the Tower after being arrested for attempting to brand the king a bastard and have his half sister, Mary, crowned queen. Dominic now believed, as most did, that the Duke of Norfolk's fall had been cleverly manipulated.

"What say you, John Dudley?" Rochford asked after the reading of the charges.

"My Lord Chancellor," Northumberland responded, rising. "My lords all," he addressed the others of the jury, "I say that my faults have ever only been those of a father. I acknowledge my pride and ambition and humbly confess that those sins have led me to a state I do greatly regret. But I have not and could never compass a desire to wish or inflict harm upon His Most Gracious Majesty. My acts were those of a desperate father to a willful son. Guildford's death is greatly to be lamented, but I do desire nothing more than to be reconciled to our king and his government."

Northumberland was led out after his speech, and the jury retired to discuss their verdict. It took far less time than Dominic was comfortable with and the outcome was never in doubt. Rochford and the twenty-year-old Duke of Norfolk (grandson of the man who had died in a false state of treasonable disgrace) were the most vehement of Northumberland's enemies, but every other lord on the jury had cause to resent the duke's arrogance and ambition. And as Dominic studied each man there, he was aware of an undercurrent of fear, deeply hidden perhaps, but real. There was not a single peer present whose family title was older than Henry VII, and most of them had been ennobled by Henry VIII or William himself. The Tudors had broken the back of the old hereditary nobility, raising instead men whose power resulted from their personal loyalty and royal usefulness. Just consider Dominic himself—grandson of a king's daughter, true, but in more practical terms only the son of a younger son with no land or title at all until William had granted them to him.

Or consider Rochford, who might have been only a talented diplomat or secretary if his sister had not been queen.

The problem with being raised up by personal loyalty was that one could as easily be unmade. And thus it was today—the jury would find Northumberland guilty because William wished it as much as because it was right. And after all, Dominic would vote guilty without more than a slight qualm, for he had ridden through the midst of Northumberland's army last autumn. He knew that it had been but a hair's breadth of pride and fear from open battle against the king.

They returned to the hall, and Northumberland stood to face the jury as, one after another, each member stood and personally delivered his verdict. Dominic saw the glint of tears in North-umberland's eyes as Rochford pronounced the traditional sentence of a traitor—to be hung, drawn, and quartered—and concluded with, "May God have mercy on your soul."

There was a tinge of triumph to George Boleyn's voice.

Elizabeth was with her brother when Dominic and Rochford returned to Richmond to report on the trial of Northumberland. They waited for the two dukes in a reception chamber of Richmond Palace known as the painted hall for the heavily coloured and gilded paneling that surrounded them.

The royal siblings were not alone, of course. There were half a dozen quiet attendants who had learned these last months to give their king his space. And Minuette was also there—though these days one hardly needed to specify Minuette's presence. Wherever William was, there was Minuette at his side. Since his recovery, the only place she didn't follow the king was his bed at night and Elizabeth wondered how long that restraint would last. Since his illness, William's devotion to Minuette had grown perilously near to obsession.

William sat beneath the canopy of state as he received Lord Rochford's official report in silence. Another effect of his illness; his characteristic restlessness was often submerged beneath lengthy periods of stillness. When Rochford handed him the execution order to sign, William took it without a word, almost as though he had no interest in the matter.

It was Elizabeth who said, "Thank you, Uncle."

That stirred William enough to say flatly, "You may go. Lord Exeter will return this to you shortly."

Rochford gave them all a long, hard look but he was not ready to bring his discontent to open argument. Elizabeth knew it was coming—this inner circle of just the four of them could not be allowed to last much longer—but for today the Lord Chancellor held his tongue. He left them alone, the attendants filing out after him.

They had always been exceptionally close—the "Holy Quartet," Robert Dudley had named them. But since his brush with death, William had kept his sister, his love, and his friend even tighter around him. Elizabeth wasn't sure if it were for comfort or protection.

Alone with those he trusted, William stretched out his legs in a characteristic gesture that made the tightness in Elizabeth's shoulders ease. She rejoiced with every little moment that spoke of William as he had been before.

"Sentenced to be hanged, disemboweled, and quartered," William said to Dominic. "I'll commute that to beheading, of course."

"Of course."

"You have nothing to plead else?"

Elizabeth tightened again. They had not told William of Robert's plea to see her, of his claim that another man had as much to do with Northumberland's fall as his own actions. But despite that silence, William knew Dominic. Clearly he sensed there was more than just his usual caution behind his friend's reserve.

But in this, Dominic did not hesitate. "Northumberland held Elizabeth and Minuette against their will. He raised an army that could only have been meant to be used against you. I have nothing to plead for him."

William nodded, then stood and crossed to the table where pen and ink waited. The three of them watched as he signed in swift bold strokes—*Henry Rex*. His father's name. His ruling name.

He handed the signed order to Dominic—always entrusting his closest friend to see his will carried out—and, as though the momentum caused by one decision made led him to another, he said abruptly, "I've settled on Easter for my return to London. We'll spend it at Whitehall and celebrate lavishly. Masques, tournaments, riding through the streets to Westminster Abbey for service . . ."

Elizabeth added tartly, still trying to gauge when and how to speak to her brother as before, "All elaborately designed to set people's minds at rest and give them reason to rejoice in their brilliant king."

Through everything—Rochford's report, William signing someone's death—Minuette had sat in perfect stillness. Another change, as though her own being was linked to William's and what he experienced so did she. Now she stood and joined William without touching him. There was something poignant almost to pain about the pairing—something indefinable that set Elizabeth's heart wringing—as Minuette smiled gravely and said to William, "The people are waiting to rejoice in their brilliant and handsome king."

William flinched slightly and, as he always did these days, kept himself angled a little away from Minuette's gaze. Keeping his left side turned always to the shadows.

The smallpox, which had covered his face and chest and arms wholly, had not scarred quite so wholly. If one looked at William from the right, one saw only the perfect face he'd been born with. And his left hand and arm had healed almost cleanly, with only a small scattering of scars. But the left side of his face . . .

Minuette was the only one who could speak of it, or touch him. She did so now, resting her hand on William's ruined cheek. "The people love you, Will, as we do. The rejoicing will be honest. What matters more than that you are still here?"

Only Minuette could make him smile these days. He did so now, and Elizabeth thought if only he could be brought to smile more, to be himself more, to quit brooding on the scars, that people would hardly notice them. *We see what we expect to see,* she thought. *Will must make people expect to see only the king and all will be well.*

Dominic waited for her in the Richmond gardens. It was well after dark, but Minuette knew every line and shadow of her husband and the dark was their ally these days. Their only ally.

It was all supposed to have been over by now. They had wed secretly (and illegally and, according to the Protestants, heretically) last November, with every intention of confessing to the king at Christmas. Then William had been stricken with smallpox. And in the space of days when they had feared for his life, plans and confessions had fallen to the wayside.

But not their marriage. And not their love, Minuette thought as Dominic wrapped her in a tight embrace, his cloak covering them both. She rested her head on his shoulder and let herself be at momentary peace. Her only peace in an increasingly troubled world.

"What will happen to his sons?" she asked quietly. She did not need to specify Northumberland's sons; Dominic read her these days with an ease that went beyond familiarity to almost uncanny.

"It is the duke himself people hate. His sons will remain in prison for now, but I suspect they will be safe. Not their lands or titles, though—there will not be another Duke of Northumberland for a long time. But I think John Dudley would count the title well lost if it saves his sons."

"Does he still expect to be pardoned?"

She felt Dominic's shrug. "I suppose I will find out when I deliver the order tomorrow."

"I'm sorry it has to be you."

"Better me than Rochford. At least I will not gloat quite so openly."

She drew a little away, so she could see his face—or at least its outlines—as she asked, "What are you going to do about Robert's accusations?"

"When am I going to tell Will about them, do you mean? One step at a time, sweetheart. First let's get him back into the world. It's almost spring, which means campaigning, which means we'll find out if the French intend to continue their aggressions. I'm watching Rochford, but honestly, after destroying Norfolk and Northumberland, who is left for the man to bring down?"

"You," Minuette answered softly but resolutely. "And me. Rochford does not trust your influence with the king, and he despises me heartily." She hesitated over the next part, but someone had to be sensible. "Do you never think that, rather than being our enemy, we could turn Rochford to our best ally?"

Against William, she meant, or at least the king's anger. Because William was going to be angry. He was going to be furious when he found out they had married behind his back. While Minuette was secretly betrothed to William himself.

How had they come to this, the lies and the betrayals? She often wondered what she could have done differently. But she and Dominic had made their choices and they could not be unmade. All that could be done now was to mitigate the damage. And for that, they would need allies.

Elizabeth was the most obvious, but Minuette could not burden her with this when she had been so worried about her brother. Besides, she had her own touchy royal pride and might not be entirely understanding. But Rochford was, above all, practical. Add in the fact that he wanted nothing more than to ensure his nephew did not marry a common girl for love alone, and he seemed the perfect choice to counsel and aid them.

If only Dominic could be persuaded. Because there was the not inconsiderable fact that, if Robert Dudley were right, then it had not been Northumberland who had ordered Minuette poisoned last year: it had been Rochford.

She read Dominic's resistance in the hard lines of his chest and shoulders and was not surprised when he shook his head. "I do not trust Rochford in the least, and I will not attempt to ally myself with a man who may be a traitor simply because it is convenient for me."

There had been no chance of a different response. Where Rochford's core principle was practicality, Dominic's was honour. He would never use a man he despised simply because it could benefit him. Minuette had not really expected him to agree. She had only proposed it so he could not accuse her later of acting on impulse.

She could never regret being married to Dominic, even if it had been hurried and secret and perhaps wrong. She could not regret a moment of the brief weeks they'd had together at Wynfield Mote as husband and wife. There were no such moments now, except in dark corners where the most they could manage were a few guilty kisses. But from the moment William's eyes had opened and his slow recovery had begun, Minuette had felt a great looming pressure that spoke of unavoidable disaster. She didn't know what form it would take or when it would strike, but every choice she made each day seemed designed only to plug a leak in the flood that threatened to overwhelm them all.

Once she'd been confident in her ability to find a solution that would preserve not only themselves as individuals, but their friendships. Now her confidence was gone and when she wept, which was often, it was for a tangle of troubles far beyond her abilities to solve.

At such times, there was a terrible whisper in her head, poisonous and treasonous, that would not leave her alone. *If only William had not survived the pox . . .*

She buried herself in Dominic's arms once more to shut out that thought. William had survived and she was glad of it, and if there were terrible prices to be paid in future she would pay them with a clear conscience.

"It will be all right," Dominic whispered, his hands stroking her hair. "It shall all come right in the end."

And there was a measure of how the world had upended itself: that Dominic had all the confidence and she all the doubt.

"After the execution, I will speak to Robert again. Perhaps his father's death will loosen his tongue," Dominic said.

And if not, Minuette thought, *I shall have to make my own choice about whether to approach Rochford.*